# a Bargain with the Rake

## SADIE BOSQUE

First edition

Editing by Tracy Liebchen
Cover art by The Brazen Wallflower Designs

This book was professionally typeset on Reedsy.
Find out more at reedsy.com

*To my dear grandfather who always listened to my stories, no matter how long, and let me be exactly the way I am. You are forever in my heart.*
*May your soul rest in peace.*

# Contents

# Acknowledgement

To my fabulous Beta readers:
Nicole Yost
and
Michelle Lokeigh

The story would not be the same without you. Thank you, for making my experience in publishing a novel unforgettable.

# Author's Note

*This work of fiction contains adult content, strong language, off-page death, and violence.*

*Reader discretion is advised.*

# Prologue

*All troubles begin with a lady*, Gabriel thought grimly as he held a pistol in his shaking hand. Cold sweat ran down his forehead as his stomach twisted and churned inside.

At least, all *his* troubles began with a lady.

First, Lady Wakefield, one of his former lovers, had sicced her husband on him once he severed their association. Poor bastard was so wrapped around her finger he didn't understand what was going on or what Gabriel's crime against his wife was. After that incident, Gabriel had wanted nothing to do with the lady. However, when Gabriel's friend Clydesdale needed a favor from her, Gabriel knew he could procure it easily if he promised one last tumble. He couldn't very well refuse to help his oldest friend.

Then Lady Stanhope, a young and eager tigress of a woman, who always threw flirtatious glances at him, accosted him in the ballroom of the aforementioned Lady Wakefield, at the same time as his planned assignation with the mistress of the house. Gabriel was bored, so he decided to have a tryst with her before Lady Wakefield arrived. Predictably, he got caught, and this little error earned him two invitations to a duel from the aggrieved husbands—which he, of course, ignored—and one letter from Gabriel's sire. The Earl of Winchester was cutting Gabriel off.

His latest troubles, however, all began with one particular lady. *His* lady. If he was honest, the entire ordeal at Lady Wakefield's ball and what followed was actually her fault, too, even if not directly.

He'd done it for her. Everything he'd done recently had been for her.

He wiped the errant drop of sweat out of his eye and concentrated on his target some twenty paces away. Today, he would die for her, too.

# Chapter 1

*Two months earlier...*

L    ightning split the sky, illuminating the dark street. A
     tiny figure stood on the doorstep of Gabriel's house,
     pounding wildly at the door.

The raindrops ran in rivulets down the figure's cloak. A small, soaked valise lay at their feet, and a horse tethered to a nearby tree whinnied uncontrollably. All of that and the fact that it was the middle of the night made Gabriel, Viscount St. Clare, deduce that the visit was unplanned.

It wasn't the first time he had come home from a late-night rendezvous to find a potential lover waiting at his doorstep—or in his bed. This night, however, was his only live-in servant's night off, which meant nobody could enter Gabriel's house without his knowledge. The cloaked figure didn't look like a potential lover, though. If not for the tiny size, he'd think it was male. *A boy?* Gabriel cocked his head to the side, and water streamed down his hat. He shook the excess water off his shoulders and hurried toward the distressed mare.

He patted the animal consolingly before addressing the shadowy figure still knocking relentlessly at his door. "You might want to put the horse in the stables if you are planning to enter," he shouted over the noise of the rain.

The figure turned and peered at him from beneath the hood. Gabriel could not make out facial features or anything else in the dark, so he gave up trying. He had no wish to interrogate the poor fellow in the drizzling rain. He also didn't want to torture the animal, who'd be forced to soak under the tree so much longer. Besides, if this person wished him harm, it wouldn't be the worst day to enact this wish.

Until a few weeks ago, Gabriel had been a respected viscount, a revered member of society. He was welcomed in all the clubs and ballrooms across England. Then, he had opened his cold heart to a friend in need—or rather a friend's relative in need—and ruined his good name.

To be fair, his name had never been associated with anything good. Debauchery, roguery, and mayhem were more likely associated with St. Clare, but at least he could afford it.

Now, after the fiasco at Lady Wakefield's ball, he was left without an allowance from his father, the earl, and shunned from good society for dishonoring young wives and refusing to duel. None of that would've mattered to him if he hadn't been refused credit in gentlemen's clubs and gaming hells following his disownment by his father.

His lovers were the only ones who hadn't turned their backs on him unless he made them do that during their tupping.

They even offered to sustain him financially for the sole benefit of being serviced by him in bed.

*Like a mistress.*

Gabriel almost laughed out loud. He knew some rakes lived like that, but he couldn't. He valued his independence, in and out of bed, too much to agree to such conditions.

Gabriel slowly untethered the horse. "Let's go 'round the back." He tipped his head toward the stables and walked the animal there without checking if his night visitor followed him.

He settled the mare into the stables, woke up his poor stable boy to rub it down, and turned to the unwelcome guest. His visitor stood in the doorway, huddled under a cloak, shaking, presumably with cold. The view was pitiful. Even more pitiful than Gabriel's own predicament.

No, this person was probably not there to murder him. What did they want then?

Gabriel passed the visitor on the way out and called for them to follow him. He entered his house from the back door and kept it open for the mystery guest. St. Clare shook off his coat, took off his hat, placed them on the chair, and looked around. It was dark, and he had no idea where to find the candles.

Since his finances had taken an enormous hit, he'd let go of all his servants, except for a valet, a cook, a groom, and a stable boy. The cook had her own residence, and she usually left for her home after supper. His valet, Edward, who had also taken on the responsibilities of a butler, had gone to visit his sick mother in the country for the weekend. Which meant Gabriel was on his own to navigate through the house.

He groped through the side table and somehow found a

candle and a tinderbox. After he lit it, he waved to the cloaked stranger to follow him. He heard the chatter of the stranger's teeth and realized the poor creature was frozen solid. It explained the lack of conversation.

Gabriel wasn't too eager to talk just yet, either. They walked through his townhouse in silence until they reached his chambers. He entered the sitting room and proceeded to light the fire. After he was done, he turned to the visitor.

"Wait here if you wish. I'd like to put some dry clothes on." With those words and without a backward glance, Gabriel entered his bedroom through the adjoining door.

The absence of his valet left Gabriel to fend for himself in the wardrobe department as well. He took off all his sodden clothing and left them hanging on the chair, then found his banyan and threw it over his naked form, loosely tying it around his waist. Gabriel returned to the sitting room, not caring about his half-naked appearance for his late-night visitor. His banyan gaped open, showing off his bare chest. His feet and ankles peeked out from under the robe when he walked. But if the visitor was offended by his state of dishabille, they were more than welcome to sod off his property.

Gabriel walked through the door, turned to the fireplace, and froze in surprise as the cloaked figure carefully drew the hood back, revealing a shock of long, curly, flaming red hair.

Gabriel stared at the young woman, who stood with her back to him and extended her hands to the fire. Anticipation flared deep inside his crotch. Perhaps this *was* a new lover who'd come to warm his bed. Gabriel bit his lip and craned his neck to better see her face. The moment he did, he sobered immediately.

4

# Chapter 1

"Well, well, well," Gabriel drawled, recognizing his visitor at last. He didn't believe for a moment that she was there for a late-night tryst, which immediately dowsed any flicker of anticipation he'd had just a moment ago. There wouldn't be any entertaining her in his townhouse. Not unless he wanted to die at the end of his friend's pistol.

Lady Eabha Montgomery, the granddaughter of the late Duke of Somerset, and currently the Duchess of Somerset in her own right, was untying her cloak, in his sitting room, all bedraggled.

Still, her head was held high as if nothing untoward was happening. As if she hadn't come knocking on the door of a notorious rake in the middle of the night during a heavy rain.

Gabriel crossed his arms and regarded her with narrowed eyes. "If it isn't the pain in my arse, the sole reason for my downfall, the weapon of my destruction—"

"D-don't be melod-dram-matic," she interrupted him with a stammer. Her teeth were still chattering from the cold.

Gabriel gritted his teeth and held back the urge to throw her out on the doorstep and leave her there, come what may. She was cold, and she wanted something from him. At least that last bit had him curious. And even if she was the reason that he'd gotten mixed up in a mad scheme a few weeks ago and subsequently got shunned from society, she wasn't entirely at fault.

Oh, very well, it wasn't her fault at all. He was the weapon of his own downfall. All he had to do was grant a personal *favor* to Lady Wakefield during her ball, and in return, she would invite the duchess's guardians to the ball. This would have allowed the duchess to elope with her suitor. Only Gabriel had gotten bored and arranged a tryst with Lady Stanhope at the same time and gotten caught.

The frustrating part was that the tryst wasn't even satisfying, and the duchess hadn't eloped with her fellow. So it had all been for naught.

No matter whose fault it had been, Gabriel really wasn't in the mood to grant another favor to the troublesome duchess. Just having her in his bedroom was dangerous enough.

In any case, he'd known the lady ever since she was a young girl, and he couldn't very well let her freeze to death on his doorstep. His best friend, the Earl of Clydesdale, wouldn't be too happy with it, either. He was the husband of the duchess's cousin and was very fond of her. Gabriel pressed his lips together in irritation and studied the lady before him.

In the warm glow of firelight, he could see her appearance more clearly. Her cloak—which still covered her from head to toe—was sodden, the hem was covered in dirt, and her hair was soaking wet and plastered to her head and face. Her forest-green eyes were rimmed with red, heavy shadows beneath them, and her usually lush pink lips were blue and trembled lightly.

With a sigh of resignation, he invited her to sit in the chair in front of the fire and collapsed into another chair across from it with an audible 'oomph.' He wanted to show her with every gesture that she was an unwanted guest, intruding on his solitude. Not that she hadn't known that already.

She looked around, then draped her cloak on the back of a chair. Gabriel's eyes widened as he saw what she was wearing.

No wonder he hadn't immediately recognized her as a lady. Underneath the cloak, she had on a white linen shirt—a masculine shirt—and dark brown breeches! They were tucked into a dainty pair of women's riding boots, which were covered with mud and had probably soaked her feet.

Gabriel fought to conceal his surprise. If he seemed indifferent to her plight, she might just leave him alone.

"Feel free to start speaking, darling," he said, feigning nonchalance. "We don't have all night. Unless you are interested in some late-night exercising, in which case, I'd ask you to make haste as well."

He punctuated his words with an appraising gaze he sent her way from the top of her head to the soles of her boots.

The Duchess of Somerset regarded him with a haughty, bored look, the one she'd probably learned from her grandfather while she was still in her crib, and carefully lowered herself into a chair. The effect was somewhat ruined by a shiver that passed through her. Probably the warmth of the fire chasing away the chills.

"My lord—" she began.

Gabriel interrupted with a scoff. "By all means, let's be formal," he said sarcastically. "Since you are in my bedchamber in the dead of night, you might as well call me Gabriel."

"This isn't your bedchamber," she said skeptically, looking around.

"My bedroom is through these doors." Gabriel gestured with a wave of his hand. "This sitting room is part of a bedroom suite."

"Very well." She demurely folded her hands on her lap, a picture of a proper young lady in a devil's den. "Gabriel, in that case, you can call me Evie."

"I'll call you whatever I like, pet." St. Clare sent her an appraising look again.

"Right. I forgot; it's too much of trouble for you to

remember a lady's name. Isn't it?" She had the gall to smirk at him.

"Listen, love, you showed up at my house, in the middle of the night, after being the reason for the ruin of my reputation"—she gave a ladylike snort. Gabriel narrowed his eyes—"my reputation, which led me to the loss of my fortune. So, you better get to the point and then get out."

"I believe your reputation was ruined long before I was born, m*y lord*. But I concede, I played a part in the loss of your fortune, however unwittingly. And that is the reason I am here," she said with all the dignity of a queen.

"Oh?" He raised his brow.

"I came here to propose a bargain." She looked at him down the length of her pretty freckled nose. A queen offering her lowly servant a scrap of leftover food. Then she ruined the effect by sneezing into her sleeve. Twice.

Gabriel rolled his eyes. "For God's sakes, get rid of those sodden boots of yours and sit closer to the fire."

He got to his feet and walked to his bedroom door. He showed up a moment later with an afghan wrapped over his arm.

Evie had already moved the heavy chair closer to the fire and snuggled in it, drawing her feet under her buttocks. He knelt before her and tucked the blanket around her, taking advantage to caress her tiny waist and hips.

Another shiver passed through her. He walked to the sideboard, filled a glass of whisky, and handed it to her.

"Drink." He stared right into her surprised, wide eyes.

"I don't—" She tried to hand the glass back to him, but he turned and settled back in his chair.

"Drink. You need to get warm and fast. Otherwise, you'll

catch a cold. And trust me when I say I shan't be sitting by your bedside feeding you chicken soup."

She grumbled something under her breath, then took a sip and started coughing as the burning liquid passed through her throat.

Gabriel chuckled. "A little more," he coaxed, and to his surprise, she obeyed, taking another sip before lowering the glass to the floor. "You were saying?"

"Yes, right." She cleared her throat. "I have a business proposition for you."

"Business proposition? Does it involve asking another woman for a favor? Perhaps in return for a tryst at her ball? Because if so, I refuse. Once is quite enough."

"I promise you, this proposition doesn't involve any trysts."

She was calm and composed again, hands demurely folded on her lap. Only the red in the crests of her cheeks signaled the warmth of the whisky coursing through her blood. Her lush lips returned to their regular rosy pink. Her flame-colored hair started drying and curling at the ends. She was the picture of innocence, somehow mixed with pure seduction. Although for Gabriel, even a saint would be the perfect picture of seduction.

"Then, I am definitely not interested," he said.

"I promise you will find it worth your while."

"Very well." Gabriel let out a weary sigh. "Go on."

"As you know, I am a duchess in my own right," she said, looking him squarely in the eyes.

He did know that. It was a rare occurrence indeed when a female became an heir to the peerage. Thus were the terms of the Somerset title upon its inception, though. And Gabriel had to agree. There was no better lady to become a duchess.

Evie was born for the role.

He made sure not to react to her words, however. He knelt to take his glass of whisky back and took a sip.

"Other than the title and the lands, my grandfather left me quite a lot of money," she continued.

St. Clare relaxed, lounging in his chair. The picture of boredom. He took another sip of whisky. The familiar burn of spirits gave him comfort.

"But until I turn five and twenty, I do not have access to any part of my inheritance. The only other way to get to it is for me to get married."

"What do I have to do with any of that?" He took another sip, getting more bored by the moment.

He studied her lips while she spoke. A lush, pretty mouth. He knew of more pleasurable ways she could use that mouth than talking.

She smiled then, and he caught his breath. Such a beautiful curve of lips she had. He would enjoy watching those lips close on his—

"I came to propose marriage."

Gabriel choked on his sip of whisky. "You what?" he asked hoarsely in between fits of coughs.

"Marriage," she answered without blinking an eye. "It would be a marriage of convenience, naturally."

"Naturally." He stared at her in disbelief.

"Just listen, please." It didn't sound like a plea, more like a command. She raised her right hand, thrusting an elegant index finger up in the air. "First, since your preferred lifestyle of debauchery was ruined because you tried to help me, I know you would like to get it back. As my husband, you will be free to use all the capital I own and get back to the lifestyle you love so much. Second"—her middle finger joined her first one—"I have a few estates, including my favorite mansion in Sussex, which means I shall not get in the way of said lifestyle. Third"—she whipped up her forefinger to join the others—"being married will grant you a reprieve from the ladies who ever wanted to ensnare you for themselves. And as an added boon, being married to a duchess will get you back in the good graces of society."

"If I wanted to get married, do you think I'd still be sitting here?" He gestured to the bare walls of his townhouse.

Evie didn't follow his gesture with her gaze. She just stared at him intently. "All the other women would want something from you. Fidelity, loyalty, love."

"Exclusive access to my bedroom."

"Right, I want none of that."

Gabriel fought not to feel offended. He leaned forward, propping his elbows on his knees. "And what do you get out of it, pray tell?"

"Independence," she answered evenly. "You promise to stay out of my life, let me live the way I want, do with my part of the inheritance, my estates whatever I want, and I shall do the same."

"That's it?" he asked skeptically. "We get married. I get part of your generous inheritance, you retreat to Sussex or one of your other estates, and we never see each other again?"

At Evie's nod, his eyes narrowed in mistrust. "What's the catch?"

"There is no catch." She licked her lips nervously, drawing his already restless eyes to them.

His gaze traveled lower to the delicate length of her neck, to the masculine garment hiding her feminine delights. He

11

raised his eyes back to her lips.

"Will we be having marital relations?" he asked in a husky voice. "Because if so—"

"No," she answered a little too swiftly, cutting him off. He noticed her breathing quickened, too.

"No," he repeated thoughtfully and met her gaze. "So you want a *mariage blanc*? What about an heir?"

Evie looked away. "I shall not be"—she waved her hand toward the bedroom—"doing that with you."

"But you mean to have children, yes?" He scoffed. "How very entertaining. So, you mean to drop a cuckoo in my nest?"

"No," she said after taking a long breath. "I do not plan on having children."

Her answer placated him somewhat. He settled back in his seat and studied her carefully. She fidgeted in her seat.

"Why the haste? You are what? Three and twenty?"

"Four and twenty."

"Then you have less than a year to get your hands on your rightful inheritance. Why not wait?"

"The reasons are my own. But if you must know, I want to get my hands on my inheritance before my guardian squanders it away. And before he forcefully marries me to someone else." She paused. "Someone worse."

Gabriel snorted. High praise indeed. She did have a point, however. He needed money. She had money. He never wanted to get shackled to a wife. She proposed an arrangement where she'd leave him to his own devices. The bargain seemed too good to be true, but he wasn't about to look a gift horse in the mouth.

"Very well," he finally said. "But I have one condition."

She looked at him curiously, all wide-eyed innocence.

# Chapter 1

"If you ever change your mind about having children, you come to me."

Her eyes widened further, almost comically so.

"What?" He shrugged nonchalantly. "I am going to be an earl. I am not anxious about having an heir, but as long as there is one, it might as well be mine. Besides, I don't like the idea of my wife cuckolding me."

She laughed. A beautiful, seductive sound. "As opposed to the other way around?"

Gabriel leaned forward so she wouldn't see the tent forming under his banyan. "Listen, sweet, those were your rules. You're the one who insisted on me continuing my debauched ways after marriage."

"And if I insisted on fidelity? Would you have agreed?" She cocked an eyebrow.

"I suppose you will never know now, will you?" he said with a satisfied smirk.

# Chapter 2

vie sat in a chair in the bedchamber of the most notorious rake in the country. She was tired and hungry. Her leg muscles ached from the tortuous journey from Carlisle to London. She was lucky the man even come home tonight, or she'd have died out on the street during the thunderstorm.

Everything had seemed to be going so well after she left for her Somerset estate with her guardians. They'd apologized for pushing an unwanted marriage at her, said she'd have her own pick of suitors next season. But then their sons arrived, and she noticed the extra attention, the courting behavior. Her heart had fallen as she realized this was their ploy all along, to marry her to one of their sons and keep the title and inheritance in their family.

She might even have considered the match if not for the promise she'd made to her grandfather, but the last straw was the conversation she'd overheard between Lady Montbrook and her son.

## Chapter 2

*There are only two ways you can become a duke. Either marry the girl or kill her.*

After that, Evie hadn't waited to see which path her cousin would take. She'd collected her most necessary belongings and ran. She'd taken a horse from the stables and galloped until her mount was too tired to continue. After that, she traveled by a hackney.

She'd dressed like a man and hidden her bright hair under a tall hat, but even then, she'd started drawing too much attention. So, after a while, she'd hired a mount again and galloped the rest of the way astride a horse. As athletic as she was, she had never before ridden at such a grueling pace and for such a long period.

The danger for a lady traveling alone on such a long stretch of the road was indescribable. Of course, there was a possibility nobody had suspected she was a lady. Still, the only reason she could find for making it this far unscathed was the providence of God. She had a pistol in her valise, but she hadn't had to use it even once. It was quite possible that looking as she did, dirty and disheveled, nobody thought she had anything of value to steal.

Now she was finally safe. She'd told this gorgeous creature of a man her conditions, and he could either take them or leave them. If he left them, she would probably die out on the street because she had no strength to even move from this huge, comfortable chair. No, she wouldn't marry her odious cousin, no matter what. The dukedom belonged to her. Besides, she'd made a promise to her grandfather to marry for love, hadn't she?

Evie felt her eyelids getting heavier by the second. Through the haze of a dream, she heard a pleasant, masculine rumble, but she couldn't make out any words anymore. Suddenly, she was being lifted by a pair of strong arms and cradled to a rock-hard chest.

"What are you...?" She gave a half-hearted protest, but her strength had finally left her, and she lowered her heavy head onto a comfortable male shoulder. She inhaled a familiar scent of aloe wood and spice and snuggled further into the crook of Gabriel's shoulder.

"We'll talk about it tomorrow," he said, his voice rumbling through his chest. "For now, you sleep."

The warmth of his body left her as he lowered her onto a soft mattress, and she whimpered in protest. Gabriel chuckled, covered her with a warm blanket, and in a moment, she was asleep.

\* \* \*

Evie woke up with a start. She sat up and groaned from the ache in her muscles. The rigorous ride across the country hadn't gone unnoticed by her body. Something heavy fell from her chest onto her lap, causing her to hiss from the pain. She looked around and took in the unfamiliar room.

She was in a bed, surrounded by dark green drapes hanging from the canopy. The room itself was decorated in gold and dark green tones. She looked to the left and saw a man lying in bed with her. Naked. And he wasn't covered by blankets at all.

Gabriel.

His strong, beautifully shaped buttocks and muscled back were rising and falling with his every breath. His golden mane of hair had fallen over his face, covering his handsome features.

She had an inexplicable urge to reach out and move the lock of hair away from his face and then trace the muscles on his back. She licked her lips as she continued studying his naked form. Well, she thought ruefully, she was lucky he wasn't sleeping on his back.

*Thank God for small mercies.*

Gabriel St. Clare was a tall, lean, beautifully complexioned man in the prime of his life. His features were gorgeous, and he was often likened to an angel, though he had the reputation of a devil. Many ladies had ruined their reputation for a night in his arms. And as much as Evie tried to fight her attraction to the man, it was no use. She'd loved him almost from the moment she first set her eyes on him.

He was handsome, funny, and quite clever. She had never stood a chance. And now she was going to be his wife.

She continued studying his form with avid interest. His arm, lying on her lap, was well-muscled and bulky, his fingers lean, and—

Her eyes widened in horror as he flexed his arm and drew her closer to him.

With an unladylike squeak, she fell on the pillows, landing a few inches from his face. He scraped his hair back from his eyes and smiled his devilish smile at her.

"Good morning, love," he said with a husky, sleepy voice that sent involuntary shivers down her spine, and something warm passed lower, through her midsection.

"What?" She jerked up again, her lower back protesting in pain. She ignored it and looked down at herself.

She was still fully clothed, in her filthy garments, no less. At least he hadn't tried to undress her. She drew a breath of relief. He'd acted like a gentleman.

"Surprised I didn't strip you naked?" he asked with a husky chuckle, as if reading her mind. "I do have scruples, believe it or not. I never bed an unconscious woman. That's where I draw the line." He bared his white teeth in a smile. "Or, an unwilling woman," he said with a nod and sat up.

To do that, he had to turn around and reveal his front in all his masculine glory. Evie hastily turned away.

"And as far as I understood by the bargain we made last night, you are indeed unwilling," he continued, as if nothing indecent was going on. As if he weren't utterly naked.

He got up and walked to a nearby chair, which contained his clothes. Evie ducked her head and developed quite a fascination with the beautifully embroidered pattern on the counterpane while he drew on his breeches.

"You," he said conversationally, "need a bath."

Evie's head shot up, her cheeks burning from humiliation. She saw a devilish gleam playing in his eyes.

"I'll have Ed run it for you. He should be back by now from his nightmare of a vacation. I'll also tell my cook, Matilda, to prepare us some breakfast." He stretched, showing off his hard, lean abdomen. Evie's mouth watered just by looking at him. "Tell me, how do you want to do this? A big church wedding, or should I get us a special license?"

"*No!*" She shot off the bed the idea frightened her so much. "No license, no banns. We are eloping," she said in a rush, untangling herself from the sheets.

Gabriel raised an eyebrow in question.

"My guardian." Evie swallowed before continuing. "He has connections. He will find out. It's been days; he already knows that I ran off... He'll be keeping track of anyone trying to get a special license."

"Fine," Gabriel said after drawing a long breath. "Then we leave after breakfast." He went to the door and paused with his hand on the door handle. "Does he have any reason to suspect you'd come here?"

The best Evie could muster was a nervous laugh and a shake of her head. Nobody could imagine such madness from Evie. Not even her best friend, Samantha.

"Good."


A bath was brought in a few moments later, and Evie lay soaking in it, letting her tired muscles warm and her body relax while her mind simply shut off for a moment. She knew she didn't have a lot of time; they needed to get a move on, but she couldn't quite make herself get up yet.

Her guardian had probably reached London by now. She wondered if he'd already checked with Sam and Evie's distant cousin, Julie. There was really nowhere else she could go.

Montbrook would soon start looking into the friends of her friends. And if so, it was just a matter of time before he came knocking at St. Clare's door.

At that precise moment, a loud knock at her door startled her.

"Are you going to be bathing all morning?" her savior called, irritation in his voice. "I thought you were in a hurry to leave."

"I am," she answered, already scrambling from the bath. "I just needed some time to… uh… never mind. I'll be out in ten minutes."

"You better be," Gabriel grumbled and stalked away from the door.

Evie got dressed in record time, especially considering the

lack of a maid to help her. She wore one of three gowns she'd packed into her valise and a pair of satin slippers. Yesterday's attire was given to Gabriel's valet to wash, press, and clean. Evie was certain he wouldn't have any problems with it since the clothing was made for gentlemen.

Evie sent a quick prayer of thanks to her grandfather for teaching her to ride astride when she couldn't quite grasp the sidesaddle and never caring one whit about how unladylike it was, or scandalous even. She wondered for a moment if she should change into masculine garments again so that they could pose as two traveling gentlemen riding on horseback all the way to the Scottish border. It would be faster, too, than using a carriage. No matter how her muscles ached and how tired she was, efficiency was the key.

Evie caught her wet hair in a quick bun at her nape and came down for breakfast. Gabriel wasn't there, but the sideboard held fried eggs, several strips of bacon, fried tomatoes, and some oatcakes. Evie's stomach grumbled at the view of the food. She sat and finished the plate off in minutes she was so hungry. She was draining the last drops of tea when Gabriel came in.

"That was rather fast," he drawled.

Evie turned to him and beheld his surprised features.

"I feel like I haven't eaten in days," she said, wiping her mouth with a napkin. "Should I change into gentlemen's attire again? It would be faster—"

Gabriel stopped her mid-sentence by raising a hand. "No gentlemen's attire, no riding on horseback. We are riding in style, or not at all."

"But—"

"And no arguing." He handed her a light shawl that was

draped over his arm. "We shall be Mr. and Mrs. Swift, and you will wear a turban on your head when we are out of the carriage to conceal your flaming red hair so that we don't raise any suspicions if your guardian decides to send someone on your trail."

Evie took the turban cloth and looked it over. "Didn't I say my independence was part of our bargain? All I get instead is being ordered around."

"You'll get your independence after I get my money, understand? Until then…" He raised his hands in a shrug. "I put your valise in the carriage, so as soon as you don the turban, be out on the street so we can leave."

"Just one more thing. I need to send a note to my friend. She will worry."

St. Clare expelled an impatient breath. "Fine, but be quick about it. My study is this way."

\* \* \*

They set off not long after that. As soon as the carriage left London, Evie took off the turban. She didn't want people to see her flaming hair peeking out of Gabriel's carriage window while they were still in London, but it was heavy and uncomfortable.

They traveled for a long time in silence. She was staring out the window while Gabriel alternated between studying the scenery and her.

"Didn't you bring a novel or embroidery with you to pass the time?" he asked.

"No, I don't do those things in a carriage. I get nauseous. The only way for me to be well is looking out the window."

"Is that why you traveled by horse and not by mail coach to London?"

"One of the reasons, yes. I did travel by mail coach part of the way, but a young lady traveling alone is very suspicious." Evie shrugged. "Besides, it was faster on horseback."

"You could have been robbed, or worse, by brigands. Have you thought of that?" Gabriel sounded irritated. *What did it matter to him?*

"But I wasn't," she said calmly. "I am here, and everything worked out well, didn't it?"

A short silence followed, filled only by the sounds of carriage wheels and horse hooves.

"Did you send a note to Lord Clydesdale?" Evie asked.

Gabriel nodded. "I sent a note to him this morning. Said that I was summoned by my father to Winchester. If your guardian decides to look there, I wish him luck."

They proceeded the rest of the way without conversation. The carriage was jostling them this way and that, making any kind of effort to converse uncomfortable. Gabriel sat in the seat across from her. He lowered his hat to his eyes and seemed to be dozing most of the way. Evie wondered how anybody could sleep in conditions like these and kept her eyes on the horizon.

They stopped several times during the day to change the horses and stretch their legs. Sometime after eight o'clock in the evening, they reached a tiny inn, a bit out of the way from the main road. St. Clare checked them in as Mr. and Mrs. Swift and ordered their supper and bath to their rooms.

Evie was extremely tired, so she even contemplated going to bed unbathed and hungry for the second night in a row. But the lady in her won out. She picked at the food while waiting for the hip tub to be brought in and filled with hot water.

Gabriel entered the room just as the last bucket of water was emptied into the bath. He took off his jacket, hat, and cravat and draped them over the chair by the window. He came closer to the table and studied Evie's plate.

"You haven't eaten much. I thought you'd be hungry."

Evie wrinkled her nose, "I do not eat much while on the road."

"You don't do a lot of things while on the road, do you?"

Evie sighed and rubbed her eyes with her fingers. "I don't. I'm too tired from jostling around the carriage, and my stomach is too churned to keep down much of the food."

"More for me." He settled at the table across from her. "Feel free to have a bath while I eat."

Evie raised a haughty brow at that.

"Very well." He stood and moved his chair so his back was to the bath. "I'll have my back turned, but that's the most I can do. You have nothing to be embarrassed about, I assure you. I've seen so many women naked that nothing can surprise me. Besides, I am too hungry to care about your little naked bottom."

Evie frowned at him, but she was too weary to argue. "Just keep your back turned until I'm done," she grumbled and stood from the table.

Evie undressed as fast as she could and lowered herself carefully into the bath, watching Gabriel all the while, afraid he would decide to take a peek. She lathered herself with soap several times, washed her hair, and got out of the bath before he finished his supper.

"That was fast." He turned to look at her as she wrapped a

towel around her.

"You said you wouldn't look."

"I said I wouldn't look until you were done. And you're done." He studied her toweled form. "You need to eat better. You're too thin."

"Thank you for being so kind, but you don't have to worry about me."

"With the way you take care of yourself, no wonder you are skin and bones. I only hope you'll be well enough when we get to the border and won't be swaying with the wind."

Evie drew in a breath. She didn't have the energy left to spar with him. Instead, she went to her valise and took out her night shift, hair comb, and toothbrush. She took care of her nightly ablutions while he got undressed and got himself into a tub. Gabriel was humming some tune under his breath, and the pleasant timbre of his baritone quickly lulled her into sleep.

# Chapter 3

By the time Gabriel was done with his bath, Evie was fast asleep. After watching her lithe, fit body trot around the room with nothing to cover it up but a towel, he was certain he wouldn't fall asleep for quite some time. How in the hell did she expect them to travel over a sennight together, staying in inns, sharing a narrow bed, and not succumb to the demands of the flesh? As it was, his flesh was hard, hot, and aching for her touch.

He wasn't mocking her when he said she was too thin; she was. But she was also athletically built, and if that towel was any indication, she had small but perky breasts. Add to that milky white skin and golden freckles scattered around her body, and she looked absolutely delicious. She was going to be his wife, too. And he wasn't allowed to have a taste. Not fair.

He lay on the other side of the bed from her and tried distracting himself with thoughts of some non-arousing things, like what his father would say when he found out about his marriage. How Clydesdale would work himself up into a fit when he realized he'd married his wife's cousin. He thought about the upcoming three-day journey in a closed carriage with an innocent seductress until they reached Scotland. At least three more nights in a bed with her. Her red hair tousled on the pillow, her sweet body resting just a few inches away, the scent of her skin mixed with soap arousing his—

Blast! He turned on his stomach and buried his head into his pillow.

He needed to do something about his erection. He couldn't possibly spend the entire journey with it. Perhaps at the next inn, he would find some serving girl or a village woman willing to spend a few hours with him. Yes, he would do just that. Next time they stopped for the night, he wouldn't spend it sleeping chastely in bed next to the seductive little vixen.

This night, however, was torture. He tossed all night, turning this way and that, bumping into her and brushing various parts of his body against her warm skin. She seemed not to notice. In fact, she slept like a log, while he managed to doze only a short while close to dawn.

The next day, Evie woke up, all fresh and rested. And in contrast, he was surly and sleepy. Because of this, he spent most of the day sleeping in the carriage. When he wasn't sleeping, he managed to coax a little conversation from his bride-to-be.

Evie was a little more talkative than the day before, and by suppertime, she was in higher spirits than when she showed up on his doorstep two nights ago. She was turning into the Evie he knew.

They'd met for the first time when she was about seventeen

years old, when Clydesdale had just married his wife, Julie. But Gabriel didn't really remember her back then. His first conscious recollection of her was at her coming-out ball.

She had been standing in a circle of gentlemen, flanked by her grandfather, the formidable duke, and her cousin's husband, the Earl of Clydesdale. She wore a pale emerald gown with a high neckline, full sleeves, and a modest design.

Innocence incarnate.

Her golden-red hair had been gleaming in the candlelight, and her eyes were glowing with joy. That was the moment he'd realized he needed to stay away from her. That mix of innocence and seduction spelled trouble for him every time. Not that she was interested in him, but he knew he could seduce her in no time.

But even guarded by two of the most redoubtable men in England, one of whom held the most respected title and the other being his best friend, he knew it would amount to nothing should he ever seduce her. So he'd stayed away. And now he was about to marry her.

He braced himself for a nice and long pummeling by his best friend. But her grandfather was no longer there to protect her. That job was his from now on.

Somerset had doted on his granddaughter. That was apparent to everyone. It was a constant cause for gossip. He did anything and everything for her. She was rich, beautiful, talented, and adored. A path to ultimate disaster.

But somehow, she'd turned out to be one of the sweetest young ladies of the *ton*. Untouched by the ugliness of envy and greed, she was generous, sincere, and lovely. She'd adored her grandfather, too.

Now, as Gabriel was gazing at her, he noted that the

shadows under her eyes weren't the result of a few sleepless nights; they were a sign of her deep sorrow.

She looked at him at that moment and smiled.

"I understand that the scenery gets boring," she said, her lips twitching in the beginning of laughter. "But could you maybe stop staring at me? I don't suppose I am more interesting than hills and sheep."

"Oh, you are most definitely more interesting than sheep," he said without taking his intent gaze off her face. "Tell me, how does the beloved granddaughter of a formidable duke turn up under the guardianship of a weasel such as Montbrook?"

She sighed heavily and looked away. She was silent for several long moments before finally answering. When she did, her face took on a sorrowful look that strained her features, which made him regret the question.

"He is the only relative from Grandpa's side. And I don't have any aunts or uncles. Our family was very small. When my grandfather married, he probably thought he'd have a bevy of children." She smiled then, lost in a memory. "Their marriage was a scandalous one. My grandmother was the daughter of an Irish merchant and my grandfather a newly titled duke. Grandpa always said that I am the spitting image of her."

"She was quite a beauty, eh?" Gabriel grinned.

Evie turned to him then, a genuine smile playing on her lips. "That's what Grandpa always told me. I imagine that I reminded him of her. That is why he loved me so. Her name was Niamh. Which meant radiant, bright." She paused for a moment, looking back out the window. "They eloped too. But theirs was a love match."

## Chapter 3

A long pause followed while Evie stared out the window, lost in thought. Gabriel didn't interrupt. He was genuinely interested in her story.

"Her fragile health only worsened after she gave birth. So after my father was born, they decided not to have more children. They were happy with their little family. My grandfather doted on his only son. I suppose he always thought my father would take over the Somerset title. Since they were both healthy and strong, he imagined that I would marry long before..." She paused, shook her head, and cleared her throat. "Nobody could have predicted my parents' carriage accident or my grandfather's health issues. And most of all, the treasure of Somerset, unmarried, on the brink of spinsterhood."

She smiled again, only her smile had a bitter twist to it.

"Why haven't you married already?" he asked, suddenly curious. Year in and year out, dozens of suitors had trotted in her wake, worshiping the ground she walked upon, and yet year after year, she remained unwed.

"I was looking for love." She looked up at him with such sadness in her eyes he wanted to weep. "My grandparents married for love, and my parents did too. I lived surrounded by it..." Her face closed, became stony and emotionless, the true duchess in all her grandeur. "I took it for granted," she said quietly.

"No need for that," he said quickly, trying to lighten the mood. "It's not too late. You still have two nights to fall in love. I promise to step aside for true love."

She chuckled lightly, just as he hoped she would. "I am afraid even I am not naïve enough to believe in love at first sight. And for what it's worth, I am not regretting my decision to marry you."

She looked at him as if she was waiting for him to return her sentiment. But how could he? By marrying one of the most marvelous women of the *ton*, he was single-handedly ruining her chances at love and marital bliss. He'd also agreed never to take her to bed, a sentiment he regretted even more than his promise to marry her.

In several more hours, they made it to their next rest stop. The rain was beginning to pour with all its might, and the skies were dark and ominous. Usually, Gabriel enjoyed thunderstorms, which were at least some variation to constant dull weather. Not when he was traveling, however.

He booked a room for them with the innkeeper, and all the while, the bar wench winked and smiled at him in a blatant invitation. Gabriel resolved to take full advantage of her right after supper.

He ushered Evie into the room and looked around. The bath was brought in, and the footmen were rushing back and forth, filling the hip bath with steaming water. Their supper was cooling on the table next to the bed.

Evie was wet, and her shoes were caked with mud from the short walk from the carriage to the inn door. Her teeth were chattering too, and she flinched with every sound of thunder.

"Are you well?" he asked, looking worriedly at her profile. "You seem—"

"I am. It's just… Never mind. I'll feel better after a bath and supper. Do you mind if I bathe first? You can have your supper with your back turned, and I'll…" She gestured to the bath. "It's just that I am cold and dirty. I can't possibly eat like this."

# Chapter 3

"Certainly."

He turned his chair to face the window and listened to her disrobe, the traitorous sounds of fabric peeling off her body and leaving her skin absolutely naked.

He couldn't help but imagine her pulling the gown from her shoulders, then pushing it to the floor, peeling her chemise off her wet body. He didn't hear her take off her stays; he could only imagine that she hadn't worn them the whole day.

If he turned his head just a little, he would see... He heard a splash, signaling that she lowered herself into the bath, and he closed his eyes. This was torture. His fork fell to his plate with a clatter. He stood, not bothering to finish his supper, and walked to the door.

"A-are you leaving?" She stammered out the words.

"Yes, I was—" Gabriel paused with his hand on the door handle and turned to look at her.

Her expressive eyes were wide with horror, her lips parted. Just then, another boom of roaring thunder shook the inn roof. Evie visibly flinched again.

"You are not afraid of a thunderstorm, are you?"

Evie swallowed audibly and shook her head. His gaze narrowed on that light ripple in her throat.

He forced himself to meet her eyes. "You *are* afraid!"

"I..." Evie lowered herself deeper into the bath water, making herself as small as possible, and closed her eyes. "Maybe," she finally said with a grimace.

"Do you want me to stay?" He turned to face her, leaned his back against the door, and regarded her lazily.

Evie took a long breath and just stared at him. Gabriel smiled inwardly. She was too proud even to admit she was afraid. But saying that she needed him was completely beyond

31

her. Suddenly, he wanted her to admit that she needed him. Badly.

"You know," he drawled. "I needed to take care of something, but if you want me to stay, all you have to do is ask."

He took on a deceptively leisurely stance, raised his hand, and studied his nails, waiting for her move.

"Would you please stay here?" she finally muttered under her breath.

"You want me to stay," he said as loudly as he could without shouting. "Here."

"Yes," she answered irritably.

"Let me get this straight." He flicked an invisible speck off his shoulder. "The shy and proper Lady Eabha Montgomery is asking me"—he pointed at himself—"a notorious rake, to stay here with her and watch her bathe?"

A sponge flew out of her hands and landed squarely in the middle of his chest, wetting his shirt. He caught the sponge in his hands as it bounced off his body.

"And she wants me to lather her with soap. Mmm, how tempting."

"I've changed my mind; please go away." Evie covered her face with her hands and lowered her head under the water.

Gabriel chuckled in delight. Despite his teasing, he couldn't very well leave a woman when she was clearly in distress. Besides, he was having far too grand a time making her blush. In the candlelight, she blushed an alluring color of strawberry pink.

The bar wench forgotten, Gabriel pulled his wet and soapy shirt off his back and moved toward the bath just as she emerged from under the water. She regarded him warily as he came to a stop a few inches from her bath and lowered himself to sit beside her. He put the hand that held her sponge into the water.

"Do you need me to give you a nice scrub, too?" he asked, a charming smile on his lips.

"No, I need you to go away."

The thunder crackled then, making her flinch again.

"You see," he drawled, weaving the sponge in the water. "I don't think you do. I think you want me to stay right here."

"Not right here." She gestured around her bath. "Right there." She pointed her finger in the direction of the table. "Preferably with your back turned."

"What's the difference?" He shrugged and dropped the sponge in the water. He raised his hand and clutched the bath rim. "We are going to be married soon. I might as well see you naked."

"I think you've seen a fair share of naked women in your lifetime. It is only right that there is one woman you don't get to see." She smiled her smug smile at him.

"Don't you think it unfair that the only woman I don't get to see naked would be my own wife?"

"Unfair?" She tapped a forefinger on her plump lips, looking thoughtful. "No. Ironic?" She made a gesture of weighing things in her hands. "Maybe. Poetic? Definitely." She smiled her beguiling smile at him and gestured to their supper table. "Now move, please."

She used that commanding tone again as if he were a petulant child or a disobedient mare. He unfolded himself and meekly strode in the direction of the table.

"Besides," she continued conversationally, making splashing sounds while lathering her arms with soap, "you agreed on our terms. You could have negotiated. But you didn't."

"Are you saying," he said, sitting down in his chair and looking at her over his shoulder, "you would have negotiated sleeping with me if I insisted upon it?"

She threw him another one of her superior smiles. "I suppose you will never know now, will you?"

Gabriel chuckled as he settled in his chair. As strange as it was, he actually enjoyed the company of this sharp-tongued virgin. Maybe it wasn't so strange, since everyone in the *ton* adored her. Suitors, their mothers, fathers, and other relatives—everyone loved her. He just hadn't thought that a seasoned rake like him would be charmed by this innocent girl.

She was extremely beautiful, and her thin, athletic body aroused him, but that was no news. He felt this way about almost any female. He was a rake. But he'd turned down a good long tumble with a bar wench for sitting in a chair and sparring with her, and he wasn't even regretting it.

"When you came to my doorstep the other night, it was raining too. Weren't you afraid then?"

"I was, but I had no choice, did I?"

"Hm. So tell me the story?"

"What story?"

"Of darling little Evie being left out in the storm that led to this unreasonable fear."

"It isn't unreasonable. The lightning can strike at any place and just burn you. I've read that it can even travel inside the house if the windows are not covered."

Gabriel chuckled. "Ridiculous."

"No, it isn't. And there is no story. I was always terrified of storms. My grandfather encouraged me to learn about them. He even bought me books about the phenomenon, hoping knowing what caused it would remove my *unreasonable* fear. But all it did was worsen it."

Gabriel laughed again.

"You can laugh all you want," she grumbled. "But you won't laugh if it ever strikes you."

Gabriel turned his head toward her. She was lathering her hands with a great deal of concentration. "You traveled alone from Carlisle; I wouldn't peg you for a fearful one."

She shrugged. "Everyone is afraid of something. For instance, what are you afraid of?"

Gabriel scratched his jaw in thought. "I suppose I am not afraid of anything."

She laughed. "Impossible."

"I am not; there is really nothing that frightens me."

"And as a child? Were you afraid of anything then?"

"No." Gabriel turned away.

"Come, little Gabriel never ran into his parents' room at night because he had a bad dream?"

She was teasing. He knew it. And he'd love to keep her talking because she didn't seem to notice the rumbling thunder anymore. But his childhood was something he wasn't willing to discuss.

"No," he said and stood from the table. "In fact, little Gabriel spent most of his childhood in the Eton boardinghouse."

He walked to his valise and started rummaging through it, looking for his robe.

"Hm," she said but didn't pursue the topic. "It must be exciting to live in a school away from your parents with a bunch of boys."

He grinned as he put on a robe. "Yes, it was. We were into all kinds of mischief."

"Truly, such as?"

Gabriel sat back down at the table and proceeded to tell her about the pet turtle he and his roommate hid in their room at Eton. She told him about a tabby that had fur almost the same shade as her hair and how everyone called them twins. They discussed books they had read as children and the adventures they had dreamed of having once they grew up.

He wanted to be a pirate and roam the seas. She wanted to travel across America on horseback with Indians.

The conversation easily slipped off his tongue. She was so easy to talk to, never judging, always ready with a joke and a smile. She was so warm and affectionate toward his childhood self that he forgot to be self-conscious, to pretend, to put up a façade.

When she was done washing, she stepped out of the bath, and he tortured himself with the naked visions of her in his mind's eye again while she dried and dressed. Then they traded places as she ate and he bathed.

When the maids cleared their room of the bath and food, he sat in bed in his night robe and watched his bride. Evie combed her hair near the fireplace in her fresh day gown, yellow with tiny, embroidered ornaments at the hem and bust line. The storm seemed to have calmed, although the rain beat an incessant staccato on the inn's windows and roof.

Gabriel watched her with avid interest. She was too enticing for her own good. Her long, flaming hair curled as she brushed it. And he finally understood why young ladies always had their hair bound in public.

It was like an aphrodisiac. He imagined wrapping his hands in her curls, drawing her close. *Damn it.* Would his thoughts ever get out of the gutter? He tried to divert his musings.

36

## Chapter 3

"Tell me, love. What was with the men's clothing you were wearing the night you came to my doorstep?"

As an attempt to get his thoughts out of the gutter, it failed miserably. He suddenly remembered her in men's breeches, her buttocks swaying invitingly, the gentle curve of her hips enhanced by the garment. He closed his eyes tight.

Evie wasn't looking at him; her gaze was focused on the fire, her hands working on brushing out the tendrils of her hair.

"I told you, it is suspect for a lady to travel unaccompanied. So I had to pass for a gentleman. Besides, it is quite uncomfortable riding astride in skirts unless you pull them up and bunch them at the waist."

This wasn't helping. Now he was imagining her exactly like that, with her skirts lifted, bunched at the waist, or even tossed over her head. He could do so many pleasurable things to her in that position.

He cleared his throat. "Where did you learn such a scandalous activity as riding astride?"

She laughed. "My grandfather taught me. He said I begged him until he relented, although my mother used to say that I didn't ever have to beg for anything. He did whatever I asked."

"You spent quite a lot of time with your grandfather," Gabriel observed, glad to pull his thoughts to safer pastures.

"Quite." She smiled at him, still brushing her hair. "As soon as I was born, he basically appropriated me from my parents."

She laughed softly again. Gabriel didn't think he'd ever heard a lady laugh as much in one evening. The main trait of all gentle society was to wear an air of boredom, to never show their emotions.

And there she was, laughing openly, at herself, at her family, at him. Everything made her laugh or at least smile. She was a breath of fresh air for his stone-cold heart and cynical attitude.

He remembered his sophisticated lovers. They would pretend to be intrigued, act coy, and always aloof.

He found a return smile on his lips this entire evening, as well. When she wasn't jostling in a moving carriage, she was a delight. He loved every minute he spent with her. Even his aching erection didn't bother him that much.

He winced. *Much.*

"They loved me too, of course. But they had each other." She threw a glance over her shoulder. "Grandpa didn't have anyone, so he poured all his love into me, I suppose."

How lovely it must have been to grow up surrounded by an adoring family. Gabriel thought of his cold and distant father. No. He didn't know what it felt like to be loved.

Surely, his lovers adored him, worshiped him even, but they hadn't really known him enough to love him.

Oh, they loved his sexual prowess, his looks, his wealth when he had it, his title. None of them knew him well enough to love him for him, though.

Evie got up, obviously done brushing and drying her hair. "What time are we setting off tomorrow?"

"It depends," he answered thoughtfully. "If the morning is sunny, the roads should be passably dry by mid-morning."

She frowned at the thought. "I wish we could get there sooner."

"Don't worry, love," he said as she blew out the candle and climbed into bed with him. "You'll be married to me in no time."

"I can't wait." She yawned and turned her back on him.

## Chapter 3

"Good night."

"Good night," he answered with a sigh and resigned himself to another sleepless night.

# Chapter 4

Evie moaned at pleasurable sensations. She was in a state of half slumber, having an incredibly pleasant dream. Hot hands were caressing her body, touching her most indecently, and yet she couldn't help but enjoy the feeling. She'd had similar dreams before, but this time, it was a little different.

The hands were expertly flicking her nipples, cupping her breasts in a way that shot wicked sensations down her belly. Her nipples turned into hard, aching peaks, and she leaned firmer into the caress, wanting more of the contact, needing more of the contact.

She felt a tingle low in her belly, demanding something. Evie whimpered and shifted restlessly, pressing her buttocks against something hard and hot behind her. One hand moved down from her breast to caress her ribcage, her belly, and lower still.

Evie caught her breath as the hand cupped her most intimate place. She was jolted awake by the sensation and jumped in reaction, but arms as hard as steel and hot as coal kept her in place.

This wasn't a dream anymore. Evie's eyes widened. She was being caressed so intimately by… She managed to collect her wits enough to remember that she was sharing a bed with a notorious rake!

But it was so delicious that for a moment, Evie was tempted to stay in bed and let him do whatever he wanted with her. As long as he didn't stop.

But as pleasurable as the sensations were, she knew this wasn't right; she needed to get out of bed.

She wriggled again, and her buttocks ground against a hot, hard rod. Her breathing grew heavy, either from shock or from excitement. Her body felt like it was on pins and needles.

She squeaked and managed to untangle herself from Gabriel's grip. She shot out from the bed and stared at him wide-eyed.

Gabriel groaned and propped himself on one elbow, looking as confused as she felt. His hair was falling over one half of his face, his lips were plump, and his chin was covered with light stubble. All in all, he looked sinfully delicious yet boyishly innocent. Evie had an inexplicable urge to crawl back into bed and kiss him senseless.

"What?" Gabriel rubbed his eyes with his knuckles. "What happened?"

His voice, low and hoarse from sleep, sent a pleasant tingle down her spine. His untidy appearance gave him a roguish look and somehow made him so much more handsome. The unfairness of it all, of him looking so gorgeous, of her wanting him beyond reason, made her irritable.

"What happened?" she gasped, fairly bristling with indignation. "You tell me!"

"What are you talking about?" He looked extremely confused, and understanding finally dawned on her.

He was so used to spending his nights with his lovers that he was caressing her in his sleep, without even realizing what he was doing. Here she was enjoying his touch, wishing she could spend eternity in his arms, and he was asleep! He wasn't even touching her; he was touching some other woman in his dreams.

"Never mind," she grumbled and turned away from him.

Tears of indignation burned at the back of her eyes. She didn't know whether to laugh or cry. Hadn't she been affronted just a moment ago that he was touching her so scandalously? And now she was upset that he wasn't aware that he was touching *her*.

*Oh, Evie, you are such an idiot.* She rummaged through her valise, took out her brush, poured cleaning powder on it, and walked to the washbasin. Gabriel groaned and collapsed back on the bed, throwing one arm over his eyes.

"Something's bothering you," he said.

She threw him a glance over her shoulder. A sheet covered him from thigh to abdomen. The rest of him was naked.

"Dm lws shep laken?" she asked while brushing her teeth.

Gabriel chuckled. "Did you say something?"

She spat and turned to face him, her hands gripping the washbasin from behind. "I said, do you always sleep naked?"

Gabriel took his arm from his eyes and surveyed his appearance. With a shrug, he returned his arm to cover his eyes. "I do, actually. I don't own a nightshirt. I went to bed in a robe last night, but I obviously took it off during the night without realizing it. I'm not used to restraining clothing while

I sleep."

"Obviously not," she muttered under her breath.

"You see," he continued, as he sat up in bed, regarding her intently. "I am not used to sleeping in a bed with a woman without... actually bedding her."

Evie felt a fierce blush creep up her neck and onto her face. Curse her fair skin.

"You are shameless," she said, for lack of a decent reply.

"I have to be. I'm a rake, remember? Couldn't go far with shame pulling me down."

Evie looked down at her feet. She could practically feel his gaze like a caress.

"Tell me," he coaxed. "What did I do?"

Her head shot up. "Nothing."

"Look, I am really not used to this. I spend almost every night with a woman. So, if I did something untoward in my sleep, it was an involuntary reaction. Nothing personal."

Evie felt as if a huge boulder was stuck in her throat. *Nothing personal.* Of course, it wasn't personal.

"I promise to get us separate rooms at the next inn," he continued.

*So you can bed some willing woman.* Evie finished his sentence in her head.

The thought shouldn't have bothered her so. There was a reason she'd struck this deal with him. If he never bedded her, she wouldn't grow even more attached to him. She needed to let him do his business with other women. If she allowed him an inch, he would take over not only her heart but every corner of her mind.

Just like he said, he was used to bedding various women every night. Expecting him to behave differently on this trip was setting herself up for disappointment. She had been in love with him for as long as she could remember, and she always knew who he was and that her fairytale love match was doomed.

But no, she'd promised her grandfather to marry for love, and she'd do it even if it killed her. And it very well might.

Somehow, when Gabriel was just a distant figure passing at the edge of her life, it was easier not to pay attention to his trysts. Now that they were traveling together, it was painful to even contemplate. And she was about to marry him.

*Oh, Evie, what are you getting yourself into?*

"Good," she said and nodded for emphasis. She walked up to the chair that held her clothing and started pulling on her gown. She heard the rustle of bedsheets. Gabriel was probably up and getting dressed as well. She kept her back turned as she dressed and arranged her hair, trying to ignore the sounds of Gabriel putting on his clothes, shaving, and walking around the room.

"I am going to order us some breakfast and then get the horses ready. Meet me downstairs."

Gabriel left, and Evie sagged against the wall. Her lips curled downward, her brows furrowed. Why did she always have to suffer? Why did she have to fall in love with the least attainable man in London? She heaved a sigh, pushed off the wall, and proceeded to collect the rest of her things. Whatever the answers were to her questions, she wasn't going to find them in this old inn.

They started their journey right after breakfast. The carriage was slow because the roads hadn't dried out as much as they'd anticipated, and it jostled even worse than before in the thick mud. Still, Evie didn't want to waste any more time than necessary. The faster they got to Scotland, the faster she'd be married and free of the Montbrooks.

She wouldn't have to worry about them catching up with her and dragging her kicking and screaming back to Carlisle. Or worse. What if they caught up with her at the border? They could marry her off to their odious son right then and there. She shuddered at the thought.

"Are you cold?"

Evie directed her gaze to the tired-looking viscount sitting across from her. Despite the weary lines about his eyes, he looked as bored and elegant as ever. She imagined she looked green from wanting to cast up her accounts, weary from the jostling, and overall tired from the journey. Oh, how she wished to be on horseback right now instead of this.

"No," she answered and returned her gaze to the horizon. The more her gaze wandered from the window, the worse she felt.

"Are you certain?" His voice took on a genuinely worried lilt.

"I am."

Gabriel drew his breath to say something more when the carriage suddenly and violently drew to a halt. Evie flew from her seat and right into his arms with a grunt. He held her close, his arms locking around her body. Evie inhaled his comforting scent and inwardly cursed herself. Even as simple an action as holding her when she fell caused her to melt.

He gently set her aside, looking her over with a wandering gaze. "Are you hurt?"

"No, I'm—" She blew a loose tendril of hair from her face, feeling heat climb up from her neck. "What happened?" She looked around the unmoving carriage.

"I shall go check," Gabriel said and exited the vehicle.

Evie looked out from both of the windows, but she couldn't see anything. After a few minutes, the door flew open, and Gabriel poked his head in.

"An axle broke on one of the wheels."

Evie's eyes grew wide. They were stuck on the muddied road in a broken carriage.

"We are already several hours away from the last village, and if memory serves our coachman, there's another village, Forton, some ten miles ahead."

Evie absorbed the information, trying to understand what he was telling her.

"There are two ways out of our predicament," he said. "One, we send our coachman to Forton, so he can get help. On horseback, it'll take him about an hour to get there, maybe an hour and a half in this mud. Fetching another carriage to get us and coming back for us will take longer, though."

"We'll be stranded here for hours," she finished his thought.

"Exactly."

"What is another option?"

"We can leave the carriage here. We both have just small valises with us. We can load them up and travel to the village on horseback. Then send some people to fix our carriage and bring it back. But either way, we'll have to spend the night in the village."

A delay she possibly could not afford. But there was nothing they could do about it now.

"We'll have to share a horse too," he said with an apologetic smile. "Our coachman will take the other one. We don't have any valuables in the carriage, so it doesn't make sense to leave him here alone."

Another hour in his arms. Another opportunity for her fanciful thoughts to get away from her. She sighed with resignation.

"Very well," she muttered as he helped her out of the carriage. Gabriel was right; they couldn't leave the poor coachman alone on the road. She'd just have to keep her wits about her.

Gabriel swung up on the horse and helped Evie up into his lap. She was sitting with her backside propped against his left thigh and her legs swinging over his right leg. He put his right hand over her waist, propped her back with his left, and urged the horse into a canter.

It wasn't the most comfortable position for Evie, so she wiggled and shifted in her seat.

"Would you care to cease doing that?" Gabriel said on a hiss.

"Doing what?"

"Wiggling your bottom. Repeatedly. It's very... er... distracting."

"Distracting?"

"Uncomfortable," Gabriel muttered.

"Well, it is not exactly a picnic for me here either," she complained. "Do you think it's comfortable being propped sideways on a human being?"

Gabriel gave a soft laugh. "How about you try to relax? You can rest your head against me, like so"—with his right hand, he pressed her cheek against his shoulder—"and try not to move."

"Splendid," she muttered against him.

They rode in silence for a little while. The horse's unhurried pace and the warmth of Gabriel's embrace started to lull Evie into sleep. She slipped her right arm around his back and pressed herself closer, cushioning her head against his chest. His left arm tensed around her, and he pressed her closer.

His scent, his warmth, enveloped her in its comfort. She sighed and relaxed against him, pretending that he held her close because he wanted to, not because he had to, that they shared a horse not because they had no choice, but because he couldn't spend a moment apart from her.

One more daydream wouldn't hurt, right?

She was drifting off to sleep when she heard distant thunder rumbling. She immediately tensed.

"Wonderful," Gabriel muttered under his breath. Evie felt a wet drop on her hair, and then another, and another until a heavy rain descended upon them.

"Hold on to me," he said over the sound of rain and urged the horse to a gallop.

About half an hour later, they were standing on the doorstep of a tiny inn, drenched and dirty up to their waist.

"Why is it," she asked after running into an inn and shaking her hair off of excess water, "that I seem to be constantly wet around you?"

He cocked an arrogant brow at her. "I get asked that all the time."

She threw him a suspicious gaze, and he laughed heartily.

Gabriel was soaked in rainwater. His hair was plastered to his face, his coat clung to his wide shoulders, his breeches outlined every muscle of his thighs, and rivulets of water trickled down his face.

All in all, he looked magnificent. Why? Evie had no answer to this question. It was one of those unfair truths of the universe. It bestowed beauty upon the undeserving. The more bedraggled he looked, and the less put together, the more his natural beauty shone.

Evie couldn't seem to take her gaze off him. Which was absolutely unfair and completely one-sided.

Since they'd dismounted, he had looked at her only once, to make that scathing comment to her remark. Now he headed to the innkeeper without a backward glance.

Well, what did she expect from the notorious rake? Besides, she probably looked a fright.

\* \* \*

Gabriel walked to the reception desk and away from the seductive vixen he was traveling with. It wasn't enough that he'd spent an hour on horseback with her backside pressed against his inner thigh, the scent of her soap and skin under his nostrils. Now, she stood in the doorway bunching parts of her gown that were plastered to her skin, unsuccessfully trying to wring the water out of her clothing.

The only thing she managed to do was give Gabriel an aching erection. He almost groaned and forced his thoughts to return to their predicament at hand.

He approached the innkeeper in the crowded hallway, but he didn't have time to ask anything as the innkeeper said in a raised tone of voice, "There is no more room. I am sorry, folks, but you'll have to disperse."

Groans and exclamations of outrage followed this announcement. The innkeeper was about to leave, but Gabriel caught him by the arm.

"Here, good sir, you wouldn't turn away guests of noble

origin, now would you?"

"Who?" The innkeeper frowned at Gabriel's rain-soaked appearance.

"Look there. The beautiful young lady by the doorway is my wife. We've been traveling from London nonstop."

He turned to Evie.

She was still shaking out her skirts; her gown was dirty almost to her waist, her bodice soaked, and her hair, darkened to the color of burgundy, was plastered to her head. She looked pitiful but also magnificent. With her hair messy and tangled over her shoulders, her sodden gown outlining every curve of her athletic form, and her chin lifted up in defiance, she was like a warrior queen from the Highlands.

The innkeeper didn't seem to see her the same way, though; he looked her over with an unflattering gaze. "Noblemen, eh? Then I'm the pope." He turned on his heel and stalked out of the common room so fast Gabriel had barely opened his mouth to retort.

The door opened, and their coachman walked straight to Gabriel. "My lord, I took care of the horses and found willing bodies to fix the axle on the morrow. However, it looks like we'll have to spend the night here."

Gabriel scoffed. "Unfortunately, it doesn't seem like there's a place here."

"There's a space in the stables—" The coachman grimaced and clamped his lips shut.

Gabriel stifled a bitter laugh. With how things were going, they might just have to spend the night in the stables.

"You take the stables." Gabriel patted the coachman on the shoulder. "And I shall see if I can procure a place for the duchess and me."

He walked to Evie and plastered as optimistic a smile as he could on his face. Apparently, he failed because Evie blinked at him, looking worried.

"There's no room here," he said and rubbed his hand over his face.

"What do you mean, no room?" She looked at him in misery.

"I mean, they are full. There is no extra room, no bed, not even a bloody closet." He heaved a long-suffering sigh. "There's a place in the stables. I offered it to our coachman, but if you decide you want it instead…"

Evie looked out the window at the gray wall of rain and shuddered.

"Bloody hell, you're freezing," Gabriel said and put his hand on her cold and sodden sleeve. "Come."

He led her to a small reception area and sat her on a chair next to a fireplace.

"I'm thinking a night in the stables is not such a bad prospect if the alternative is to freeze to death in the rain," Evie said, settling into the chair.

"During the thunderstorm." He smiled his wicked smile at her.

"Preying on my weaknesses. It's not charming," she said.

"You sit here. I'll see what I can find for us for the night."

He beckoned the coachman to join them in the room. "Look after her, will you?" He flipped him a coin and walked away.

Gabriel wrapped his coat closer to him and walked out of the inn into the heavy rain. What a brave little duchess he was taking for a wife. Any other lady would be having conniptions by now.

Yet, she didn't cry; she didn't scream in frustration, and he would wager his future inheritance that she would have gone through the storm if he said this was her only choice. She, who flinched with every sound of thunder. The thought was ridiculous.

Gabriel looked around at the dull scenery. He didn't have a plan, so he did the only thing he could. He went knocking on people's homes and telling them their unfortunate story, exaggerating here and there, omitting a few facts, and using his considerable charm in order to find a dry, warm place to spend the night.

The cottages were small and didn't have any room. The third house he approached had six inhabitants, and they only had enough space to sleep on the floor. They directed him to a small shabby cottage a few houses past, at the edge of the village.

The widow Jane's place.

Gabriel knocked on the door and was greeted by a tiny elderly lady. She was wearing a gray gown, gray slippers, and a gray shawl about her shoulders. Because of their proximity and his tall form, she had to crane her neck all the way back to look him in the eyes.

"A handsome devil, aren't you?" she said in lieu of greeting and cocked a brow. "Did they send you to seduce me out of my house?" She gave a low cackle of laughter as she looked him up suggestively. "If I were but a few years younger." She huffed. "These days, all I am interested in is a dominoes game and a cup of honeyed tea. Do you play?"

"Erm…" For once, Gabriel didn't know how to answer. Perhaps all of his charm and wit were frozen by the icy rain or jostled out of him by the horse. "I would love to engage you in a game of dominoes," he finally said. "But we'd need lodging for a night as well. I'll pay you."

She huffed again. "Pay me?" She looked him up and down again. "With what exactly?"

"I'm sure we can work this out, ma'am," he said with a crooked smile. "But you see, my lady wife is waiting at the inn. They didn't have a spare room, and I don't think she can travel any farther… in her condition. I am begging for your kindness to let us spend the night."

The old lady's eyes widened at that, and she sobered. "Well, why didn't you say so right away? Standing here, flirting away." Gabriel pursed his lips so as not to laugh. Widow Jane waved her hand in the direction of the inn. "Go get your lady now, will you? I'll prepare a clean bed for you two." With that, she disappeared inside the house, and Gabriel was back in the rainy street.

He hurried through the drizzling rain toward the inn. Once he reached it, he opened the inn door with a crash. Gabriel was cold, hungry, and tired. All he wanted was a dry bed, dry clothes, and possibly a nice hot bath. He was irritated and angry at the weather, at this damn trip, and most of all, at his father. If he hadn't cut him off, none of this would have happened.

He entered the small reception area where he'd left Evie and froze at the door, a sense of peace assailing him.

She was sleeping curled up in a chair by the fire. She looked so innocent, with such a peaceful look on her face that he wanted to cuddle up next to her and fall asleep beside her. Forget the hot bath and dry sheets. Just a snuggle with this fiery angel was enough. He sighed and stepped inside quietly. He needed to wake her, or she risked catching a cold.

# Chapter 5

E vie heard the sound of birds chirping. She opened her eyes and looked around. She was in Peacehaven, surrounded by rose bushes and other flowers. She squinted at the bright sun and smiled, lifting her face toward it.

"You'll get even more freckles," said an achingly familiar male voice. "Not that I care, but your mother is going to complain."

Evie turned toward her favorite person in the world.

"Let her complain, Grandpa," she said, chuckling. "She says I shan't find any suitors with my freckles. But really, do I want a husband who will only appreciate me as long as I am not all spotted?"

"You sure don't, Flamebird." He laughed huskily and sat next to her.

Evie rearranged her skirts, so Somerset had more room to sit. "Shall we go to the tower today?"

"Do you want to?" he asked.

"I do." She smiled up at him. "You can tell me the story again."

The duke laughed again. "You know the story by heart, darling *girl."*

*"I know I do." She looked at him with all her love for the dearest man. "But I love to hear the way you tell it."*

*"Very well, Flamebird." He stood and towered over her, shadowing the sun. "Lead the way."*

*She looked at him, confused. Something was different about him at that moment. His beautiful features were shadowed; he looked almost foreign.*

*He put his hand on her shoulder. "Evie," he said. "Wake up."*

"I'm not…" she began and opened her eyes.

She was jostled out of sleep, bewildered. She looked around, not recognizing where she was. It took her a moment to realize that the person towering over her and shaking her awake wasn't her beloved grandfather, but Viscount St. Clare, and she wasn't in her cozy garden by the sea in Peacehaven, she was at a dingy inn, asleep in the chair by the fireplace. She rubbed her eyes with her knuckles and sat up.

"I'm up," she said, not completely out of her dream state.

She cast about the inn for the familiar form and the husky, gravelly sound of her grandfather's voice, but he was gone, and the dream was gone too. She was left alone in this miserable reality.

She wanted to bury her face in her hands and stay in her dreams forever. But she had to move. So, she got up and put on the most brilliant smile she could muster.

"Did you find a place for us to sleep?"

"I think you've managed that well by yourself," Gabriel answered, indicating her state of half slumber.

"Oh, apologies." She laughed. "It's the fire. It lulled me to sleep and gave me a false sense of security."

"No need to fret," he answered. "Our coachman was looking

after you." He extended his hand. "Come, now. I've found us lodgings for the night."

"You did?" She put her hand in his and let him pull her up to her feet. She ran her fingers through her hair, brushing it away from her face.

"Yes, but I was cold and miserable and, in my haste to get us a roof over our heads, I might have told a couple of lies." He took their valises and shuffled toward the door.

"What kind of lies?" she asked.

He turned to her, a wide grin on his face. "It's better if it comes as a surprise to you. Just remember, you have to agree with whatever I tell you."

"That's not fair—" she began, but at that moment, he opened the door.

The wind howled into the inn, and the rain whipped in their faces, so no further conversation was even remotely possible.

By the time they reached the cottage, they were both wet to the bone. Evie's teeth chattered so violently that she was worried she'd break them.

"It's pissing down there, isn't it?" a croaking female voice called from somewhere inside the house. "Well, don't just stand there; come on in."

Gabriel didn't even hesitate. He entered further into the house, sloshing water and dirt in his wake.

Evie paused in the doorway, looking down at herself. "We'll get everything wet," she said helplessly.

"Don't you worry about that, my child." The weathered old woman turned nurturing and soft at the sight of Evie. "I prepared my finest guest room for you," she said, taking Evie by her hand and leading her away. "I have just one anyway, but you wouldn't want to stay away from your husband now, would you, child?" she asked mildly, patting Evie on her arm. "In your condition, after the horrible journey you must have gone through, he must be by your side if you need anything."

"Actually I do not mind…." Evie said before throwing a scorching gaze toward Gabriel. "My condition?"

"You are a thin little thing too, like a twig. You need to eat more, dear," the woman continued as if Evie hadn't spoken.

"That's what I keep telling her," Gabriel interjected and earned himself another glare. "Well, I do." He raised his shoulders in a shrug.

They finally reached a small and cozy little room on the first floor of the cottage. It was a bright, cheerful room, done in whites and pinks, with flowers adorning every surface. The bed was small but tall. It looked so incredibly soft and warm that Evie wanted to groan. She already imagined herself snuggled beneath the warm covers, fast asleep. The fire crackled comfortably in the hearth.

"There's a dressing room just behind that door." The woman indicated a door by the bed. "I am heating you some water so you can have a bath, just to warm yourself. Then we can have some tea in the kitchen."

Evie left her side to stand by the fire. Gabriel walked toward her, put an arm around her shoulders, and rubbed her upper arm in a show of husbandly solicitude. Evie tensed at the contact before letting herself relax in his arms.

"Then we can have a game of dominoes," the widow added cheerfully.

"I don't think my wife—" Gabriel protested, but Evie interrupted him.

"That would be lovely," she said, twisting in his arms and

giving the old woman a warm smile. "Thank you so much for your generosity and hospitality."

"You are most welcome, my child." The old woman regarded them both with fond eyes. "I shall leave you now. You need to change from your sodden clothes as soon as possible. We don't want you to catch a chill now, do we?" With these words, the old woman shuffled away, closing the door behind her.

Evie stared at the closed door as if transfixed for a few moments before rounding on Gabriel.

"My condition?" she asked, narrowing her eyes on him. "What condition is that, exactly?"

"I think you know the answer to that," he said, not bothered by her outrage at all.

He moved away from the fire and started taking off his clothes one by one and making a small heap on the floor.

"You told her I am with child," she accused, still staring at him. "I do not even look like I'm with child."

He raised his head and looked her up and down with an assessing gaze. "You certainly don't, but we can tell her we just found out."

He shrugged and resumed taking off his clothes. Off went the waistcoat. Next, he tugged his shirt free of his breeches.

"Why did you have to lie to her?"

"Listen, pet, I was tired, hungry, and freezing my bollocks off while you were peacefully slumbering by the fire. I think I deserve some gratitude, not accusations."

He pulled his shirt from his back, and the sodden garment joined the growing heap on the floor. Evie had trouble averting her gaze from the gleaming wet muscles on his back. Her mouth began to water, and a peculiar heat started gathering between her legs. She regained her composure when he reached for the falls of his trousers and quickly turned to face the fire.

"You are right," she said. "I apologize."

"Truly?"

"Yes. Truly. It's just… She seems so very nice. I don't feel good about lying to her."

"Listen, love, we would have to lie to her about our relationship anyway; what's one more lie in the grand scheme of things?"

"You could have told her we were siblings, then the extra lie about my condition would have been unnecessary."

She looked at him again. A horrible mistake. He was standing buck naked, facing her. After three days of travel and sharing his bed for three nights, she still hadn't seen him fully naked, at least not from his front.

Her gaze instantly went to the spot between his legs. It was a curious sight. That part of his body seemed to have a life of its own. It had been saggy and limp when she first set her eyes on it, but it started swelling and growing in an upward direction with each second. Her eyes widened, and her mouth formed a silent 'O'.

Gabriel laughed, and she tore her gaze from his groin to look at his face. She felt the heat creep up her neck.

"You were saying?" he asked, not at all embarrassed, standing there, still naked, hands on his hips, displaying all his manly glory.

Evie could have died from mortification right then and there. She'd been caught staring like a wanton or a trollop. She wished the floor would open up and swallow her without a chance of being spit back.

Evie covered her face with her hands and turned around with a whimper.

Gabriel just chuckled. The insufferable man. Of course, he wasn't embarrassed. Half of England's population had probably seen him like this. She, on the other hand, was mortified.

This was the first time she'd ever seen a male fully naked up front. And she didn't know what to think. Gabriel was lean and muscled, like the statues she'd seen in museums and books. But the difference was in that private part of his body. They didn't look like that on the statues. And they definitely didn't move.

*Of course, they didn't move, you ninny head; they were statues!*

"Like I said," Gabriel said in his hard-measured tone. "I wasn't thinking straight. Besides, I think I can play adoring husband more than a concerned brother. I've never played that role before, you know."

"You haven't exactly played the role of the husband before now, have you?" she said, her voice muffled through her hands, which were still covering her face. "And," she continued stubbornly, "you promised me a separate bed!"

"Afraid you won't be able to keep your hands off of me, eh?" he asked with a chuckle.

"Believe me," she said as emphatically as she could. "That will not be a problem."

"I shan't touch you either, so relax," he said, suddenly irate. "Now," he said, coming closer to her. "Keep still while I unfasten your bodice. You look extremely chilled."

About forty minutes later, Evie was washed, dressed in a dry day gown, with plaited hair. She came downstairs to see

Gabriel helping the old woman in setting the table.

She raised her brow at the unlikely tableau. Gabriel was not the kind of man she would imagine knew anything about the etiquette of setting the dinner plates, but the old woman didn't seem to protest.

"May I help?" Evie asked when she neared the table.

"Don't you worry about a thing, child," the woman said. "You need to rest; your husband will take care of you."

Evie swallowed an urge to laugh. Didn't the woman know she had a viscount, an heir to an earldom, in her kitchen, running around like an errand boy?

Gabriel didn't say a word of protest. He was amicably discussing something with the old lady, being his most charming self. Evie smiled and sat at the table.

"My old Mr. Travis was the one who cooked in our house," the old lady said. "He was working as a footman for the old baron but spent quite a lot of time in the kitchen just watching the chef cook. That's where he learned all his recipes." She put a pie on the table. "All I can make is a half-decent eel pie and a stew."

She cut the pie and put the pieces on everyone's plates. She sat at the head of the table, and Gabriel sat across from Evie.

Evie looked at her plate. *Wonderful, another eel pie.* Would she ever have a decent meal on this journey? She picked up a spoon and dug into the stew and buttered bread rolls.

"This is delicious, Mrs. Travis," Evie said.

The woman cackled. "Nobody ever calls me Mrs. Travis. Never did. I was born in this small village, and everybody just called me Jane. When my husband died a few years back, people started referring to me as Widow Jane. I don't mind either."

"Thank you, Widow Jane." Evie felt uncomfortable addressing the woman so familiarly. But if that's what she wished, then she would comply.

"I've lived in this cottage since I was born," the widow continued. "Mr. Travis was born on Baron Bingham's estate and moved in with me once we married. My parents died young, and I inherited this cottage from them. Unfortunately, my little dwelling is not bringing the baron enough profit. And he wants to run me out of my land!"

"Ahh," Gabriel drawled. "That's why you were so sour toward me when I first came over?"

"They tried to force me out, then tossed some food scraps on my property so the vermin would run me out, but they haven't succeeded yet."

"When is your lease up?" Evie asked.

Unfortunately, she knew that sooner or later, the old woman would have to comply. The land was not hers. It was the baron's. She was just leasing it from him.

"I have a lifetime lease. That's the issue. They can't raise the rent; they can't make me leave."

Evie looked at her in disbelief. She hadn't heard of such a thing before.

"It was given to the first settlers," Widow Jane explained. "And since my family were the first settlers, we just transfer the lease in our wills. Of course, I have no one to transfer the lease to, but the least they could do is let me die in peace." The old woman nodded to herself.

"Can they?" Evie looked at Gabriel. "Can they run her off her property?"

"Not legally, no." Gabriel cleared his throat. "But there's more than one way to get rid of someone."

"And didn't they try it all?" The woman scoffed. "The only thing they haven't tried was seducing me out of the house. I thought that was a clever one." She looked suggestively at Gabriel.

Evie raised her eyebrow and looked questioningly at him. Gabriel waggled his eyebrows at her, smiled, and regarded the old woman.

"Would it have worked?" he asked in a mock seductive voice. Evie rolled her eyes.

Widow Jane laughed her croaking laugh. "Maybe if I was younger. You are a handsome devil. Too handsome for your own good." She looked over at Evie. "That child of yours is going to be even more so. Just look at you two. What was God thinking putting the two of you together?"

Evie felt herself blushing. *What indeed?*

"And what are you two doing traveling these roads?" Jane asked. "Where are you headed?"

Evie looked at Gabriel, hoping he would take on concocting a story for them.

"We are on our way to visit family," he said, clearing his throat. "Evie's family lives in Scotland, you see. She wanted to tell them in person the big news." He smiled affectionately.

"Scottish, are ya?" Jane eyed Evie suspiciously. "I would have figured Irish."

"My grandmother was," Evie answered without thinking.

Jane laughed at that. "What a combination, eh? Scottish and Irish. Wouldn't tell by the accent, though. You"—she turned to Gabriel—"got yourself in some big trouble, young man."

"Yes, ma'am," Gabriel answered with a grin.

Oh, he was acting smooth. He had the old woman wrapped

around his finger in no time. Not that Evie could blame her.

"Done with your pie?" Gabriel suddenly looked at the untouched pie on her plate.

"I'm…" She looked at him, thinking hard about how not to offend the old lady. "You know I stopped eating fish since my condition got apparent." She was suddenly grateful for his lie. "My appetites changed drastically," she said, looking at the widow, "and fish makes me nauseous."

"Oh, why didn't you say so!" The old woman was on her feet and grabbing Evie's plate before she could respond. "Let me bring you more stew. Or would you rather have some tea? I can bake us some buns. I am good at baking, you see."

She didn't wait for Evie's response and went to put a kettle on the stove. "I have the dough ready right here." She started whipping out the dough and some other ingredients for the buns.

"That's not necessary," Evie assured her, mortified that she made the woman work to please her again.

"Buns would be lovely," Gabriel drawled, interrupting her.

Evie threw him a chastising gaze. He raised a brow at her, and Evie sighed.

For a privileged viscount, it was natural to have everybody running around to please him. Evie, although a granddaughter of a duke, had been raised in a different household.

Her grandparents had it tough at the beginning of their marriage, doing a lot of menial work themselves. When they did come into money, they didn't forget their roots, instilling the love of labor in their children and making sure they were grateful for what they had because any day, it could just disappear.

Evie loved helping the cook in the kitchen and learned

to clean after herself. Respect was taken seriously in the Somerset household. That was why all the servants loved him and, by extension, doted on Evie.

The evening stretched on as they played dominoes, then had some tea with buns. Widow Jane also went down to her small garden after the rain calmed and collected some berries.

Evie wanted to help her, but she protested vigorously, taking Gabriel with her instead. Evie laughed to herself. The old woman was already in love with the charming viscount.

Finally, the old widow got tired and sent them upstairs to rest. By that time Evie was ready to fall off her feet. She washed up, dressed in her shift, and climbed up on one side of the bed.

Gabriel, however, had other plans. Once he got ready for bed, he took one pillow and an afghan resting on the chair and settled on the floor.

Evie sat up and looked over at him. "You are going to sleep there?" she asked, surprised at his behavior.

"Mhm," was all he said.

"I thought you said you could control yourself not to touch me?" she asked, still sitting, bed covers clutched to her chest.

"I can," he said and turned to his right side, facing away from her. "I am just tired, and I need rest. I don't want to have to be woken up in the middle of the night in case my hand accidentally brushes your side."

"Last time, it wasn't just your hand brushing my side—" she started defensively, but he interrupted her.

"Sleep, Evie. Tomorrow will be a long day."

Evie set her lips in a pout, not that he could see her, and settled back in her bed. She'd gotten used to his comforting warmth at her side. Not having Gabriel in her bed already felt strange.

# Chapter 6

The next day, they still couldn't get out on the road. The roads were still very wet, and even though the villagers fixed the axle, setting off could get it broken again in no time and possibly cause an injury this time. The rain stopped by midafternoon, though, so Gabriel hoped the roads would clear by the next morning.

It was a beautiful afternoon, although a bit chilly, so to idle away some time, they went out for a walk around the village grounds. The air was fresh with a hint of rain; the birds were chirping in the trees; the sky was clear.

Widow Jane gave Evie her old gray wrap to keep her warm. Gabriel asked for an old cape, which the widow quickly drew out from her late husband's wardrobe, so he wouldn't stand out. Now, Gabriel and Evie looked just like regular village folk, having a walk in the countryside.

Evie silently walked by his side, outwardly serene, but there was a certain tension in the air. Waves of unease were radiating off of her. Now that they'd spent some time together, he'd started to get curious about her situation.

He knew her well enough. They had met plenty of times in the last seven years, ever since Clydesdale married her cousin. He knew her grandfather, Somerset, when he was alive. And he knew her guardian, Montbrook. What he didn't know was the whole situation.

Some things just didn't add up in her story. If the prospect of marrying Montbrook's choice was so horrifying, why didn't she worry about it before Somerset's death? It wasn't like he was in perfect health. He had been over eighty when he died, after all.

Gabriel knew she had recently been betrothed to a soldier, and they even tried to elope in a wild scheme that got Gabriel involved and ultimately got him cut off. And now, she was unmarried, running from her guardian to Scotland, to marry him, Viscount St. Clare, a notorious rake, of all people, and bribing him to do it too. He had so many questions to ask her.

"So, no fish, huh?" he asked instead.

"Pardon?" She looked at him bewildered, a frown between her brows.

"Fish," he repeated. "Makes you nauseous?"

"Oh, that." She waved her hand dismissively and gave a tiny giggle. "I detest it. Always have."

"Why?" He looked at her while they walked, studying the subtle changes in her features. She was very easy to read. Every emotion was clearly written on her face. Although, he would have to conclude, only the emotions she was willing to share. She seemed to conceal quite a lot.

"It's several things. First, there's the taste. All fish have this aftertaste... I cannot explain it, like eating ink or something."

"Ink?" He made a thoughtful expression as if he were actually contemplating the ridiculous statement.

"I know, I know, it's ridiculous. But I can't help it." She grimaced.

"And second?" he prompted.

"The texture, I suppose," she answered thoughtfully. "I don't like the way it feels in my mouth."

Gabriel almost choked on air. He swallowed about a dozen lewd comments about what *would* feel good in her mouth, but he supposed she wouldn't understand them, anyway.

"You are very picky, aren't you?"

"I am not spoiled if that's what you mean." She immediately took offense.

"Oh, you are definitely spoiled, love. But no, that was not what I meant. I mean, you are picky about everything. Your gowns are not only well-tailored and the height of fashion, but they are also only the ones that flatter your figure, your coloring, and bring out the best in you."

"Why would anyone want clothing that doesn't do that?" she asked defensively.

"Most people don't know what does. But then, some people do not care." She took a breath to say something, but he interrupted her once again. "You're picky about food, which side of the carriage you sit, hell, even the side of the bed you sleep on."

"That's not picky!" she argued. "I cannot face the back of the carriage, or I get sick. And I need to see the sun while I travel, to see the passing of time. Regarding the bed…." She paused as she saw his smug, smiling face. "Very well, maybe I am picky," she grumbled in defeat. "Is it so bad?"

"I suppose not," he said thoughtfully and scratched his chin.

69

"Not in most cases anyway, yet here you are, walking with me down a shabby village path, waiting for the roads to dry so we can elope and get married in Scotland because you couldn't pick one suitor out of a hundred while you had the chance."

She took a deep breath. "You didn't have to agree, you know," she said quietly.

"That's not what I'm saying," he soothed. "I just want to know why."

"I've already told you." Her tone turned self-mocking. "I was waiting for love."

"And there wasn't at least one suitor worthy of your love out of all who courted you?"

"It's not about being worthy. Many would say that my grandmother wasn't worthy of my grandfather. But they loved each other dearly. They were happy. I think it has to do with the possibility of being happy together. And I think I can be very happy being married to you," she said with a coquettish smile.

"You do?" His heart gave a curious jolt.

"I do." Her smile broadened to a grin. "I shall be free to do what I please, take care of my estates the way I see fit, and live at my most favorite place on earth—Peacehaven. And I shan't have to go through any more social seasons."

He decided to let the insult slide. Why he thought it an insult, that she expected happiness away from him, he decided not to analyze at the moment.

"I thought you loved the *ton*. You looked like you thrived in social settings," he countered.

She gave a delicate shrug. "I love dancing. It was one positive thing out of being so sought after. I never had a free dance at the ball. I love the theater, art, and rides in an open barouche. Perhaps, I do thrive in social settings. But I never felt like I belonged there."

"Truly?" He was genuinely surprised by her remark.

She nodded. "It is really difficult to find a genuine connection with people when most ladies envy you, and most gentlemen are after your dowry. The conversations just become noise, and you grow accustomed to blocking it out. Perhaps, once I am married, this is going to change too." She paused. "I didn't think you found yourself comfortable among the *ton* either."

"Why would you say so?" he asked, truly curious to hear what she thought about him.

"You don't have many close friends. Except for Clydesdale, that is. The rest are either your enemies or your lovers." She laughed sweetly.

He couldn't help but laugh along with her. "Well, it is difficult being friends with men you are cuckolding." He shrugged.

"You probably wouldn't do it if you wanted them as friends. You haven't cuckolded Clydesdale, have you?" That wasn't said as a question, more like a statement. And he appreciated her faith that he had at least one virtue. He didn't betray his friends.

"I don't think Julie would be interested," he said evenly.

"Oh, she wouldn't. No, she is definitely in love. I envy that, you know. Real love." She looked up with her innocent eyes and smiled at him with a wistful expression on her face.

He cleared his throat and tried for a careless tone, "What about the soldier?"

"The soldier?" she repeated, wrinkling her brow.

"The one you were betrothed to," he reminded.

71

"Oh!" She laughed merrily. "Well, that's the most engaging story, actually. He was in love with Samantha, my best friend. They are living happily in Bedford, I believe."

"So, you weren't in love with him?"

"No." She shook her head. "It was going to be a marriage of convenience. Similar to ours. But my best friend fell in love with him during our courtship. It wasn't meant to be." She lifted one shoulder in a delicate shrug.

"Lucky me." He scoffed.

For some reason, it pained him that he was the last choice. After hundreds of suitors and the failed courtship, he was her last resort. On the other hand, he was glad that he was the one who got to keep her. Let the *ton* die of envy.

"Were Montbrook's suitors so much worse than me then?"

"They truly were." She laughed. "One was the old and lecherous Lord Lansdowne. Another was their son. Which was bad enough on its own, but Lady Montbrook wanted to control every aspect of my life. If I had married him, they would have taken over the dukedom too."

"Would it be so bad to have fewer responsibilities?"

She looked at him as if he was addle-brained. "These are my grandfather's lands we are speaking of. I am not giving them up, not for anything. Besides, I've seen how they've run the estates ever since taking over the guardianship. They've done enough damage as it is. And—" She pursed her lips suddenly.

"And what?"

"Nothing." She shook her head. "Lady Montbrook is the head of that family, and she can be quite ruthless."

Gabriel threw her a curious frown. *Ruthless?* He didn't have time to pursue the matter, though. At that moment, a young woman waved at them and hurried their way.

"You're new here," she said, still several feet away.

"We're just visiting," he called out in return.

"Visiting whom exactly?" she asked, picking up her skirts and coming closer.

"Mrs. Jane Travis," Evie said with a smile.

"Mrs. Jane…" The young woman's eyes widened. "Widow Jane? We did not know she had family."

"Very distant," Gabriel assured her. "Gabriel Swift," he said, inclining his head. "And this beautiful young lady is my wife. Mrs. Swift."

"You don't say." The young woman eyed them jovially. "It is rare we get fresh, young blood around here. I'm Molly," she said, straightening her hair with one hand. "So, you're married. What a pity." She smiled up at Gabriel, and out of the periphery of his vision, he saw Evie roll her eyes.

"A pleasure, Miss Molly." He took her hand and bowed over it.

The young woman giggled. "Are you coming to the dance, then?" she asked, still looking at Gabriel and completely ignoring Evie.

"The dance?" he repeated, raising a brow.

"Yes, there is a dance at the inn tonight. You should come." She giggled again.

"Thank you for the invitation; we wouldn't miss it for the world." He took Evie by the arm and inclined his head toward giggling Molly. "My dear wife loves to dance."

\* \* \*

They arrived at the dance fashionably late. The villagers didn't seem to know of the fashion because the old inn was crowded to the ceiling. Evie wore what Gabriel assumed was her best gown of the three she'd brought on this journey. It was a green gown with a square neckline, high bustline, and gathered puffy sleeves. He could see that she even wore a corset, as her bosom was thrust higher than usual. The only thing different from the usual Evie he knew was the turban she'd carefully woven around her head.

Gabriel knew she was beautiful, but with a bit of polish, she was simply breathtaking. Gabriel, on the other hand, had opted to wear all black, except a green waistcoat, white shirt, and crisp white cravat. He'd pulled back his hair, and Jane had even shined his boots. He looked to all the world like the haughty aristocrat he was.

Jane refused to go to the dance, citing her age and being weary of large crowds, but she admonished them to bring gossip.

As soon as Evie and Gabriel showed up at the inn, the entire ballroom's attention was riveted on them. They stayed apart from the main crowd for a moment before the woman who'd invited them, Molly, found her way through the crowd and took it as her job to introduce them to everyone.

Although Gabriel tried his best to adopt his least sophisticated accent, nobody was fooled. The villagers quickly realized they were dealing with an aristocratic couple and surrounded the newcomers, asking them millions of questions.

Evie was quickly commandeered for a dance, and from then on, she never left the dancefloor. She was a graceful dancer, as well as a remarkable conversationalist from what he saw. Anyone dancing with her was all smiles and laughter, and after the dance, they looked at her with a love-struck expression on their faces. Gabriel was tempted to find a looking glass to check if he was wearing the same idiotic expression on his face as everybody else. Evie was simply charming.

Gabriel turned away from her and went to ask Molly to dance. As they danced, the woman openly flirted with him, while others winked and batted their eyelashes in an invitation from the sidelines.

Gabriel was used to it. Women always pursued him. The only difference, this time, was that they thought he was married, and it didn't seem to matter.

"I don't mean to be too forward, but would you like to step outside with me?" Miss Molly said as the dance finished, and he escorted her to the edge of the dancefloor.

Her cheeks were flushed, her eyes batting in seductive invitation. For a moment, Gabriel was tempted to say yes. But when he raised his head, he saw Evie on the arm of a gentleman, laughing as she walked back to the dancefloor for another dance.

No, he couldn't do it to her. A quick rut in the shadows would feel good for a moment, but then this woman would look at Evie with pity and contempt. She would gossip, and the entire ballroom would be giggling behind Evie's back for the rest of the evening.

"I would love that," he said, "but perhaps some other time."

Gabriel turned on his heel and stalked to the card room. At least there, he would be less likely to be accosted by eager women.

Gabriel played and chatted with the townsmen for a while, quickly realizing that Widow Jane's predicament wasn't a solitary case. Since the new Baron of Bingham had inherited the village of Forton, he'd raised the rent and endeavored to drive early settlers away since he couldn't do the same to them. The estate was in shambles.

Gabriel knew that the economy had suffered after the war, and while progressive landowners did their best to care for their tenants, the wastrels such as Bingham and probably Montbrook saw to capitalize on them instead.

Not for the first time, Gabriel wondered which kind of master he would become upon inheriting the earldom. He'd avoided his father and his responsibilities long enough, but could he do it for much longer? Would his vendetta against his father result in causing suffering to innocent villagers?

A few hours later, he peeked his head out of the card room and saw Evie winded, aggressively fanning herself and looking about for an escape. She was encircled by a great number of men from the ages of sixteen to about one hundred.

Gabriel made his way to her and stopped by her elbow.

"I apologize, gentlemen," he said loudly. "I'd like to steal my wife for a moment."

He gave them a charming smile and led Evie away from the crowd.

As soon as they exited the inn from the side door onto the balcony, Evie breathed in heavily.

"Oh, thank God," she said on an exhale.

"Gabriel is fine." He grinned at her.

"That's blasphemous!" Evie gave a burst of choked laughter.

"Not a believer, don't care."

"You are a heathen!" Her eyes widened in surprise.

"Come now, don't act so surprised! You know all about my debauched and libertine ways. Do not tell me you thought I was a true Christian."

Evie huffed delicately. "I didn't think about it."

"What about you?" he asked after a brief pause.

She let out a small, self-deprecating laugh. "I am a believer. A Christian.  Like my parents and grandparents."  She shook her head a little as if dispelling some thought. "My grandfather used to tell me stories about Angels. Do you know that Gabriel is the name of one of the archangels?" She smiled as she turned to him.

Gabriel nodded, mesmerized by the sight of her. Her eyes were glinting with mischief, her cheeks flushed, her mouth curved in a sensual smile.

"How come you are named after an archangel, your title is *Saint* Clare, yet ironically you are far from divine?"

Gabriel looked away from her and stared into the darkness beyond the balcony. "Maybe I am fallen."

"Then maybe a more appropriate name for you would be Lucifer."

She smiled and followed the direction of his gaze. They were standing side by side now, leaning over the banister.

"Well, if it makes you feel any better at all, I shall one day become the Earl of Winchester," he said, without looking at her. "So, a little less saintly. And a little more worthy of you, my little duchess," he added after a short pause.

She gave a wistful sigh. Her brows drew in a frown as her thoughts drifted to some unpleasant subject. He decided to dispel the atmosphere.

"Have you ever been kissed?" It was the first question that came to his mind, but he mentally kicked himself.

It had done the trick, however; she immediately turned to him.

"Kissed?"

"Yes." He turned to her also. "On the lips, by a man."

She snorted. "Of course."

"Did you like it?" He raised a brow.

"Why…" She looked confused and embarrassed, and heat was slowly creeping up her neck. "Why would that matter?"

"So… no?"

"I can't think how that's any of your business." She raised her chin defiantly.

"I am willing to wager my entire cut of your dowry that you will enjoy my kiss."

She laughed nervously. "Ladies don't wager. Besides, why would I want you to kiss me?" She started biting nervously on her lower lip, and her eyes lowered to his mouth.

He smiled. "To pass the time." He shrugged. "To see what you'd be missing with your bargain of never sleeping with me."

"What does that…?" She looked up at him then, worry creasing her eyebrows. She was so adorably innocent. He just wanted to gobble her up.

"I'll show you," he said in a seductive half-whisper and lowered his head.

# Chapter 7

I t was a soft, sweet brush of his lips against hers. Blink, and she would miss it. Evie closed her eyes and gathered the pleasant sensations around her like a blanket. She heard him chuckle, but before she could open her eyes, one more brush followed. And another, and one more.

Suddenly, he opened his mouth over hers and licked her lips. The tingly sensation was so unexpected that she almost fell. Evie raised her hands and clutched his shoulders.

At that exact moment, his arms snaked around her waist. He licked the seam of her lips, then concentrated on one corner. With a whimper, she opened her mouth, and his tongue darted inside. He did a slow and sensual sweep inside her mouth that dulled all her other senses. She lost all control of her actions, clutching him tightly, letting him do whatever he wanted with her.

She felt his hand slide down and squeeze her bottom. With that motion, he brought her body closer to his, making her feel his heat from the tips of her toes to the top of her head.

A hot, hard bulge poked at her stomach, and it curiously sent a jolt of desire through her body.

Gabriel grabbed her tightly by the nape of her head, angling her for better access for his tongue. He was kissing her fiercely and rubbing her against him in sensual movements that robbed her of any rational thought. She didn't hear anything beyond her own whimpers and his groans of satisfaction.

The next moment, it was over.

He broke the kiss so abruptly that she gave a pitiful whimper and tried to clutch him back closer.

He chuckled and lowered his head to her ear. "The ball is over. We need to go." He drew away, straightened his clothes, and offered his arm as if nothing had happened.

Evie was still dazed and confused. She was certain her turban was falling out of her pins, and her gown was rumpled. Her lips felt swollen and aching. She was aching in other places, too, with a sensation she hadn't felt before. In contrast, Gabriel was the picture of a self-possessed, perfectly groomed gentleman.

When her senses returned to her, she noticed that the music had ceased playing. A buzz of people talking and filing out of the ballroom meant that Gabriel was right. The ball was over. She composed her features, took a deep breath, and placed her hand in the crook of his arm.

They didn't talk during their walk to Widow Jane's house.

When they entered their room, the air was filled with tension. Their earlier kiss lingered between them. Evie wondered if Gabriel felt as uncomfortable and self-conscious as she did.

Probably not. He'd done it a million times. She walked

farther into the room before turning to him. He still stood by the door, or rather leaned his back against the door, with his eyes closed.

Evie needed to undress, so she untied the laces at her bodice and slowly took it off.

She turned to Gabriel. "Do you mind undoing my stays, please?"

"Yes." Gabriel's voice was hoarse and barely audible.

"Pardon me?" She furrowed her brow.

Gabriel cleared his throat. "Apologies. I meant no, I don't mind. Turn around."

He came closer and started undoing her stays as she stood with her back to him. His fingertips brushed against her chemise, and the tingly feeling traveled low down her body. His breath worried the wisps of hair at her nape, and goosebumps covered her skin in reaction.

She caught the corset against her as it sagged so it still covered her upper body. She heard his sharp intake of breath as he bared her chemise. They both stood there for a few energy-charged moments before he finally stepped away.

She turned to him, still clutching the stays tightly to her body.

"We can't do this," he said as he turned to the door. He ran his fingers through his hair. "If you wish to stay a virgin, that is."

"We can't do what?" she asked, confused.

"This." He gestured, encompassing the room in one swooping motion. "Sharing a bed, kissing, undressing in front of each other."

Evie protectively clutched her stays tighter to her.

"I'm not like most men, Evie," he continued. "I am used

to bedding women every night, and my body is missing the feeling fiercely. So…" He swallowed audibly. "Unless you want to end up on the bed with skirts over your head, you better steer clear of me."

She didn't have time to respond to his unfair demands as he left the room and shut the door behind him with a decisive click.

Evie stood there in the middle of the room, still clutching her stays to her chest and trying to resolve her feelings. She was tingling all over from the simple act of having him unhook her corset. Her body had been acutely aware of him ever since that devastating kiss and refused to let go of that knowledge. Now he wanted to cut communication with her. And probably sleep with other women from this moment on.

The thought depressed her more than she was willing to admit. He would spend the following nights in bed with other women, hugging them tightly to him, touching them like he had touched her that first night they spent together. She covered her eyes with her hands, letting go of her corset, and it fell with a loud thump.

What was she thinking? They'd made a deal: He would marry her, then she'd leave to Peacehaven, and he would continue his debauchery in London and wherever else he pleased. That was the only reason he was marrying her. And if she let him get closer to her now, she was bound for heartbreak later. As he said, he was used to having a different woman in his bed every night, and it was unlikely to ever change. No, she shouldn't let him even further into her heart. With his smooth words, his roguish smile, caring attitude, and those sensual lips…

She closed her eyes tightly and shook the thoughts from

her head. *Don't be a ninny, Evie! Those lips will never be just yours; the man will never be one you can rely on. Just let it go.*

It was easier said than done, however. She changed into her nightgown, packed all of her belongings for an early morning start, performed her nightly ablutions, and stared out the window half the night. She finally lay in bed and spent several hours tossing and turning. But Gabriel did not return to their room.

Finally, with the first light of dawn, just as Evie fell asleep, the door to their room opened, and Gabriel walked inside.

"Good morning, love!" he said jovially. "I brought you chocolate."

He put a cup on the bedside table with a loud smack. Evie flinched and flung her arm over her eyes. "What time is it?" she grumbled in her sleepy voice.

"Just before dawn." He paused for a moment. "Come now, get up; we need an early start if we want to get to Scotland on the morrow."

He sounded too cheerful for that time of the morning. And considering her sleepless night, she didn't appreciate his good humor. She wanted to shout at him that he was the reason she'd slept so badly and ask where he'd spent last night, but she knew she had no right. Instead, she sat up in bed and regarded him from beneath her hooded eyes.

"Please, leave. I need to get dressed now."

"I'll get our carriage ready. Be downstairs in half an hour." With these words, he left the room.

\* \* \*

Evie said goodbye to Widow Jane, promising to visit as soon

as she could, although she knew it to be a lie. Widow Jane instructed her to eat well and take care of the babe and hugged her tight.

Evie fairly melted into the embrace. It felt so good to have an older soul worrying about her again. She missed her grandfather so much, and her eyes watered at the thought.

"Oh, don't cry, child!" the widow croaked. "We'll see each other soon, right?"

Evie just nodded and climbed into the carriage.

\* \* \*

That night, Gabriel rented them separate bedchambers. Evie still didn't know where he'd spent the night before, and if she were honest with herself, she didn't want to know. And if she were even more honest, then yes, she did want to know, but she was afraid to ask.

She knew logically that she had no hold over him, no right to him, and what's even more, she'd be better off to never feel that she had. But she couldn't shake this awful gnawing feeling in the pit of her stomach.

*Mine*, it screamed at her. *He's mine.*

She'd never felt that sort of possessiveness over anyone before. Well, maybe it wasn't bad to have these feelings toward her husband-to-be? She realized that she was justifying something that would only have awful consequences for her. Feeling possessive over Gabriel would lead to a disaster.

Evie had a bath and supper in her room alone. She drew the curtains down and started to prepare for bed. The fire was blazing in the hearth as she sat beside it, brushing out her hair. She was lost deep in thought, of what she could not remember, when she was jolted by the frantic knock at her door.

"Evie, it's me. Let me in," came the hushed voice of her future husband. She looked down at her gaping dressing gown and back at the door.

"I am not decent," she said with a frown.

"Don't be ridiculous. I've seen you in all states of dishabille already. Make haste now; it's important."

Evie stood, chewing on her lip. Hadn't he been the one insisting on maintaining a proper distance between them?

She placed her brush on the mantel and padded barefoot toward the door. The moment she unlatched the lock, the door flew open. Gabriel rushed through and locked it behind him. He put an ear to the wood for a moment before turning back to her.

"Listen," he said carefully, raising both his hands in a calming gesture. "Do not panic."

"If you didn't want me to panic, that is the worst thing you could have said to me right now," Evie hissed, her eyes darting frantically from his face to the door and back again.

He was still dressed in the suit he was wearing earlier on the road. He was rumpled and worse for wear, his cravat mussed as if he'd tugged on it repeatedly. His hat and gloves were missing.

"I was downstairs, drinking." Now that he mentioned it, she noticed an alcohol smell on his breath. "And two travelers came in looking for a young woman with bright red hair."

Evie's eyes widened slightly, and her mouth fell open. It couldn't be.

They'd reached her. They'd finally found her. It was over.

"Don't!" he said harshly. He put his hands on her arms and

shook her a little. "Don't you dare freeze on me."

Evie quickly nodded, frantically searching his face for any indication of assurance. She found it in his stony features of absolute resolution.

"We are getting out of this," he said confidently.

Evie took a deep breath. "What do you want me to do?"

"I want you to get dressed quickly." He nudged her toward her valise and sat in the chair she'd vacated several moments ago. "I've asked my valet to pack the rest of our things and set out in a carriage back to London tomorrow morning."

Evie paused in the act of airing out her gown and regarded him over her shoulder with raised eyebrows.

"We are setting off on horseback. Right now," he answered her unspoken question.

*On horseback.* She didn't have her gentlemen's attire with her. Gabriel had insisted she leave it in London. Evie opened her mouth to say just that, but he interrupted her.

"I've asked for two horses to be saddled. Do not fret; one will be a sidesaddle." He winked at his last statement.

"Sidesaddle?" she muttered to herself, placing the gown on the bed and undoing her dressing gown. "Would you mind turning away?" She threw the question at him over her shoulder.

"I do." She heard him grin. Evie sighed and let her dressing gown fall to the floor. After traveling with him across England, she somehow didn't feel at all embarrassed to be standing in front of him in a translucent chemise. If he didn't care, neither would she. "I can't ride," she muttered as she drew the skirts over her head.

"Excuse me?" he asked, confusion in his voice.

"I said," Evie muffled out from inside her overskirts, "I can't ride."

She turned as her head appeared from under her skirt and drew them down to her waist. She took the bodice and crammed her arms into the sleeves.

"Button me up, please." She walked toward him and turned her back.

Gabriel brushed her hair over one shoulder. This entire scene, her dressing in front of him, him buttoning her up, was so casual and felt so natural, as if they had been doing this for years. It truly felt as if they were a married couple.

"What do you mean, you can't ride?" He stirred the wisps of her hair at the nape of her neck with his breath. "You rode at least part of the two-hundred-mile journey from Carlisle on horseback, didn't you?"

"Astride," she clarified.

Gabriel made quick work of her buttons. She assumed a lot of practice accounted for his deft fingers. He took her by the shoulders and turned her to face him once he was done.

"You mean to tell me that you are perfectly capable of riding astride, and yet you've never learned to ride sidesaddle?"

Evie shrugged. "It was too difficult for me as a child, and Grandpa didn't want to torture me with it."

Gabriel chuckled into his fist.

"I can ride sidesaddle, but not well. And I'd rather not risk breaking my neck," she said defensively.

"You are incredible," Gabriel said with a slow smile. But his features darkened momentarily. "Well, you can't ride astride in this, and I don't think I can get you any decent male clothing that'll fit you at this hour. You'll have to ride with me."

He took her valise and peeked out of the room. Then he stepped out, looked around once more, and waved for Evie to follow him. She managed to hastily weave the turban around her head and covered her shoulders with an old shawl Widow Jane gave her for the road in the hopes of appearing older than she was.

They made it downstairs without an incident, and once they reached the horses, Evie was able to breathe again.

"I'll mount first," Gabriel warned. "Then you step on my foot, and I'll pull you up."

Evie swallowed and nodded. As soon as Gabriel mounted, he leaned in and stretched his arms toward her. Evie struggled to get her foot up on the stirrup with Jane's shawl and her gown on. She untangled the shawl and threw it at Gabriel.

"Hold it for a moment, will you?"

"You should have left it," he grumbled, trying to fold the cloth into some semblance of order.

"I would have if I didn't need a disguise, and this turban—" Evie was aggressively picking up her skirts and trying to hold her turban in place with her shoulder at the same time. She was interrupted by a slurred male voice coming from somewhere above.

"Oi!" the voice called. "What are you doing there?"

"What's it to you?" Gabriel called back.

"Where are you off to in the middle of the night?" the man continued interrogating.

"Late for my aunt's funeral," Gabriel called back and turned back to Evie. "Will you hurry?" he hissed between his teeth.

"Fine!" Evie yanked her foot up and stepped on Gabriel's boot.

She held up both her arms for Gabriel to lift her. He took her by her wrists and pulled her up with great force. She landed on his thighs with an audible oomph.

## Chapter 7

Evie almost fell backward, and if it wasn't for Gabriel's quick reflexes, she would have. He placed his arm around her and pulled her toward his chest. The motion resulted in Evie's turban unwinding and landing on the ground, leaving her glorious fiery hair spilling down her shoulders.

# Chapter 8

"It's her!" the slurred voice shouted from above.

Gabriel cursed, spurred the horse on, and galloped away.

Evie clung tightly to Gabriel's chest, pressing her cheek into his vest. That man yelling from the window was definitely the one sent after her. He was probably not alone, either. The sly Lady Montbrook would rather see her dead than married, evidenced by the thugs she'd sent after her.

And they'd found her.

"Everything is going to be well," Gabriel shouted over the sounds of the wind and horse's hoofs. "He was too drunk to follow us at such a pace."

Evie nodded against his chest, although she wasn't so certain he was correct. Either way, this would all be over soon.

With incredible luck for the second time in a sennight, Evie traveled during the night and wasn't accosted by brigands. Her luck was bound to run out soon. She prayed it wouldn't happen before she married.

They arrived in Gretna Green with the first light of morning. Gabriel stopped the horse near a blacksmith shop. According to gossip, that's where people got married in Scotland.

Gabriel hopped down from the horse, then took her by the waist and lowered her to the ground. His hair was mussed from the wind, his golden mane dirt-streaked and no longer shining. His cravat was gray and rumpled as if it had been balled in a fist for several hours. The rest of his clothing wasn't well groomed either, his boots taking most of the toll. His eyes were red-rimmed, his face covered with grime.

Evie looked him up and down, laughter bubbling from inside of her. She put her hand to her mouth and proceeded to laugh in earnest.

"What?" Gabriel frowned down his length and looked back at her.

Evie couldn't stop laughing. The nerves, the lack of sleep, and their journey were finally taking a toll on her sanity. "You"—she paused for air—"you look hideous."

Gabriel huffed a tiny chuckle, looked himself over once again, and then looked back at her. "You, my darling, are not looking any better."

"I know!" Evie hugged her stomach and wheezed with laughter. "But you…" She tried to catch her breath unsuccessfully. "You're supposed to be this handsome rake… Seducer of innocents." She doubled over again. "Look at you!"

Gabriel finally joined in on the laughter. "You are supposed to be a diamond of the first water, the haughty duchess. What would your hundreds of suitors say?"

Evie rubbed her eyes, wiping the tears. "They would run

like wild dogs were on their tails." She stopped, and her eyes widened in horror. "Oh, my God, my hair!"

She put her hands on her hair and realized no amount of palming would ever do it any good. She couldn't see it, but it felt like she had a bird's nest on her head. She leaned her forehead against Gabriel's rumpled, dirty waistcoat, shaking with laughter.

"Some bride and groom, huh?" she said between chuckles. "Samantha and I wagered that whoever married last between the two of us would have to wear a gown the color of manure." She looked down her length. "She'd be delighted to know that she got her forfeit."

"Well, at least right now, we are a perfect couple." Gabriel placed his arms around her and rubbed her back with a soothing motion. "Are you ready to become my lady wife?"

Evie shook her head against his chest. She then drew away and wiped at the place her forehead was touching a moment ago. "I just smeared the dirt here," she said, grinning.

"Look at it this way. Maybe nobody will recognize you now. I mean, your hair does not shine anymore. It is almost ordinary, a dull red now."

Evie smiled at the implied compliment.

Gabriel extended his hand. "Shall we?"

Evie took his hand, and together they walked to the blacksmith's door. Gabriel gave it a loud knock.

*No answer.*

He knocked again.

*Still no answer.*

Evie broke out in hysterical laughter again.

"Would you cease that?" Gabriel couldn't hold back his own laugh.

"It's barely dawn," she said between the laughs, trying to catch her breath. "Normal people are asleep at this hour, and we're banging—" Evie couldn't finish the sentence. Her breathing grew heavy. "If anybody sees us like this, they'll assume we're robbing them."

Evie leaned her back against the cold stone of the building next to the door and finally caught her breath.

"Gabriel," she said, and he looked at her quizzically. "What if they catch us in the meantime?" She tried to frown, but she was too tired to exhibit any emotion except for nervous laughter.

"We'll just tell them we're already married." He shrugged and mirrored her pose next to her. "Don't worry about that, sweet. I'll get us properly married." One side of his mouth kicked up in a smile.

They looked at the small cottages of the village, the beautiful greenery covering them, the sun rising slowly above their roofs. It was a beautiful morning.

"Did you ever think this was how you were going to get married?" Evie asked, staring straight ahead.

"To be honest with you, I thought I would never marry."

"Why not?"

He shrugged. "Didn't have many good examples of marriage, I guess. Besides, after cuckolding as many husbands as I have, believing in the sanctity of marital vows…" He grimaced. "Besides, I was never eager to beget an heir. I'd hoist the title onto my cousins if I could."

Evie couldn't imagine not caring for her lands. She loved all of her grandfather's estates and the lands surrounding them. She cared for the villagers, the animals, and the gardens. She couldn't imagine not having that, living constantly in

93

London's social world. As much as she loved the dancing and entertainment London offered, she couldn't live without the freedom the country granted her and the intimacies of knowing her neighbors.

"Your father might have disagreed with it," she said.

"Oh, he would." Gabriel nodded with a bitter grimace on his face. "His land, estates, and horses are all he cares about. I am just a tool to look after all that after he dies."

"I'm sure that's not true," she countered softly.

"And I am sure you don't know my father." He stepped away from the wall. "Listen, we can stand here till the cows come home. Or, we can go to the inn, clean up, and return at a more decent hour." He dusted off his pants, avoiding her gaze.

"I want to get married as soon as the blacksmith gets here," Evie said with a frown.

"And if we're being pursued, do you want to be caught out on the streets with nowhere to hide?" he asked irritably.

"No need to be snippy," Evie grumbled as Gabriel went to untether the horse.

He looked both ways before deciding on the direction and walked toward the heart of the village.

"Do you even know where we are going?" Evie asked, following on his heels.

"No, but I don't think we have much of a choice. It's either forward or backward, and we are not going back. Besides, if this place is as notorious for its elopements as we were led to believe, there are bound to be plenty of inns."

\* \* \*

Gabriel's guess turned out to be correct. They found an inn rather quickly. The village of Gretna Green was not very big but picturesque. The inn they stumbled upon had only one room left. Since they were not planning to spend the night in it, Gabriel decided it was fine for both of them to occupy it for a few hours before they wed.

They refreshed themselves quickly, just washing off the grime from the road with wet cloths, wiping the dust off their clothes, and cleaning their boots. It didn't do much good, but Evie didn't want to change and sully the only relatively clean gown she had left. True, it was her wedding day, but she was so dirty it didn't really matter what she wore. She braided her hair as Gabriel ordered them some breakfast.

Evie was too nervous to be hungry, but she knew she needed strength to get through it all, so she chewed reluctantly.

Once they were done with breakfast, they went to the smithy again. And several short minutes later, Evie was standing toe to toe with Gabriel St. Clare, holding his hand and looking into his solemn blue eyes. Recalling her romanticized notions of a grand wedding to the man she loved, she was tempted to laugh again.

She'd always dreamed of an emerald gown to match her eyes, a pearl necklace, and a coronet. Instead, she was wearing the worst of the three gowns she brought with her on the journey. It was dirty at the hem and dusty everywhere else. Since the simple wipe-off didn't really clean it, it was difficult to even recall what color it was.

Instead of a huge procession and a priest at St. Paul's cathedral, they stood in a tiny smithy, with no one but a huge Scot in front of them. His hands were as big as hammers; his ginger beard was long and thick. He looked formidable with a frown marring his face.

No, this wasn't her dream wedding. But at least she was getting her dream man.

Evie concentrated on the face of the man she'd traveled over three hundred miles to marry. His eyes were red-rimmed, his face sullen. But a light smirk played about his lips. Evie smiled lightly. She wasn't making a mistake, was she?

"Do you have rings?" the blacksmith asked.

Gabriel shook his head. The blacksmith nodded and started the ceremony.

A few brief sentences from the blacksmith and a couple of lines of vows later, they were married. The blacksmith bound their hands with the knot over the stone, and that was it. From this moment on, they were bound for life.

"Do not untie this knot until ye consummate the marriage," the blacksmith said with a smirk. "Bad omen."

Gabriel raised a brow at her, and Evie shook her head with a smile. There would be no consummation of the marriage for them. They'd just have to take their chances with the old superstition.

The moment they exited the smithy, Gabriel looked down at her.

"Are you certain you're willing to risk the bad omen? Because—"

"There they are!" Gabriel was interrupted by a loud shout. They turned to see a short man running in their direction. The same man who'd spotted them by the inn the night before, only now he had a knife in his grip. Two more men were coming toward them from either side, each of them holding pistols in their hands.

"But... we haven't even untied the knot yet," Evie complained.

Gabriel clutched her hand in a harsh grip and shoved her behind his back. She hit his shoulder blade with her cheek and whimpered.

"Apologies," Gabriel whispered, "but stay back, do you hear?"

"But—"

"No buts, I'm your husband now, and you promised to obey me just a minute ago."

"That—"

"Not. A. Word," he hissed each word between his teeth and then addressed the men in his most sophisticated accent. "What can I do for you, gentlemen?"

"You can hand over the lass; that's what you can do," the biggest one sneered at him.

"I'm afraid I can't do that," Gabriel said with a shrug. "I shan't be handing over *my wife* to anyone."

"She's not your wife yet," the smallest one yelled. "Not unless you managed to bed her right there on the wedding stone."

All three men guffawed, and Gabriel joined in with them. Evie clutched his right arm in a vise-like grip and peeked out from behind him. Gabriel ran a thumb over her hand in soothing motions.

Evie relaxed under his ministrations, her logic returning to her. She slowly but determinedly started working on the knots. If they untied themselves, they'd be able to run easier.

"We precipitated our vows." Gabriel shrugged. "Even if we didn't, there is no way for you or anyone else to dissolve this marriage. Not unless you prove me incapable to consummate it. And if you know who I am, you will have no doubt I do not have this issue. So, I'd suggest you return to your master and say that the woman he's after is another man's property now."

*Property?* Evie stopped midway through untying the knot and shoved him slightly between his shoulder blades. His hand tightened around her arm in warning.

"But we don't know who you are," the third man said with a shrug. "And I don't care. Our job is to get the lass. And we'll get her."

Evie untied the knot at that moment and freed their hands. She rubbed her sore wrist, then fumbled in her reticule before stepping forward.

"How much?" she asked, holding her hands behind her back. "How much did he pay you? Because I can pay you more."

The men's eyes glinted with greed.

Gabriel quickly shoved her back behind him. "Do not move," he whispered fiercely. "Until I tell you to."

"Let the lady speak," one of them shouted.

Evie couldn't believe he wasn't going to let her pay them with her money! Although, now that she thought about it, as of two minutes ago, all her money belonged to him. Or, to use his words, was his property. Was he really that greedy, that he'd sacrifice their lives for a few extra coins?

"Leave her out of it. Deal with me." Gabriel threw the words at the thugs. At that moment, Evie heard the door open behind them, and a huge shadow cast over them. She turned and saw the blacksmith, the man who'd married them, step out onto the porch.

The thugs staggered back as one and looked at each other.

"A problem here, laddies?" he boomed as he stepped beside

Gabriel.

Evie peeked out from behind Gabriel's shoulder again. He snaked his arm behind them both and gripped her tightly so that she was plastered to him.

"No problem. Just chatting with the happy couple," one of the thugs answered.

"Stay back. The moment I let go of you, you run to the inn and lock yourself in our room, understand?" Gabriel said in a quiet whisper so that only she could hear, as the thugs continued their conversation with the blacksmith,

"What—"

"Don't argue, for once. Just do as I ask."

"Gabriel, I have a pistol," she whispered through her teeth. Evie didn't see what was going on between the thugs and the blacksmith, but the voices grew louder, the argument becoming more heated.

Gabriel paused in stunned silence for a moment before wiggling his fingers. "Give it to me and leave."

"But—"

"What do you think will happen if they catch you? I want you out of here, hear me?"

Evie begrudgingly handed the pistol to him.

"You are not breaking off one of my marriages," the black-smith called louder.

"The moment I let go, you run." Gabriel patted her back lightly.

Blood rushed loudly through her head. She could hear the voices, but she couldn't distinguish what was being said. In the next moment, Gabriel let go of her abruptly and took a step forward.

"Go!" he yelled without looking at her. A gun fired, and

she raced in the direction of the inn.

# Chapter 9

Shots fired from different sides all at once. Gabriel and the blacksmith dived in different directions. The biggest thug staggered back but didn't fall. Blood dripped from his shoulder.

"You shot me!" He seemed quite surprised that Gabriel hadn't missed his target.

Gabriel had missed the man's heart on purpose. He was an excellent marksman, but he didn't find killing a human to be an honorable duty. Although, for Evie, he could probably revise his beliefs.

Gabriel got up, confident that the thugs had emptied their pistols. "I think you better leave, now."

"Bugger all." The smallest thug took out a knife and charged at Gabriel.

Gabriel blocked his attack and threw a blow to the side of the thug's face. All the days spent in Gentleman Jackson's were finally paying off. The thug staggered to the side and sat on the ground.

Gabriel turned to see that the blacksmith had felled one of his attackers and was fending off the bigger one.

"Oi! My wife's already safe at home; you might want to give up!" Gabriel yelled. The thug got distracted, just as he planned, and the blacksmith used this moment to plant a major blow to the thug's jaw.

In a flash, Gabriel felt himself being thrown to the ground. He rolled in the dirt, and a moment later, his previous adversary straddled him and punched him in his face.

*Not the face. My face is my only asset.*

Gabriel blocked one more hit and rolled, reversing positions with his attacker. He hit his assailant on the nose, his own knuckles screaming with pain. Hitting a person in the face with bare knuckles was not something Gabriel regularly did, and he immediately wished to never do so again.

Unfortunately, his attacker didn't subside after taking a punch, and Gabriel was forced to drive a couple more shots to his jaw and cheek. The adrenaline overtook his body, and he didn't feel the pain anymore. He was governed by the drive to silence the man beneath him, to stop him and all others from coming after his Evie.

A moment later, he felt huge hands dragging him off the limp body on the ground.

"It's fine; he's done for," the blacksmith said roughly.

Gabriel nodded and wiped the blood off his face. His hand was bleeding and swollen, pain radiated from his fingers, and his nose was in agony as well.

"I'll have the boys take care of them. But you can't go to your bride looking like that," the blacksmith continued, looking Gabriel over from head to toe. "Come, I'll clean you up." He beckoned Gabriel back to his smithy, and Gabriel followed.

"I know just the thing to make the pain go away," the blacksmith said as Gabriel returned to the stone over which he had been wed a few minutes ago. The blacksmith rummaged through the cupboard and, a moment later, returned to Gabriel and put a bottle of fine scotch on the wedding stone with a loud clunk.

\* \* \*

Evie ran panting back to the inn. She mounted the stairs, hiking up her skirts high and taking two steps at a time. The innkeeper probably thought her deranged. She didn't give a fig about that. She needed to come up with a plan and fast.

There were three bandits, and two of them had pistols and were rather large. Even if Gabriel evaded the bullets, she was certain he would lose in the hand-to-hand battle. The blacksmith looked capable enough, but Gabriel was a gentleman. He wasn't groomed for a street fight.

Evie got to the room and looked around. Surely, Gabriel had a pistol lying around somewhere. She walked to his valise and started sifting through his things.

She shouldn't have left. Perhaps she could help fight them off. If she found a stick big enough to hit someone, or perhaps... She stopped and expelled a deep breath. Or she would've distracted Gabriel and got him killed. There were three thugs. One of them could have grabbed her, and Gabriel wouldn't be able to do anything about it.

Had he hit his target? She didn't know whether he was a good shot or not. She knew he always refused to duel. Perhaps that was because he was a poor marksman.

What if he got shot and killed because of her? *What if he*

*gets killed now while I sit here contemplating the possibility?*

Evie resumed looking through his things.

She found a pistol at the bottom of his valise and carefully took it out. It was large and heavy, a lot different from her tiny one. Evie cursed under her breath. Heavy or not, foreign or not, she needed to figure out how to use it. Or Gabriel would be dead.

She checked the gun and groaned in frustration. It was empty.

Right. She needed to find gunpowder. She went back to rummaging through his valise, tears of frustration burning her eyes. Even if she found the powder, she'd have to clean the gun and load it, and it would take a lot of time. Curse Gabriel for not thinking ahead.

She shook herself. Now was not the time to get irritated. Perhaps she couldn't load the gun, but she needed to find something she could use to help him.

Evie paced back and forth from the window to the door of their room, thinking of a plan. *Oh, blast it all, I shouldn't have left! He could be dead by now, for all I know.*

Resolute to get back, she flew to the door, opened it… and beheld her husband.

Gabriel stood with one hand on the door jamb, his head hung, and his shoulders slumped; he looked as if he was about to drop to the floor. His hair was mussed and smeared with blood. His face was bloody, too, including a bruised lip with a cut in the corner of his mouth. His shirt was torn and bloody, his waistcoat and jacket missing.

"What—" Evie began, but he made two steps and fairly collapsed into her arms. Evie caught him heavily, her knees bending from his weight. "What happened to you?" she finally asked.

"What do you mean?" He righted himself and stared at her as if she'd just asked the most ridiculous question.

"I mean, why are you wobbling on your feet? Were you shot? Did you lose a lot of blood? Where else are you hurt?" She started patting his upper body.

"I'm fine." He made a few more steps and collapsed on the bed.

Evie stared at him, her eyes wide. He didn't seem to be bleeding. There were no obvious wounds on him except for his face. She blinked, just to clear her mind and vision. When that didn't help, she went over to the door and locked it. She went to the washbasin, wet the cloth, and came over to sit by Gabriel's side.

He looked at her then, a stupid grin on his face. "I saved you," he said and then flinched, touching a hand to his bruised lip. "I think I deserve a reward for my heroics."

"I think you already rewarded yourself for your heroics." She grimaced, smelling alcohol on his breath. "When did you have time to drink?" She raised her arm and pressed the cloth to the corner of his lips. He took her hand in his and guided it away from his face. There she was marching off to save him, worried sick, and he was drinking! How long had she been looking for a gun? Surely not enough for him to get foxed.

"The blacksmith. He said it would help heal the wounds." He shrugged.

Evie brought her hand back over to his face and started cleaning him off. "Well," she said wryly. "Looks like that didn't work."

"It did." He flinched when she touched the cut at the corner of his lip. "Until you did that," he added grimly.

"You need your wounds cleaned. You don't want the dirt mixing with your blood and forever sticking to your face, do you?"

She slowly cleaned his face, then went to the washbasin to clean the cloth and returned again.

"My face is not the only part of my body that's hurting." He narrowed his eyes at her suggestively. "Will you clean me all over?"

Evie looked at him mockingly. "I might, but you will not like the method I use." She continued to minister to him, moving the cloth down to his neck. He caught her arm again and tugged at her so unexpectedly that she fell against his chest with a yelp.

"Kiss me," he whispered, looking into her eyes. One of his arms tightened around her, holding her close to his chest. With another hand, he brushed the wisps of her hair away from her face. The movement of his fingers was so deft and gentle that it made her shiver. "I saved you, didn't I?" He shrugged good-naturedly. "I think I deserve a little kiss for my efforts."

Surrounded by his heat, his husky voice penetrating her to her bones, she couldn't protest even if she'd wanted to. But she didn't want to protest. The truth was, ever since the country dance, she couldn't stop fantasizing about their kiss at every free opportunity she got.

"Just one tiny kiss," she said, trying to look resigned.

"Just one," he whispered, staring at her lips.

Evie slowly lowered her mouth and moved her lips gently over his. The kiss was so light; it was barely a brush. Gabriel groaned.

His hand settled at the nape of her neck, and his mouth

moved demandingly over hers, brushing over her lips, sipping on her mouth. She didn't know what to do. She just froze with her eyes closed and her lips slightly parted.

"Kiss me back," he whispered as he brushed light kisses on top of her mouth, at the corners of her lips. She opened her eyes and looked at him, feeling dazed. He smiled at her then, his smile predatory. "Just do as I do," he whispered and caught her upper lip between his and gave a light tug. When she repeated his action, he did the same to her lower lip, lightly sucking on it. She reciprocated.

"Open your mouth," he whispered against her lips, and then he caught both of her lips with his parted mouth and licked at the seam. She opened her mouth, and his tongue took advantage and entered her, taking a bold, proprietary sweep inside her. He licked at her, teased her, drawing circles and taunting her to do the same. She shyly let her tongue touch his.

The next moment, everything changed. The arm circling her gripped her tight, and suddenly she was under him. His weight was crushing her to the bed, his knee settled between her legs, and his free hand moved from her cheek to her neck, shoulder, and lower. In the meantime, his tongue continued his insistent invasion.

He started moving over her with a persistent rhythm of his hips, rubbing his pelvis against hers. With his every movement, she felt a hard, hot bulge insistently probing against her center. She felt hot all over. The strange ache originated somewhere low in her stomach and moved even lower.

She gripped at him, frustrated, wanting something… more. She heard her needy whimpers and moans while she copied his movement and started moving her hips rhythmically against him as his tongue plunged in and out of her mouth. She felt wetness accumulate in her most private place, and she felt embarrassed and confused. Suddenly, she struggled to catch her breath. His weight was crushing her, and the unknown feelings overwhelmed her. She tore her mouth away from his and shoved at his chest.

She braced herself for his anger. She'd acted like a complete wanton, and now she was pushing him away. An embarrassed blush covered her face and neck.

Gabriel rolled away from her and lay on his back. "I apologize," he said hoarsely.

Caught by surprise, Evie looked up, blinking stupidly at him. He sat up and raked his hand through his hair. "I got carried away. I shouldn't have done that," he said without looking at her.

Evie didn't know what to say to that. Did she say it was fine, even if it wasn't? Should she say the fault was hers, even though she wasn't certain it was? Even if she knew what to say, her tongue refused to cooperate after that moment of pure red-hot passion. Her body still tingled all over.

Gabriel stood and walked to the washbasin. He splashed his face several times with the water, then stood in silence, his hands braced on the washbasin, his head bowed.

Evie took the time to sit up on the bed and adjust her clothing. She was in the process of re-pinning her hair when he finally spoke.

"We should head back to London." His voice was still hoarse. "I'll wait for you outside while you change."

Evie opened her mouth to reply, but Gabriel walked swiftly to the door and exited the room without a backward glance.

# Chapter 9

### * * *

What was it about the girl that made him all randy with just one kiss? He couldn't quite figure it out. He was always easily aroused. That was not new. But he enjoyed kissing and foreplay as much as he enjoyed the act itself and sometimes could spend hours indulging in it. With her, he just wanted to throw her skirts up and have his way with her. It was probably the dry spell. He'd get himself a nice, willing woman at the next village and…

He looked up at the window of the room they'd occupied at the inn. He didn't want any random woman. He wanted his wife. *How bourgeois.* He smiled to himself.

No, he wouldn't be able to bed anyone else until their wretched trip was over. But he couldn't have her either. Luckily, London was full of women willing to fill his bed. And once Evie moved away, he'd be free to do as he pleased, without the thoughts of her intruding on him all the time. Now that he was rich again, he could indulge in as many lovers as he wished without feeling like a whore.

Gabriel washed with the frigid water by the inn and changed into cleaner clothes. The water helped sober him up, and his bruises seemed to hurt less.

When he was more or less presentable, he went to the inn counter to find them a carriage. He could not ride with her on his lap anymore. That was just plain painful now. Since Gabriel had let his carriage go back to London, however, they needed to find themselves another vehicle. And Gabriel knew just where to find one.

His wife owned an estate in Carlisle. All they needed was to get there, and afterward, they'd travel back to London in style. In the duchess's carriage. Perhaps they would even have outriders with them. The thought landed a satisfied smirk on his face.

No carriages were available for lend, but to his luck, he found an elderly couple who were traveling south toward Lancaster.

Evie was out by the time he strapped their valises on the outside of the elderly couple's carriage. She looked at him questioningly as she made her way toward him.

"I've found us a ride," he said merrily, waggling his eyebrows at her. "Mr. and Mrs. Adley, I am pleased to introduce you to my wife, Evie St. Clare, the Duchess of Somerset." He smiled at the elderly couple and then looked at his wife's dumbfounded expression. He realized this was the first time she had been introduced officially as Evie St. Clare. For some reason, he realized that he liked the sound of that. True, she would never carry his title, not that he wished she would. He wasn't fond of it, either. Perhaps he could wear hers?

"A duke and a duchess, my-my." The elderly woman clapped her hands.

"No-no, my dear wife is the duchess. I am a simple viscount. My lady wife," he said and turned to Evie. "Mr. and Mrs. Adley were gracious enough to give us a ride all the way to Carlisle. I told them we had carriage trouble on our way here that probably won't get fixed soon." He winked at her and reached to hand her into the carriage.

"A pleasure to meet you, Mr. and Mrs. Adley." Evie smiled at them sweetly. "How generous of you to give us a ride." She climbed into the carriage and eyed the interior in horror as she realized the elderly couple had taken the forward-facing seats.

Gabriel instantly recognized her distress. "You see"—he turned to the elderly couple—"my wife is in a delicate condition, oomph!" He earned a jab in his ribs from his wife's elbow but continued. "She gets ill in the rear-facing seat. Is it too much trouble if she switches seats with one of you?"

"Oh, of course, my dear," both of them grumbled as Mr. Adley vacated his seat and sat opposite his wife.

"Thank you, I appreciate it very much." Evie smiled at the elderly couple and shot daggers at Gabriel with her gaze once she was seated.

"Oh, not at all. I might be old, but I still remember what it's like to be with child," the woman said kindly.

"But we never traveled when you were in a delicate condition," the old man noted. "The young people today are not afraid of anything. And to be accosted by thugs! My-my!"

Gabriel had to tell a tale of a broken carriage and thugs to explain their disheveled state, his bruised face, and their lack of a vehicle.

"You must be careful with that," Mrs. Adley agreed. "All kinds of misfortunes happen on the road. And you are much too thin for your condition; you must eat more. Here, I have some biscuits in a basket somewhere."

"Thank you for worrying, but eating during travel makes me ill," Evie said apologetically.

"That is why one shouldn't travel in your condition," exclaimed Mr. Adley.

Gabriel shot her a laughing gaze while Evie narrowed her eyes on him.

"They are right, you know," Gabriel drawled. "You need to eat more."

"Thank you, dear," she said pointedly. "I would rather have

a nap, if you don't mind."

"Oh, of course," Mrs. Adley chimed in. "When I was carrying my first child, I used to sleep in all sorts of situations. One time, I fell asleep during a dance, on the dancefloor!"

With that came a story of every single time Mrs. Adley was with child—which was a lot—and how that affected her moods, her lifestyle, and her eating habits. As it turned out, the Adleys had eight children, so the narrative went on for a while.

# Chapter 10

T hey reached Carlisle in a couple of hours. The Adleys were nice enough to drive them right up to the front steps. Travel with the Adleys turned out to be not as grueling as they'd first thought. The elderly couple were lively and talkative. Contrary to Evie's usual sullen mood on the road, she almost didn't notice the sickness and constantly laughed at their jokes, listened attentively, and told them stories of her childhood.

She liked to chat with them. They seemed to be people who did not dwell on the past and did not curse their lives for turning them old. They genuinely loved their children and grandchildren, which warmed Evie's heart.

For as long as she could remember, since her grandfather's death, she couldn't talk about him without tears in her eyes. Now, as she recalled some of the stories, the time they'd spent together, she found herself smiling.

Gabriel did not join in on their stories of grandparents' and grandchildren's escapades. He laughed at their antics but did not add to the conversation.

When they finally arrived at their destination, she didn't want to leave. She'd rather travel with them all the way to London than confront the Montbrooks. But that wasn't an option. She needed to get her lands back.

"This is odd. I didn't feel ill throughout this journey. It was lovely," Evie said as they were saying goodbyes.

"It's the ginger root," the woman said. "I always add it to my biscuits for spice, and it helps with the nausea."

"Truly? I never knew that. You might have saved my life."

They said their goodbyes and stepped out in front of the Somerset manor.

"Are you ready?" Gabriel asked and took her hand in his.

Evie squeezed his hand. "Yes, let's take my inheritance back."

With a nod, they both stepped up to the door and knocked.

Deafening silence greeted them. Evie frowned and knocked again, only harder. No answer.

Evie looked at Gabriel, panic settling inside her. Gabriel silently squeezed her hand and knocked again. When it was obvious that no one was going to answer, Gabriel bade her to stay by the door and went to check all other entrances to the house. He even knocked on the windows.

By the time Gabriel returned, Evie had made herself comfortable on the front steps. He didn't have to say anything. She already knew the answer.

The mansion had been vacated.

Where had all the servants gone? What had happened here? When she ran off two weeks ago, it was bustling with life.

Gabriel sat next to her and raised his eyes heavenward. "At least, it's not raining."

## Chapter 10

Evie gave a small chuckle. "There's an inn in town. Some three miles away. We might be able to get a room there. But if I remember correctly, the summer fair should be going on around this time. Which means—"

"Which means that the inn might be full," Gabriel finished for her and got up. "Well, no need wasting our time here. I don't think anybody is coming to let us in." He stretched an arm toward her. "How are you feeling?" he asked with such a concern in his eyes that she worried she looked even worse than she felt.

"I am well. I am just worried. Where could Montbrook have taken all my staff? It's not necessary to move them to London since every estate has its own set of servants. If I hadn't left—"

"You'd be married off to one of his sons."

*Or worse.* Evie's stomach clenched at the unpleasant thought.

"You're right. No point in dwelling on the past and what could have been. We better move if we want to get into town before dusk."

The road to town took over an hour. By the time they got there, they were dusty, and Evie's feet burned.

As they reached the fair, they entered the area surrounded by tents, watching families go from one tent to another, buying trinkets, food, dancing, and having fun.

The smell of street food surrounded them, and Evie's stomach grumbled in hunger. She was usually giddy at the prospect of spending time at a fair. Now, however, the noises of the crowd were irritating. She slowed her steps before stopping completely and refusing to move.

Gabriel looked at her inquiringly.

"I am tired, Gabriel," she breathed. "There is no way I am going to live through this fair if I don't eat something."

Gabriel cupped her cheek tenderly and ran his thumb back and forth over her skin. "Poor darling. Don't fret; your husband will take care of you."

Evie looked up at Gabriel's worry-filled eyes. *My husband.*

"Come." He put his hand over Evie's shoulder and led her away.

Gabriel seated her on the trunk of a tree a few feet away from the fair and placed the valises close to her feet.

"Stay here. I'll go fetch us some food," he said absently as he looked over the tents.

As soon as Gabriel left, Evie stretched out her legs and groaned. She rotated her neck and shook out her sore arms. This journey had been torture, and they were only halfway through. On the other hand, she was glad to get a few more days with Gabriel. She sighed and looked up at the sky. The sun was still up but ready for its eventual descent.

She sat on the trunk watching as people laughed, chatted, and enjoyed the fair. She tapped her foot in time to the music that was playing on the other side of the tents. Her thoughts were somewhere far away. Suddenly, she noticed a shadow covering her, and she looked up to see an old gypsy woman standing in front of her.

"Do you want to know your fortune?" she asked in a harsh, gravelly voice.

"No, but thank you." Evie bit her lip as she stared into the eyes of the gray-haired, colorfully dressed old woman. She was thin but well-dressed. She was clearly not a beggar. Nevertheless, Evie knew that most of the villagers relied on fairs as their big earning nights. She searched through her purse and found a shilling. "Feel free to take this, though." She placed the shilling into the woman's hand.

The older woman grabbed her by the wrist and turned her hand palm up. "You give me money"—she took the shilling into her hand but didn't let go of Evie's wrist—"I give you your fortune. No charity!"

"Very well," Evie agreed, her lips twitching.

The woman regarded her palm curiously. "You had bad fortune recently. *Bad.*" She emphasized the word with a shudder. "Someone wants what you have." She looked at Evie and nodded menacingly. "Bad people. You have an angel looking out for you. But be careful, girl. Bad people will want to take your angel away. You need protection." The woman handed her a little cloth with a design of an eye in a triangle. "Come by the tent; we shall pick you protection, especially for you."

"Thank you." Evie smiled at the woman, recognizing the oldest ploy of fortune-tellers. Predict bad luck and sell a trinket as protection. "I shall stop by the tent," she lied.

The older woman nodded, pacified, and walked away.

Gabriel rejoined Evie in a few minutes with meat pies, a couple of apples, and two mugs of ale.

"I wanted to grab us some fish pies," he teased, handing her a portion of the food. "But opted for a minced lamb instead."

He settled on the tree trunk across from her and took a bite of a pie.

"Mmm..." he moaned in satisfaction.

Evie smiled at his obvious enjoyment of food and bit into her own piece. She was starving, so she ate in silence, breathing in the fresh air, listening to the faraway music. Her mood brightened after a few bites of food, and Evie swayed with the music while she ate.

"Dancing already?" Gabriel grinned at her. "I'd take you for a dance, but I'm afraid it won't be that easy with the valises hanging off both my arms." He gestured toward their luggage.

"I'd much rather we find a place to sleep."

"Right." Gabriel finished the last bite of his pie, dusted off his hands, and got up. "Should we go looking for an inn, then?"

Evie swallowed her own last piece of pie as she nodded. She got up and shook off her skirts. "Do you need help with the valises? I can carry one." She reached for her own valise, but he brushed off her hand.

"You are offending my gentlemanly sensibilities." He took both of the valises in one hand and offered her the other.

As they walked through the crowd, they caught a few curious glances their way. Evie smiled and greeted the villagers politely, but she was not certain they recognized her in her bedraggled state. She had wrapped Jane's shawl as a turban over her head for good measure. She loved the villagers, she truly did, but she would rather not answer the uncomfortable questions now, as tired as she was.

After passing several inns, they reached one where a woman checked out just as they entered.

"The room is being cleaned," the inn owner said to them. "As soon as we put some fresh linens on it, you'll be able to settle in."

"Good. Excellent. Would you be so kind as to order us a bath as well?"

As the inn proprietor nodded, Gabriel handed him their valises and asked him to place them in their room as soon as it was ready. He then turned to Evie. "Well, it looks like our room won't be ready for some time. How about a dance?"

Evie was too tired to dance, but she wouldn't refuse Gabriel in a million years. "Absolutely."

Her eyes sparkling, she took his arm, and they headed toward the music.

The dance floor was filled with villagers. The musicians played lovely country tunes neither Evie nor Gabriel knew the moves to. So they just stood opposite each other and tried to imitate what other people were doing. They laughed uproariously as they got every move absolutely wrong. After they bumped into three couples, they decided to leave the floor.

They were still laughing as they reached the edge of the woods. They could still hear the music and the laughter accompanying it.

"No people to bump into here." Gabriel shrugged. "Care to join me in this dance?"

"Here?" Evie's eyes widened, and she swallowed a chuckle. "Now?"

"No place like here, no time like now."

Gabriel offered his arm with a flourish. Evie laughed and placed her hand in his. They danced, twirled, and laughed to the music. By the end of the second dance, Evie was laughing so hard she doubled over and leaned her back against the tree.

Gabriel took her by the shoulders and looked into her laughing eyes.

"You," he said, looking at her closely, "have the most beautiful laugh."

Evie smiled self-consciously. "And you," she retorted, "have the smoothest silver tongue." Her eyes danced with laughter, but his gaze suddenly concentrated on her mouth.

"Do I?" he said absently. "Care to test that theory?"

She blinked up at him, not sure about his mood, as his face moved perilously close to hers. He stopped when his mouth was a hair's breadth away from hers. Then he raised his smoldering eyes to hers. Evie swallowed audibly as she stared into his hypnotic gaze, transfixed. Gabriel braced both hands on either side of her, his body not touching hers anywhere. And yet, she felt his warmth all over. Unable to bear more torment, she leaned up on her toes and kissed him. She felt him smile before his mouth closed on hers in a demanding, scalding kiss.

Evie clutched at his lapels, holding on to him like he was a lifeline. She opened her lips to him and allowed his tongue access to her mouth. Her hands traveled up his chest as she placed one hand over his neck and ran her fingers through his hair with the other. A tingly sensation ran through her fingers. Gabriel groaned as he moved his hands down to her rear and gathered her close, rubbing her pelvis against his hot, aroused length.

Evie fit her body to his, rubbing her own body all over him, clutching him closer to her, unable to get enough of him. When he tore his mouth from her, she whimpered from the loss. But instead of raising his head, he traced his mouth down to her neck, placing tiny bites on her skin, suckling on her pulse at the base of her throat. His hands moved up to the bodice of her dress, and he started tugging it down.

"Gabriel," Evie breathed, unable to think.

"Yes, sweet?" Gabriel succeeded in freeing one of her breasts from the bodice and licked at her hardened nipple.

Evie whimpered at the sensation. Then he took the nipple into his mouth and sucked on it, rolling it with his tongue.

# Chapter 10

A breathy moan escaped her as she melted into his arms. Gabriel tugged the bodice lower, freeing her other breast and repeating his earlier ministrations while squeezing her other nipple with his thumb and forefinger. Evie felt feverish. A peculiar ache settled low in her most private place. She wriggled in frustration.

Gabriel bunched her skirts in one hand and tugged them up before wedging his thigh between her legs. He moved his thigh, introducing unknown sensations at the core of her. Then he returned his mouth to her lips in a passionate kiss.

He devoured her, all the while moving his thigh against her center, sending hot waves of pleasure through her body. Evie's skin grew hot, and sweat covered her body. The tingly feeling originating at her center started spreading through her body as she writhed, riding him.

Needy whimpers and moans started escaping her mouth, and she clutched Gabriel closer to her while still moving against him, chasing the fluttering sensations, wanting more, needing—

A small cry escaped her lips as a feeling of pure bliss surrounded her. She closed her eyes tight and clutched at Gabriel, needing him closer, while her entire body pulsated from the inside. When she opened her eyes, she was breathing heavily, her body buzzing with the aftershocks of pure bliss.

Gabriel watched her, his breath coming in fits, his wintry blue eyes dark, like the sea during a storm. He slowly took her by her waist and set her aside, all the while looking down at the ground, unable to face her. Evie waited for her heartbeat to slow. When that didn't help, she tugged her bodice up and started adjusting her clothes. Gabriel turned away, raking a hand through his hair.

"We should do something about this, Evie," he said with his back still to her, his voice hoarse. "I mean, we are obviously attracted to each other. There is no point in denying that." He cleared his throat and looked at her over his shoulder. "I want you too much to keep traveling with you and not do anything about it."

Evie licked her lips in a nervous gesture, which drew his gaze immediately to her mouth.

"Fuck." He shook his head and turned away. "If you still want me to not act on it, we need to spend as little time as possible together."

Evie swallowed audibly. She didn't want to spend time away from him. During their travels, she'd learned to love his lewd sense of humor, his warm gaze, his seductive smile. She loved that she could talk to him about anything, and he wouldn't dismiss any topic as not for a lady's ears. He didn't care to offend her 'delicate sensibilities' and treated her as an equal. She even enjoyed his teasing, the way he coerced her to eat more, the way he worried over her. And most of all, she enjoyed his kisses. A little too much.

She also knew that way lay heartbreak. They would be back in London in several days. After that, she'd be back at Peacehaven, and he'd be back to his many conquests. She couldn't get attached to him. She had to stay away for her own good.

She understood that logically, and yet her heart refused to cooperate. That's why she stood there, mutely looking at her handsome husband, wishing they could be married for real, wishing he could have loved her. Her foolish, foolish heart.

Gabriel recovered first. He turned to her and extended his arm. "Let us go," he said soberly. "Our room must be ready."

## Chapter 10

They walked toward the inn in silence. The moment they reached the main floor, Gabriel disengaged from her side.

"I need... some time. Fresh air perhaps," he said, not quite meeting her gaze. "You go up to our room. I shall be there shortly."

She nodded, but he didn't see it. He was already walking away.

# Chapter 11

Gabriel left the inn at a brisk pace. Spending the night in the same room as Evie, watching her bathe again, would be torture the likes of which he had never experienced before. He stood quietly in the garden, waiting for his arousal to subside. He wanted to wait until he knew she'd be in bed, asleep. The less temptation he faced, the more sanity he would be able to preserve by the end of the trip.

He took out a cigar and lit it, watching the ambers glow in the dark. He didn't smoke very often, but tonight, it seemed like the right occasion. He walked around the garden, trying unsuccessfully to divert his thoughts from his enticing wife. His wife, who at this moment was probably bathing in steaming water, her cheeks flushed, her skin warm and wet…

He shook his head but was unable to rid himself of the thoughts of her. He flicked the cigar away and expelled a deep sigh with the remnants of smoke. Gabriel leaned his back on the side of the wall, thinking about the way she'd kissed him just now in the woods, how her breasts had tasted in his mouth. With a groan, he undid the falls of his breeches, and his aroused length sprang out instantaneously. God, how he wanted her. He took himself in hand and started rubbing his cock in an erotic rhythm.

Gabriel imagined Evie on her knees in front of him, holding his cock, then he thought of Evie's hot lips on him, of her silky hair beneath his fingers. He would hold her tighter in his grasp, her wet tongue circling the head of him. He quickened the pace, thrusting his arousal into his hand. He imagined himself moving his cock between Evie's wet lips. The way she would feel in his arms, around him, under him. In a short burst of bliss, he spilled himself into his hand and stood, breathing heavily.

He heard a tiny gasp and looked in that direction, only to see his wife watching him, her hand covering her mouth.

"Damn." The foul curse left his lips without a thought.

Evie watched him wide-eyed for a moment, then turned on her heel and stalked away.

Gabriel entered their chamber a few minutes after Evie. She'd managed to change into her nightgown, crawl into bed, and pretend to be asleep. Gabriel came closer to the bed and sat at the edge.

"Do you want to talk about what you saw?" he asked quietly.

"No, thank you. I just came to let you know that supper was getting cold while you—you, well, you know." Evie grimaced and turned to her other side.

"You don't have to be embarrassed by what you saw."

Evie scoffed. Of course, he wasn't embarrassed.

"It's natural," he said conversationally. "When you spend time with a person you desire, you start to feel... uncomfortable. Your skin starts to crawl when they are near, and your temperature rises."

Evie felt like squirming, and goosebumps covered her skin.

"It is nothing to be ashamed of. However, sometimes it reaches a point when you just need a... release. And you either take a partner to bed or... do what I did." A pause followed.

Evie's mind went blank, and she didn't know how to react to what he was saying. She finally turned to him. "If it doesn't matter whether you do it yourself or with... with a partner—"

Gabriel's lips twitched slightly. "It does matter. It is much more pleasurable with a woman. With a willing woman," he corrected himself. "You can do this yourself too," he added with a sly smile.

"I don't think...." Her face scrunched up thoughtfully again. "How?"

Gabriel let out a laugh. "Do you want me to show you?"

Evie felt her face heat. "No, thank you." She turned her back to him again.

Gabriel patted her on the arm and sauntered to the supper table.

\* \* \*

Evie tossed and turned that night, unable to fall asleep. In comparison, her husband was snoring softly, contentedly lying on his side. She turned to him, watching his muscled back, and had a sudden urge to trace his muscles with her finger and then to press up against him, rubbing herself over him like a cat.

Evie shook her head and turned away. Ever since the *event*

she'd witnessed in the garden, she felt uncomfortable in her own skin. Her nipples hardened and chafed against her clothes. She wanted to take off her chemise so it wouldn't rub against her sensitive skin. More than that, she wanted to envelop Gabriel with her body, throw her leg over his hips, and press herself close to him. She wanted him to touch her everywhere but especially between her legs.

*When you spend time with a person you desire, you start to feel... uncomfortable. Your skin starts to crawl when they are near, and your temperature rises.*

It was like he was describing the effect he had on her. Did he truly feel the same when he was around her?

*You can do it yourself too.*

His words rang through her mind. She slowly ran her hand down her stomach and pressed a hand between her legs. She almost moaned. She quivered, but it felt good, the feeling of having something against her center. She pressed herself harder against her palm and took a deep breath. She then quickly removed her hand and threw a sideways glance at her husband.

*What am I supposed to do next?*

Suddenly embarrassed that she'd even attempted this with Gabriel lying right next to her, she pulled her hand away and turned on her side. Would he be appalled at her wanton behavior? She scoffed. He'd probably urge her on. She sighed and shifted one more time, determined to get some sleep after all.

\* \* \*

The next day, Gabriel rented a pair of horses and an old

curricle for lack of a better vehicle.

Evie was overjoyed. She wrapped Jane's shawl around her head and sat there grinning, looking around at the countryside. Gabriel couldn't help but smile as he looked at her.

The wind, the loud sounds of horse hooves, and the carriage wheels prevented any meaningful conversation, but Evie managed to jump up once in a while and yell at him to look at the sun, or the funny-looking cloud, some sheep, or anything else she encountered. She was completely different from the subdued, sickly-looking girl who suffered in a closed carriage.

Gabriel prayed it wouldn't rain until they got to their destination for the night. Moving in a light curricle, they could run horses at a much faster pace, which meant they would be able to reach London almost twice as fast.

The sun was already setting, but Gabriel refused to stop at any of the nearby villages. With such a speed, they'd be able to get to Warwick by nightfall. There, he could finally enjoy a nice bed at the Marquess of Vane's house, provided he was in residence. Gabriel envisioned a soft feather mattress and a huge four-poster bed, and he almost groaned out loud, so delightful the image seemed to him.

He was jolted from his daydreaming when the horses suddenly whinnied and shied, threatening to overturn the curricle. Evie grabbed the handles in front of her as Gabriel tried to calm the horses, to no avail. One of the animals reared, successfully overturning the curricle on its side and sending both Evie and Gabriel skidding to the ground. They landed solidly in the mud.

"Are you hurt?" Gabriel asked.

"No, I'm well." Evie tried to sit up in the slippery mud,

unsuccessfully.

At that moment, three men jumped out from the side of the road, pointing their guns at them. Gabriel groaned in frustration. Why did this keep happening to them? And why did he never have a gun with him when it did?

He did have a pistol under his seat, but with the vehicle overturned, he had no way of quickly grabbing it. Moreover, even if he was lucky enough to pull it out before one of the bandits shot him, he'd never be able to outgun all three of them. He raked his hand through his hair before raising his arms in surrender.

"Take whatever you want, and be on your way," he said calmly, more for Evie's benefit than for the thugs'. Evie shifted closer to his side. One of the bandits sneered at her.

"Whatever we want? What if we want her?" he said mockingly. Gabriel felt Evie burrowing herself into his side.

"That would be a grave mistake," he said calmly. "Take the money." He slowly reached for his purse inside his coat, jingling with change, and threw it to the bandit. "And you'll leave unharmed."

The bandits guffawed in answer.

"And what if we don't?" the one closest to Evie said, moving even closer to her side.

"You don't want to do this." Gabriel regarded him lazily. "Harm her, and you'll be hunted for the rest of your lives."

"Such an important little treasure, is she?" asked the man who looked like he could be their leader.

"She's a duchess," Gabriel said dismissively.

"Is she now?" The leader looked around the scene. "Traveling in a frail old curricle? With no outriders?" All three bandits laughed loudly. "And you be the prince?" More laughter followed.

"It doesn't matter whether you believe me or not." Gabriel shrugged. "The truth is, you should leave us both unharmed, and you know that."

"We also know"—the bandit took a step closer—"that she must have some jewelry in her purse." The bandit looked Evie provocatively up and down her dirt-streaked length. Gabriel put a protective arm around her shoulders.

"Give him your purse, love," he murmured in her ear.

She looked at him pleadingly. "It's all our money…" she began, then flinched, realizing she'd said the wrong thing. It only made the thugs want her purse more. She drew in a long breath and threw her purse over at them.

"Excellent," one of the bandits intoned. "To the horses!"

They mounted the animals that were tethered beside the road and cantered away, leaving Gabriel and Evie penniless, sitting in the dirt next to the overturned curricle.

"Bullocks!" Gabriel closed his eyes in agony.

He should have stopped at one of the closer villages. His foolish dream of a nice, warm bed vanished. Looking as they did now, they would be turned away from Vane Manor in a heartbeat.

A light chuckle from Evie returned him to the present. He looked over at her in surprise. Her shoulders were shaking, and she was visibly trying not to laugh. He raised a brow at her, his own lips twitching with laughter. She looked at his puzzled face and doubled over, laughing even harder. Gabriel joined in the laughter. Her amusement was infectious.

Evie tried to get up but slipped and fell squarely on her buttocks, her hands flailing at her sides. She looked around her, stunned, and then dissolved in a new fit of laughter.

"A d-duchess," she said between laughs. "Sitting in a puddle of mud, on an empty road." She raised her hands, looking at her dirt-covered palms, and continued laughing.

"Well." Gabriel chuckled, finally managing to get up. "At least you are in good company."

He extended her a muddied palm. She took it, and he pulled her to her feet. She was covered in dirt from feet to waist, her hands dirty up to her elbows. Some spatters had even got on her shoulder. She pushed a lock of hair from her face without thinking and got some dirt on her nose, cheek, and hair. Evie looked at her hand in frustration and then at Gabriel.

"Do I look as awful as I think I look?" She bit her lower lip in uncertainty.

Gabriel smiled at the picture she made. Pure innocence completely ruined and covered in dirt. And all it took was for her to elope with him.

"Yes," he said, nodding in confirmation. "Bright side? No bandits are going to attack us now."

She sputtered a laugh and pushed at his waistcoat with her dirt-covered hands. Then she bent down, took some more dirt, and threw it at him playfully. Gabriel tried to duck, but she got him in the neck and his chin.

"Now," she said, looking completely satisfied with herself, "you look just as bad."

Gabriel laughed out loud. "You," he said, coming close to her and taking her by the shoulders, "are beautiful. Even covered in mud." One side of his mouth kicked up in a sardonic smile. "I, on the other hand, must look like the devil."

He looked at his palms and shook his head.

"You look like you always do." She smiled broadly. "Like an angel. Albeit fallen. In the dirt." She sputtered a laugh again.

A beautiful, infectious sound.

Gabriel looked at her in amazement. Any other lady he knew would have been swooning about fifty miles ago, even before they reached Scotland. And here she was, with no close relatives other than her terrifying guardian, married to the most notorious rake in London, covered in mud in the middle of the road next to the overturned curricle, laughing like she hadn't a care in the world.

"As much as I am enjoying your attitude…." He looked at the horizon and tipped his head toward the dipping sun. "We need to get moving."

"Right." She took a deep breath, visibly holding back another spout of laughter. "How do you propose we do that? Do you want me to pull on the carriage or push?" She raised her brow, her eyes dancing in merriment.

"No." He put his hands on his hips. "I want you to ride." He tipped his head toward the horses. "Astride."

Her mouth fell open in astonishment. Then she ran an appraising eye over her gown and shrugged. "I suppose I can't do any more damage than has already been done."

Gabriel smiled. Would she ever stop surprising him?

He boosted her on top of the nearest horse and went toward the other one that had slightly wandered away. In the meantime, Evie had hiked up her skirts to her thighs, so she could sit comfortably astride. She let her skirts fall when she settled in, but he could still see her slim legs up to her knees. He shook his head. *What a tease.*

"So," she said conversationally when he mounted his horse and caught up with her. "Do you have any idea where we are going?"

Gabriel thoughtfully scratched his chin. "No, unfortunately,

I don't have any clue."

Evie laughed and threw him a whimsical look. "If it doesn't rain, we can sleep under the stars." She shrugged and looked at the clear sky. "The stars are beautiful."

"You'll freeze." He looked her over, taking in her light summer gown and mud-covered half-boots.

She shrugged again. "I used to spend nights under the stars with my grandfather when I was little."

"You did?"

She made a sound of acquiescence. "I loved watching the stars. Of course, Grandpa would bring me home and tuck me into a warm bed after I fell asleep." She smiled slyly.

"He doesn't sound like a regular duke to me," he said thoughtfully.

"I never thought of him as one. He was just my grandfather." She paused in thought. "He worked a lot. I remember that clearly. Especially when I was a small child. But he always found time for me. He used to climb the ruins with me, swim in the lake, and show me an old tower on our estate. He told me a tale about it."

"Let me guess. A princess lived imprisoned in the tower. Then one day, a handsome prince saved her?"

Evie laughed. "No. Actually, not quite like that. You got the beginning right, though. A princess was imprisoned in the tower. But once she grew up, she escaped. And then took over the kingdom and ruled forever."

Gabriel snorted a laugh. "Well, I am not surprised you grew up as fierce as you did, with stories like that."

Evie smiled. "That's what he always said he wanted me to be. Fierce. He took care of me, yes, but he never sheltered me. He wanted me to be strong, independent. I still can't believe he's gone, you know."

The sadness in her voice gripped his heart in a cold vice.

"Sometimes I wake up and think, I'm going to go down to breakfast, and he'll be sitting there, reading his morning paper, waiting for me to go riding with him." She shook her head and smiled at him. "I am getting maudlin. You don't need to hear this."

"I think it's wonderful," he said absently.

Evie raised a brow at him. "What is?"

"Your relationship with your grandfather."

Evie nodded mutely.

"Sometimes I wish…." He shook his head. "Now I am getting maudlin."

"No, please. What were you going to say?" She tilted her head in interest.

"Sometimes, I wish I had a family like that," he said with a shrug. "It's an empty fantasy, hardly worth entertaining. How many families like yours do you really know? They are like unicorns. Or God."

Evie laughed hard at that. "Don't be blasphemous. I know you are a heathen, but you are talking to a believer." She smiled at him coyly.

"Why?" He looked curiously at her. "How can you still be a believer after everything that happened to you?"

"That's not fair. You cannot be a believer when times are good and stop believing when they are hard. It doesn't work that way."

"How does it work then?"

Evie tilted her head in thought. "I suppose having faith means trusting that everything you're going through is for a reason. Trusting that it makes you stronger, cleverer, and brings you closer to your destiny." He looked sardonically at her. "I know. You probably don't believe in destiny, either. But that's what I choose to believe. When times are hard, I have to believe that there will be benefits in the end, that I am just where I am supposed to be at this moment, and that I haven't strayed from my path. God deals us the cards, and I believe it's up to us to make the best of it." She shrugged lightly. "It isn't magic. You cannot expect God to intervene when something bad happens. You have to trust that God gave you the instruments to deal with this hardship and that if you move past it, there will be rewards in the end."

"That's... very philosophical," he said with a smile, and she laughed again.

"Similarly, you can't just expect a caring family to happen upon you. I think if you want a caring family, you just need to create one yourself."

He looked at her, startled. Was she saying what he thought she was saying?

"Look!" She pointed at the forest up ahead. "I think I see a river flowing there."

"And?" He frowned in question.

"And, we can clean ourselves there."

"In a cold river. At night."

"Exactly. Listen," she said seriously after a pause. "I have a shilling sewn into my pocket, but even if it does get us a room, no inn is going to let us in. And I am not sleeping as dirty as I am now. Do you have a better idea?"

Unfortunately, he didn't. His only plan was to go to Vane Manor. But if they got there looking like beggars from St. Giles, they might not even be admitted. There was no guarantee the marquess was even in residence, and his staff would definitely turn them away. The marquess was a recluse and rarely left his estate, but it'd be just their luck not to encounter him inside.

With a sigh, Gabriel turned his horse toward the river.

"You don't look even a little bit excited about the swim in the river," Evie observed.

"You won't be either when you feel how cold the water is."

Evie scoffed. "Somehow, I am more afraid of having mud stuck in my hair. A little cold water I can handle."

Gabriel raised his brow at her. "Have I ever told you that you are the most surprising woman I have ever met?"

"No, you haven't told me that." Evie didn't look at him. She just smiled and cantered on.

"Well, you are. Every time I think this will be the final straw, and she is going to have conniptions—" Evie laughed merrily, and Gabriel waved his hand at her. "And there you are, smiling and laughing as if it is the most fascinating adventure you've ever been a part of."

"Well, first off, I do not have conniptions. And second, it *is* the most fascinating adventure I've ever been a part of. All my life, I have been cherished and protected. As much as my grandfather encouraged my adventurous spirit, he never let me out of his sight. I loved him for it, I truly did, but at the same time, I always wanted something more. Something a bit more dangerous, a bit more exciting."

Gabriel grunted. *Cherished, protected.* And now, she'd married the biggest scoundrel in England, and in less than a fortnight, he'd brought her to this low state. He wasn't ready to take on the responsibility for another's life. He shouldn't have married her. He didn't deserve a wife, much less a treasure like Evie.

"Want to race to the river?" she said, successfully pulling him out of his dark thoughts.

"Oh, don't think I'll let you win just because you are a lady." He nudged his horse forward, and they both galloped in the direction of the river, the sound of laughter ripping through the cold night air.

Gabriel reached the river clearing first, but as he stopped, Evie ran right past him and led the horse a few inches into the river. The animal immediately bowed its head and started drinking.

"I win!" she shouted. Gabriel gave her a sardonic look. "What? I said, race to the river, not to the clearing. So, I win."

Gabriel shook his head and laughed. "Fine, you win. What's your forfeit?"

"Hm." Evie furrowed her brow thoughtfully.

"See." Gabriel jumped down from his horse. "I already knew my forfeit as I started racing."

"What was it?" Evie guided her horse back to the bank, and Gabriel helped her down. He held her by the waist a little longer than was necessary, unwilling to let go of her warm body. She felt too good in his hands, like she belonged there.

"I'm not going to tell you," he said a half-octave lower.

"Then why bring it up?" Laughter danced in her eyes.

"I'm not going to tell you," he repeated as he walked away from her and took off his coat and boots, "until you agree that the victory was mine. You won on a technicality." He continued stripping away his clothes and stood on the bank in his drawers.

"I am not that curious," she said, but her eyes betrayed her as her gaze ran over his half-clad body. Gabriel smirked.

She swiftly turned away, looking for a place to sit. Gabriel came up behind her and started undoing the buttons of her gown.

"What would you want if you could ask for anything? Good or bad, big or small? Even if it seemed impossible?"

"Right at this moment, I would ask for a big hearty meal," she said with a chuckle.

Gabriel laughed merrily. "You are completely different when you're not traveling on the inside of a closed carriage. I like it. Fine, you will have your meal, I promise you."

"Wait, was that my forfeit?" She fidgeted to turn and face him, but he held her tight as he pushed her gown down, successfully trapping her arms with the sleeves, and continued undoing her stays. "If I didn't ask for it, would you not provide me with food?" she said, trying to sound pitiful, although he could hear a smile in her voice.

"I would. You are my wife, after all, and I promised to protect you. I suppose protection from hunger is also somewhere in the vows."

Evie giggled in response. "Then, I would like to change my forfeit to something less attainable."

"Like what?" Gabriel finished undressing her, leaving her in her chemise, placed her clothing on a nearby boulder, and turned to face her. He carefully sat her down and crouched in front of her, unlacing her half-boots.

"Hm..." She tapped her finger against her chin. "This is too hard. I don't think I want anything material. I am rich. I have six estates, and plenty of gowns. Anything I do not have, I can buy."

"And what immaterial thing would you want?"

He took off her half-boots and looked up at her. Evie had a wistful expression on her face. She gazed silently into his eyes as if trying to communicate something to him wordlessly. Then she smiled. "Go into the river, husband, I need to take off my stockings, and I am not doing it in front of you."

Gabriel gave her a swift smile, ran into the water, and dived headfirst. He came back up and shook out his hair with a tortured sound.

"This water is like ice!" he shouted.

"Thank you. Now I don't want to go in," she shouted back.

"I am afraid you don't have a choice, my dirt-stricken wife. You are a viscount's wife, and you need to look the part."

Evie scoffed audibly. "I am a duchess! I believe marriage to you lowered my status, so I can look a little bedraggled."

Gabriel laughed and waved toward her. "Come now, before I freeze to death."

Evie slowly made a few steps into the water. Her eyes widened, and her lips parted in shock before she turned and ran back up the bank, screeching. "I am not—" she said but didn't finish her sentence as Gabriel reached her, took her into his arms, and carried her back into the water.

Evie screamed her heart out and laughed while Gabriel carried her until the water reached his waist. He then unceremoniously dumped her into the river. Evie came up sputtering, and he doubled over in laughter.

"Oh, you..." Her teeth chattered, preventing her from speaking quickly. "You are going to answer for that!"

She lunged at him, but he caught her in his arms and started rubbing her arms and back. "You better get clean, quick," he said, chuckling, "before you turn all blue."

He held her tightly in his arms, caressing her body in an attempt to warm and clean her at the same time. The water was icy cold, but he felt himself warming up.

"I forgot the soap in my valise," Evie said on a moan.

Gabriel placed a soft kiss on her hair. "Do not worry, my dear wife; your servant will get it for you."

He swiftly walked away into the frigid night air. Good. He needed to cool down, perhaps even freeze. That ought to help his need for her to subside.

\* \* \*

After cleaning up hastily in the frigid water, they ran out of the river like the devil was on their tracks. Water was cascading from Evie's hair and down her body. Her breasts were peeking out from her wet chemise, and she was certain Gabriel could see all the other parts of her body very well too. He was standing on the bank and studying her intently, his gaze locked on her as if he was preparing to devour her.

Evie hastily crossed her arms over her breasts. Gabriel finally looked up at her face.

"My apologies, I got distracted." He smiled wolfishly, not looking apologetic one bit. "We need to get dressed in dry clothes as soon as possible." He turned around as he was speaking and got some of his dry clothes out of his valise.

Evie followed his lead, although her teeth chattered, and her hands shook from the cold. She was barely able to strip off her wet chemise and put on a dry one when her fingers refused to cooperate.

"Blast," she whispered, trying to wring the excess water from her hair. Her dry chemise was getting wet all over again. She felt Gabriel come up behind her. He gathered her against his chest and started rubbing her arms and body in warming gestures. After a minute or two, she started warming up, so she relaxed against him, her back against his chest, the back of her head resting on his shoulder. Gabriel slowed his movements, not rubbing her body anymore but moving his hands in a gentle caress.

A light sigh escaped Evie as she closed her eyes. She didn't feel cold anymore. As a matter of fact, a strange warmth originated somewhere inside her and traveled through her body.

"Better?" Gabriel whispered in her ear.

"Mmm..." Evie mumbled a sound of acquiescence.

"Good," Gabriel whispered and nipped her earlobe.

Evie felt she should be offended by the liberty, but she was too relaxed to care. Gabriel moved his mouth lower and kissed where her jaw met her neck, then lower still, kissing her neck open-mouthed. He drew little circles with his tongue as he traveled down to her shoulder. His hands, in the meantime, traveled upward and cupped her breasts; his thumbs caressed her hardening tips.

One of his hands moved lower and pressed lightly on her abdomen so that her behind was pressed against his crotch. She felt a hot, hard protrusion probing at her buttocks. She stiffened, and Gabriel stilled his movements, just letting her rest against him. After a moment, he let go of her and stepped back.

Evie felt the earth move from under her feet. She stumbled forward, feeling dazed. What was that?

Gabriel cleared his throat. "We need to get moving if we want to get anywhere before midnight," he said, his voice hoarse.

Evie nodded, although she was not sure he was looking, and proceeded to put on the rest of her clothes. She couldn't believe he'd recovered that fast from the encounter. Her limbs still trembled, and her legs felt like wool. He, however, quickly finished dressing, collected both valises, and threw them over the horses' backs. By the time Evie finally threw on her gown, he was all ready for the journey. Gabriel helped her with the fastenings on her gown, and they started forward.

"Where are we going?" Evie asked as they moved in silence for several minutes.

"I have a friend—and I use the word friend liberally here—who lives nearby. We might as well try our luck in case there's a warm bed for us there."

Evie frowned at him. "Couldn't we have taken a bath there?"

"There's no guarantee he'll be in, and even less guarantee that we'll be admitted by his staff looking the way we did. Not that we look much better now."

"So, who is this friend?" Evie asked curiously. She rarely saw Gabriel in the company of men. In fact, the Earl of Clydesdale seemed to be the only person he actively socialized with.

"The Marquess of Vane."

Evie frowned in thought. "I don't think I know him." She prided herself on knowing every person in polite society by name.

"You wouldn't." Gabriel shrugged. "He's a recluse and a hermit. I don't think he's been to London in all the time you've been out in society. He married when he was young."

She nodded as the dark, tall silhouette of a castle made itself known. "We are here," she said in relief.

"Indeed." Gabriel urged his horse into a canter.

# Chapter 12

Evie stood shivering on the doorstep as Gabriel knocked on the door for the third time. They couldn't be this unlucky. It just wasn't possible. Somebody had to answer them. She chafed her hands over her arms and was ready to cry in frustration when the door finally swung open, and a tired-looking old man peered at them from the inside.

"The household is asleep," he said in a pretentious tone, looking them over with a disgusted gaze.

"I am a friend of your master. Please tell his lordship that Gabriel St. Clare is here to see him."

The butler looked down his nose at him. He was about to close the door when a low, deep voice sounded from behind him. "Who is it, Monroe?"

"A gentleman who claims to be your friend, my lord, and a lady beside him. They do not look respectable."

Evie narrowed her eyes on the old butler, but she couldn't even scrounge up any indignation. They truly did not look respectable at all.

Gabriel wrapped his arm around her shoulder and pulled her closer to him. "You're cold," he said into her hair. Evie took a deep breath and inhaled his scent. She was just relaxing into him when a vast shadow appeared in the doorway.

"Ah, St. Clare, it is you!" came the dark voice of the marquess. "And you brought your..." He paused, clearly searching for a polite way to call her a strumpet.

Evie couldn't fault the man. The way she looked now, especially leaning into Gabriel's side, in a bedraggled state, she'd mistake herself for a harlot too.

She disengaged herself from Gabriel's side and curtsied. "A pleasure to meet you, my lord."

"Vane, meet my wife," Gabriel said sharply. "Will you keep us outside all night, or can we count on your hospitality?"

The man reared back in surprise. "Of course." He opened the door wide and watched them come in with his brows drawn low over his eyes.

Evie shivered as she entered the house and finally took a look at their host. He was extremely tall, about a head taller than Gabriel. His shoulders were wide, and his demeanor dark and menacing. Evie instinctively inched closer to Gabriel's side.

"A pleasure to meet you, Lady St. Clare." He took her hand and bowed over it.

"She's a duchess," Gabriel said briskly.

"I thought you said—" The marquess frowned from Gabriel to Evie.

"In my own right," Evie added, and the marquess lifted his brow. "The Duchess of Somerset, a pleasure to meet you." It was a rare occurrence, to be sure, so his surprise was understandable.

"The pleasure is all mine, I assure you. Monroe, tell Mrs. Ainsworth to prepare the best room for our guests," he addressed the butler, then turned back to Gabriel as the servant scurried away. "I am certain you don't want to spend the night away from your wife."

"Actually, we are quite starved. Do you think your servants can send up a meal to our room now and possibly a bath in the morn?"

"Certainly." The marquess reached out a hand and rang the servants' bell. "Will you tell me what you're doing here in the dead of night with a single valise and looking like drowned rats?" He lifted his brow, and Evie struggled to stifle a chuckle.

Drowned rats, indeed.

"I shall gladly regale you with our tale over a glass of your fine whisky," Gabriel said.

The housekeeper silently appeared by their side, and Gabriel took Evie's hand and bowed over it. "I trust you will be pleased to adjourn to our quarters, my dear wife?"

Evie bit her lip so as not to laugh. "Certainly, my dear husband. My lord." She curtsied toward the marquess, who was observing their exchange with an unconcealed look of astonishment on his face. If he was truly Gabriel's friend, then it must come as a surprise indeed to find him suddenly shackled with no grandeur.

\* \* \*

Gabriel settled comfortably in a large armchair by the fire and shivered pleasantly. Vane passed him a glass of whisky and sat across from him.

"So," he said, eyeing him curiously. "Do tell. What in the devil is going on? Are you truly married? Or is she some doxy you picked up along the route home?"

"Tread carefully, my friend," Gabriel warned in a low voice. "She is my wife and a duchess. Nothing I've said is a lie."

The marquess raised his brow. "Wouldn't be the first time."

Gabriel waved his hand dismissively. "No, this time, it is real."

"Well, she is beautiful, I'll give you that."

Gabriel scoffed. *Beautiful.* "She is gorgeous."

Vane tilted his head and studied Gabriel curiously. "Are you in love then?"

One side of Gabriel's mouth kicked up in a smile. "No. I did not succumb to the disease yet. But if I was to choose, she would definitely be on the list of people I could fall in love with."

"Hm." Vane leaned back, continuing to stare at Gabriel intently. "And how many people exactly does this list contain?"

Gabriel stood and walked to the sideboard. He filled his glass once more. "How have you been, Vane?" he asked, instead of giving an answer. "Are you ever going to rejoin us in the social whirl?"

Vane ran a hand through his hair, looking miserable. "It seems like I do not have much of a choice."

Gabriel raised a brow. "What happened?"

Vane heaved a long sigh. "It's Millicent."

"What about Millicent? She is not out in society yet, is she? I'd think she's too young." Gabriel chuckled at his own joke, and Vane just regarded him wearily. "Good God, you're not truly venturing her into society, are you?"

"Heavens, no, St. Clare. She is five years old!"

"Oh, good. I thought I became too old and hadn't noticed. I even started reevaluating my life."

"I doubt it," Vane grumbled.

"So, whatever's wrong with Millie?"

"Nothing's wrong with her. She's a perfect angel. But she's growing up so fast, and I do not completely understand her at times. She doesn't suffer any governess I hire for her, she skips her schooling, she rebels at etiquette lessons—"

"Shouldn't we all?"

"Do not encourage her when you see her tomorrow."

"I would never!" Gabriel took a sip to hide his grin.

"I think she needs a mother."

Gabriel almost choked on his drink. "You're looking for a wife," he said in between the fits of coughs.

"Not yet. I've been avoiding it, although my servants have been hinting at it for a good year or more. I think I'll have to heed their implied advice."

"You are too familiar with your servants."

"And don't I know it. It's too hard not to be, though, when one spends most of one's time at one's estate." Vane heaved a sigh. "But the truth is, they are right. There are things I cannot talk to Millie about, things she'll have to know about before she has her debut. It's a decade in the future, but she needs to learn things now. I am not going to be here forever either. What if I perish before her debut?"

"Good gracious, man."

"You have to think about these things when you're a parent. You'll understand soon enough."

Gabriel sipped on his drink silently. He wasn't about to tell the marquess about the bargain he'd made with Evie. No children were part of it, unless, of course, she changed her mind. He heaved a sigh.

"Apologies for keeping you so long," Vane said, misinterpreting his sigh. "You must be tired. And I am keeping you from your gorgeous young wife. Why are you still here?"

*If you only knew.* "You're right." Gabriel stood briskly and put the glass on the side table with a loud clunk. "I'd better go and… debauch my wife."

"Don't be too loud."

Gabriel winked at his friend and walked out of the room.

Gabriel woke up to the feel of a comforting weight across his waist and a warm bundle tucked against his side. He opened his eyes to see his wife had thrown her leg over his waist. Her nightgown collected at her thighs as she lay half on her stomach, her hair strewn about his chest, her pillow nowhere in sight.

Gabriel chuckled. The duchess was a fussy sleeper, apparently. At least in a large bed. He traced his hand up Evie's bare leg until he reached one firm, delectable buttock. He pulled until Evie lay on top of him.

She stirred but didn't rouse. He ran his hands up and down her back, then proceeded to massage the muscles of her thighs, kneading her buttocks, caressing her back. Evie moaned and shifted on top of him. Gabriel was already hard, but her action just made him strain painfully. He lifted his hips, his cock touching the side of her thigh, and groaned.

How he wanted to get rid of the sheets between them, rip off her nightgown, and enter her in one swift thrust. It wouldn't take him long. He'd do it in one quick motion. If he just moved—

## Chapter 12

Evie moved her pelvis against him, and Gabriel forgot his thoughts. His hands tightened on her buttocks. God, how he wanted her.

He turned on his side, taking her with him. Evie finally opened her eyes and regarded him sleepily. Gabriel took the hem of her nightgown in his hand and slowly, carefully raised it to her waist. Evie gaped at him, breathing heavily.

He slowly lowered his hand and traced one finger up her inner thigh, not taking his gaze off her. "Turn around," he said, his voice hoarse.

Evie blinked and stilled, the only indication that she heard him the quickening of her breath.

"Do not worry. I shan't break our bargain. But I can make you feel really, really good. Trust me," he added at her silence.

Evie lowered her eyes, and for a moment, he thought she'd refuse him, but she shifted and turned on her side, her back to him. Gabriel snaked his hand around her waist and pressed her flush with his body. Evie burrowed even closer to him, pressing her body to his. Her soft bottom was cradling his hot length, and Gabriel had to grit his teeth to keep himself in check. He lowered his head and inhaled her lovely scent, burrowing his nose in her hair.

He slowly moved his hand up to her breast. The moment he cupped her, Evie tensed. Then she relaxed and threw her head further back against his shoulder. Gabriel took it as a sign of encouragement. He sucked on his thumb and ran it over her nipple, rubbing it up and down, causing it to rise proudly with his skillful ministrations. He snaked his other hand from beneath her waist and drew her closer to him, then lowered his hand to her most private place. He heard her moan as he cupped her there and rubbed her slowly.

"Gabriel," she moaned sleepily.

Gabriel ran his finger up and down her folds, making her squirm and whimper. He groaned, feeling the wet evidence of her desire on his hand.

"Shh... I shan't do anything you don't want me to. I promise," he said in her ear, then kissed her temple, behind her ear, then moved lower to her throat. "Let me touch you," he coaxed silkily against her throat.

"Oh, Gabe," Evie moaned and moved her pelvis against his hand. Gabriel let out a groan and sucked on the side of her throat to keep himself from moaning. He grazed her silky skin with his teeth and had the satisfaction of hearing her whimper in pleasure.

"Let me touch you, darling." He brushed kisses on the side of her neck. "I shan't hurt you. I shan't enter you either. I just want to feel you; I want to come to completion with you."

Evie stiffened at his words.

Gabriel pressed his cock firmer to her buttocks. "This part of me," he said in a husky whisper, "it needs to touch you. It wants to feel you," he said, getting hotter by the second.

Evie gave a slight nod. Her acquiescence was so unexpected that he froze for a moment before reacting.

"Are you sure?" he asked again.

"Yes." Evie's agreement was more of a moan than a word.

He realized that she was as aroused as he was. With one hand, he caressed the inside of her leg; with the other, he put his cock between her hot thighs and groaned in satisfaction. His wife whimpered as she pressed her thighs together. Gabriel kissed her behind her ear, then nibbled on her earlobe, all the while shifting his hand back to her breasts, caressing them each, in turn, playing with her nipples. His other hand was moving over her most sacred place. A place he wanted to touch, taste, penetrate. He bit down on her shoulder and cupped her between her legs. He heard her gasp as she arched her back and squeezed her thighs tighter. His cock gave a pleasant jolt.

"My God, you're lovely." Gabriel soothed her shoulder with his tongue as he started moving his hips against her thighs in a suggestive rhythm. She was getting wetter as he played slightly with his fingers, circling her swollen nub. He felt ecstasy rise up as he continued his movements. A few more thrusts and he'd be in bliss. Their grunts, moans, and whimpers blended together so that he didn't know who made which sound. And it didn't matter. Only this feeling of blended bliss mattered. Just a few more thrusts and—

Loud barking and the sounds of footsteps running down the hall jolted Gabriel to his senses.

"Button, come back!" a young girl screeched. And then someone scratched violently at their door, and more barks followed.

Gabriel cursed loudly, still holding the aroused body of his wife in his arms. Evie jumped in reaction to the hubbub outside the door and rolled away from him, drawing her nightgown down over her hips. Gabriel closed his eyes in agony. His cock still pulsed with need, so he turned on his stomach with a groan.

"Button! Down to breakfast!" the girl commanded.

Instead, it seemed that *Button* ran down the hall, jumping and barking. The damned dog had no manners. Gabriel growled in frustration into the pillow. The mood was definitely broken. Evie scurried from the bed and locked herself inside the washing closet.

# Chapter 13

Evie sat at the breakfast table politely conversing with their host, relaying the tale of their trip as if nothing was amiss. As if they hadn't spent the morning writhing against each other in bed. Gabriel could hardly concentrate on the conversation. His mind was still in their bedroom. Evie turned to him briefly, caught his intense stare, and her cheeks heated before she turned away. So, she wasn't as composed as she'd like him to think. Gabriel smiled in self-satisfaction.

Tiny footsteps sounded in the room, preceding heavy thumps and loud barking. Gabriel turned to regard the intruders of the morning—Lady Millicent Townsend and her dog Button. The dog ran past Gabriel and settled next to her master, wagging its tail. It was white with black spots and almost the size of a small pony. *Button* indeed.

Gabriel scowled at the animal but stood to greet the young lady.

"Millie, what did I say about Button at the dining table?"

Vane said sternly.

Button looked pleadingly at him, and the marquess sighed.

"He insisted on seeing you, Papa," the girl answered.

"I'm sure he did," Vane grumbled.

Millie's gaze ran warily over Gabriel and Evie. She ducked her head and sat to the right of her father.

"Did you greet our guests, Millie?" Vane asked.

Millicent pursed her lips. "Are you my new governess?" she asked in a half-whisper, looking suspiciously at Evie.

"No, I am not." Evie stood from her chair and sank into a perfect curtsy. "I am the Duchess of Somerset. But my friends call me Evie."

Millie looked at her in awe. "A duchess," she murmured.

"And this is my husband, Gabriel," she continued.

Gabriel sketched a bow.

"Are you a duke?" Millie tilted her head, gazing at Gabriel.

"No, my lady. I am just a viscount."

Millie scrunched up her nose, thinking.

"Now, shouldn't you introduce yourself?" Evie asked.

Millicent studied Evie begrudgingly but finally scooted from her chair and sank in a careless curtsy. She tripped, almost toppling over, but caught herself on the side of the table and sat back down.

Vane's eyes widened as he studied his daughter. He then turned to Evie. "This is the first time she's ever done that around guests."

Evie ignored the marquess and instead spoke to his daughter. "See, in polite society, ladies curtsy to their guests, and the higher the rank of the lady, the more gracefully she moves."

Millie seemed to contemplate this for a moment. "Why is your husband a viscount if you are a duchess?" she finally asked.

"I am a duchess in my own right. I inherited the dukedom from my grandfather."

"My father is a marquess," Millicent said, proudly puffing out her chest. "Will I be a marchioness then?" She picked up a fork and chased the food around her plate.

Evie pursed her lips in thought. "No," she finally said. "It is very rare for women to inherit a title."

"Why?" Millie asked around the bite of food.

"Millie, you have to chew and swallow before you speak," Vane admonished her.

Millie threw him a disgruntled glance. She looked at Evie, but the latter waited for her patiently. Millie swallowed and addressed Evie once more. "Why?"

"This is the way of the world," Evie said.

"It is stupid," Millie answered.

Evie grinned. "I am not disagreeing with you."

Millie chewed thoughtfully. "Can I become a duchess when I grow up?"

"Yes, if you marry a duke."

"What if I don't want to marry a duke?"

Evie chewed thoughtfully before answering. "Sometimes, the Queen can create a title to bestow an honor upon someone. Perhaps if you're distinguished in some way, the queen can create a title for you."

Millie's face lit up at the thought.

"Please, do not encourage her," Vane said quietly.

Evie pursed her lips and gave a conspiratorial wink toward Millie. The girl giggled merrily and proceeded to eat her food.

Vane and St. Clare exchanged a look. Evie was wonderful

with the girl. The marquess was probably thinking the same thing. She would be a lovely mother.

Gabriel sucked in a breath. Did she want children? He knew what their bargain entailed, but he wondered whether she was changing her mind.

Evie continued an animated conversation with Millie while Button shifted to sit beside her and placed his head on her lap. Gabriel shook his head in wonder. Everyone flocked to her. Gentlemen, matrons, children, and, as it turned out, even dogs loved Evie.

And she was his.

He smiled, then shifted his gaze and collided with Vane's amused one.

*Damn*, the bastard had caught him admiring his own wife. Gabriel shifted uncomfortably in his seat. Perhaps it wouldn't be so bad to claim Evie as his, to have her on his arm. Having her by his side would make many society functions more bearable and nights more pleasurable. He took his cup of tea and hid his face behind it as he drank, hoping that nobody would guess the thoughts that were going through his mind.

After breakfast, Gabriel asked Vane to spare a carriage and two fine mounts for them to continue to London. He'd leave them at Vane's London townhouse upon their arrival. The latter agreed, so Gabriel settled Evie in the carriage and regarded their host.

"Thank you for your hospitality. If you're ever in London, I shall be sure to repay it."

"I might take you up on your offer, but perhaps I need the help of your wife."

Gabriel raised his brow in question.

"You saw how she was with Millie. I am convinced more

than ever now that the right female influence is what Millie needs."

"Well, you can't have my wife," Gabriel said, only half-joking.

Vane puffed a laugh. "I didn't think I could. But perhaps she can help me find one of my own."

Gabriel patted Vane on his shoulder. "Call on us when you come to London," he said and hopped into the carriage.

He settled down against the seat and thumped on the roof. Only then did he realize that even if Vane did come to London, Evie would no longer be by Gabriel's side.

\* \* \*

Evie rested her head against the carriage seat, her eyes closed, her mind busy with the events of the morning. She could still feel Gabriel's hands on her, his hot, hard shaft moving between her thighs. She felt liquid seep out of her center, and she tensed. Just the thought of him sent her mind reeling. What would the act feel like? Should she just give in and damn the consequences?

"What are you thinking about?" Gabriel asked her suddenly.

Evie opened her eyes in the dimly lit carriage. Her cheeks were burning, and she only hoped Gabriel couldn't decipher her thoughts. "How did you know I wasn't sleeping?"

"Your breathing," he said with a smile in his voice. "I already know the depth of your breath when you're asleep, wife."

Evie smiled in answer. It was definitely a strange journey. She felt like they had been on it forever. It was almost unfathomable to think that tomorrow they'd reach London and then go their separate ways.

"I was thinking about Widow Jane and her predicament."

"What about it?"

"She was truly kind to us. I would love to do something for her and the other villagers. You saw the conditions they live in. Happily dancing away in a rotting inn and walking around the muddy village."

Gabriel heaved a sigh. "Yes, I saw. But short of buying it out, I don't see how you could help them."

Evie raised her brow, although she was certain he didn't see it in the dim carriage interior.

"You are thinking of buying it, aren't you? Just remember, Bingham will try to drive a hard bargain. Unless, of course, you try to win it from him at cards. He is a big gambler."

"Like you?" She smiled.

"No, there is no bigger gambler than me," he said proudly, and she laughed.

Her stomach rumbled then, and she pressed a hand to her belly, embarrassed.

"Hungry, are you?" Gabriel said with a smile in his voice. "Do not worry, we shall stop for the night soon, and I shall buy you supper."

"But we don't have any money. Unless you borrowed from the marquess. My shilling would get us either a place to sleep or a meal."

Gabriel threw her a wounded look. "Do you insinuate I cannot care for my wife without outside help? No. I always keep a few coins in a separate pocket while traveling. The brigands aren't the only thieves on the roads. Sometimes I get robbed in the most unexpected places." He grinned at her.

"Don't tell me." She rolled her eyes and looked away. "I have to say, I am going to appreciate food more after this journey."

"Even fish?" Gabriel smiled.

Evie grimaced. "I doubt I'm ever going to tolerate fish."

"Imagine we are stranded on an uninhabited island. There are only coconut trees on land and fish in the ocean." He looked at her in challenge. "Will you eat the fish I catch, or will you eat your coconuts all day long?"

Evie laughed merrily at that question. "Well, I imagine I would have to concede to your fish. As long as you cook it too. I am drawing a line on raw fish."

"Fair enough." Gabriel nodded. "I'd feed you."

"Thank you." Evie chuckled. "I suppose I lucked out picking a husband who can fish and cook."

"Oh, those are not the only things I can do." Gabriel waggled his eyebrows at her.

"Somehow, I am not surprised." Evie laughed.

* * *

They reached London just before sunset the next day. Gabriel hopped down from the carriage and assisted Evie in getting down. She raised her head and studied the facade of Gabriel's townhouse. The last time she'd been here, it was pouring rain. The building looked dark and ominous. This time, it didn't look any more inviting. Or perhaps it just reflected Evie's mood. She was weary and all too aware that she'd have to leave Gabriel soon.

"It is probably cold too," Gabriel said, looking at Evie apologetically. Her misery must have shown clearly on her face. "Not the ideal environment I'd wish to bring my new bride to. I suppose now I can afford to hire more staff for this house," he said with a shrug once they entered the pitch-black townhouse. He rang the bell by the door loudly. "Let's hope my valet has returned before us and is sleeping peacefully."

While they shed their outer clothing, his valet appeared in the hall, stumbling in his haste.

"My lord, Your Grace!" He bowed as he came toward them. "Welcome back home."

*Home.* Evie's heart skipped a beat.

"Please prepare our chambers and two hot baths," Gabriel said in an offhand manner. "I'll show Her Grace her chambers."

"A bath would take hours to heat, my lord," the valet said apologetically.

"Forget the bath then. Just warm up the rooms, will you?"

"Certainly, sir." The valet hurried past them at a near run.

"Shall we?" Gabriel offered his arm.

Evie took it weakly as she moved with him toward the stairs.

"Are you feeling well?" he asked with a worried frown.

"Yes, just… tired." Evie tried to smile, but it felt more like a grimace. She looked away. The long trip had finally worn her down. She'd tried to stay cheerful and optimistic all the way, but now that they'd reached their destination, she finally let herself drop the façade and feel the entire weight of the cumbersome journey.

"You need to rest. Not the best introduction to my husbandly duties, was it? Not much for providing comfort for my wife," he said gently and looked at her searchingly.

Evie was too tired to show any kind of emotion.

"You will have a large, warm bed. Clean sheets. A warm hearth, and I shall order you a bath first thing in the morning," he continued when she remained silent. "My cook makes the best breakfast. I'll ask for extra sweet buns. I know how you like them."

By the end of his monologue, they reached the viscountess's chambers. "This room had been vacant for a long time before you crashed into my townhouse," he said with a smile.

Evie managed a weak smile for his benefit, then entered the room and closed the door, leaving him on the other side of it.

\* \* \*

Evie came downstairs the next day feeling rested and cheerful. She had slept for almost twelve hours. Then, she'd soaked in the bath for about an hour. Her clothing lay on the edge of her bed, magically clean and pressed. The poor valet had probably worked on that all night. She smiled to herself. He definitely needed a promotion. Washing and pressing feminine garments were probably not part of his job description. But she was grateful to have clean clothing after a relaxing hot bath.

As she entered the dining room, she saw the side table was filled with breakfast foods. The dishes were set for two at one side of the table, but Gabriel wasn't there. She picked up her plate and filled it with warm buns, eggs, and different meats. She was so hungry; she thought she could eat a horse. The cook came in with a hot teapot a few minutes later.

"Good morning, Your Grace." The cook curtsied and filled Evie's cup. She placed the kettle on the side table and stood there watching Evie eat. Evie raised her head to see the cook grinning.

"I apologize. I do not remember your name," Evie said.

The cook blinked and then smiled. "I'm Matilda, Your Grace."

"Thank you, Matilda." Evie smiled. "Everything looks delicious. But you don't have to wait on me. I can pour my own tea."

"Oh, no, it is my pleasure. I was waiting for the day the master would finally settle down. This house definitely needs a mistress," she said with a hearty nod.

Evie felt self-conscious and guilty for letting this kind woman think she would have a mistress. But she didn't have the heart to contradict her.

*Let Gabriel deal with his servants,* she thought glumly. But the truth was, she wasn't so sure she wanted to leave anymore. The days she'd spent with Gabriel had been the most exciting adventure of her life. Yes, she was bedraggled, tired, robbed, starved, and brought to the end of her strength by the time they came to London. She was also exhilarated.

She'd danced with Gabriel at the fair, swam in the freezing river under the stars, galloped away from pursuers, and gotten married in the smithy by a burly Scot. She had been kissed and caressed expertly by a notorious rake; she'd felt passion the likes of which she had not known existed. She felt alive. She also felt safe and secure. She felt... at home.

The thought hit her unexpectedly. She no longer considered Peacehaven her home. She considered this man, this rogue and libertine, her haven now. And he was her husband.

At that moment, the object of her thoughts entered the room. She started guiltily, afraid that he could see her musings on her expressive face.

"There you are," he said cheerfully as he took his place at the head of the table. He gestured for Matilda to bring him

161

some tea.

"You haven't eaten yet?" Evie asked in surprise.

"I have, but that was a while ago. You slept a lot." He grinned at her. "Are there any more scones left?" he addressed the cook.

"Of course." Matilda ran to the side table and brought him several scones.

"I was in my study, notifying your solicitor of our marriage," he said, after taking a bite of a scone and a sip of his tea. "He is going to prepare all the documents and alert your cousin of our arrival this afternoon."

"Oh." Evie was quickly jolted back to reality. *Of course.* This was why he'd agreed to this whole sham. Her inheritance. Not that she held it against him. She'd like to wrestle her lands, her home, out of the odious Montbrooks' hands as soon as possible too. It just wasn't her first thought this morning. "Good," she said, swallowing her disappointment. "What time shall we leave?"

Gabriel took his watch out of his pocket and squinted at it slightly. "In about two hours. You have enough time to get yourself in order and even have another snack." He smiled, looking at her full plate.

"Now that I am not jostling in a carriage for hours a day, I feel like I could eat an elephant. Everything is delicious, Matilda."

"Thank you, Your Grace." The cook beamed at her.

"That will be all, Matilda." Gabriel gave her a look full of meaning. She curtsied hastily and hurried away from the room.

Gabriel cleared his throat loudly. Evie looked at his beautiful face and saw hesitation and uncertainty in his eyes.

His blond hair glinted in the morning light, and his attire was impeccable. He looked once again like the stunning rake he'd been when she first met him. Only now, she could see vulnerability deep in his blue eyes.

"I know that we agreed that once we arrived in London, you would retire to your southern estate, and I would remain here...." He paused as if searching for words. "But you need new gowns." He waved a hand toward her bodice, and Evie couldn't help but look down at the day gown she'd worn at least four times during the last ten days. "And I need new staff for my townhouse," he continued carelessly. "Maybe we can strike another deal. I shall order you a new wardrobe, befitting the wife of a libertine viscount. I shall even pay for it, not taking it out of your allowance. And in return, you will stay here a while and help me fill this house with worthy servants. I am sure I know nothing about running a household," he finished on a strangled note.

He was asking her to stay. She looked at him, carefully placing her fork on the side of her dish. He was asking her to stay in London with him. And he was nervous about it. It couldn't have been her imagination. The servants, the gowns... It was all an excuse to keep her with him. She could barely swallow her elation.

She pretended to consider it before replying. "I need to think about it," she said slowly, although she was bursting with joy on the inside. But then she remembered her Peacehaven tenants, the people who relied on her there, her servants at other estates, especially Carlisle. They all suffered from Montbrook's rule. There was a lot to take care of. "There are people who depend on me," she added lamely.

"Of course," he said courteously. "Take your time."

# Chapter 14

That afternoon, Matilda, the only female servant in the house, helped Evie dress and made an intricate coiffure, all the while chattering about how happy she was to finally have a mistress in this house of debauchery. How glad she was that she didn't have to feed another of her master's arrogant lovers and how she was hoping against hope for a friendly yet efficient household staff. Evie sat silently, afraid to build up too much hope for the friendly cook. Things were too uncertain between her and Gabriel.

Evie wore one of her better gowns and came downstairs to meet her husband, who was pacing like a caged tiger. He stopped in his tracks when he saw her and stared at her for several seconds, giving her an appraising look.

"You look beautiful," he finally said.

Evie smiled brightly at him. He reciprocated with his boyish grin, not the one he used for the *ton,* but the one he used in his moments of unguarded happiness. The one that made him twenty times more attractive to her.

"You too," she said, coming down the stairs.

"Are you ready?" He offered his arm, and she took it.

"No," she said on an exhale. "But the quicker we deal with it, the better everything will be."

"I hope so." He gave her a gentle look before moving toward the waiting carriage.

It took them about thirty minutes to get to the Somerset townhouse. Evie knew she'd find her guardian there unless he'd emptied this house the same way he had her Carlisle estate. She couldn't fathom what damage he could have done to the place while she was away.

The journey seemed extremely long and yet not nearly long enough for Evie at the same time. She closed her eyes and took a deep breath before extending her hand toward Gabriel, who was helping her out of the carriage.

"Everything will be fine," he whispered close to her ear as she took his arm, and they moved toward the beautiful townhouse she'd once called her home.

An elderly butler she did not know answered the door and ordered them to wait for his lordship in one of the drawing rooms. Evie looked about the familiar room, a lump forming in her throat. Everything was achingly dear to her and yet completely foreign at the same time. The scents were different; the energy in the room was cold as if it hadn't been used in a long while.

Evie remembered sitting on the windowsill, reading her books behind the curtains, and how her grandfather would charge into the room looking for her. How they laughed together, having warm conversations by the hearth. She closed her eyes, trying to clear her thoughts.

"Welcome back home."

She whirled around and saw the thin, ramrod-straight figure of Lady Montbrook. Evie's heavyset cousin, Lord Montbrook, stood a few feet behind her in the doorway.

"Please, sit down." Lady Montbrook gestured toward the sitting area in the middle of the room.

Evie swallowed hard. Seeing her cousins after everything that happened sent her blood boiling.

Evie felt a supportive hand land solidly at the small of her back. "Are you doing well?" Gabriel lowered his head toward her as he whispered the question.

Evie nodded and moved toward the sofa. Gabriel sat beside her, snaking his arm around her waist. Lady Montbrook looked them over with narrowed eyes before lowering herself to the chair across from them.

Lord Montbrook settled nearby. "When I received the note from your solicitor and his subsequent arrival, I didn't believe my own eyes and ears," he said, looking at them suspiciously. "You truly are married."

"We are," Gabriel answered firmly.

"Evie, dear, you didn't have to elope. If you truly wanted to marry this—*this libertine*—all you had to do was ask. We would have protested, naturally, but we only want what's best for you," Lady Montbrook said.

"Do you?" Evie's nostrils flared at this fake show of solicitude. "That's not what I heard you telling your son."

"Whatever you think you heard, you must be mistaken. Surely our prospects couldn't have been worse than *him*?"

The show of contempt toward Gabriel sent Evie grinding her teeth. "Nobody could have been better than him," she said vehemently.

"I heard your finances struggled, St. Clare," Lady Montbrook addressed Evie's husband for the first time. "But I didn't think you were that desperate."

Evie's nostrils flared at the insinuation. Of course, it was true, but stating it in such a way, as if there was no other reason Gabriel would ever marry her, ignited her temper. Gabriel squeezed her waist gently and took her right hand in his free one.

Lady Montbrook followed the action with her gaze. "Surely you could find some other way out of your predicament."

"I could," Gabriel agreed readily. "But none more pleasant."

"My husband will have to look into the legitimacy of this marriage before I hand you our money and the lands," Lady Montbrook replied with a nasty twist to her lips.

"Are you insinuating my inability to bed my wife?" Now it was Gabriel's turn to be angry. "Do you not know of my reputation?"

"The money is not yours," Evie said calmly. "Neither is the title. It has always been mine. You were my guardian, but now that I am married, *I* am within my right to collect my inheritance." She noticed Gabriel's soft smile directed toward her from the periphery of her vision. "This call today is just a courtesy on my and my husband's behalf. I shall be taking over the lands starting today. The money will be transferred with my solicitor, Mr. Barrel's, approval." Evie stood, forcing her husband and Lord Montbrook to follow her.

Lady Montbrook also stood slowly. "Are you so afraid to prove the legitimacy of your vows?"

"I do not have to account for anything regarding my marital state," Evie replied. "What is curious, however, is after we got married, we were accosted by thugs who said they were sent to stop the marriage. By you. You wouldn't know anything about it, would you?"

Montbrook slowly turned toward his wife, suspicion clear on his face.

She huffed indignantly. "Your insinuation is not only rude but damning. You should apologize!"

"Of course." Evie smiled. Apologizing was the last thing on her mind. "And I suppose you didn't let go of all my Carlisle servants, either?"

"They were a lazy brood. I am surprised anything got done around the house. You should be thankful for everything I did while you were under my care."

Evie swallowed a nasty retort. She would act civilized, just as her grandfather taught her. "I am thankful. That is why you have a fortnight to clear out from the house." She paused and threw her cousin a condescending look. "It was... satisfying to see you again."

"Until next time, Montbrook." Gabriel tipped his head lightly in their direction and led Evie out of the room.

Once they left the house, Gabriel caught her in his arms and whirled her around. Surrounded by the reassuring heat of her husband, Evie relaxed, clinging to his neck. Gabriel carefully lowered her to the pavement, chuckling lightly. "You," he said, placing a brief kiss on her mouth, "were incredible."

Evie smiled up at him, still holding on to his arms. "Thank you," she said, suddenly feeling shy.

"I don't think I've had that much fun putting someone down since...." He frowned in thought. "Well, since the fight with their thugs, actually." He smiled down at her, then led her to the carriage. "Actually," he continued casually, handing her into the carriage, "I don't think I've ever had as much fun as I've had since you burst into my townhouse demanding marriage."

Evie laughed at that. "Likewise," she said cheerfully as he climbed into the carriage and sat beside her.

Gabriel signaled the driver to move and regarded her intensely. The charged silence made Evie uncomfortable, but she couldn't seem to stop staring into the unfathomable depths of his deep blue eyes.

Gabriel lowered his gaze to her mouth. "I'd like to kiss you," he finally said hoarsely.

"Very well," Evie answered as if mesmerized.

Gabriel raised his shocked gaze to hers, but he didn't linger. His mouth caught hers, and he was kissing her deeply, fiercely, passionately.

He gathered her close to him, his hands scouring her body. Evie ran her hands up his arms. One settled on the back of his neck while the other sifted through his hair, massaging his scalp, gliding through his thick, silky locks.

She felt Gabriel's tongue penetrate her mouth and move inside as if he owned her. Tasting her, devouring her, licking her. One hand on her waist, he placed the other on her bottom and squeezed hard through the layers of her skirts. Evie moaned and heard an answering groan coming from deep inside his throat. Gabriel nudged her even closer to him until she was straddling his hips. They both fought with her skirts to arrange them such that they weren't in the way.

During the struggle, one of his hands found its way beneath her skirts, slowly traveling up her leg, leaving goosebumps in its wake.

"Gabriel." Evie tore her mouth from his with a moan. She felt frustrated and confused. Gabriel lowered his mouth to her shoulder and suckled her, occasionally grazing her skin with his teeth.

"I want you," he said hoarsely while looking deep into her eyes. "God, how much I want you."

Evie didn't know what to say to that. Her breathing was labored, her breasts frantically rising with every inhale. Her nipples chafed against her bodice, aching for his touch. He kissed her collarbone, then moved his mouth lower. Evie heard herself groan, and then she yelped as she realized that his hand had moved perilously close to the juncture between her legs.

"No," she said, with her eyes wide.

"Why not?" he asked gently, looking at her as if she was the only thing that mattered in this world.

"I feel… It's—" she mumbled, getting red from embarrassment. "I'm wet," she finally forced out. "There. I need to…" She struggled to leave her position on top of him, embarrassed and mortified that she'd actually said those words out loud.

Gabriel gathered her closer with one hand while the other squeezed her bare thigh under the slit of her drawers. He lowered his head to her shoulder, and… laughed. He was shaking with laughter. The insufferable man. Evie renewed the struggle to leave, but he bit on her shoulder playfully.

"Shh," he said, raising his head and regarding her with laughing eyes. "Sometimes, I forget how innocent you are." He caught her lower lip between his, then playfully licked it. "You are supposed to be wet there," he finally said with a smile.

"I am?" Evie frowned at him, confused. This wasn't the first time she'd felt like this. In fact, the longer she spent time with Gabriel, the more this phenomenon occurred. But the thought of him touching her there, while she was in this state, felt embarrassing.

"Yes, sweet." Gabriel moved his hand upward until he cupped her between her legs.

Evie let out a moan of satisfaction. The feeling of his strong, hot hand on her was magical. His skillful fingers played with her there, spreading her wetness, separating her folds.

Evie gripped him like he was her lifeline while experiencing wild, unfamiliar sensations. He moved his thumb toward the sensitive nub above her folds, and Evie stiffened. She threw back her head, writhing against him.

"It makes it easier for me to enter you," he said.

Evie lowered her head and opened her eyes. His thumb continued doing wicked things to her, and she breathed heavily, blinking at Gabriel and curling her fingers into his coat with his every movement.

"Let me inside you," he said hoarsely.

Evie slowly shook her head.

Gabriel intensified the movement of his thumb while his other fingers played with her folds. She felt empty at her center, needing more of him. She pressed herself against the heel of his palm and rubbed against him.

Gabriel chuckled. "You will feel better if you allow me in. I promise."

The heat was building inside Evie, and she whimpered in frustration. "Yes," Evie breathed out frantically. "Please, just do… something."

Gabriel kissed her neck and plunged a finger inside her.

Evie stiffened and inhaled sharply.

The feeling of having him there was strange yet satisfying. Gabriel continued his ministrations and plunged a second finger inside. Evie stiffened again, feeling a slight burning and stretching at her center.

"I don't think…" she started.

"Don't think," Gabriel coaxed, kissing her cheeks, her chin, her shoulder. "Feel," he said hoarsely as his clever fingers continued their exploration down below.

He plunged his fingers deeper, then retreated just to plunge inside again. Evie was lost in the feeling of bliss and pleasure. She didn't even realize that she was moving her hips, riding his fingers, stimulating her heightened senses. He was kissing and licking her, all the while sending her to the wild corners of pleasure with his clever hands.

Suddenly, Evie felt something rising inside her. She felt tickled from the inside, in her stomach, and down lower. The feeling made her writhe and strain as she whimpered in Gabriel's arms.

"Shh," he whispered in her ear. "I know what you need. Don't struggle for it. Relax."

"I can't," Evie whimpered, her breathing labored, a moan coming out of her with her every breath. She needed something, and she needed it now. Evie cried in frustration.

"I've got you," Gabriel said, his voice strained as if from hard labor. "I've got you."

Evie shut her eyes as a feeling of white-hot pleasure originated somewhere from inside her. It traveled throughout her body, sending her to some other universe among the stars. She threw her head back and let out a short scream.

A second or a lifetime later, she opened her eyes and crashed into the soulful gaze of her husband's blue eyes, looking at her with wonder. They were both panting, looking at one another in the most intimate moment of Evie's life. He hugged her close to him with both arms as she placed her head on his shoulder.

She half lay there, still straddling his hips, her body plastered to his, her head under his chin, listening to the wild beating of his heart. His aroused length poked into her most private place, which now absolutely belonged to him.

No wonder women lined up to get into bed with him. The unwanted thought crept into her mind. He probably did this to all of them. Maybe this wasn't even the only thing he did. As far as she knew, men didn't use their fingers but the hot, long shaft between their legs. Something that she'd seen him stimulate with his hand.

*You can do it yourself too,* he'd said to her back then. Was this what he'd meant? But even now, she couldn't imagine herself doing anything like this to herself, much less finding it pleasurable.

Her thoughts came to an abrupt stop the moment their carriage did. Gabriel uttered a curse as he lowered his hands from her. Evie scrambled from his lap and tried to adjust her clothing as the carriage door opened.

Gabriel's cravat was mussed, his hair messy, his breeches straining. He took a deep breath and jumped down, then helped her down, holding her tightly by her waist with both his hands. He lowered her to the pavement and kissed the top of her head.

"Come." He gave her a nudge at the small of her back and followed her inside the townhouse.

Gabriel's valet took their outer clothing, and they climbed the stairs in silence. The moment they turned into the hall leading to their respective chambers, Gabriel whirled around on her. He caught her by the waist and gave her a hard, possessive kiss.

Evie responded instantly, her body curving against his, molding to his hard exterior. He backed her slowly against the wall, then gathered her buttocks and pressed her against his arousal. Evie moved her pelvis against his, marveling at the feeling of pleasure she gathered from the simple movement.

She licked at his lips, then lowered her mouth to his strong chin, then lower to his neck. She had a strange urge to know his taste, to suck him in. A low growl came from Gabriel as he moved away from her. He was breathing heavily, visibly fighting for composure.

"Come to my room," he said as he lowered his forehead to hers.

Evie closed her eyes briefly. Could she really refuse this man?

"Come to bed with me," he said, his voice hoarse and uncertain.

Evie gave a slight nod. Gabriel let out a long breath. Then he smiled, took her by the hand, and led her to his chambers.

# Chapter 15

Millions of thoughts raced through Gabriel's mind as he led Evie to his room. What if she changed her mind? What if she didn't know what she was agreeing to? Everything rested on this one night. If this went well, then maybe he could convince her to stay with him. Or for him to move with her. For them to stay together.

What if she didn't enjoy it? The self-doubt and anxieties that hadn't plagued him for years rushed inside his mind. All the thoughts ran through his mind.

All the thoughts except for one.

Gabriel opened the door for Evie and saw her stop cold with one foot inside the doorway. She then retracted her step and backed away. Gabriel regarded her curiously, then peeked inside his room and closed his eyes in agony.

Justine, a curvy brunette, was lounging on his bed. Naked. She stood and walked toward him, her lush hips swaying, her round breasts bouncing with each step, her nipples perked up in excitement.

"You are finally home, dear." She threw her arms around his neck before he realized what was happening. He placed his hands against her belly to push her away, but she clung to him, moving her pelvis against his still-aroused length. "I see you are happy to see me too," she said in a sultry whisper and nipped on his earlobe. Gabriel pushed her as gently as he could with his anger rising. "Who's that?" she said, and he turned to regard the horror-stricken face of his wife.

"I'm..." Evie found her voice a moment later.

Gabriel, as silver-tongued as they come, couldn't seem to find a thing to say.

"I'll leave." Evie whirled around and hurried away from the room, from the hall, and probably from the house.

Gabriel didn't move a muscle. Justine raised a questioning brow at him.

"That was my wife," he said in a strained voice.

"Your what?" Justine screamed.

"My wife," Gabriel repeated more assertively. "Who let you in here?" he asked as he moved deeper into the room. He scrubbed his hand over his face. This was a nightmare.

"Nobody needs to let me in," Justine said defiantly. "I know my way through the back of the house."

"Well, I should have changed the locks," he said angrily. He knew Justine didn't deserve his ire. She wasn't the only woman to use his back door to visit him. His door was permanently open to all his lovers. But why had she come today, of all days?

"What, got married, and suddenly you're too good for me?" Justine walked to the chair angrily and started putting on her clothes.

"I apologize," Gabriel said, staring out the window. "I

shouldn't be angry with you. I just... I didn't think you'd be here."

"The moment I saw your carriage return, I came to see you. Or did you think just because you lost your fortune, I'd stop coming?" She turned to him then, understanding dawning in her eyes. "That's why you married, isn't it? Did you promise her fidelity?"

"No," he said, not clarifying which question he was answering.

"Then it's not a bother." Justine came close to him and plastered her body to his, her breasts pressed against his back. The action she knew would have his blood boiling. Somehow, it didn't arouse him at that moment. All he wanted was to hold his slim, tiny wife.

"It's over, Justine." Gabriel turned to her and regarded her coldly.

Fury ignited in her eyes. "You can't just end it like that!"

"I just did," he said darkly.

"At least let's do it one more time. I can't bear to live without knowing one more night of passion with you," she purred, playing with the lapels of his jacket.

"I'm certain you'll get by." Gabriel retracted her hands from his jacket and strode out of the room. "I trust you can find your way out," he threw over his shoulder as he left.

Gabriel found Evie in the garden. She was sitting on the bench, staring blankly into space. He stood quietly, watching her, drinking her in. He didn't want to disturb her; she looked so peaceful. He imagined her sitting like that on the bench in her garden in Peacehaven, with a view of the sea. And he realized he had no right to keep her here. Not in the middle of the messy break-ups with his numerous lovers.

Not exposed to the scandals he had gathered throughout his lifetime. Facing the hatred of other men and jealousy of other women. He was an idiot, believing that he could give her something better than she already had. She wanted freedom. Not being imprisoned against her will in a large dirty city, chained to the most scandalous lord London had ever known.

He came closer to her and sat down on the bench beside her.

"I didn't know she was here," he said after a moment of silence.

Evie didn't say anything. She just nodded.

"I didn't—" Gabriel let out a frustrated breath and raked his hand through his hair. "She's gone now."

Another nod.

"Will you say something?" He looked at her, part irritated, part hopeful that she still wouldn't leave him. He didn't deserve her, but what if it didn't matter to her? His hopes crumbled as she turned to him, her face serene.

"I am leaving tomorrow morning," she said quietly. "Does it matter what I say?"

"It matters to me." He looked searchingly into her eyes but couldn't find anything there.

"It wasn't pleasant, seeing her there," she finally said, looking back into the void. "But I can imagine that she isn't the first, and she won't be the last."

Gabriel closed his eyes in agony at her matter-of-fact tone of voice.

"These past few days were truly amazing. I loved every second. I shall never forget them." Her last words were like a knife through his heart. "I shall always be grateful to you."

"You are saying goodbye," Gabriel observed dryly.

"We had a bargain." She finally found the courage to look at him, but Gabriel couldn't hold her gaze. He looked away and took a deep breath as she continued. "It is better if we stick to it."

Gabriel sat stonily as she kissed him lightly on the cheek and stood. "I want to take your driver and a carriage to see my cousin if you don't mind. The Countess of Clydesdale."

All Gabriel could do was nod in response. He sat there on the bench as she left the garden; he continued to sit there staring into space when he heard his carriage move away, and he was still sitting there when his valet finally came to announce that the solicitor had come to discuss the terms of his marriage.

\* \* \*

"You married that… that libertine and rake?" Julie was pacing in front of the fireplace, unable to either hold her surprise in check or to sit in one place. "Why? Why him?"

"Who else would you suggest?" Evie cocked her brow.

"Anyone else!" Julie yelled.

Julie, the Countess of Clydesdale, was Evie's distant cousin, but they were very close friends and confidants. Evie had been Julie's only ally when she was in a difficult situation years ago. She was the only one who'd stood by her when the rumors about her simpleminded sister settled and everyone turned away from her. And Julie was forever devoted to Evie in return.

She was also the reason Evie had met Gabriel in the first place. He was the best friend of her husband, the Earl of Clydesdale.

"Don't get me wrong, I like Gabriel as much as the next man, but to marry him, Eves!" Julie resumed pacing in front of the hearth.

"Don't be dramatic, Julie. It is a marriage of convenience. I needed to get out from under Montbrook's rule, and I found a way to do it. You did the same thing when your father forced you to marry someone. And the Montbrooks were going to marry me to their son. If not him, then Lansdowne! I just know it." She omitted the death threat, not willing to trouble her cousin even more.

"Oh, that awful Lansdowne. Will he ever marry some old hag and leave the young brides alone?" Julie said irritably. Evie couldn't help but chuckle at the indignant tone of her cousin. "That is not funny," Julie continued sternly, making Evie roll with laughter.

Evie was glad to be around her cousin. She needed a laugh and to take her mind off of things, especially after what she'd witnessed in Gabriel's townhouse.

Julie's lips twitched in an answering smile, but she sobered quickly. She walked to the chair Evie occupied and crouched in front of her. "Oh, Eves, you are always so cheerful, so lighthearted, no matter what happens. I just don't want your spark to die out."

"It won't." Evie smiled at her cousin.

"Gabriel doesn't treat women very well." Julie frowned at her.

"Oh, is that why women are lining up at his doorstep?" *Or his bedroom.* Evie stifled a grimace and forced out a smile for the benefit of her cousin.

"That is exactly what I am trying to tell you. He uses them, then discards them without a second thought. Do you know how many women threatened suicide if he left them? And did he care? No!"

"Well, he can't leave me. I am his wife." Evie shrugged lightly, feigning nonchalance.

Julie took a deep breath. "I know he is very charismatic and persuasive. He is also charming and handsome—"

"Are you trying to dissuade me or endorse him?"

"He is like a snake from the garden of Eden. He slithers into your life, seduces you, and leaves you to fend for yourself, ejected from the garden!"

Evie took several even breaths before answering. "He is not as bad as all that," she said carefully.

"I knew it!" Julie jumped to her feet and resumed pacing back and forth in front of Evie. "He seduced you, didn't he? Oh, that sly—"

"Julie, calm down. Please?" Evie indicated the seat in front of her with a nod. "Just listen to me!"

Julie took a deep breath and did as Evie asked.

"I sought him out. He suffered because of our ploy last year—"

"It wasn't our fault he—"

Evie stopped Julie's protests with a staying gesture. "He needed money. I needed a husband. I know he is Clydesdale's best friend, and he wouldn't risk upsetting that friendship by treating me badly. He is also used to his bachelor lifestyle in London, so he won't care what I do back in Peacehaven. I thought it all through. Please, give me some credit." Evie hoped she was assuring her cousin because she barely believed her own words. This might have sounded like a solid plan to her a fortnight earlier, but now?

Julie looked at Evie for a short moment before replying.

"Of course, I trust you. I know how smart you are and that you wouldn't make hasty decisions… But I know what your grandfather wanted for you. I know what you have always wanted."

Evie's eyes filled with tears. "We don't always get what we want." She smiled sadly. "I have more than most women."

Julie regarded her with worry shining in her dark blue eyes. "Have you talked to Samantha yet? She is extremely worried about you, you know."

"No, I haven't. To be honest, I don't even know where she is right now. I haven't had the chance to communicate with her much since Montbrook took over the Somerset estates." She paused and swallowed the hurt in her chest. "I sent a note to her London residence about two weeks ago."

"Yes, I know. She showed it to me. The same note I received about not worrying about you because you were eloping?" Julie's lips twitched in laughter. "Let me tell you one thing, that did not succeed in ceasing either of our worries."

"I am sorry." Evie chewed on her bottom lip.

"Don't apologize, sweetheart. You were in a difficult situation, and you took the opportunity to get out of it. We worried about you, but we were fine."

Evie nodded thoughtfully. "How is Sam?"

"She looked good, happy, healthy. She said she needed to speak with you. Some news or some such, but she is in Bedford now."

Evie pursed her lips in thought. "I wish I could see her sooner. But I have to go and take care of my people. They've been neglected quite enough. I am moving to Peacehaven on the morrow." She looked at the fire thoughtfully. "Do you mind posting a letter from me to Sam?"

"Absolutely not." Julie got up from her chair. "Let's go. You better use Robert's study for that."

Evie looked around the quiet townhouse as they walked down the hall. "Where are the children?" she finally asked. "I assumed they were in the nursery, but it is too quiet for that."

"Robert took them for a ride in the park." Julie waved her hand dismissively.

"And Mary is still in York?"

"Yes, but she and the dowager will be traveling here soon."

"Is the season over then?" Evie asked, walking beside her cousin. She knew Mary tried to avoid the crowded season. The *haut ton* didn't take well to her.

"Yes, the final ball happened a few days ago."

"Oh, good."

"You'll need a new wardrobe next year. You can wear bright colors now that you're a matron."

Evie smiled, remembering her constant complaints that she wasn't allowed to wear bright colors. Before they made it to the study, they heard the loud sounds of voices coming from downstairs.

"Oh, God, the family is back." Julie grinned openly. "Let's go say hello." She took Evie by the hand and fairly dragged her down the stairs. As soon as the children saw them, they charged at them at top speed. Both of them jumped on their mother, clinging to and hugging her.

"Auntie Evie!" The eldest boy, Jared, hugged Evie tightly while Julie picked up her little daughter, Victoria.

Clydesdale came up behind the children and gave his wife a soft kiss on her lips. "Hello, darling." He looked at her with so much love in his pale gray eyes that Evie's heart constricted. That was all she'd ever wanted for herself. A husband who looked at her like that, and children who hugged and kissed her after a short separation. A loving family.

"And if it isn't our runaway bride," Clydesdale observed as he took in Evie's appearance. "Are you well?" he asked gently.

"Yes, she is good and healthy, and we'll meet you in your study to share all the gossip once you hand these little monsters to their governess." Julie gave Victoria back to him.

The little girl squirmed and turned in her father's arms. "Aunt Evie—"

"I want to go with you—" both children yelled at the same time.

"You need a bath before supper, or you are not eating," Julie said sternly.

The children growled in disappointment. Jared shuffled up the stairs to his room. Clydesdale gave one more kiss to his wife's forehead and followed his son up the stairs, carrying the little girl.

Evie regarded Julie in wonder. "I don't know how you do that."

"Do what?" Julie led her toward the study.

"Deal with them so easily."

"It comes with practice. Once you have children, you'll understand," she said, then turned to Evie, biting her lip. "Shoot, I am sorry. I don't know if you... If Gabriel..." She looked so worried and apologetic that Evie wanted to laugh.

"Don't worry, Julie. It's fine. I don't plan on having children." She swallowed and put a wide smile on her face. "He did offer, though."

"I bet he did," Julie grumbled, which just made Evie laugh.

Clydesdale joined them shortly in his study. Julie had brought him up to date on the issue of Evie and Gabriel's marriage by the time Evie finished addressing her letter to her friend Sam. Clydesdale looked at her then, a frown of concentration marring his brows.

"You are telling me you traveled over ten days alone with Gabriel, and nothing untoward happened between you two?" He cocked a brow at Evie.

Evie's traitorous mind selected that moment to remember all of Gabriel's penetrating kisses, the way he'd brought her to bliss in the carriage. She felt her skin growing hot. "Nothing untoward," she said unconvincingly.

"Right. I'd like to have a talk with your *husband* if you don't mind. I'll go with you when you leave for home."

"It'll have to wait." Julie took her husband by the arm and massaged his muscles. "Evie is staying for supper. Right, Eves?"

Evie nodded her acquiescence. She'd rather spend her last evening with Gabriel, but she wasn't quite ready to face him after this afternoon. Besides, she'd missed her cousin.

During supper, Evie told them all the adventures she and Gabriel had gone through on the way to Scotland and back. She told them all the stories, including Widow Jane, the thugs who were after her, how they got robbed, and even washing up in the river at night, omitting the most intimate details.

Clydesdale regarded her thoughtfully while Julie gasped and laughed as the story went on.

"Oh, my," Julie finally said, laughing. "This does sound like a romantic tale."

Clydesdale scoffed.

"You should publish it in the paper," Julie continued, ignoring her husband.

Evie drew a deep breath. "No, thank you. I would rather

return to my quiet existence at Peacehaven."

"Who is representing your fortune in the marriage contract?" Clydesdale asked from the head of the table.

"Grandfather's solicitor, Mr. Barrel," Evie said.

"You don't mind if I take a look at it, do you?"

"No, I don't. But why?"

"I trust Gabriel more than anyone, but I would like to look out for you," Clydesdale answered.

Evie put her fork down and regarded him curiously. "You are his best friend. And yet, even you don't think he'd be fair to me," she said accusingly. Somehow it chafed her that everybody, and especially his best friend, mistrusted him.

"Gabriel is a good person. I wouldn't be friends with him if he wasn't. He is also selfish. He likes to indulge in pleasurable activities and doesn't think of the consequences. You don't know him as I do."

"And you don't know him as I do," she countered, earning curious glances from both of her hosts. "I appreciate you looking out for me, but what's done is done. Gabriel is my husband now. We made a deal, and we'll stick to it. I trust him with my fortune, and I trust that he will keep me safe from the Montbrooks or anyone else for that matter," she said assertively.

That earned her another peculiar glance from Julie and her husband.

"You're right," Julie finally said and earned a doubtful gaze from her husband. "Well, she is. She is a married lady now, and we need to respect that. There is nothing we can do except make the best of this situation." She looked at her husband and smiled widely. "For instance, your dear friend is now our relative."

# Chapter 15

"Splendid." Robert rolled his eyes. And both women burst out in laughter.

# Chapter 16

Gabriel sat at his desk, flipping through the late Duke of Somerset's will.

"These are all her assets and lands?" He cocked a brow at the solicitor.

The solicitor nodded.

"Does Evie know what she inherited?" Gabriel asked.

"Yes. To my understanding, late Somerset prepared Lady Eabha—pardon me, the duchess—to run his estates. We had several meetings with her present in the room."

"Hmm." Gabriel continued studying the documents. The list of her assets was extensive. He wasn't certain he'd be able to take care of it all, but his wife... Well, he wouldn't be surprised if she ruled all of it blindfolded.

"Since there was no marital contract drawn up, everything in there now belongs to you," Mr. Barrel, the solicitor, said tightly. "Including, but not limited to, a seat in the House of Lords on behalf of the Somerset title."

Gabriel snorted. He hadn't set foot in the House of Lords

even as Winchester's heir. He wouldn't start now. Unless she asked him to.

"Can we draw up the marriage contract now? Post marriage?"

"Technically, everything now belongs to you, so if you want to allocate the duchess a yearly allowance—"

"No, I don't want to give her an allowance," Gabriel interrupted briskly.

The solicitor fought for composure, but it was evident he was shocked by Gabriel's attitude.

"I want you to open a bank account exclusively in her name and transfer all the funds there. She will be in charge of all her estates, and she can even take the seat in Parliament, although I doubt she'd be willing to rub elbows with all those sweaty old lords," he said in an offhand manner.

Mr. Barrel's eyes widened briefly. He composed himself and adjusted his spectacles on the bridge of his nose. "You won't take a penny from her accounts?"

Gabriel scratched his jaw thoughtfully. He didn't want to take as much as a coin from Evie's purse. He wanted to show her that although he'd married her for money, that was no longer the reason. He needed to be a better man for her, to dig himself out of this bind by himself, without her support. If he couldn't solve his own monetary problems, what could he truly offer her? A broken, empty household with just a couple of servants?

He shook his head. "Not a penny."

The solicitor adjusted his spectacles again and wrote something down in his notebook.

"What do you know about Montbrook's finances?" Gabriel asked as he lounged in his chair.

"Not much. He had a low to average income. He did try to gamble against the duchess's inheritance once or twice but wasn't allowed to take more than the allowance granted by the will, which I believe is ten percent. He hasn't made any grand purchases since becoming the guardian to the duchess. On the contrary, as far as I heard, he let most of the previous servants go and hired his own."

"He let go of *all* of the previous servants?" Gabriel stopped playing with the quill, put his elbows on the table, and leaned forward.

"Most. He's done it quite recently too. I believe some estates still have a skeleton staff that is the same, but most are gone. Most of them had served the Somerset line for generations. Some were too old to find another placement."

"Why would he do that?" Gabriel asked.

"I am afraid I do not know."

Gabriel thought for a moment before regarding the solicitor with a curious stare. "Since you represent the Somerset title, I assume you will continue working for my wife, yes?"

"It would be my honor, my lord."

"Good then. I shall let my wife make all the decisions from here on out." He closed the ledgers and set them aside.

Barrel nodded and scribbled something else in his notebook. "Is there anything else?"

"Yes." Gabriel nodded slowly. "I have a special request for you."

* * *

It was long past suppertime when Gabriel finally heard the carriage wheels and horse hooves outside of the townhouse.

Evie had finally returned home. He had paced back and forth in his study for hours, looking out the window every ten minutes.

He'd wanted to go to Clydesdale's townhouse himself and bring her home, but he knew he had no right to do that. *But what if something happened to her?* The nagging voice inside his head didn't give him a moment's reprieve. *It's not that late. She probably stayed for supper. Besides, Clydesdale wouldn't let anything bad happen to her.* He tried to reassure himself, but it barely worked. Just as he'd decided he would finally go and track her down, the carriage rolled into the driveway.

He walked into the hall to greet his wayward wife when he saw the tall figure of his friend in the doorway.

"Ahh, Rob, good to see you," he said somewhat tersely.

"Gabe." Clydesdale gave him a short nod.

Evie looked from one man to another, then shook her head and walked to the stairs. "I shall retire now if you both don't mind. Today was quite exhausting." She smiled at Gabriel as she walked past him. He sent her a gentle look before regarding his friend again.

"Shall we adjourn to my study?" He led the way at Robert's nod. "Would you like some whisky, or brandy perhaps? I've got this new supplier; his brandy is magnificent," he said as he entered the study and walked to the sidebar.

"No, thank you. Perhaps you have some scotch?" Robert replied as he settled in the chair across from the table.

"Scotch it is then." Gabriel filled two glasses and brought them to the table. He handed one to Clydesdale and sat comfortably in his chair. "Come to wish me felicitations, have you?" he asked with a sly smile.

"Not quite." Robert took a sip from his glass and looked at

Gabriel in concentration.

Gabriel cocked a brow at him. "Oh?"

"You should have come to me, Gabe," Robert said in ominous tones. "The moment Evie appeared on your doorstep, you should have come to me."

"And risk Montbrook finding out where she was? Did she tell you what happened? He sent thugs after her, ready to murder anyone who stood in their way."

"And yet here you are, unscathed."

"I had help." Gabriel carelessly waved his hand.

"You had no right to marry her," Clydesdale said darkly.

"You are the one who has no right to tell me what I did or didn't have the right to do. She chose me. She came to me for help, and I agreed. I didn't do anything wrong, and neither did she." Gabriel's temper started to rise.

"She was desperate, Gabe! You should have known that. You took advantage of a beautiful young girl in peril, just like you always do."

Gabriel landed his glass on the table with a loud thud.

"You should have brought her to me," Clydesdale said more softly. "We would have come up with a better plan."

"Oh, would you now? And what would you have her do? Hide away until her twenty-fifth birthday? Murder her guardian?" Gabriel's face started turning red.

He'd expected his friend to be angry with him, but he hadn't expected himself to get worked up over his accusations. Clydesdale was right, after all. Gabriel had ruined more than one young lady. He had no reason for getting defensive about this. And yet, the thought of relinquishing Evie bothered him too much for rational thought to take over.

"Don't be ridiculous, Gabe—"

"No, let's hear your better plan, Robert. What would you have done to help her?"

Clydesdale shifted uncomfortably in his chair. "I don't know."

"Oh, you don't know," Gabriel jeered. "Now, *that* would have helped her splendidly. It would also have wasted just enough time for Montbrook to find her. And we would have no right to keep her with us. Now, I do," he said heatedly.

Robert watched him for a moment, lost in thought. "What happened on that trip to Scotland?" he asked, tilting his head. "You seem... different."

"Tired." Gabriel relaxed in his chair. "I am just bloody tired. I barely slept through that trip. Today wasn't a picnic either." He scrubbed his face with his hand and took a sip of the scotch.

"What happened today?" Clydesdale raised a brow in question.

"Nothing you should worry yourself over." Gabriel let out a breath and regarded his friend wearily. "Why are you here, Robert, to debate the unchangeable?"

"No." Clydesdale cleared his throat. "Actually, I wanted to talk to you about this bargain you two made up."

"What about it?" Gabriel asked, taking a deceptively relaxed pose.

"According to Evie, you are allowed to continue your debauched ways once she moves back to Peacehaven."

"So?" Gabriel picked at an invisible speck on the sleeve of his coat.

"So, I want you to promise me you won't make a spectacle of her."

Gabriel looked at his friend with a stony expression on his

face, his anger boiling from the inside.

"I shan't tell you how to live your life, Gabriel, but I don't want her to face the embarrassment from the *ton* when they discuss another one of your conquests."

"Oh, so it is fine for you to have a mistress after marriage, but not for me?" Gabriel said venomously.

"I was an idiot," Robert said evenly. "Julie didn't have anybody to look out for her, so she had to do it herself. Evie has me. And I shan't let you mistreat her."

"I wasn't going to," Gabriel said evenly.

"Truly? Because scandal and you usually go hand in hand."

"I think that's enough insults from you for one day. Is there anything you want, or can I throw you out of my house yet?"

"Don't be an arse, Gabriel—"

"Isn't that the pot calling the kettle black?" Gabriel cocked a brow at his friend. A tense silence sizzled between them. "Look, Rob," Gabriel finally said, taking a deep breath. "I know you worry about her, but you don't have to. She took great care of herself while getting rid of her guardian. She took splendid care of herself during the journey with a notorious rake. And she will be quite fine on her own from here on out."

Gabriel finished his glass of scotch in one gulp to drown the bitter taste in his mouth.

Clydesdale watched him with narrowed eyes. "And you?"

"And I"—Gabriel stood and went to the sideboard for a refill—"shall not stand in her way."

"You know you are going to be the most notorious couple of the *ton*," Clydesdale said, lounging in his chair lazily. He stretched out his legs and crossed them at the ankles, looking extremely comfortable. "You will be the envy of every beau who has ever proposed to her, and there were dozens."

"I can imagine," Gabriel grumbled under his breath, taking a sip of his scotch.

"Rumors will be following your every step," Robert continued.

"So what?" Gabriel threw nonchalantly.

"So, Evie will be propositioned from every corner by the same husbands you once cuckolded."

Gabriel's hand froze with his glass halfway to his lips.

"Now that she's married, she is fair game for the mistress seekers." Clydesdale shrugged as if he didn't care.

"They can proposition her all they want. She wouldn't agree to them," Gabriel said, sounding uncertain to his own ears.

"Oh?" Clydesdale cocked a brow at him.

"She lasted almost two weeks of one-on-one travel with me. She can withstand some other fop." He drained his glass and went for another refill.

Clydesdale chuckled lightly. "You are not as unaffected as you want to seem, my friend," he said, humor dusting his tone.

"What are you talking about?" Gabriel turned to him, a glass of scotch in his hand.

"I'm talking about Evie and how you didn't return unscathed from the trip with her."

Gabriel suddenly felt tired and weary, or perhaps the scotch had kicked in and relaxed his guard.

"Did you see the girl?" He scoffed. "Nobody would return unscathed after one look at her, let alone ten days. At least I married her." He smiled at his glass of scotch and took another sip.

"You are in love with her," Clydesdale observed dispassionately.

"I wouldn't use the word love." Gabriel shrugged. "Infatuated is more likely. Although, I don't think I've ever been infatuated with anyone. So, who am I to judge?"

"And you're just going to let her go?" Clydesdale looked at him questioningly. "The first time you feel deeply about a girl, you marry her and let her go?"

Gabriel smiled sadly. "That's what she wants."

"Since when do you care about other people's wants?" Clydesdale snorted.

"You said it yourself. I am not fit to be her husband. I don't care for anyone but myself. Scandal follows me around like a shadow. There's really no upside for living with me." Gabriel shrugged. "She is better off without me."

Clydesdale looked at him with a thoughtful frown on his face. "Listen, Gabe. I know I might have come a bit strongly about this, but I care for Evie a lot, and I wouldn't want her to get hurt. She clearly cares about you, too."

Gabriel's head shot up at that.

"However," Clydesdale continued slowly, "don't make any move unless you're certain. Don't give her false hope. If you are not planning to be with her forever, don't seduce her."

Gabriel scoffed and downed another glass of scotch. Clydesdale followed the movement of his hand and then slowly walked toward his friend. He took the empty glass from Gabriel and placed it face down on the side table.

"And please don't drink anymore." He patted Gabriel on the shoulder and walked toward the door. "I want you to know that my initial impulse to come here was to check if you'd emptied Evie's coffers. But I can see that you care for her. So, I shall trust you. But if you ever hurt her, I shall not hesitate to break your beautiful face." He grinned openly at Gabriel's miserable grimace and walked out the door.

# Chapter 17

B y the time Evie woke up, her carriage was already
packed and ready. Her own carriage. Somerset's
carriage, the one her grandfather used to travel in
when he was alive. Her heart constricted at the memory. She
ran a hand over the shiny surface, smiling as if seeing a good
friend for the first time in weeks. Her old driver was at the
reins, a couple of footmen who used to work at Peacehaven
stood guard, and even her elderly housekeeper bustled around
the vehicle. The latter was about to travel in the carriage with
Evie.

Evie could not believe what she was seeing. Four outriders
were lining up to journey with her, too. Where did all these
people come from? She had asked Gabriel to prepare a vehicle
for her last night, but she'd imagined she'd travel in one of
his carriages with a maid. Instead, there was all this. Her
insides warmed at the thought of how much trouble he'd
gone through to ensure she had a comfortable ride home.

She'd walked into Gabriel's room earlier, his study, and all the other rooms she could think that he might be in, but he was nowhere to be found. Evie noted the readiness of her ride and took a last look at the townhouse; she hadn't had enough time to call it her home.

"Leaving without saying goodbye?" a dear, deep voice called from behind her.

She turned and saw Gabriel leaning against the carriage in a casual stance, feet crossed at the ankles, arms folded on his chest, his golden blond hair gleaming in the sun, a relaxed smile on his lips. God, she was going to miss those lips. Oh, who was she kidding? She was going to miss all of him. A lot.

"I didn't think you were home." Evie smiled slightly.

"I wasn't. Had a last-minute errand to run. Your solicitor did a great job procuring your old staff for you." He shrugged and pushed off the carriage.

"My solicitor?"

"Yes, he will speak with you at Peacehaven once he rounds up the rest of your runaway staff. You will have some busy days ahead of you, running all your estates."

"Did you go through the marital contract with him already? I would have liked to be present during the negotiations."

One side of Gabriel's mouth kicked up in a smile. "I did not strip your accounts naked if that's what you're worried about."

"You are a master at stripping things naked, as I recall," she said saucily, and he laughed.

"Perhaps some things." He came closer to her. "Nothing is final without your signature, so not to worry. Are you ready for your trip?"

Evie nodded, still smiling. Because if she didn't, the alternative would be to bawl her eyes out. Gabriel took one of her hands and placed a warm kiss on her knuckles. Evie swallowed, trying very hard not to give in to the urge to cry.

He handed her into the carriage, but instead of closing the door, he leaned in.

"I've got a present for you," he said shyly. She could have sworn he looked embarrassed and out of place. "It's a tiny thing...."

Evie stared, wide-eyed, as he handed her a piece of ginger root. She blinked and looked at him questioningly.

"Remember, Mrs. Adley said it helps with motion sickness? I know she had hers in biscuits, but I was told just a nibble before you start the journey should settle the stomach just as well. I don't know if it's true, but it couldn't hurt, right?" He grinned, reached up, and gave her a soft kiss on her cheek. "Farewell, Lady St. Clare," he said, his voice husky.

He tipped his hat, shut the door, and signaled for the driver to get moving before Evie could even open her mouth to reply.

*Lady St. Clare.* The name rang in her ears. The name she would never be called by, but the one that warned her that she was leaving something important behind.

\* \* \*

Melancholy ate at Evie most of the trip, but the closer she got to Peacehaven, the giddier and more excited she became. She could smell the musk of the sea, could hear the splashing of the waves. Her heart beat louder in her chest with anticipation. She was back home.

Evie was almost hanging out of the carriage window as they neared Peacehaven. The sun shone brightly in the sky, shooting sparks off the mansion's roof. The sparkling white Georgian facade with Greek columns and angel figures on the walls of the manor made it look like a fairytale palace. Surrounded by colorful, lush gardens and overall greenery, the place really did look like a heavenly garden.

By the time the carriage stopped, Evie's cheeks had started to hurt; her grin was that wide. As she stepped out of the carriage, her elderly butler greeted her from the steps of the house, bowing deeply. She entered the hall, and more of her old servants lined the space. She whirled around, taking in the walls, the paintings, and the people inside her favorite place on earth. Tears collected at the corners of her eyes as servants bowed to greet their mistress.

Evie walked around her house most of the day, making certain everything was where it was supposed to be. Just before sundown, she went to her favorite spot, a cliff with a bench overlooking the sea. She sat down and listened to the sounds of birds chirping, waves splashing, and the wind whistling. If she listened intently, she just might hear footsteps and then the sound of her grandfather's lovely voice.

"I miss you," she whispered into the void. "I wish you were here. But I am well now. I'm even married. And no, he doesn't love me. But you don't have to worry. He's a good man." She smiled to herself.

"He's an idiot if he doesn't love you," a male voice said from behind her, and she nearly jumped out of her skin. She turned to regard the caretaker of the estate.

"Mr. Cromwell! What a pleasure to see you. I was going to walk over to your cottage a bit later. I just arrived this afternoon."

He nodded. "I was doing the rounds when I heard you'd

arrived. Thought I'd find you here."

Evie smiled. "You know me well."

"So, I saw Monsterbrook's servants were kicked out on their arses. The place is rightfully yours again."

Evie giggled at the nickname. "Right you are, sir, I am the mistress of this place once more. Would you like to have a seat?"

"No, I'd rather stand. My knees can't take too much bending back and forth," he said in a rusty voice. "So, tell me about this idiot husband of yours."

Evie laughed merrily at Mr. Cromwell's cranky tone. "He's a good man, Mr. Cromwell. He helped me get back everything I own from Montbrook. He stood up to him for me and made sure I was comfortable here."

Old Cromwell scoffed. "That doesn't excuse his leaving you here all alone, does it?"

"That was our bargain." Evie shrugged.

"Bargain." He scoffed again. "If that'd been me, and I got a girl like you, I would've never let you go," he said, turning toward the sea.

"And you didn't," Evie said mildly.

"That's right. And I've lived the best life I could." He nodded thoughtfully, and Evie knew that he wanted to believe that was true. Mr. Cromwell's wife had died decades ago from scarlet fever, and his only son died during the war. The missive came several months before Evie moved back to Peacehaven after Somerset's death. "Don't get me wrong, I enjoy our conversations and spending time with you, but you are young, vibrant, and beautiful. You are the one who should be living her life to the fullest. Preferably with your husband. Especially if he's such a paragon of good as you

202

describe him."

Evie laughed sonorously. "Did I give you that impression of him?" She raised a brow. "On the contrary, he is the devil himself, the most notorious rake and scoundrel London has ever seen." Her lips twitched with renewed laughter as Mr. Cromwell regarded her curiously. "He's beautiful as an angel, though," she added, pursing her lips in contemplation.

"You are a perfect match then," he said evenly.

"Why is that?" She grinned widely at her friend.

"Because you are also as handsome as the devil, but you're as innocent as an angel. You two will cancel each other's faults. And," he added, smiling, "because you have never talked about your previous suitors like you talk about him."

Evie looked down at her hands. That's because she'd never felt anything for those suitors. Nothing even close to what she felt for Gabriel.

"The most important part is that now I am in possession of my estates, and we can proceed with grand plans of revitalizing this village. There's a lot to do. I shall invite my solicitor to move here with his family so that I can run my lands from here. I shall still visit my other estates, but I do not need to stay in London anymore." Evie smiled broadly, but her chest constricted, making it difficult to breathe. With self-inflicted exile, she ran the risk of never seeing Gabriel again. Was that truly what she wanted?

"I shall leave you to contemplate your predicament alone, my dear. It's getting dark, and I don't want to catch a hole in the ground and injure my horse." Mr. Cromwell beat his hat over his thigh and put it on. "Do not sit out here alone for too long. The sun will be down soon." He tipped his hat to her and walked away.

Evie turned back to gaze out at the sea. She'd spent one night without Gabriel and already felt ghastly. Was she ready to spend an eternity without him?

\* \* \*

Every day in the next fortnight went the same way. Evie met with her solicitor every morning; she went into town to greet her villagers and bring them supply baskets every afternoon, then she locked herself in her grandfather's old study and worked on new plans for her lands, read papers, and studied the ledgers, trying to figure out the best avenues to invest in. Her grandfather had taught her well, but it was one thing to play pretend and sit in on meetings with him, throw in advice and feel like she'd solved a major problem, but another thing to do it all by herself. She doubted every decision she made; she calculated and recalculated the costs of everything thousands of times until her head hurt, but she still didn't know what she was doing.

Evie leaned her head against the huge leather chair in the study one evening, inhaling the familiar scent of the room. *Oh, Grandpa, how I wish you were here now.*

She took the candle from the table and shuffled out of the room. The household was asleep, so there were no sounds other than her solitary footsteps. Evie trailed slowly up the stairs and turned into the family wing. She paused beside her door, hesitated for a moment, and walked on. A few doors down, she reached her grandfather's bedchamber and entered.

The glow of the candlelight only partially illuminated the dark room. She walked farther into the room and stopped, looking around.

The room looked the same, felt the same. The same curtains adorned the windows as the ones she used to hide behind when she was a child. The same coverlet lay on the bed as the one she used to tack on her back, pretending to be the queen with a long trailing gown. The same portrait of her grandparents hung on the wall across from the bed as the one she used to gaze into, wishing she'd known her grandmother better.

Now both of her grandparents stared from it, smiles on their faces, looking happy and in love. Evie wiped at her cheeks, only now realizing that tears were falling uncontrollably from her eyes. She placed the candle on the bedside table and climbed onto the bed, burrowing herself into the pillows. The scent of clean sheets and Grandpa's cologne hit her senses hard.

"Grandpapa, did I make a mistake?" she asked, looking at the dark portrait in the shadows. "I mean, I know I did. But which one? Marrying a man who would never love me back or leaving him behind?"

No answers came from the dark; the portrait didn't move or whisper, her grandfather still looked lovingly at his wife, but his voice echoed in her mind. "Love is the most important thing in the world."

\* \* \*

Evie stood in her garden the next morning, overseeing the planting of new rose bushes when she heard a carriage rattle up her driveway. Puzzled, she hurried up the path leading to the front of the house. Who could have come to visit her?

Was it Sam? She doubted she would have had time to make the journey, unless, of course, she'd jumped in her carriage the moment she received Evie's letter that she was back at Peacehaven.

But when Evie rounded the corner, a completely different picture rose before her eyes. A beautiful black lacquered carriage with the Winchester family crest ornamented her doorstep. A young and sinfully attractive gentleman jumped out of it and turned to her as if he knew she was standing there by the side of the driveway, watching him.

Viscount St. Clare, her husband.

She hurried toward him, trying to moderate her steps, while in reality, she wanted to run to him as fast as she could and fall into his arms.

He grinned at her as she reached his side and took both her hands in his big and warm ones. "Glad to see me, my lady wife?"

"Welcome to Peacehaven, my lord," she said with a bright smile on her face and curtsied without taking her eyes off him. She had a terrible feeling that if she averted her gaze, he would disappear, and this all would prove to be one long hallucination. She hoped it wasn't so. "What brings you here?"

"Missing my wife and wishing to see her isn't enough?" He cocked a brow at her, and she simply stared.

Was he serious? Did he really miss her as much as she did him?

"Well, if you must know, I am here because we've been summoned." He finally let go of her hands, and she realized he'd been holding them all that time. He dipped his hand into his coat's inner pocket, took out a letter with a broken seal, and extended it to her. "My father, the Earl of Winchester, would like to meet you. With all haste," he added dryly.

"Is this a good thing?" she asked, perplexed.

"Depends on your definition, but no, not in my dictionary, it isn't. He probably just wants to inquire about our progress on his heirs. But do not fret; we shan't be staying there long. We'll arrive, make our introductions, and take our leave."

He'd just gotten here and already couldn't wait to get rid of her.

"We'll be traveling all the way to Winchester to stay but a day?"

"Trust me; you wouldn't want to stay longer," he grumbled.

"Fine, when do we depart?"

"As soon as you pack a small valise, we can be on our way. It's a two-day journey to Winchester from here, so you'll need some more clothes."

Evie smiled tightly. "Let me get ready then."

She turned on her heel and walked up the steps of the house, not bothering to check if he followed her or remained standing by the carriage. She was unaccountably vexed that he didn't deem it necessary to kiss her after the long separation, while that was all she had dreamed about.

About two hours later, Evie sat opposite Gabriel in the carriage as it swayed forward.

"Just like old times, isn't it?" he mused, grinning at her.

"Mm, yes," she agreed. "I do hope we shan't get robbed this time."

"Oh, no need to worry. I know these roads like the back of my hand." He smiled and looked out the window.

Evie sat fidgeting with the ruffles of her gown, thinking desperately about what to say to her husband. And as often happened in these situations, not one thought crossed her mind. The silence was deafening.

"So, tell me—"

"How is—"

They both started at the same time and laughed. He waved his hand, indicating for her to proceed.

"No, please, you go. I insist." She smiled because she really didn't know what she was going to ask him.

"How is the estate?"

"Oh. It's good. Prospering. I've taken the reins of all my properties, and although I find running six estates challenging, it is also very fulfilling."

"Splendid. Splendid," he said, idly rotating his walking stick in his hand. "I have all the confidence in you."

Evie smirked. *I don't.* "How is... how are things in London? I assume you've resumed your... err... customary activities." She frowned down at her hands, kicking herself mentally for such a revealing question.

"I've been quite busy," Gabriel said, and Evie felt her heart sink.

"Oh," was all she was able to say.

"But it's not what you think," Gabriel said with a smile in his voice.

"How do you know what I think?"

"Oh, trust me. I know." He grinned at her and waggled his brows. "Actually, I've been working on revitalizing my accounts. Looking into prospects on where to invest, believe it or not."

"Not." Evie smiled. "Where did you get the capital? My solicitor told me you didn't take a penny from me, which by the way, I meant to speak with you about."

"There is nothing to discuss; that money is yours. And contrary to what you might believe about me, I am not a spendthrift. I do have some savings. Or I do now, as I've sold my curricle and a couple of other things. Granted, I would never know what to do with that money other than gamble it away—which I do rather splendidly—but I am determined to change my irresponsible ways. Do not tell my father. He'd be too pleased to hear this."

"Why?"

"Well, he was always spouting about the responsibility I have to his title, which I think is bull crap, considering he never cared a whit for the responsibility he had to his son, but I digress."

Evie licked her lips, studying Gabriel intently. "Why do it then? If not for your title, or to impress your father and regain your fortune."

"Because, my dear wife, I couldn't very well let you carry all the burdens and have the ton gossip about who wears the breeches in our household. They would be surprised to find out that both of us do." He grinned, and Evie shook her head, smiling.

*Dear*, she'd missed him.

# Chapter 18

Two days later, they were rounding the drive to Winchester manor. Gabriel fidgeted in his seat. He hadn't been on these premises for over a decade, and he'd spend another decade, or ten, without visiting it if he could help it. He peered out the window to see the dark brown exterior, the sun illuminating statues on the pediments of the main hall, and sighed. He'd remembered the place just as it was. Nothing seemed to have changed, and he was willing to wager his father hadn't changed either.

Something else caught his attention, and he almost fell out of his seat. *Carriages.* Not one, not two, but several carriages were lined up in front of the main entrance. People were filing out of them and entering the mansion.

"That bastard," he muttered.

Evie turned her attention from the window overlooking the hills and regarded him curiously. She hadn't spoken for the past several hours. She nibbled on her ginger root from time to time and looked out the window. Somehow, he remembered their previous trip to be full of adventure and excitement. He'd completely forgotten how subdued she'd been inside the carriage.

Now she studied him across the carriage, a slight frown marring her brow. "Is something amiss?"

"Amiss?" He scoffed. "I should say so. That scheming son of a whore has organized a party in our honor, it seems. It's another of his schemes to keep me longer on his estates, no doubt. I'll be damned if it works."

Evie's face turned troubled, and he wished he hadn't said what he did. "Would it be so very bad then if we spent a little more time here?"

Gabriel heaved a long-suffering sigh. "I suppose not," he grumbled at last. "I just really would rather avoid my father's company as much as possible."

"Oh, no!" Evie exclaimed, looking out the same window as he. "So many people!"

*Finally*, she was getting the predicament they were in.

"I didn't bring my ball gowns." She looked so forlorn he wanted to laugh.

*Gowns, of course.* The diamond of the *ton* could not be caught dead wearing the same thing twice among polite society, could she? And he supposed by her light valise that she hadn't brought more than four. "I wish I would have known about it beforehand. I would have packed accordingly. Why didn't your father tell you that there were going to be guests and perhaps a ball?"

"Because, my pet, he knew that I wouldn't have come if I'd known this to be the case."

"Why not?"

Gabriel grimaced. "I am not on the best terms with my sire,

211

I am afraid. I haven't spent much time here since I was a child, and I am not looking forward to it either."

"We can't leave early now that the entire *ton* has arrived at the house party, which I assume is in our honor."

"No, we can't," he agreed. *Cunning bastard.*

Gabriel alighted from the carriage as it stopped and helped Evie descend before turning toward the house. Gabriel was about to knock when the door opened and his father's butler, Wilson, appeared on the doorstep.

"Master Gabriel." He bowed low. "Pardon, I meant Lord St. Clare. And Lady St. Clare." He bowed again before Evie.

"It's the Duchess of Somerset, actually," Gabriel corrected, took his wife's arm, and led her up the steps. "I assume our chambers are prepared, Wilson?"

"Certainly, my lord." Wilson bowed again, then snapped his fingers, and two strapping footmen appeared at his side. "Please show Lord St. Clare and Her Grace, the Duchess of Somerset, to their chambers. And bring their trunks in."

They followed one of the servants up the stairs while another hurried to their carriage to get their valises. Evie was looking around in wide-eyed awe. The Winchester house was much more impressive than his townhouse lodgings, he had to agree. His father was an art collector, and one couldn't take a step without seeing an exquisite painting or a marble statue of some sort. The walls were tall and gilded with gold, the ceilings painted with angels and cherubs in the Garden of Eden. Evie stumbled on the steps as she was staring at the ceiling, and Gabriel caught her swiftly, pressing her closer to him.

Evie giggled as she looked into his eyes. "This place is gorgeous. I wonder why you wouldn't want to come here," she said in a dreamy voice.

"The house itself has nothing to do with my reasons. I am glad you like it," he said, looking ahead. "This will be your home one day."

He felt her hand tense on his arm at his last words and wondered if she liked the idea of living here with him or if she would rather stay at her Peacehaven estate. He didn't like this mansion. And he didn't lie; it had nothing to do with the house itself, although he would rather avoid it. But if it made her happy, he'd move here in a heartbeat.

As they climbed to the second floor, they turned left into a wide corridor decorated with more paintings, plush ottomans, and benches placed against the walls, as if for people to sit there. Gabriel wondered if they had ever been used. He stopped at the door to his wife's chambers and turned to Evie.

"These are your quarters, my lady," he said with a slight bow. "If you need me, I shall be in the next room; it's adjoined with yours." He smirked at her raised brows, sketched a bow, and walked away. Sleeping in the room next to her would prove a trial to him, he knew.

\* \* \*

Evie came downstairs on the arm of her husband an hour later, all freshened up and wearing a clean gown. None of the gowns she'd brought with her were fancy enough to entertain. Only one was fit for the supper table, but even that one was just serviceable and simple. She wore it in lieu of anything else and wondered how she would manage during the rest of the days of the party. She grimaced at the thought of wearing the same evening gown over and over again. No, she, who was known as the most fashionable lady of the *ton*, couldn't do that. Especially not at the party in her honor. She would die of embarrassment.

She cursed her tendency to overlook the necessities for the trip. Twice already, she was traveling with Gabriel with not nearly enough clothing.

They reached the tall, dark wooden doors of what Evie assumed was the earl's study, and Gabriel stopped dead. He looked at her sideways and squeezed her hand.

"Are you ready?"

Was there a note of uncertainty in his gaze?

The earl had asked Gabriel to bring his new bride to his study before supper for introductions, and she hadn't thought anything of it. Of course, she knew the discomfort with which Gabriel talked of his father. The fact that he hadn't come home for over a decade spoke for itself, not to mention the tension it must have caused when the earl cut off Gabriel's funds. But her always confident husband, the angel with the devilish attitude, looked extremely nervous now.

Evie gave him a reassuring smile. "Of course, my dear."

Gabriel smiled back at her and knocked on the door.

"Come," a deep male voice beyond the door called, and she started at the harsh sound. She held her head high as she entered the room on her husband's arm.

The study was spacious and long. At the far corner stood a large mahogany desk, and a proportionally large gentleman was sitting behind it. Evie had to blink a couple of times. The earl's posture, the way he held himself, everything about him was extremely familiar. In fact, as the man stood to greet them, she believed she was staring at her husband some thirty years into the future.

She smiled at the thought. The earl was tall and stately and quite large. His form was athletic, and he moved with fluid grace. But for all the similarities, the earl's face was harsh, his mouth hard. His nose was overlong, and he had quite a few worry lines on his face. Even the only feature on his face that actually reminded her of her husband was different. He had the same winter-blue eyes as Gabriel, but his were frosty.

Gabriel stopped a few feet from the desk and sketched a formal bow. Evie sank into a curtsy at his side and smiled up at the serious face of her husband's father, her father-in-law.

"My lord," her husband said. "Let me present to you my bride, the Duchess of Somerset." Evie's eyes widened as she saw the man's face break into a smile. His formerly cold eyes took on a warm glint. "My lady," Gabriel continued, "this is my father, Lord Winchester."

"A pleasure, my lord." Evie curtsied again. To her surprise, the man walked around his desk until he stood in front of her and took her hands in his.

"The pleasure is all mine, I assure you, my child. Aren't you lovely?" he said, studying her intently. She felt Gabriel stiffen at her side. "Tell me, how did my buffoon of a son manage to sweep you up? I wasn't certain he had enough wit to propose to such a fine lady as you." The statement was meant as a jest, and Evie's smile brightened at the friendliness of the earl's tone.

Based on all she knew from Gabriel, this was the last thing she'd expected from the meeting. She was warmed by his greeting and decided to keep the flow of the conversation. "Alas, you were not wrong," she said, grinning up at him. "It was I who proposed to him." The earl's eyes widened, and

Gabriel cleared his throat.

Winchester laughed heartily. "At least he wasn't foolish enough to turn you down."

"He couldn't afford to, my lord. Lucky for me, you cut him off."

The earl gave a bark of laughter. "I believe luck is singularly on my son's side, my child." The earl smiled down at her warmly before turning to look at his son, his brow raised. "Well, it seems you chose well."

"Yes, thank you," her husband replied dryly. "Can we leave now?"

Evie thought the earl would be hurt, or surprised, at the dryness of Gabriel's tone, but he didn't miss a beat. "It would be extremely rude if you did. Didn't you see, we have a house full of guests? People who've come from all over England to celebrate your nuptials."

"How lovely," Gabriel said in a flat tone, and Evie swallowed a chuckle.

"The party starts tonight, with a ball," the earl declared.

"A ball?" Evie was not laughing anymore. "But... But..." She looked from one gentleman to another. "I have nothing to wear."

"Yes," Gabriel said without taking his eyes off his father. "See, we were only supposed to stay one night."

"Nonsense," the earl declared, then turned to Evie and repeated, "Nonsense. I am sure we can do something about your attire, my child. In fact, I think we still have my late countess's old gowns. They are a little out of fashion, but surely nothing can mar the perfection of a lady such as you." He smiled at Evie, and she turned to gauge Gabriel's reaction. He was staring ahead with a stony expression on his face.

"Thank you," Evie said and almost choked on the word. Somehow it all felt very wrong now. "That would be lovely."

The earl went to the servants' bell and rang. He'd barely turned when a portly old lady entered the room. By the state of her attire, Evie guessed she was the housekeeper.

"You rang, my lord?" she said with a curtsy and kept her head down.

"Yes, Mrs. Ford. Please, take my daughter-in-law to the old countess's chambers and pick out a gown for her to wear for tonight's ball."

The housekeeper raised her head at the mention of her late mistress but quickly lowered her gaze as if looking straight at her master would turn her to ash.

"I am sure they won't fit perfectly, but you have my permission to mobilize as many maids as you need to adjust it. Just make certain it is ready by eight o'clock tonight."

"Yes, my lord." The housekeeper curtsied again.

"My child," the earl addressed Evie. "Please, go with Mrs. Ford. She'll make sure you're presentable for tonight's festivities. Well, even more presentable than you already are," he added with a warm smile.

"I can escort my own wife," came the hard voice of her husband beside her.

She looked up at him, startled.

"No need to get in the way of feminine business, son." The earl waved his hand dismissively in the same good-natured tone as if he didn't notice his son's frostiness. "Besides, I have issues to discuss with you. Important ones."

"Oh, I don't doubt it," Gabriel replied dryly, and Evie wanted to shake him.

What was wrong with him? The earl was going out of his

way to be hospitable and polite, and here he was scoffing at his every word. She frowned, but before she could form any words to either chastise her husband or reassure him, the housekeeper opened the door and looked at her expectantly.

"Right," Evie muttered under her breath, then turned her smile toward her husband. "I shall see you at supper," she said brightly.

Gabriel turned to her slowly, but to her relief, he looked down at her with a soft smile. "Until supper, my lady wife," he said and winked at her.

Evie stifled an urge to giggle. She then turned to their host, curtseyed, thanked him for everything, and sailed out of the room.

# Chapter 19

Gabriel stared into his father's icy gaze. His father, whom he hadn't seen in a decade. His father, who'd cut him off with a single note, refusing to hear any of his explanations. The same father who now played a considerate host and a doting father-in-law to his new bride.

"I suppose I should be grateful you're polite to my wife," he said. "Although I must say it came as a surprise. But then again, you did want me to settle down, give you an heir and a spare for your darling estate."

"You always were cynical." Winchester shook his head.

"Is it me being cynical then? I thought it was very realistic of me. Considering you've never before wanted me to show my face around here."

"That is not true, and you know it. I called upon you before—"

"Yes, to instruct me on my duty, to force upon me this chunk of land so I could die looking after it, forlorn and alone, just like—" He stopped mid-sentence, his gaze intense upon his father's dark face.

"Just like me." His father nodded, suddenly looking old and weary. "Son—" he started, but Gabriel interrupted him with a harsh scoff.

"You've never called me that before, either. I suppose this year is full of firsts."

"You have every right to be angry with me."

Gabriel laughed sharply. "Thank you for giving me permission. Very benevolent of you."

"You don't need my permission for anything anymore. You've grown into a fine young man—"

"Fine. Young. Man," Gabriel said quietly, enunciating every word as if trying to decipher their meaning. "Do you know this is the first time you've ever called me that?"

"I've made a lot of mistakes." Gabriel scoffed again, but the earl continued. "You are not so innocent yourself. But I am the parent, and I should have handled everything... better." He said the last words slowly, as if unsure what he was about to say. "Why don't we start anew?"

"Why?" Gabriel narrowed his eyes at his father. "Because suddenly I am married? Because you're hoping I shall finally beget you a brood of heirs? Well, I am sorry to disappoint you, *Father.*" He spat the last in his father's face. "But ours is a marriage in name only. There will be no heirs."

The earl reared back as if he'd hit him. "It didn't look like a marriage in name only to me. You're taken by the girl, and she you. I could see that."

Gabriel laughed harshly. *I could see that.* In what, all of five minutes they'd spent in his study? "Well, it seems to me it's time for you to get spectacles, old man," Gabriel spat, turned on his heel, and stalked away.

## Chapter 19

*** 

"He could see that," Gabriel muttered under his breath as he stalked up the stairs, taking them two at a time. He sprinted down the corridor to his own chambers but stopped in his tracks as he was about to pass his wife's sitting room. The door was slightly ajar, and he saw a flurry of movement, could hear the rustle of fabric. Gabriel paused for a moment before entering the room. One of the maids hurried inside after him, carrying a load of fabrics. She shut the door behind them as she entered.

Evie looked up at the sound. She was surrounded by maids, poking at her and pinching the fabrics on her body. She was wearing a shimmering golden gown, with a bodice lined with gemstones and a greenish-blue trail. She looked absolutely gorgeous.

Evie smiled shyly as she saw Gabriel and self-consciously pressed her bodice closer to her body. The gown was definitely too big for her, although Gabriel hadn't noticed it up until that point. It was wide at the bodice—his little wife had tiny breasts, and she was lean and athletic, while his mother must have been a curvy woman. He didn't remember his mother, and he didn't think he'd ever seen her likeness in this gown either.

He looked over her body slowly, then raised his eyes to hers. Her gaze was full of vulnerability and uncertainty, and he hated seeing her like that. He didn't think he'd ever seen that look on her before.

"You look—"

"I know, hideous—"

"—gorgeous," they said at the same time.

221

"What?" Her eyes widened, and he stepped closer.

"The golden fabric," he said as he came even closer, his hips almost touching her skirts. "It suits you. Who knew? I guess I'll have to order you a complete wardrobe in that color."

Evie let out a giggle. Gabriel noticed the maids scattering away, leaving them in privacy.

"It's—you don't think it's too much? Too shiny?" she asked, biting on her lower lip.

He looked down at her gown as if considering her question. "No," he answered, shaking his head. "Not as bright as you, love."

Evie smiled at him then, in such a way that made him want to kiss her until they both forgot their names. He'd been dreaming of this, of being close to her, touching her, kissing her all the way during the ride.

Now, as he stood in front of her, he could finally make his dream come true. He leaned closer to her, so close that their mouths were almost touching. But as he was about to close the distance between them, she reared back and cleared her throat.

Just as well, Gabriel thought glumly. He wouldn't be able to stop at one kiss, anyway.

"Wh—What…" Evie stammered as she tried to collect her thoughts, and Gabriel grinned. "Why were you so stiff with the earl earlier?" she finally asked, and the smile died on Gabriel's lips.

"It's a long story," he said with a dismissive wave and sauntered about the room, looking around.

"Surely not so long that you can't reveal it to your wife?"

Gabriel heaved a sigh. "It's not a very interesting story either." He shrugged. "The earl has always cared about his estates much more than he cared about me. He sent me off to school when I was seven—too early for anyone really—but I was a small child, much too small for my age, too small compared to other children."

He grimaced slightly as he came toward her vanity and took one of the jars from its surface and studied it intently, although, in reality, he couldn't even understand what he was looking at. "I was bullied there, obviously. Everyone was. But I was just…" He left his sentence unfinished, trying to explain to his innocent wife how cruel boys can be, especially to a new boy, and the smallest, weakest boy was not something he looked forward to. "When I wrote to him, asking to take me back, he refused. He said that if I was to be a man, I should learn how to stand up for myself."

He felt Evie's fingers prying the jar away from him. "At seven years old, he expected you to stand up for yourself against the boys much bigger and older than you?"

"Well, it wasn't such a big deal after all," he said, turning to her and tucking a wisp of hair behind her ear. "I did take care of myself, I learned how to fight, or don't you remember how I held my own against Montbrook's thugs?"

"You had help." Evie grinned.

"Either way, the rift between my father and I only grew after that. He wasn't interested in anything I had to say, he punished me for little transgressions, and he didn't really want anything to do with me until I finished university and established my own lodgings in London. Even then, all of our communication went through his solicitors and stewards." He put his fingers on her chin and forced her to meet his gaze. "But I don't want to talk about it anymore," he whispered and kissed her on the lips.

The sensation was so sweet and pleasurable, he almost groaned. God, how he'd missed her lips. The taste of her was so delicious and pure, the feel of her was so soft and tender. She wasn't as lost in the kiss as he because she pulled away and studied his face for a moment.

"Why did he do that?"

Gabriel expelled a breath. "I don't know. I presume I reminded him of my mother."

"But why—"

He cut her off with another kiss. This time, he licked across her lips before plunging his tongue inside her and sweeping over her mouth in little circles, making certain she knew he owned it. Her mouth, her body, was his. With a small moan, she surrendered and pressed her body closer to his, as if acquiescing to his demand, as if she heard his thoughts and agreed with him.

He moved his hand lower and dipped it inside her loose bodice, running his fingers against her breasts, thrust unnaturally high by her corset. She moaned, but instead of moving closer to him, she pushed at him. Gabriel looked at her with a frown. She was breathing heavily, trying to regain her composure.

"Not now," she whispered. "I need this gown ready for the ball."

Gabriel smiled wolfishly and traced her cheek with his thumb before planting another demanding kiss on her lips.

When he raised his head, Evie still had her eyes closed, and she was holding on to his shoulders as if she might fall if she let go. Her lips were soft and swollen from his kisses. All he wanted was to take her in his arms, cross to the door adjoining his chambers, and make long and unhurried love to her.

Only one thing made him stifle his impatience. It was not the fact that the maids were waiting outside the door, not the fact that she needed to get ready for the ball or else they'd be late. What held him back was the fact that she didn't say no. She said, "Not now." And that he could wait for.

\* \* \*

Once the gown was ready and her hair bound, Evie peered into the looking glass and smiled. She looked like fire, radiant and bright. She would draw every eye in the ballroom, even more so than she ever had. Just as well, this was her wedding ball, after all. She grinned at her own reflection, picked up her skirts, and twirled, enjoying the swishing of skirts, the bright colors that flashed in front of her.

A knock sounded at her door.

"Are you ready, pet? We are already la—" Gabriel opened the door and stepped in. He froze in his tracks, his mouth hanging open. Evie smothered a chuckle at the expression on his face. "Or perhaps we don't have to go at all. We can stay in," he said, slowly running his gaze over her body, his voice turning husky.

The maids giggled as they scattered away, and Evie felt herself grow hot with embarrassment.

"You shouldn't say such things in front of the servants," she said weakly.

"Why not?" He stepped closer, and Evie danced away from his reach.

She picked up her fan, flicked it open, and regarded him from beneath her lashes. "Let's go, husband, or we'll be even later."

Gabriel growled. "I'd rather stay here," he said as he stalked toward her again, but Evie evaded him once more and walked toward the doors.

"I am not missing my wedding ball because of you, my lord," she said with a haughty air.

"I liked it better when you called me husband," Gabriel said behind her, and she smiled. She liked it better, too.

They walked through the corridor in silence and were soon standing on top of the stairs as the butler announced them for the first time.

A hush enveloped the ballroom, and hundreds of heads whipped up at the announcement. Every eye in the ballroom was on them. Ladies were whispering behind their fans and fanning themselves vigorously. Gentlemen bowed their heads to listen to the whispers, all the while watching the approaching couple.

Evie smiled brightly as they stepped down the stairs into the crowd of curious people. The first bars of a waltz struck, and her husband claimed their first dance, not giving a moment for the people to start approaching them.

Evie turned to Gabriel as he enveloped her in his arms and looked into his eyes. He held her close to his body, a little too close for propriety, but then she'd married a notorious rake, hadn't she? She could feel his hands on her body as if they burned through her fabric. His scent of aloe wood, spices, and him, enveloped her like a fog. They were dancing and gazing into each other's eyes, not even attempting to speak.

From the periphery of her vision, Evie saw people continue to whisper and watch them with their mouths agape. Evie always loved attention, and this was too much not to enjoy.

She smiled widely, and Gabriel winked at her. He spun her around the ballroom with effortless grace. This was not the first dance she'd ever danced with him, but this time, as he stared right through to her soul and held her close, she knew he was rightfully hers.

When the music finally ceased, Gabriel leaned in and whispered into her ear, "Soon."

Her breath caught in her throat, all her thoughts disappearing like a puddle on a sunny day.

The next moment, they were accosted by a throng of people offering their felicitations, asking loads of questions, and eventually drawing them apart.

\* \* \*

"Your Grace, may I have this dance?" A gentleman bowed before her, and Evie accepted his offer with a smile. She left a throng of people behind, moving to the dancefloor on the gentleman's arm.

"Mr. Darby," she said as they reached the dancefloor and stood opposite each other. "A pleasure to be dancing with you again."

The young gentleman grinned, obviously pleased that she remembered him. "Actually, it's Lord Bingham now," he said as they started the dance. "Inherited the title quite recently."

Evie raised her brows. He was Bingham? The lord Widow Jane and the entire village of Forton had complained about? "Oh, my condolences for your loss," she said.

He waved her sympathy away. "My father was sickly; it was his time to go."

They continued dancing in uncomfortable silence for

several beats.

"Lord Bingham, does the small village of Forton belong to your estates?" she finally asked.

"It does." He nodded. "Useless little piece of land does not bring any profit. But I am going to make it bring profit, just you see."

"How are you going to do that exactly?" She smiled at him, although she wanted to kick him instead. She knew how, by robbing his tenants and booting them off their homes.

"You just know that I shall. Nothing to worry your beautiful little head with."

Evie's smile turned tight. "I assure you, I am quite capable of understanding the intricacies of landowning. I am a duchess."

"I am certain your husband takes care of all—Oh, pardon, I almost forgot. You married St. Clare." The man laughed, and Evie boiled from the inside. How dare he criticize Gabriel when he was treating his tenants worse than cattle? "If you ever need help, it'll be my pleasure to go over your estate matters with you. For a certain… price." He looked her up and down suggestively, and Evie's stomach churned unpleasantly.

"Whatever you think I need help with, I assure you, I don't."

"Oh, I wouldn't be so final with your words, Your Grace."

Thankfully, the music ceased, and Evie didn't have to retort. She curtsied sharply and turned away from him. Another gentleman approached her before she even made a step.

"Your Grace, would you do me an honor of gracing me with this dance?"

Evie smiled and nodded. "Lord Stanhope, a pleasure."

He led her farther into a throng of dancers, and they stood opposite each other. Evie curtsied, and they started to dance as the orchestra struck the first tune.

"You look exquisite," Lord Stanhope said a few moments later. "You've always been beautiful, but now you've blossomed, like a flower in an English field in the summertime."

Evie smiled coyly. "Thank you. Your wife must appreciate your flowery speeches."

"Perhaps, but I've never told her that her eyes remind me of emerald waters."

"Oh, no, how did she survive without such a flattery?" Evie laughed in earnest, and her dance partner smiled wolfishly.

"Spouting flowery nonsense is not the only thing I am good at." Lord Stanhope winked at Evie. They clasped hands and were dancing in a circle around each other. Stanhope imprisoned Evie's gaze with his, burning a hole in her eyes with his intensity. Evie felt decidedly uneasy.

She cleared her throat and licked her lips before attempting to speak. Stanhope's gaze fell to her mouth, then traveled down to her bosom.

"What marvelous things keep your wife happy then?" she asked with a tight smile, trying to dispel the tension.

Stanhope leaned closer to her then and whispered into her ear, "Meet me at the gazebo after this dance, and I'll show you."

Evie's eyes widened in shock. Had he just proposed what she thought he'd proposed? Luckily, they got separated by the dance, and Evie was swept into a twirl by another partner. The momentary reprieve helped her collect her thoughts. After a few more steps, she and Stanhope were reunited.

"I don't think my husband would appreciate my absence from the ballroom," Evie answered with a haughty air, and Stanhope laughed loudly as if it were the drollest thing he'd ever heard. People around them turned at the sound.

"Mark my words, my darling," he said in a low voice. "He'll be doing the same thing, only perhaps in a different part of the estate."

Evie's stomach churned at the idea. She unconsciously turned her head in search of her husband but could not see him anywhere.

"Do not twist your head so," her dance partner continued. "I am sure he is indulging in some fine young lady as we speak. Or do you not know the man you married?"

Evie swallowed but refrained from answering. Another twirl away from her dance partner allowed her to breathe easier. She looked around the room. Still no sign of her husband.

It couldn't be. He wouldn't do that to her, would he? He wouldn't be spending his time with another lady while she was in the next room. During their wedding ball, no less.

Evie bit her lip. *Or do you not know the man you married?* Of course, she knew. In fact, their bargain gave him leave to continue indulging in every other lady of the *ton* and beyond as much as he wished. It was probably the only reason he'd even agreed to their marriage. Of course, he was courteous toward her; he kissed and touched her like she was the only woman who mattered, but surely he did that to every other lady he knew.

She felt ill. She was sure her face was ashen, too.

"Gazebo in five minutes?" Stanhope winked at her once more as they reunited in dance again.

"I am afraid you've misconstrued my interest," Evie said as evenly as she could. "I am not interested in clandestine meetings with gentlemen who are not my husband."

Stanhope laughed again. Evie's skin crawled with unpleasant shivers at the sound. "How bourgeois," he said with a wide smile. "By the end of this house party," he said, and they were separated again. Evie's mind was frantic, and she kept searching the room for a sign of her husband. She made a couple of steps and drew closer to Stanhope once more. "You will change your mind," he continued.

The dance ended at that, and Evie curtsied mechanically. Stanhope bowed, moving his head closer to Evie's. "Mark my words," he whispered, turned on his heel, and stalked away.

Evie stood on the dancefloor, surrounded by crowds of people dispersing after the dance. All the sounds receded to the background, her vision blurred before her eyes, and her breathing was coming up in shallow gasps. She was on the verge of tears, she realized in horror.

"Your Grace." Another gentleman bowed before her. "May I have this dance?"

# Chapter 20

E vie left the room, tears burning at the back of her eyes. What had just happened? She had never felt so powerless, so alone, and troubled in her entire life. She loved balls, loved dancing, and indulged in the compliments of the gentlemen. The moment she'd gotten married, however, everything changed.

She had danced three dances after Stanhope, and every lord she danced with made it his duty to proposition a tryst or throw lewd comments her way. Now that she was married, it seemed that they considered her an available female to prey on.

Wasn't it supposed to be the other way around? Wasn't she supposed to be under the protection of her husband? She pressed the backs of her wrists against her eyes, and tears soaked her gloves. Oh, what had become of her life?

Evie rested her head against the wall, feeling defeated and weary. She heard the ballroom doors open and close and fast-approaching footsteps in her direction. She instantly pushed away from the wall and straightened. She needed to get back to the ball. God forbid it could be one of her eager 'suitors' interpreting her defection from the ballroom as assent to his lurid proposition.

She turned and almost ran into the wall of a man's chest. She started with a squeak and jumped back. Firm, masculine hands grabbed her by the arms and held fast. Evie was about to scream when she raised her head and saw worried ice-blue eyes searching her face. *Gabriel.*

"Is something amiss?" he asked, his gaze still running over her in concern.

"No, I'm—no." She smiled weakly and relaxed in his hold.

"You don't look well." He frowned down at her. "Did something happen? Did somebody upset you? Were you hurt?"

Evie took a deep breath and looked away. What was she supposed to say? *No, nobody physically hurt me, but I got propositioned by every lord in the room for a lurid tryst in the garden*? Did one even speak of such things with one's husband?

"I am fine." Evie finally looked up into her husband's eyes. "Truly. I just needed some air."

Gabriel's grip on her gentled, and he started running his thumbs over her upper arms in a comforting gesture.

"Good," he said. Then he made a step toward her and cuddled her close to his heart.

Evie laid her head against his chest and snaked her arms around his waist. She heard his strong, sure heartbeat, and the world righted itself. She was in his arms, which meant everything was safe again.

He caressed her back in light soothing motions, holding

her tight in his embrace. Evie felt his kiss on her hair. Then he placed his cheek over the top of her head.

"Where have you been?" she asked, her voice muffled against his waistcoat.

"What do you mean?" His voice held a note of confusion.

"I didn't see you while I was on the dancefloor."

"I was watching you," he said against her hair, and his voice rumbled through every nerve in her body, making her shiver.

"You were? From where?"

Gabriel eased her away and looked down at her. "From the shadows. I am not much of a dancer, and I tried to hide away from the incessant questions of ladies and gentlemen. They seem quite curious at the idea of the notorious rake marrying the diamond of the *ton*." He grinned at her, and Evie couldn't help but smile in response.

"Are you sure nothing is bothering you?" Gabriel asked with a frown and swept a lock of hair away from her face. "You look troubled. And you never look troubled, not in all the years I've known you."

Evie's heart swelled at the idea that he'd been watching her from the shadows all through the years they'd known each other. It was probably not true. He hadn't really noticed her much in prior years, but just the thought made her all warm inside.

"Let's go," he said and extended his arm to her.

"Where?"

"To dance," he answered with a grin.

"Didn't you just say you didn't like to dance?" Evie raised a brow at him.

"I did. And I do not," he said as he took her hand and tucked it into the crook of his arm. He turned toward the ballroom.

"But what I've realized today is that I enjoy watching you dance with other gentlemen even less."

Evie let out something between a snort and a laugh, and Gabriel raised his brow at her.

"Apologies." She covered her mouth with her hand as she chuckled again.

"Why is this funny to you? I am suffering, watching my wife in the arms of other men, and you laugh at me," he said with such an air of righteous indignation that she laughed again. He shook his head reprovingly. "You enjoy seeing me suffer, do you?"

"Not at all." She smiled up at him. "But if you do have to suffer a torment, I'd rather it be in my arms."

"I'd rather suffer every kind of torment in your arms, too," he said, lowering his voice to a seductive whisper.

They reached the dancefloor at that moment, and Gabriel swept her into the dance. They didn't talk much, just smiled into each other's eyes, occasionally murmuring something about the surrounding couples or the decor of the ballroom. Evie couldn't hide her joy. If she thought she loved to dance before, it was nothing compared to the feeling of being the sole point of Gabriel's attention. Of the anticipation of his every touch, every gaze. She didn't want the dance to end.

However, the last bars of the melody struck, and Evie lowered herself in a curtsy. Gabriel caught her hand and pulled her closer to him.

"Next is the second waltz of the night, I believe," he said into her ear.

"We can't dance two dances in a row." Her eyes grew wide even as a bright smile split her lips.

"Why not?" he said, looking intently into her eyes.

"It's—It's against the rules," she hissed in a scandalized whisper, and Gabriel laughed. The music started then, and he collected Evie against his chest, slowly moving his hand up her arm, weaving his fingers through hers.

"How improper of me," he murmured, still staring into her eyes as he made the first move of the dance.

Evie followed his lead effortlessly. His moves were sure and fluid at the same time. Evie found her body listening to his command, moving with him without conscious thought. It was as if they'd danced like this forever.

He kept staring into her eyes, and Evie couldn't quite take her gaze away from him either. His hand burned through the layers of her bodice, stays, and chemise at her waist, heating her body. Her cheeks flushed, and she was sure she was about to burst into flames. The entire world melted away as they danced in complete silence, lost in each other's gazes. The flicker of thousands of candles fed into the illusion that they were dancing on clouds, among the stars, alone.

The romantic atmosphere must have muddled her mind because before she knew it, the words that had burned in her mind for seven long years almost escaped her lips. "Gabriel," she breathed, "I—"

Thankfully, the music stopped at that moment, and Gabriel was forced to a halt as well. The room buzzed around them as people started leaving the dancefloor, and Evie was jolted back into reality. With horror, she realized that she'd almost professed her love for Gabriel, right there, in the middle of his father's ballroom.

He bowed then and took her arm. "Yes?" he asked as he led her away from the dance floor. "What were you going to say?"

"I—" Evie frowned, trying to grab on to any other thought, but her mind came up blank. "I am quite parched," she finally said.

"Say no more." Gabriel grinned down at her. He brought her to his father's side and bowed to her before turning to his father. "Watch her for me, would you?"

He took Evie's hand and placed a kiss on her knuckles, then left with a wink.

Evie fanned herself vigorously as she felt her cheeks burning. She turned and saw the Earl of Winchester watching her with a sly smile on his lips.

"It is rather hot in here, wouldn't you say?" she asked, just to distract herself from blushing even more.

"Indeed," he said and turned to watch the crowd. "You and my son look perfect together on the dancefloor."

"Thank you, my lord." Evie lowered her gaze, cursing her idiot heart for leaping in happiness at his words.

"Nonsense, child," he said with a dismissive wave. "We are a family now. No need to stand on formalities. You can call me papa, or father, if you prefer it better."

Evie looked at him, wide-eyed.

"Unless, of course, you're uncomfortable with that," he corrected himself after clearing his throat.

"I would be honored to call you father," Evie said as she felt her eyes water. She hadn't realized how she'd missed having an affectionate older relative. That feeling that someone older and wiser was looking out for her.

"I knew Somerset," he said. "Admired him. He was one of the most progressive and caring landowners I knew. Loved his family too. Was notorious for it."

Evie smiled, although her eyes filled with tears like they

always did at the thought of her grandfather. "I hope I shan't let him down."

"Impossible. He wouldn't have left you with the burden of the title if he wasn't certain in your abilities."

"Thank you."

"But if you ever run into trouble, or if you have any questions, know that you can always come to me. I shall gladly impart any knowledge I possess."

"I would love that. I have been going over matters for a few weeks now, and I am questioning my every decision."

Winchester laughed. "It's a good sign!"

"Is it?"

"Yes, you should never be overly confident in your decisions. People's lives depend on those choices. If you are questioning yourself, it means you care. It also means that you might come up with better alternatives. Why don't you come to my study tomorrow after breakfast? We can go over any questions you have, and we shall see if I can help you."

"I would be eternally grateful."

"No need for that," Winchester dismissed with a wave of his hand.

Evie's heart swelled with gratitude. But she remembered the rift between the earl and her husband and hesitated. "Gabriel might not be too fond of the idea of us working together."

Winchester huffed a laugh. "I hoped you'd persuade him to join us. He seems to hold you in high esteem. I shall be honest, we don't have the best relationship, and it's my fault, really. But I dared to hope you might help us mend the rift."

"I shan't ask him to do what he doesn't want," she said.

"You are protective of him. That is good. I hoped he'd find

a lady of your fine character, someone who cared for him, perhaps even loved him." Winchester studied her curiously.

Evie cleared her throat. "You said the poor relationship between you and your son was your fault. How is that?"

Winchester heaved a sigh. She expected him to get irritated at her nosiness, but he spoke eagerly. "My wife, his mother, was a flighty lady, like a wind. Nothing about her was constant. I loved her more than I've ever loved a soul," he continued, his eyes taking on a dreamy look. He shook his head as if clearing away the memories. "I thought she would change after we married. That she'd be a devoted wife and mother." He grimaced.

"She did not?" Evie asked, immersed in the earl's recollections.

"No, she did not. She continued having her liaisons all throughout our marriage. And I forgave her every time."

Evie's eyes grew even wider. She wondered why he was confiding in her so openly. And then she thought of Gabriel. Would he do the same? The thought brought a sharp pain to the region of her heart.

"I begged her to be discreet," the earl continued. "But discretion was not in her nature. She got with child while I was away on a trip. Everyone knew the child was not mine." He shook his head in shame.

"Do you mean Gabriel?" Her mouth fell open.

"No." The earl laughed. "No, Gabriel is mine. However, I had my doubts at the beginning as well. Her second child was not, however. She died in childbirth."

Evie gasped, and the earl turned to her. "There were many rumors after that. Some said I killed her for infidelity; some even condoned the idea. Most people questioned Gabriel's parentage, as did I for a while. I was grieving, alone, confused, and left to care for a small child by myself. A child I didn't know how to raise. I was afraid he'd turn out just like his mother, but I saw more and more of me in him every day. And that's where it all went wrong."

"How so?"

"You see, Gabriel is the spitting image of his mother. I was afraid he'd grow up to be exactly like her."

Evie cocked her head to the side. *He is like her, isn't he?*

"So when I saw a feature, some speck of resemblance he had to me, I tried to reinforce it. I tried to discipline him as hard as I could, forcing so much responsibility on him, so much pressure on the little child that he naturally rebelled. I was young and proud and couldn't have a son who was as flighty, disloyal, and irresponsible as my wife. What I did not realize, however, was that Gabriel resembles his mother only outwardly. His character, his spirit, his mind—all mine. Perhaps not the best endorsement either."

Evie laughed. "He has your eyes."

Winchester nodded. "That he does. And my heart. He is devoted, loyal to a fault. His last downfall is the result of that, I think," he said with a shake of his head.

"He did it for me," she said softly, then added with a short laugh. "In a way."

The earl looked at her quizzically but said nothing. At that moment, Gabriel appeared at her elbow with two glasses of wine. "Here you are, wife," he said with a grin as he extended the glass.

"Thank you, husband." She smiled right back at him. From the periphery of her vision, she saw Winchester's satisfied smirk.

* * *

Something was wrong. Gabriel could see it on Evie's face. He'd noted it ever since she danced with Bingham. The toad must have upset her. However, it must have been not just him. After all, the men Evie danced with had all been cuckolded by Gabriel at one time or another. It would be very difficult to find a gentleman whose wife Gabriel hadn't tumbled.

Then he turned his head and saw them. The Montbrooks. Of course, she'd be upset they were there. Why didn't she tell him? Gabriel cursed under his breath. He spun to face the earl.

"You invited them?"

"Whom?" Winchester frowned.

"The Montbrooks," Gabriel gritted between his teeth.

Evie craned her neck, searching the crowd.

"Of course, I invited them," his clueless sire answered. "They're the closest family members of your wife."

"I am her family now," Gabriel said sharply. He took Evie's hand and put it in the crook of his arm. "If you'll excuse us, we have to be somewhere else," he said and led Evie away.

"It's not a problem, Gabriel," Evie said after they made several steps. "We should probably greet them, anyway. I mean, your father is right. No matter what transpired between us, they are still my relatives. We cannot cut or avoid them, or the rumors will be unbeatable."

"Maybe you haven't realized this by now, wife, but I do not give a fig about rumors."

Evie smiled up at him. "That's why you have me. To care about things you don't give a fig about."

Gabriel gave a short laugh. "And why is it a good thing?"

241

"Well, it will make you more respectable in the eyes of the *ton*. Isn't that one of the reasons you married me?"

Gabriel looked at his wife thoughtfully. He had thought he wanted her inheritance; he'd contemplated that her respectability might help him make his way into the *ton*. Having the most beautiful lady on his arm was enticing on its own, but having a duchess would open a lot more doors.

However, he had to be candid with himself. The moment she'd revealed herself in his bedroom, he'd known she wouldn't leave his rooms unattached. She'd tied herself to him by brazenly appearing at his doorstep, and he had no intention of ever letting her go.

"Felicitations to you both!" Gabriel felt the touch on his shoulder and turned. Lady Wakefield was clutching the arm of her elderly husband as she tapped Gabriel with her fan. "Oh, what a hasty marriage, wasn't it? I do wonder the reason for such haste."

"Isn't having my lovely wife on my arm as soon as possible not a reason enough?"

Lady Wakefield laughed merrily at the statement, and Evie's hand tensed on Gabriel's arm.

"Congratulations again, St. Clare, you've finally joined our ranks," Lord Wakefield said with an unpleasant smirk.

With bows and curtsies, they moved further on their promenade about the room.

"I never liked that man," Gabriel muttered under his breath.

"I wager he isn't fond of you either," Evie said, looking ahead. "You did cuckold him, didn't you?"

"What do you know about that?" Gabriel frowned.

"Only that Lady Wakefield made a fool of herself over you during her own ball last year. The one that led to the scandal and left you penniless."

"Right, and Father knows this. Why in the world would he invite this couple to our ball?"

"To show that there's no bad blood between us, I assume. Your father is doing everything right in order to put the past behind us and move on."

"He is doing everything to mask my past and pretend that I am this respectable gentleman, which I am not and will never be."

Evie stopped in her tracks, forcing Gabriel to halt too.

"What do you mean by that?" she asked, frowning at him.

"Only that—" Gabriel opened his mouth to reply but stopped as he saw the vulnerable gaze on his wife's face. He realized how that might have sounded and cursed himself for his thoughtless words. "I mean, I am not respectable. Far from it. I shall never be one of those gentlemen who does everything right, who cares about their reputation. I shall always be the devil St. Clare, the debaucher of the innocent. Even if the innocent is an equally devious wife of mine," he said with a grin.

Evie looked at him, a gentle reprieve in her eyes. Gabriel could not help but lean in, wanting to feel her lips on his again. The crowd in the ballroom be damned. He was the devil, after all. He should not care what anyone thought.

"Evie!" A chorus of feminine voices sounded at that moment, and Gabriel cursed aloud. They both turned and saw Evie's cousin, Julie, hurrying her way with her little sister, Mary, and Evie's best friend, Samantha, with her sister Isabel not far behind. So much for playing the devil.

"I shall leave you in the company of your friends," he whispered close to Evie's ear, almost brushing his lips against her skin, and sauntered away.

* * *

Evie sat in front of her dear friends in the family library. They'd left the ballroom soon after their rambunctious meeting, and Evie had decided they needed some privacy to catch up. Besides, she was really not looking forward to spending more time in that ballroom filled with hostile guests.

Samantha looked rosy-cheeked and happy. She was eyeing Evie curiously in return.

"How is married life?" Sam asked. "Oh, and what a beautiful gown you're wearing. It is not your usual style, but it looks lovely on you!"

"Thank you; it's not mine. It was Gabriel's mother's."

"Truly? That's odd. It fits you quite well."

"Well, the maids worked all day today to make it fit me. His mother was—well, bustier than I am. Although any lady would be," she added with a smile, and the ladies laughed. "How are you here? I didn't know you would be." Evie eyed all the ladies in the room.

"We would never miss your wedding ball! Lord Winchester sent Robert and me the summons and asked if there was anybody else he should invite. Apparently, he didn't know any of your friends," Julie answered.

"He could have asked me," Evie said. "Only I didn't even know there was going to be a ball in our honor. I didn't even bring any gowns, hence my current attire."

"Well." Sam looked at her from head to toe. "As I said before, you could wear a gown the color of manure and still look beautiful. But this gown is magnificent."

244

# Chapter 20

"It's very shiny," Mary said and reached to touch the fabric. "Soft," she proclaimed proudly.

"It really is." Evie smiled. "And how are you, Mary?"

Mary smiled broadly. "I love this house; it's beautiful. Many paintings here."

"Yes." Julie smiled at her sister tenderly. "Mary loves art, as you know. She might not want to leave this mansion once the party is over."

"I am certain you can stay here as long as you want," Evie said and turned back to Samantha. "Is marriage treating you well, Sam?"

"It is, although my husband can be an overprotective and overbearing arse at times."

Evie snorted a laugh. "What a compliment!"

"He almost didn't let me come on this journey! Thankfully, Isabel was with me, and she convinced him we should go."

"He is worried about you, darling," Isabel said softly. "And he has a cause to. Traveling in your con—" Isabel's eyes widened, and she pursed her lips.

Evie studied her curiously then turned to Sam, who suddenly turned red.

"Your con..." Evie's mouth gaped as she realized what Isabel was about to say. "You are with child!"

"Yes, but shush! It's still early," Sam mumbled.

"Congratulations! You must be so happy." Evie blinked back tears of joy.

"Congratulations, dear," Julie echoed.

"Thank you, I truly am," Sam said as Isabel gave her a slight hug. She turned to Evie and smoothed her skirts. "Now that we are done with pleasantries, please share."

"Share?" Evie asked, perplexed.

"Yes! How in the world did you end up marrying St. Clare? I thought you had more sense than that!" her friend cried, turning from composed to excited in a matter of a second.

Evie blinked. "Who else should I have married?"

"Anyone." Sam enunciated every syllable. "Literally anyone."

"Well, you married my first fiancé, so no, not anyone." Evie raised her brow at her friend.

"It's not like I stole him from you! You refused to marry him!"

"Nevertheless." Evie folded her hands primly. "How about you tell me about your life instead?"

"No, no, no, Evie, darling. I shall not let you change the subject so easily. Please, do tell."

Evie felt her cheeks burn in embarrassment. She'd never truly kept anything from Sam. Except for her long-standing affection toward St. Clare. They all leaned closer, waiting for her story with rapt attention. "I—very well. I shall tell you. But no scathing remarks from either of you. You promise?"

"We promise," her friends chorused with meek expressions on their faces. She wasn't fooled a bit.

Evie took a fortifying breath. "I made a promise to my grandfather. In fact, it was the main reason I did not go through with the marriage to Ashbury."

"The letter," Sam said and leaned closer to Evie. "The letter that the solicitor gave you from your grandpa. Is that what it contained?" At Evie's nod, she frowned. "Surely, he did not ask you to marry St. Clare? Why would he do that?"

"Well, he didn't. Not directly anyhow."

"How then?" Julie raised a brow at her cousin.

Evie had told her about the bargain, but she hadn't told her why she chose Gabriel.

"He said… He wrote that I should only marry for love and not accept anything less."

Her friends' jaws dropped as they tried to make sense of the words.

"Evie—"

"I know!" Evie stood and started pacing the room. "I know what you all think of him, I know who he is, and I am not making any excuses." She turned to her friends then and squared her shoulders. "I love him all the same. Have loved him for a long time now."

The look of bewilderment on her friends' faces would have made her laugh under any other circumstances, but at the moment, they were mingled with pity, and Evie couldn't stand it. Only Mary frowned in consternation, looking from her sister to Evie and then back again.

"I don't have any illusions about him. I don't expect him to be faithful or to love me in return. I've made my choice and approached Gabriel with a bargain. He is free to continue his pursuits as long as I am free to do as I please. I know, it is not ideal, but if I had to marry, it should at least be someone I love, don't you think?"

Her friends exchanged a look, and Evie rolled her eyes. "I am not deranged. You can tell me what you think."

"Well, I think that—" Julie started carefully but got unceremoniously cut off by Sam.

"Why didn't you tell me? We have been friends for so long! I've never kept anything from you."

"Oh, truly?"

"Yes!"

"Oh, truly?" Evie raised a brow, and Sam grumbled

something under her breath. "Because, as I recall, you forgot to mention a thing or two about the man I was about to marry last season."

"You were distressed at the moment, and it's not the same thing! You've kept it from me for years."

"Yes, because I knew how you'd react. I know how you feel about him, how everybody feels about him."

"Evie, dear." Julie stood and approached her slowly. "Are you sure it's love?"

"I am not a child, Julie."

Julie cocked her head to the side. "I didn't say you were. It is just surprising that you'd make that choice."

"I didn't think one had a choice in whom they fell in love with."

Julie pursed her lips.

"I love Gabriel, and I thought I'd rather spend my life as his wife than anybody else's."

"I love Gabe too," came Mary's confident voice, and Evie smiled.

"Thank you, darling. I knew you would support me, at least."

Mary stood, walked toward Evie, and gave her a hug. Evie closed her eyes and hugged her back. Mary was a ray of sunshine. It was comforting to have her support right now when her other closest friends seemed to be against her.

"You are right, Eves," Isabel said. "I think everyone in this room has made a foolish decision in the name of love once or twice. I do not know if you made the right choice or not, but arguing about it won't solve anything."

"Of course," Sam finally said slowly. She stood and came toward them. "I apologize. I was just shocked. But you are entirely correct. We don't choose who we fall in love with. And Isabel is right too. If you think you'll be happy with St. Clare, then I shall support you wholeheartedly."

Julie nodded. "Of course, we shall support you. And if you're not happy, then our husbands will beat the stuffing out of him."

Evie snorted a laugh, and all five of them fell into heaps of laughter as they hugged.

When they exited the room, however, Sam took Evie by her arm and slowed her pace.

"Evie, I know you are doing your best with this marriage, but may I remind you of something?"

Evie took a deep breath and nodded.

"Your grandfather's insistence that you marry for love wasn't so you would suffer silently by yourself; it was so you were happy. And... you promised me to do everything in your power to be happy too."

"When did I promise you that?" Evie frowned.

"Remember, before I got married? I came to see you, and you asked that same thing of me: to do everything in my power to be happy. And I said I would, only if you did the same."

Evie took a deep breath. She remembered the conversation clearly. They had both been in difficult situations back then. Samantha was marrying out of convenience, and the Montbrooks were asserting their dominance in choosing a suitor for Evie. They even moved her out of her London townhouse, so she could be easily swayed to marry the suitor of their choosing.

At that moment, Evie had vowed to herself that she wouldn't settle for anything less than love. She'd asked

Sam to fight for her happiness and promised her to do the same. And Sam was right; being married to someone she loved but living separately was not what her grandfather wanted for her.

"It wasn't easy for me either in the beginning," her friend continued. "I had to fight hard to get to the level of happiness that is now present in my life with John. He didn't make it easy for me either." Sam smiled, and Evie laughed.

No, her husband wouldn't make it easy for her either. But she could at least try. She'd resigned herself to a life of solitude and sorrow the moment she showed up on Gabriel's doorstep. But it didn't have to be this way, did it?

# Chapter 21

E vie undressed with the help of her maid, performed her nightly ablutions, and sat by the hearth, brushing out her hair.

"One hundred strokes," she murmured under her breath, humming as she brushed until she heard the adjoining door to her husband's chambers open and close. She turned and beheld Gabriel, standing by the door, one shoulder propped against the doorjamb. He had disposed of his coat, waistcoat, and cravat; his shirt was open at the collar, sleeves rolled up on his forearms.

He looked deliciously enticing. She wanted him. She wanted to give herself to him. But she promised herself not to be seduced by the devilish viscount, no matter how tempting. At least, not until her heart could afford it.

She stood and placed the brush on her vanity table. As she turned, she immediately collided with his chest. "Ow!" She staggered back a step, and he caught her by her arms.

"Steady," he said, smiling. "No need to be knocked off your

feet by my beauty."

Evie couldn't help but smile back. At that moment, Gabriel tugged on her arms, crushed her to his chest, and lowered his mouth to hers. His kiss was hard, demanding, desperate. He had never kissed her like that before. She couldn't help but sag against him and open her mouth to him. He swept his tongue inside with a groan while his hands roamed her body. Evie was ready to give up on her resolve and let him bed her right then and there. *We are married*, her treacherous mind whispered to her. *It will be so good; you won't regret it.* But she knew she would.

Evie pulled away from him with a whimper. "No," she said, panting.

"No?" Gabriel's expression was so full of surprise that she wanted to laugh. He'd probably never heard the word in his life. Not from a woman, in any case.

Evie took a deep breath before repeating more firmly, "No."

"Why not?"

She swallowed and took a couple more steps away from him. His scent, his warmth, and even the sight of him was too distracting. She turned and walked further away from him. Evie propped her back against the cool wall by the window and finally looked up at him.

"Gabriel, when we made the bargain, you promised we wouldn't be doing this."

"Forget the blasted bargain. Too many things have passed; you can't possibly be still holding on to that?"

"I am."

"Why?"

Evie let out a bitter laugh.

"You know that I love your laughter?" Gabriel asked gently

as he made several steps toward her. He stopped a few inches away. His heat and his closeness muddled her mind. He raised his hand and cupped her cheek, running his thumb over her skin in a gentle caress. "But not that laughter." He lowered his head again, but when his lips were an inch away from hers,

Evie ducked and danced out of his reach. "Gabriel, you're not listening to me."

He threw his hands up. "Fine! Tell me. What's so wrong about a husband wanting to kiss his wife?"

"What's wrong is that you don't want just a kiss. And neither do I."

"Well, that problem is easily fixed." He started unbuttoning his shirt.

Evie licked her dry lips, her eyes frantically running over every inch of his newly revealed naked skin. "There is a reason why I can't—no, I shan't spend the night with you." She paused, steeling herself to finally tell him the truth. "I love you."

There, she'd said it. The world didn't tilt on its axis; the sky didn't collapse on her, and she didn't die or turn into stone.

Gabriel's fingers stilled mid-motion.

She laughed. "I love you, Gabriel. I have loved you for as long as I can remember. Always have. And I know that if I ever spend a night in your arms, if I ever… have marital relations with you, I shall not be able to let you go."

Gabriel stood frozen in the middle of the room, his face ashen, his eyes large, his lips parted. He cleared his throat. "W-why didn't you tell me?"

"Does it matter? Would it have changed anything if I had told you earlier?"

Gabriel uncomfortably shifted from one foot to another.

Clearly speechless. A very rare occurrence with her lithe-tongued husband.

"If what you're saying is true," he finally said, "then I don't see what the issue is here. You want me; I want you. Besides, we are already married."

Evie swallowed and licked her lips again in agitation. "The issue is that I don't just want you. I love you. And after we do spend the night together, you might easily lose interest in me, but I shan't. I shan't want to ever let you go."

"Then don't." Gabriel stalked toward her and took her by the arms. "I am here," he said hoarsely. "I am not going any place. I want you as my wife, Evie. I already broke my associations with other women as soon as we reached London, if that's what you're worried about. I am not going to break your heart."

Evie noted that he didn't rebuff her claim that he might lose interest in her. She also noted that he didn't say he loved her back. "That's not all I am worried about."

"Then tell me. What are your conditions? Because I am willing to prove my regard for you."

*My regard.* Evie's heart constricted at the words, and tears burned at the back of her eyes. She took a deep breath, but it still didn't seem enough. She took another one. "There's only one way, only one condition under which I shall relent."

"Name it." He was so certain he could provide anything that her heart gave a slight pang.

"Tell me you love me," she finally pushed out past her dry throat.

A long pause followed. Gabriel seemed to freeze in place, his hands still on Evie's arms, his lips slightly parted, his eyes frantic. Evie smiled sadly and disengaged herself from his grasp.

"Evie," he finally croaked.

Evie just shook her head, walked to the bed, and propped herself on the edge.

"I am certain I'm not capable of it, Evie. You know me too well; you know how I am."

"I do," she said quietly. She lowered her head and stared down at her hands. Another long pause followed. Then Gabriel cursed and stalked out of the room.

Tears streamed down Evie's face, and she couldn't hold them in any longer. Of course, he didn't love her. She'd known that, hadn't she? Then why in her heart of hearts was she still holding out hope that he'd tell her? She collapsed onto the bed, her breath escaping on a strangled sob.

\* \* \*

Gabriel looked across the carriage at his beautiful wife. She sat, looking out the window gloomily, a ginger root in her hands. It didn't seem to help with her nausea, but she appeared to be quite attached to it.

Ever since the night of Evie's confession, the relationship between them had chilled. She still smiled and jested with people around her as if she didn't have a care in the world. As if she hadn't spent the entire night sobbing into a pillow. Because of him. He hadn't managed to sleep well that night or any night after that. He was sleep-deprived and irritable, and the fact that Evie pretended nothing had happened didn't help his mood.

She spent the rest of the house party in the company of her friends or talking amicably with old matrons, successfully avoiding Gabriel or any other gentleman in the house. The only man she didn't seem to evade was his father, the Earl of Winchester. In fact, she spent most mornings in his study, going over the ledgers and discussing business. As much as Gabriel disliked his father, he gladly took that opportunity to be closer to his wife and joined in on the morning sessions.

He loved Evie's quick mind and how she easily picked up on the intricacies of running the estates. He marveled at her ability to come up with creative solutions to mundane issues. And he was befuddled by the care she put into her every decision.

As revealing as those meetings were of Evie's heart and mind, they were even more revealing of Gabriel's ignorance. He quickly learned how little he understood the work that went into owning an estate. If the earl died tomorrow and Gabriel inherited the title, would he be a better landowner than cursed Montbrook or Bingham? Or would he become the wastrel everyone thought him to be?

Evie turned to him at that moment, gave him a polite smile, and averted her gaze once more. Outwardly, she hadn't changed her behavior toward him. She still smiled at him, talked to him, and even laughed at his lewd jokes. By all appearances, she was still the happy bride she had been during their wedding ball. But he knew better. She had put a wall of ice between them.

Gabriel didn't try to break through it, at least not yet. He knew he needed to give her more time and perhaps space. However, the thought of leaving her at Peacehaven while he went back to London made his chest burn unpleasantly. How was he to convince her that being intimate with him was better than being apart?

She'd said she loved him, but she was ready to leave him without a second thought.

*She loves me.* Gabriel couldn't believe it. Surely, she was mistaken. Nobody had ever loved him before. Not his parents, his lovers, nor his friends. They tolerated him; some admired him, and most hated him. Loved him, though? He'd never known what it felt like. And perhaps he would never find out. Not unless he persuaded his wife to stay with him.

She demanded the same from him as what she offered. But how could he? With a soul so rotten, he didn't know the meaning of love. What did it mean to love somebody?

He might not love her, but he couldn't imagine his life without her, either.

Evie turned to him again and scrunched up her nose. "Do you smell that?"

The scent of smoke hit Gabriel hard, and he stiffened in his seat. "Is it a bonfire festival? Or are your tenants burning the hay?"

Evie craned her neck out of the window. "I don't see anything."

As they neared their destination, the scent became more and more prominent. Once they rounded the hill, they were finally treated to a horrifying view. Peacehaven was on fire.

Evie plastered herself to the window, her eyes wide. "Peacehaven," she whispered.

Gabriel thumped the roof hard. "Hurry the horses, will you?" he yelled at the driver, not that it helped. They were going as fast as they could.

Evie nervously clutched the ginger root in her hands, frantically looking out the window. When they were close enough, Gabriel opened the door and jumped out of the vehicle. Evie followed, barely waiting for him to catch her. Gabriel took out his handkerchief and handed it to her.

"Cover your mouth and nose," he said and did the same with his own piece of linen.

They ran toward the house, only to see that people were standing by the building with empty buckets, helplessly watching the residence burn.

An elderly man limped toward them, his face black with soot. Evie dashed to him and took his hands in hers.

"Oh, Mr. Cromwell! Thank God you're well. Is anybody hurt?" she asked.

"Not badly, Your Grace," he said, his voice scratchy. "The cook has been burned the most as she is the one who noted the fire and started putting it out."

"How did it happen?" Gabriel interjected.

Mr. Cromwell studied him wearily. "It began in the kitchen. I do not know for certain; probably something caught fire when the cook started the breakfast."

Gabriel raised a brow, unconvinced. The entire building was taken up by smoke; even the third floor seemed to be on fire. Would an innocent breakfast fire spread so fast in such a short period of time?

"Is everybody safely out?" Evie asked the old man.

"It looks that way, my lady."

Evie raised her gaze to the burning building, a solitary tear running down her cheek.

Gabriel took Evie by her arms and turned her to him. "I shall go ask around about the details of the fire and make certain that nobody got trapped inside the house. But I need you to move farther away from the site. I don't want you breathing in the smoke."

Evie didn't answer. She didn't even look at him; her glassy gaze was concentrated upon the building.

"Do you understand what I am saying?" Gabriel shook her lightly.

"Grandpa's ledgers," Evie whispered to herself. "His letters, the portrait."

"Evie, none of that is important anymore. Look at me!"

She finally turned and regarded him as if she did not realize he was even there.

"You need to leave. Go back to the carriage, take as many people with you as you can, and stay in the village."

Evie licked her lips and nodded.

"Good." Gabriel let go of her arms and beckoned Mr. Cromwell to follow him.

He hadn't gone far, though, when he saw Evie dashing toward the house. He blinked stupidly for a moment before running after her. What in the devil was she thinking? She made it to the entrance of the side door and even stepped inside the house before he got to her. Gabriel collided with Evie's back as she stopped dead just inside the threshold.

The smoke was so thick that Gabriel couldn't see an inch beyond his nose. Gabriel grabbed her by the waist and forced her out.

"No! Let go of me!" Evie attempted to wriggle out of his hold. Gabriel bent and lifted her into his arms, then walked resolutely toward the carriage. When he reached it, he unceremoniously deposited her onto the ground.

"Are you out of your mind?" he yelled.

Evie stood, coughing and wiping at her tears.

"What in the devil are you thinking running into a burning building?" Gabriel cried, his voice getting hoarse.

"My grandfather's things! The paintings, th-the letters! His work—" She started sobbing. "I can't leave them to burn."

"They are not worth your life."

Evie pushed mightily at his chest. "I've lost everything! Don't you understand? My parents are dead. My grandfather is gone. Everyone who ever loved me"—she hiccupped—"and now my home! Every piece of memorabilia left from my family was moved here when the Montbrooks took over! And now it will all burn. I have nothing!" She kept pushing at him as she sobbed. Her hair tumbled out of her pins, her face was black with soot, her cheeks tear-streaked. "I have no one!"

Gabriel trapped her arms between them and hugged her tightly. She fought to free herself from his embrace, still beating at his chest, chanting over and over again that she had lost everything. He held her close to his heart as she wailed and cried, not paying any heed that her servants were all watching them, surprised to see their mistress so out of sorts.

Finally, her strength gave out, and she went limp in Gabriel's arms, her tiny body occasionally trembling from grief. Gabriel held her close, murmuring soothing nothings in her ear while all the remnants of Evie's happy life burned and crumbled before his eyes.

# Chapter 22

Gabriel fell onto the sofa with a loud oomph.

"Make yourself comfortable," Clydesdale said as he settled across from him on the settee. Julie's lips twitched in a smile as she sat close to her husband.

"What brings you here, St. Clare?" she asked.

"Your lovely little cousin."

"Evie? Is something wrong? I mean, apart from her childhood home burning down." Julie grimaced and shifted in her place.

Clydesdale snaked his arm around her and pulled her close. After all these years, it wasn't surprising to see his best friend openly dote on his wife. The occasional touches and kisses were always present between the Clydesdales. But had someone told Gabriel that was going to be the case seven years ago, he wouldn't have believed it.

Robert wasn't an affectionate man. In fact, he was from the coldest aristocratic family Gabriel had ever known; it was surprising he didn't freeze to death while growing up. He had also been burned by love, swore to never love again, and yet there he was, happily keeping his wife close, openly showing his affection. His love. Could Gabriel ever love that way?

"I haven't seen her since we came back from Peacehaven. When we arrived in London, she was adamant about living alone in her townhouse. She even dispatched most of her servants to my place. She cited she wanted privacy, but I am concerned. I understand the need to be alone for a while, but it's been over a fortnight. She hasn't answered any of my notes. Her servants say that she hasn't left the house during all this time. I am really beginning to worry."

"You talked to her servants?" Clydesdale raised a brow.

Gabriel just shrugged.

Julie turned to her husband briefly, and he put a comforting hand on hers. "What do you want us to do?"

"I want you to go check on her. I promised I wouldn't intrude on her solitude, but she never said either of you couldn't visit her. I just want to make sure she is well. I don't like to think that she might be sick, or—or... I don't know. I'd be drowning my sorrows in a drink right about now if I were her, but she doesn't indulge. I'd say she's galloping her frustrations out around the Serpentine... astride"—he snorted—"but since the servants said she's not leaving the house, I shudder to think what she could be up to."

Julie raised her brows at her husband, and he nodded in answer.

"Just so you know, this silent conversation between husband and wife is not at all charming."

Julie smiled. "Well, when you know someone as well as we know each other, words aren't necessary."

"I've known Clyde here a lot longer than you," Gabriel said.

"Yet we don't converse through mute gazes."

"Well, I tried a number of times, but you tend to misunderstand anything I attempt to tell you," Robert grumbled.

Julie shook her head with a smile. "I shall visit Evie this afternoon. I am quite worried about her myself. I am so glad you reached out."

"Good, good." Gabriel played with his cufflinks nervously.

"Is there anything else you wanted?" Robert raised a brow at him.

"No, that's all. It's just"—Gabriel ran a hand through his hair. *Oh, for God's sakes, just let it out*—"I'd appreciate it if you could facilitate a meeting between Evie and me. As I said, she never replied to my notes, and she is not accepting any invitations, and I—well, I'd like to see for myself that she is healthy."

Julie pursed her lips together while Robert grinned openly.

"Welcome to the land of the lovesick." Robert walked over to Gabriel and patted him on the back.

* * *

A frantic knock on the door startled Evie awake. She sat up in bed and looked around. She was in her grandfather's quarters. Ever since she'd returned to London, Evie had spent her nights in this room. No matter how hard Gabriel tried to coax her, she refused to stay with him. She had her own lodgings. Besides, she didn't want to deal with pretending that she was fine; she didn't want to feel guilt for not feeling better. She just wanted to wallow in her grief and self-pity, alone, in the peace and quiet of her home.

She had found that quiet in her grandfather's room. The

room had been locked ever since he passed away, so, fortunately, the Montbrooks hadn't been occupying it. That was why it was one of the very few rooms that still felt the same as it had before. It still had a comforting scent of tobacco and lavender. Her grandfather always sprayed his room and his pillows with lavender perfume. He'd said that it reminded him of his wife and calmed his mind.

The scent *was* calming. It immediately brought her mind to the past, when she was protected, cherished, loved—

More incessant knocking followed, and Evie frowned. She got out of bed and padded barefoot to the door. Who would be knocking so loudly in the dead of night? Was it a servant?

She opened the door, but nobody was there. She peeked her head out and saw Julie wildly banging on a door several feet away. On her door.

"Julie?" Evie croaked out in a sleepy voice.

Julie whipped her head toward Evie and visibly relaxed. "There you are!" she exclaimed and stalked toward her.

Reassured that it wasn't some annoyingly loud burglar, Evie went back to her room and huddled on the bed. "What are you doing here in the middle of the night?" she asked with a yawn.

Julie raised her brow. "The middle of the night?" She walked toward the window and pulled the curtains. Bright sunlight entered the room, making Evie flinch.

"It's afternoon," Julie said gently, then went to sit on the edge of the bed. "Darling, I know it must have been difficult losing Peacehaven, but—"

Evie bit her lip and turned away. "You don't know," she said, tears burning the backs of her eyes. "I've lost everything. Peacehaven was my last link to my grandfather."

264

"No, it wasn't. Your title, your lands, this townhouse, your entire existence is the link to your grandfather. A piece of him will always be in your heart."

Evie took a pillow and covered her face with it. "I don't need a lecture right now," she mumbled against the pillow, jumbling her words.

"What?" Julie laughed at the incoherent sound.

Evie removed a pillow from her face. "I said, this is the reason why I locked myself in here. I don't need to feel bad for feeling bad. I just want to be left alone."

A frown appeared between Julie's brows. She looked at Evie carefully, her gaze settling on Evie's puffy face and unkempt hair. "Evie, it has been over a fortnight. Gabriel came to us this morning at his wit's end. He says you don't return his notes, and the servants say you don't leave the house. Gabriel said he promised not to bother you, so he hasn't called upon you, but he is worried."

Evie let out a deep breath. "I don't want to cause you worry. Either of you. I just needed to spend some time alone. But I am well, I promise."

"Then you will come to our dinner party on the morrow?" Julie's face brightened visibly, and Evie plastered a tight smile on her face.

"Yes, I shall."

\* \* \*

Clydesdale's dinner was an unremarkable affair. The food was bland, the conversation boring, and more importantly, Evie was sitting a few seats away from him. Didn't Julie know the sole reason he'd come here was to talk to his wife? And it got even worse from there.

Evie was smiling openly at every gentleman she talked with, and it grated on Gabriel's nerves. For one thing, the smile was absolutely feigned. He had learned to discern that much. When she smiled earnestly, her eyes lit up like a million stars. Now they were hollow, cold, indifferent.

But that wasn't the main thing that grated on him. The main thing was that she smiled at him that same way. After knowing her real smile, this one was like an insult. He'd rather she screamed and wailed her frustrations, beat him in the chest, or slapped him hard across the face than see that smile, which meant she was treating Gabriel just like everybody else.

She couldn't have changed her mind so quickly about him, could she? She'd told him she loved him just a fortnight ago. Surely those feelings didn't go away so quickly. It was one thing if she avoided his gaze or refused to talk to him. Then at least, he'd know that she was angry with him. But no, she treated him just like every other man.

After dinner, the guests collected in the drawing room for entertainment and games. Gabriel saw Evie silently sneak out of the room, and he followed her a few moments later.

Gabriel looked around the hall but didn't see Evie anywhere. He knew this house like the back of his hand, and Evie did, too. So he approached the room she most likely would choose to hide in. He passed several doors and opened one on the left.

The room was sparsely illuminated by a lone candle and the lit hearth. Evie was sitting in a chair, her head thrown back, eyes closed, her neck bare to his gaze. Gabriel quietly ventured farther into the room, observing as her chest rose and fell with every measured breath. The floor creaked, and Evie sharply turned to look at him.

"It is just me." Gabriel held his hands up as if in surrender.

"Oh." She seemed to relax, so at least she still felt comfortable around him. "What are you doing here?"

"I just wanted to speak with you."

"Of course." She stiffened her spine and placed her hands on her lap, a picture of propriety. If he'd not known her taste, the feel of her as she writhed beneath him, he'd never guess by her icy demeanor today what a passionate creature she was.

He tilted his head to the chair opposite hers. "May I sit?"

"Please."

Gabriel settled comfortably in the chair, looking around and straining to find a topic of conversation.

"Mr. Cromwell," he finally pushed past his dry throat. "He seems to be settling well within my household. The rest of the servants too."

"Mm, that's good." She smiled at him, her surface smile devoid of depth, and Gabriel rubbed his forehead with his hand in frustration.

"Evie," he said. "I know that things between us aren't ideal, but I thought that maybe we could change that. Or start over."

Evie blinked at him. "What do you mean?"

"I mean, I am tired of you cutting me out of your life. I am your husband."

"This wasn't our bargain, as you recall."

"No, but—"

"Haven't we had this conversation before? I don't think I want a repeat of that."

Gabriel pursed his lips together. "Fine. But before we

married, we were friends."

"We are friends still."

"Then why are you acting as though we are strangers?"

Evie furrowed her brow.

"You don't think I notice the difference between how open you were with me before and how you treat me now? Just like another beau. I miss your real smiles, I miss your jests, your passion."

Evie scoffed. "That girl you are describing is gone now."

"No, she is not. I know you are angry with me, but just tell me what I can do to make it better?"

Evie stood so suddenly that the armchair she sat in scraped the floor. "Have you ever thought that this has nothing to do with you? I am grieving. I have lost everything that was dear to me in a span of a few months. I cannot be happy and gleeful all the time—"

Gabriel stood also. "That's not what I meant."

"No, this is exactly what you meant. You want me to go back to the cheerful and worry-free girl I was before, but the truth is she never really existed. I just learned to bottle up my frustrations and let them out around the people I loved so they could comfort me. Now I have no one! So pardon me and my grief. But if you don't want to see it, then you better not seek me out."

She walked past him, rounding him with enough space that an elephant could fit between them. *I have no one.* Her words echoed in his mind.

"You have me," he said, his voice hoarse.

Evie paused in the doorway, her hands fisted by her sides. She didn't turn. She didn't say anything. She just took a breath and stalked out of the room.

# Chapter 23

Evie lay sprawled on the bed, inspecting the ceiling with her gaze the next day. The dinner at Clydesdales' had been a trial. She wondered how she'd found it enjoyable to be around people before. Now every noise aggravated her nerves, and she found it difficult to smile.

Now that she'd appeased her cousin and was back in her hideout, she never wanted to crawl out of it again.

There was a mild scratching at the door. *Blast.* Evie sat up in bed. "Yes?"

The butler entered the room and bowed. "Your Grace, you have a visitor," he said as he straightened and stood, waiting for instructions.

Evie heaved a sigh. She wasn't ready for visitors yet. Her heart was broken into a million bits, and one fortnight wasn't nearly enough to piece it together. Why couldn't people realize that and just leave her alone? But the manners she'd groomed in herself for her entire life demanded that she receive the caller.

"Please, let them in. I shall be down shortly. Thank you."

She rang the bell, and her maid came rushing in.

"Apparently, there's a visitor downstairs for me," Evie said with a strained smile. "I need to look presentable."

Her maid looked at Evie's robe and disheveled hair in wide-eyed horror then nodded.

Thirty minutes later, Evie was dressed in a beautiful day gown, her hair was pinned in a neat coiffure, and an artificial smile was plastered on her lips. She was once again the haughty and highly revered member of the *ton*. She entered the drawing room and froze.

Gabriel turned toward her. "I thought you were never coming down." A light frown marred his face as his gaze ran over her in concern.

"Good morning." Evie curtsied.

"It's evening, my dear." Gabriel bowed.

Evie looked out the window. It was gray and gloomy, like most of the time. She heaved a sigh. "You didn't need to send the butler to fetch me. You are not a visitor here. As my husband, you are entitled to access this property without permission."

"I know, but since you thought me a guest, you got dressed for me in no time. Not that I mind you undressed, I just don't think you're in a mood for any kind of… pleasurable activities."

"I am actually too busy for any kind of pleasurable activities."

"Truly? Busy doing what?" He crossed his arms over his chest and cocked his head to the side.

Evie chewed on her lip in thought. "Going through the ledgers. Now that I've come into my inheritance, I have lots of responsibilities." It wasn't a lie; she did have lots of responsibilities. The ones she'd been ignoring for the past fortnight.

"Hm. Well, let's get to it then, shall we?" Gabriel stepped closer, forcing Evie to retreat a step.

"Pardon?"

"I don't want to get in the way, but perhaps I can help. Or at least learn. After all, I am going to inherit an earldom sooner or later, and I'd rather not make a muck of it."

"You want to go through the ledgers and my estate matters?" she asked slowly, drawing out every word.

"Why not?"

Evie scratched her brow in thought, but she couldn't come up with a reason to refuse him. "Very well. Let's proceed to my study."

They walked side by side in silence, the warmth of his body next to hers chasing away the chills. Perhaps it wasn't a bad thing Gabriel had come to visit her. She'd at least get some work done.

Evie settled in the chair behind the desk once they entered the study. Gabriel rang the servants' bell and sat across from her.

"You can't truly work on an empty stomach, can you?" He smiled at her questioning expression.

Evie didn't reply. She took out several ledgers and laid them on the desk in preparation for the day's work. Most of the ledgers had burned in the fire at Peacehaven, but some of the records were still in the townhouse. She'd have to work hard with her solicitors and stewards to get back the information that was lost in the fire. She knew that this was what she was supposed to be doing, but lately, she felt drained of energy and emotion.

"Well, what do you want to begin with? Is it calculating the crop yields, planning the renovations, or we can discuss the necessity of technological improvements in certain—"

Gabriel yawned. "Apologies, I got bored."

Evie threw him a reproving gaze. "You said you wanted to work. So let's work, shall we?"

"Is there a more exciting part to this 'work'?" He grabbed her ledger from her hands and sifted through it. "It's all numbers and statistics. Do you truly do this all day?"

"Well, yes." Evie grabbed the ledger back from him with a violent tug. "It is numbers, and calculations and guessing. This is what running estates entails. I suppose it is boring for someone like you, but this is necessary for the well-being of tenants and improving the profits on the lands. It is the difference between a landowner like Montbrook or Bingham and one like my grandfather or—" She pursed her lips suddenly.

"Or my father," Gabriel finished for her.

"He is a very clever and thoughtful landowner."

Gabriel scoffed.

"I know you dislike him, but—"

"The land is his mistress and child. Yes, I know. I suppose he is competent at what he does. But since he never paid any interest to me, I never paid any interest in his pursuits. I was too busy—"

"Wallowing in self-pity?" Evie tried to hold back laughter, but a chuckle escaped her.

"You are laughing at my expense!" Gabriel narrowed his eyes on her before grinning. "Finally."

The door opened then, and a maid brought in tea and

biscuits.

"Finally," Gabriel repeated under his breath, this time referring to the tray of food.

Evie poured the tea and returned to the ledger. "So, what do you want to go through first?"

Gabriel bit on the biscuit with a loud crunch and grimaced. He took the cup of tea and swallowed several gulps before turning to Evie. "This biscuit is abominable. How do you eat them?"

"I have never tried them," Evie said with a laugh. "What's wrong with it?"

"Well, for one thing, I think it is about a thousand years old. So it was probably prepared before any of the modern ingredients were developed." Evie chuckled once again, and Gabriel shook his head. "No wonder you are so thin you look like a light wind would blow you away. I thought you said you didn't eat well on our journey because you were ill in the closed carriage. What is the excuse now?"

Evie licked her lips. *You. My broken heart. The loss of my grandfather and everything I ever held dear.* "My Peacehaven cook is still back in Sussex, recovering from her injuries," she said instead. "My London cook was replaced by the Montbrooks, perhaps because she was too costly, and she isn't available anymore. She found a new household in no time. I really didn't want to deal with seeking a new cook, so I left the one the Montbrooks hired. As you can see, they weren't big on food."

"Well, they were big on something," Gabriel grumbled under his breath and sipped more tea.

"Since I see you are not interested in irrigation and fertilizing techniques," Evie said to change the subject, "perhaps we can take a look at some investment opportunities."

"Investments?"

"Yes, I know you took up an interest a few weeks ago. Perhaps you can walk me through some things. My grandfather left some papers about the ventures he thought would bring the most returns." She stood and took a heap of papers from the bookshelf before returning to sit behind the table. "Here, he made calculations on probabilities of their growth and—"

"No, no, and no." Gabriel shook his head and gently took the papers from her hands. "No calculations, no probabilities, none of that. Investing is a lot like gambling. You go with your inkling. The instinct. There is no way to predict which card will land on your lap—unless, of course, you cheat, which I would never do—so you take a chance based on the highest reward."

Evie just blinked up at him.

"For instance, let's say you and I were playing Vingt-Un. I deal you two cards, one is a jack, and the other is a six. Do you stay, or do you ask for another card? You could win if I have a lower value, but if I have anything over sixteen and up to twenty-one, I win."

"Yes, but if I ask for another card, I could get over twenty-one and lose."

"Correct, but if you get anything from two to five, you have a better chance of winning. What if you hit vingt-un?"

Evie chuckled. "That's pure chance!"

"Yes, and no. You could be sitting here and calculating all the odds and probabilities of hitting a vingt-un, or you could trust yourself. What is your inkling saying?"

Evie bit her lip. "It is saying that I don't actually have cards in front of me."

Gabriel laughed. "Touché. That is easily remedied, however. Do you want to play a hand?"

"But what about work?"

"It is work. Once you learn to trust yourself, you'll be able to better select the investments."

Evie shook her head. "You are the devil."

"And that's exactly why you married me."

* * *

For the next fortnight, Gabriel proceeded to visit her every day. They worked a little in the study, or she worked, and he distracted her with questions, comments, and gossip. They had tea with freshly baked buns made by Matilda, his cook, who he brought every day, and then they played Vingt-Un while discussing investment opportunities. Evie had to admit she looked forward to his visits.

Her melancholy was almost gone. Her heart still ached every time she passed her grandfather's rooms, and a slight pang in her heart reminded her of her unrequited love for the rake she'd married, but overall, she was feeling better. And so what if he didn't love her? He obviously cared for her. They had an easy friendship, so perhaps love didn't matter as much as she thought? A lot of *ton* marriages had a lot less.

She was catching up with her work, thanks to Gabriel, but she still hadn't talked even once about Peacehaven. Not with Gabriel, not with her solicitor, not even with her maid. She knew she'd have to lead the renovations for the manor, but thinking of what she'd lost always made her numb. Perhaps she needed just a little more time.

Evie lifted her head from the ledger she was perusing and

squinted at the clock on the mantel. It was past eight in the evening, past the time Gabriel usually made his appearance. Evie knew that the time would come when he started coming less and less, but she wasn't ready for that time to come now.

She stood from the table, took the lone candle, and sauntered toward her room. Perhaps she could do some reading before bed and settle in early this time. She hadn't gone to bed this early ever since Gabriel started visiting her daily. She'd only put her foot on the first step of the main stairwell when the door burst open, and Gabriel fairly leaped into the hall. The wind blew out Evie's candle before Gabriel closed the door and plunged the room into darkness.

"Do you always walk around the house in the dark?" he asked, shaking off his hat.

"No, the candle was blown out by your wind."

"My wind?"

"Never mind. Why are you late?" Gabriel raised his brow, which Evie barely discerned in the darkness. "I mean, what are you doing here so late? And I can see you are finally using the key."

"I think you butler was tired of serving me. And well, I am late today, because I need your help. Quick, go get dressed."

"What?" Evie asked but started up the steps. "What kind of help?"

"No time to explain. I need you to wear your finest gown, and please, do not tarry; this cannot wait."

"Fine. Can you at least tell me where we are going?"

"For a ride."

"A ride?"

"Do not worry; it's in a carriage. Riding astride across London would turn more than one head. Especially if you

276

wear those breeches you wore when you accosted me in my townhouse."

Evie blinked. She didn't have time to process his comment as Gabriel took her by the arm and propelled her up the stairs. Evie hurried down the hall and ran into her room, calling for her maid all the while. What could be the matter?

In about half an hour, Evie settled against the carriage seat and rearranged her skirts.

Gabriel studied her intently from head to toe. "You look beautiful."

"Thank you. Now, will you tell me where we are going?"

"Yes, we are going to a gaming club."

"What?" The words flew out of Evie's mouth before she had a moment to process her shock. *What, indeed.* "You cannot be serious," she said, a bit more composed.

"I am indeed very serious. And honestly, it might have been a better fit if you actually wore your breeches tonight since it's mostly a gentlemen's lair, but I thought it would make you suspect. Perhaps you could wear them some other time, though."

"You seem to have a slightly unhealthy fascination with those breeches," Evie said.

"Oh, no, I do not have a fascination with those breeches. I do, however, have a tremendous fascination with your bum in those breeches."

"Pardon me?" Evie's cheeks were suddenly burning red.

"Come, you've never paid attention to a gentleman's bum in his breeches?"

Evie's lips twitched in laughter. "I'll have to be honest, no."

"Well, me neither. But yours is enticingly plump."

"Err... Why are we talking about my bum?"

"Why not talk about your bum? It is plump, soft, deliciously succulent—"

"Please, stop."

Gabriel laughed huskily, and Evie's skin erupted in pleasurable shivers. *Oh, the devil.*

"Why are we going to a gaming hell?" she asked, feigning exasperation.

Gabriel heaved a sigh. "Because it is time for you to practice your skills." Evie raised a brow. "And because it's about to storm, and I didn't want you to spend the night alone."

Evie looked worriedly through the window. "It is about to storm?"

"See, my distraction technique is working; you haven't even noticed."

"Not until you brought it up," she grumbled.

The carriage halted a few minutes later, and they stood in front of a dark, ominous building with an iron door.

"Welcome to Hades," Gabriel said with a flourish.

"It is not actually called that, is it?"

Gabriel nodded and smiled. "It is. Now let's go in before it pours."

# Chapter 24

It was the ballroom at the Winchester estate all over again. The minute Evie entered the hell on Gabriel's arm, every head in the room swiveled in their direction. Even the harlots sitting on the gentlemen's laps stopped their shameless activities and stared at the newly arrived couple.

There was no rule against females in gaming hells. Hell, if that was the rule, no gentleman would ever step foot there. Ladies did find it scandalous, however. But for the wife of a devil like Gabriel, what was a little scandal?

Evie held her head high and pretended not to notice the half-clad women bouncing on the half-sprung gentlemen's laps.

She looked around the spacious, dark room and studied the walls painted with gruesome scenes from *Dante's Inferno* with avid interest. Gabriel's lips twitched in barely suppressed laughter. He'd made the right choice in marrying her. He didn't know any other lady who would calmly observe the paintings of people being shackled and eaten alive while walking through the hall of the most scandalous gaming hell.

She was perfection.

The floor was littered with their mutual acquaintances, who followed their progress, their mouths agape. Gabriel finally noticed a table with a couple of free seats and steered Evie in that direction.

"You don't mind if we join you, do you?" Gabriel asked as he sat down.

The gentlemen behind the table blinked as they saw Evie but instantly broke into stupid grins.

"Not at all." Bingham's lecherous gaze toward Evie didn't escape Gabriel, and he immediately stiffened. Evie's smile turned strained, too. Gabriel made sure to graze Evie's neck with his hand as he helped her into a seat. He then took her hand in his and placed a lingering kiss on her knuckles. The men around the table threw them speculative looks.

Gabriel leaned in close to Evie and whispered in her ear, "Show me your best game, darling."

Evie looked at him beneath her lashes and winked.

Gabriel laughed loudly before addressing the table. "Let us play."

A few hours later, the table had emptied as Evie thinned their pockets. She was a natural at this game. Of course, it helped that Gabriel had perfected the sleight of hand and always had the right card to help out his *lucky* wife.

Evie would throw reproving glances his way from time to time, but she didn't seem to have qualms about fleecing the stuffy lords.

"That's it. I don't think I have anything else to lose." Bingham threw up his hands in defeat.

Evie licked her lips and narrowed her eyes on him. Gabriel

observed her closely. She had something up her sleeve.

"How about one last wager? I'll let you win it all back," she said with a pleasant smile.

"Did you not hear what I said? I don't have as much as a penny."

"You have an unentailed property. A tiny village by the name of Forton."

"Why the interest in this worthless piece of land?"

"My husband and I journeyed through it on our way to elope. It is of sentimental value to us. If it's as worthless to you as you say, I shall be doing you a favor by taking it off your hands."

"If you bought it."

Evie drummed her fingers on the table as she studied Lord Bingham. "How about this? I win, I take it. I lose, you take all the winnings tonight, and I shall buy your land from you. For any price."

Greed shone in Bingham's eyes as he settled back against the seat. "One more game, God help me. But St. Clare doesn't play. In fact, this will be just the two of us."

Evie threw a quick glance toward Gabriel and smiled. At Gabriel's nod, the dealer dealt each of them two cards. Bingham seemed far too happy with his hand, and Evie bit her lip in uncertainty. She turned toward Gabriel and raised her brows. He understood her silent question. *What do I do?* He blinked and nodded. *Trust yourself, darling.*

Evie nodded as if she understood their silent dialog and asked for another card.

At the dealer's urging, Bingham showed his hand. He had two queens. Evie pursed her lips and slowly turned her cards, one by one. A jack, a six, and a five.

Gabriel jumped up from the chair in glee, tugged Evie up, and gave her a hard kiss on her mouth, not caring that anyone was watching, not giving a damn what anyone thought. When he raised his head, Evie laughed merrily.

"You cheat!" Bingham cried in a high-pitched voice. "You cheated! I saw you two looking at each other, giving some kind of a signal!"

"Are you accusing my wife of deceit? You better answer for your words, Bingham."

"I am certain you were the one doing the cheating, but you never know; she is your wife after all."

"Careful!" Gabriel growled in warning.

Evie put a staying hand on his arm. "We didn't trick or deceive you. And I gave you a fair chance to win it all. However, I shall be gracious, and if you call upon me in the coming week, we might discuss this situation."

"All winnings are final," the dealer proclaimed. "House rules."

Bingham's face became as red as a tomato. He stood, swaying a bit on his feet, and left the table without another word.

Evie turned her huge eyes to Gabriel, and he just shrugged. "Some people are sour losers. In any case, this shouldn't reflect on our ability to continue having a good time. Do you want to explore more on this floor, or I can show you truly devilish rooms?" He waggled his brows.

"I would rather…." Her voice dropped to a scandalized whisper. "I think I drank too much wine. I need to use the privy."

"Certainly." Gabriel turned and addressed the dealer loudly. "Which way to the ladies' necessary?"

Evie turned the color of beetroot red. Oh, the ladies of the *ton* and their ideas of modesty.

The dealer flicked his wrist, and a serving wench appeared by his side. "Show these fine people to the ladies' necessary, please."

Evie put a staying hand on Gabriel's shoulder. "I think I can take care of this business by myself," she said, still blushing fiercely.

"In a den full of randy aristocrats? I do not think so."

Gabriel took Evie by the arm, and they followed the server down the corridor. "Besides, do you truly think I do not know that ladies use the privy?"

"I'd rather not think about that."

Gabriel laughed. "After all we've been through together, this is what you are scandalized by?" He shook his head.

The 'scandalous' room wasn't too far from the main hall. As Evie entered the privy, Gabriel wandered off down the corridor, looking at the graphic artwork on the walls. It was expertly done. He would love to know the artist and have them decorate his own devil's den—his study, or perhaps the entire townhouse—with similar art. Evie might not approve, though. She'd probably want it done in more cheerful hues.

"St. Clare!" The familiar voice pulled him out of his reverie. He turned and saw one of his old gambling mates standing in the hallway. "You're back to your old ways. Who would have thought? Barely two months since your marriage."

Gabriel walked toward the man. "Actually, I am here with my lady wife."

"Where? I don't see her."

"She's taking care of some feminine business, if you must know." Gabriel tried to steer his friend away from the corridor. He didn't want his other friends accosting him in the hallway, so close to his wife. It was certain to make Evie uncomfortable.

"Truly?" The man laughed uproariously. "And you are waiting on her? Come, let's play a game of chance; she'll find her own way. Matheson! Look who I found!" More people started filing into the corridor, and Gabriel squirmed uncomfortably. If Evie exited now, she'd be accosted by a mob of drunken men.

"He's waiting on his wife to come out, can you believe it?"

"I never pegged you for a henpecked husband!"

"St. Clare is here with a wife?"

The voices roared in the hallway. Gabriel patted his friend on the back before taking him by the scruff. "Let us discuss this in the main hall, shall we?"

"But we want to see your wife."

"Not here." He led the pack away, and as soon as he reentered the main hall, more gentlemen started accosting him. Apparently, the news of Evie's spectacular win had spread like wildfire. Everyone was curious to see St. Clare and his lucky wife.

\* \* \*

Evie exited the necessities room into an empty hallway. She looked up and down the corridor but saw no sign of her husband. Perhaps he'd gotten distracted. She shrugged and made her way toward the main hall. She was about to reach the far end when a man rounded the corner and stopped in the entryway, dropping a shadow over Evie. The man took a few steps forward, crowding her in the narrow hallway.

Evie tried to make her way around him, but he seemed to follow her every step.

"Pardon me, sir, I just want to pass," she said with a frown.

"Do you?" Lord Bingham asked with a sneer.

Evie looked up and squinted at his dark features. "Lord Bingham, it is ungentlemanly of you to accost me in a narrow hallway. If you just let me pass, we can discuss whatever you like in the main hall."

"I don't think this is what you want. You've shown interest in me ever since your wedding ball. And I am willing to assuage your curiosity."

"I am afraid you misconstrued my interest. It lies solely in the small village you owned, the one which I won from you tonight." Evie backed away slowly with her every word. Bingham followed, step for step. "My husband—"

"Is too busy to notice your absence. So if you wanted a liberty, now is the time to ask for it. Nicely."

Evie scrunched up her nose in disgust. "I would rather go back to the main hall."

"And I would rather have you kiss me." Bingham made a lunge toward her.

Evie yelped as she dashed to the side and easily evaded the drunken attack.

"What in the devil is going on here?" her husband roared furiously, his voice echoing against the corridor walls. Evie turned and saw Gabriel standing in the entryway, his face shadowed in the dark.

"Gabriel." Evie picked up her skirts and hurried toward her husband. A few people peeked their heads in, curious what the hubbub was all about.

As soon as Evie reached Gabriel's side, he put a possessive

hand around her shoulders and looked down at her in concern.

"Nothing to worry about, St. Clare," Bingham slurred drunkenly. "Your wife was about to service me, that is all."

Evie flinched in humiliation and raised her eyes to Gabriel. She couldn't see his features clearly, but his chest rose on an inhale, and his hands fisted at his sides.

"Did you just insult my wife?"

Bingham seemed to finally understand that he'd gotten himself into an unsavory predicament because he stepped back. "Come, St. Clare, after all the years of debauchery, you don't appreciate a harmless joke?"

"Not. About. My wife," Gabriel enunciated slowly. "You can accuse me of being a cheat. You can even refuse to honor your forfeit. You're dishonorable; that much can be expected and even forgiven. But you don't get to touch my wife. Ever."

"Come, St. Clare, I didn't even steal a kiss."

Gabriel went very still. Evie put a hand to his chest. "He truly didn't. He didn't even touch me."

More people gathered behind them, straining to see and hear what was going on.

"My wife is off-limits."

"I understand," Bingham said hastily.

"I don't think you do. And other people won't either until they realize I am serious about this."

"Gabriel, no harm was done," Evie tried to placate her angry husband.

"I'll see you at dawn, Bingham!" Gabriel announced loudly, and a gasp sounded somewhere behind them.

"You are jesting!" Evie's mouth fell open.

"But you never duel!" Bingham whined.

"I don't duel over light skirts who throw themselves at me in the same ballroom as their husbands. Accosting my wife, trying to take a liberty against her will? That will get you a bullet in your vile, shriveled heart. And I need to make that clear. To everyone."

"I-I... I did apologize. I do apologize!" Bingham yelled.

"I accept." Evie nodded frantically.

Gabriel gazed at her gently. "I am afraid that is not enough anymore."

"Oh, for God's sake. Please, Gabriel." Evie was so irritated she was ready to stomp her foot.

"I w-will not agree to this."

"Name your second, coward."

Evie rounded on Gabriel, blocking his view of Bingham. "Gabriel, this is unnecessary. Please, let us leave now."

"There is a crowd watching us and listening to our every word, dear. They need to recognize that you, my dear wife, are not to trifle with."

"Dueling is illegal. You are creating a major scandal!"

Gabriel raised a careless brow. Of course, scandal was practically his middle name.

Evie took his hands in hers. "You might not care about a scandal, but I do. If my feelings matter to you at all, please, walk away from this. Walk away now. With me."

Gabriel didn't move a muscle.

Evie pulled out her last card. "If this is how you're going to act every time someone looks at me funny, I won't be able to leave the house again."

Gabriel looked down at her. "He didn't just—"

"You don't know what happened. He didn't even touch me."

"I didn't," Bingham agreed.

"So you are being irrational," Evie pressed on.

"If I walk away now, those people—" Gabriel tipped his head to the gathering crowd.

"Since when do you care about those people? Or do you truly hold them in higher esteem than me?"

She could see the moment Gabriel surrendered. He heaved a sigh and then narrowed his eyes on Bingham. "Don't think that this is over."

Bingham radiated relief. Evie laced her fingers with Gabriel's and led him away. The whispers grew louder with every step they took, turning into a thunderous roar. They kept on walking, not paying any heed to either the whispers or stares directed their way.

They left the hell, and Gabriel helped Evie settle into the carriage before sitting down across from her.

"What were you thinking?" Evie threw up her hands in frustration the moment the carriage lurched into motion.

"Oh, you mean why was I defending the honor of my wife?"

"My honor does not need defending."

"How many?" Gabriel's tone grew so cold that Evie felt chills racing up her arms.

"How many what?"

"How many people have accosted you with lurid propositions since we married?"

Evie picked nervously at the fingertips of her gloves.

"And do not lie to me, my duchess. I know you well enough by now to see the difference."

"I didn't keep count! Many. So what? Are you going to challenge every man—"

"I don't have to. Once should be enough to show them I am not going to tolerate any more disrespect toward you."

288

"You want to teach them a lesson. And what will it take? Will you injure poor Bingham, or do you need to kill him to get your point across? You could die doing so, or you could get sentenced to death or exiled. Dueling is illegal!"

"First of all, he dug his own grave the moment he touched you—"

"Gabriel!"

"Secondly, do you think I am doing this just for you? How am I supposed to sleep at night knowing that you might be somewhere out there, alone and unprotected! Especially since you insist on living separately from me. I need to let everybody know that if they so much as touch you or look at you the wrong way, they are earning themselves a spot at dawn. Otherwise, you won't be safe. It is my responsibility to take care of you."

"This was not a part of our bargain—"

"Oh, for the love of—" Gabriel scrubbed his face with one hand. "Would you just forget the blasted bargain?"

The carriage halted, and Gabriel took a few breaths before jumping out of the vehicle and helping her out. He reached the front door of her townhouse and waited for the butler to open it before speaking.

"We can discuss this later—"

Evie rounded on him, her face full of resolution. "Do you think I am going to let you saunter off into the night and go arrange more duels? Oh, no, you are coming with me, my lord."

Gabriel raised a brow. "If you want to make certain there's no duel at dawn—"

"I know what this means; please step inside."

Gabriel slowly walked in as the butler closed the door after him with a smirk. He stood there, obviously waiting for more instructions.

"Let the cook know she should prepare breakfast for two in the morning," Evie said, her voice shaking slightly.

Gabriel crossed his arms on his chest and raised his brow in challenge.

"That will be all." She smiled at her butler.

The man bowed and hurried away.

"What, no guest chamber for me?" Gabriel asked cockily.

"If you think I shall let you out of my sight tonight, you're sorely mistaken."

"Ahh," Gabriel drawled. "Just like the good old days. Shall I be occupying the floor once again?"

Evie took a deep breath. "That depends on your behavior, my lord," she said playfully and started up the stairs.

# Chapter 25

Evie's entire body buzzed with anticipation. She knew she was playing with fire, letting Gabriel spend the night, but she couldn't help but feel giddy at the prospect of having him by her side again.

Once they entered her chambers, Evie dismissed her maid and settled on the edge of the bed. Gabriel leaned his back against the wall across from her and folded his arms on his chest, watching her curiously.

"Just so you know, you're a prisoner in my house until you admit that dueling is a foolish solution to the problem you're trying to solve."

"Am I?" Gabriel quirked his brow. "In this case, I shall be a permanent occupant of your... err... prison. I wonder, what shall we do to pass the time?"

"Oh, come, Gabriel! Be serious for one moment."

"I am extremely, deadly serious."

"Dead is what you are going to be no matter the outcome of this duel!"

"Do not be melodramatic. Have you seen Bingham? He will delope, and I shall have made my point."

"What if he doesn't delope? What if he shoots you? Or what if he injures you, and you're required to defend your honor and kill him? What then? You're going to hang." Evie's chest heaved from exasperation. "You're not going anywhere."

"Fine." Gabriel pushed off the wall and started unbuttoning his coat. He hung it on the back of the chair and started on the buttons of his waistcoat. Evie sat on the bed, her entire body tensing as Gabriel shed one piece of clothing after another. Her mouth went dry as he removed his cufflinks and started undoing his shirt, revealing a gleaming, muscled chest. "If I am stuck here, then we might as well get on with it," he grumbled under his breath.

"I am not sleeping with you," she said with as much dignity as she could muster.

"Well, if you're planning to keep me here until I change my mind about the duel, then we are going to grow old together. The least we could do is have some fun while we are at it."

"You are incorrigible."

"That is why you love me." He grinned at her, and Evie lowered her head.

Gabriel cursed under his breath and came toward her. He stood so close that his knees brushed her skirts. Her entire body vibrated from the heat radiating from him.

"Evie, I might not love you," Gabriel said gently, and Evie felt as if a huge boulder was stuck in her throat. "But I do care about you. More than I have ever cared for anyone. And I am not about to let people mistreat you."

He offered both hands, and she took them. Gabriel tugged her up and nudged her chin so that she'd look at him. "I might not know the first thing about love, but I know that I shall rip anyone to shreds if they look at you the wrong way. You think if I don't love you, that means I don't think about you? Worry about you? Oh, I do.

"I think about you all the damn time. I wonder if you slept well and if you are warm enough. Whether you are safe or have gotten yourself into mischief. Being separated from you is like torture, and not because I cannot kiss you, although it is definitely on the list, but because I constantly worry if you've had enough to eat and if you've taken the ginger root with you on your travels. Every time it rains, I pray it doesn't storm because I know you're alone...."

Evie's eyes grew rounder with every word of Gabriel's confession. She stared at him as he held her hands in his and continued his recitation.

"So what if I don't love you? I am incapable. But I miss you with every fiber of my being. Your scent, your touch, the glimpse of you. I'm haunted by the vision of you every time I close my eyes. I crave you. Your lips, your tongue, your tasty little"—he smirked and suggestively lowered his eyes—"everything."

Evie reached up on her toes and gently nudged his lips with hers. Her heart was beating loudly in her ears, and tears burned at the back of her eyes.

"Tell me more," she whispered against his lips.

"More of what?" he whispered back.

"How you don't love me." She smiled and kissed him again. Evie opened her mouth over his and ran her hands up his chest until they settled at his nape. She kissed him ardently, weaving her hands through his silky locks.

Gabriel's hands traveled down until he cupped her by the

buttocks and crushed her closer to him. Evie moaned as she felt his hot arousal and rubbed against him.

"Evie." Gabriel tore his mouth from her. "I didn't say any of this to change your mind about the bargain."

"I know." She reached up and closed her mouth over his. She licked at him, devouring his mouth, tasting him with her tongue.

Evie whimpered in frustration, wanting more from their embrace. She pulled away and started frantically untying her bodice.

Gabriel watched her, his eyes round, his breathing frantic. "Evie, what—"

"Just—help me with this." Evie looked at him pleadingly, and Gabriel nodded. He untied her bodice and deposited it on the chair next to the bed. Next went the overskirts and stays. As soon as her underskirts were discarded, she threw her arms around his neck and kissed him again. Her hands slowly made their way down, and she fumbled with the falls of Gabriel's breeches.

Gabriel tore his mouth away from her. "What are you doing?" he asked, his breathing frantic.

"What do you think I am doing?"

"I think you're playing with fire, my dear wife." His voice was hoarse, and his gaze roamed her body.

"Good." Evie lowered her hands to the skirts of her chemise and slowly started raising them higher. She watched his breathing grow frantic, his eyes glowed with a devilish gleam, and felt a surge of power with every inch of skin she bared. His gaze followed her actions, lingering on her belly button and running over her ribcage. Evie stopped just before she reached her breasts and paused there.

Gabriel's eyes paused in their movement, too, his breath hitching as he waited for her to bare her breasts. Evie discarded her chemise in one swift motion, and Gabriel's mouth dropped open.

She slowly, sensually untied the ribbon of her drawers, and as they fell away, she stood in front of him in just her silk stockings.

Gabriel swallowed audibly. His eyes roamed her body as if he was uncertain of where to rest them. Then they settled on the junction between her thighs.

"You heard that I said I don't love you, right?"

*Oh, my poor, clueless husband.* Evie tried unsuccessfully to suppress a grin. "I know."

"And you still want me in bed with you?"

Evie bit her lip and nodded. "Yes."

"In that case…" Gabriel bent down, picked Evie up, and threw her onto the bed. He then hastily took off his boots, breeches, and his shirt and fairly fell on top of Evie.

She laughed and locked her arms around his neck. Evie tugged Gabriel closer to her and kissed him open-mouthed. She licked the seam between his lips before plunging her tongue inside his warmth. Gabriel groaned, the sound reverberating through her entire body.

Gabriel rolled onto his back, taking her with him, holding her close to his body. He took her head between his hands and kissed her fiercely, biting on her lips, then soothing them with his tongue, sipping on her as if she were a chalice of water and he a thirsty beast. Her mouth felt swollen and sensitive. His stubble pricked her skin around her mouth, adding to the fiery sensations. He ran his hands down her sides, her thighs, then widened her legs, making her straddle him.

Evie wriggled on top of him, looking for a comfortable position, and heard him hiss. She looked up, worried she might have hurt him. His eyes were closed, a grimace resembling that of pain on his face. He then opened his eyes and looked dazedly at her.

Gabriel took her by her waist and pulled her higher so that her breasts were directly in front of his face, hanging like ripe fruit, ready for the picking. He looked at them for a brief moment, then raised his head and licked one nipple. Evie felt a jolt, like lightning running from her nipple through her body and settling between her legs.

She pressed herself closer to him, rubbing her pelvis against him, and felt a liquid heat seeping out of her and soaking him. She wriggled to escape the sensation, but Gabriel held fast. He continued to lick around her nipple, nipping at it, playing with her breast before he put his mouth over her and sucked. Hard. Evie's head fell back as she let out a strangled moan. She heard Gabriel chuckle against her skin before he moved his attention to her other breast.

"Gabriel," she breathed, unable to take it anymore. She wanted something, needed something, something more. Some sort of completion to this tortuous, sensual act. The feeling that she remembered from that long-ago day in a carriage when he'd stimulated her with his hand.

"Shh, sweetheart," he whispered against her breast. "I'll take care of you."

With that, he pulled her a little more over him, sliding her center against his body. The feeling made her moan. He kissed and licked her flat stomach, then dipped his tongue into her belly button as she squirmed. He chuckled darkly before taking her by the hips and sitting her over his face. Evie yelped and caught herself against the bed frame. Her eyes widened in shock.

"What—" She was about to ask him what he was doing when she felt him lick her. Lick her. There. Right in the center. And the feeling was such a glorious one that she sobbed. Then he licked her again, and Evie forgot her own thoughts.

She heard her moans and his growls of satisfaction as he put his mouth firmer against her and kept licking at her center, drinking her in, dipping his tongue inside her. Evie moaned and felt her hips moving of their own volition, riding his mouth like a complete wanton.

Her juices trickled down his mouth, and her moans were coming out with her every breath. Then he swirled his tongue around the tiny bud at the top of her sex, and she lost all her reason. She was writhing wantonly on his face, moaning to get more, marveling at being sucked so deliciously. A moment later, bright sparks lit inside her tightly shut eyelids, and her entire body tensed while wave after wave of pleasure assailed her. She stiffened on top of Gabriel, her hips still moving against him, his tongue still doing wicked things against her center as she pulsed from the inside and felt tiny shudders going through her body. She heard a muffled cry and realized it was coming from her as she collapsed against the pillows.

When she opened her eyes, she was lying on her back, her feet braced against the bed, her knees apart, lying completely open in front of Gabriel as he kneeled before her, his manhood in hand. He was holding himself, gently, slowly running his hand up and down his shaft. All the while, his eyes never left her center. He looked up at her then, his eyes heavy-lidded, a wicked gleam playing in them. He smiled before lowering himself to her, covering her body with his. The head of his shaft snuggled against her center, the weight and heat of him exciting her senses.

"Tell me you want this." He lowered his head and scraped his teeth against her neck before sucking her in.

"I want this. I want you." Evie moaned and tightened her arms and legs about his body.

Gabriel made a thrust, and Evie felt herself being stretched by him. He raised his intense and heavy-lidded eyes to hers, his features dark and serious. Sweat was running down his forehead. He braced himself on his elbows on either side of her head before kissing her sweetly on her mouth.

"It's going to hurt a little," he whispered, his voice hoarse as if from strain.

She nodded and kissed him, plunging her tongue inside his mouth, tasting the salty essence of her own release on his tongue. He thrust again, and she felt him invading her, stretching her even more. A burning sensation appeared between her legs. She tightened her hands about his shoulders and curled her fingers into him.

Gabriel was breathing heavily, holding himself over her, his face dark with passion.

"I can't," he finally said, his voice too strained as if from great pain. "I'm sorry, I can't anymore."

*Is it over?* The thought hadn't left Evie's mind before Gabriel made one more thrust and seated himself fully inside her. Gabriel kissed her gently on her mouth, then peppered tiny kisses all over her face.

"God, you're tight," he said, as if in a great deal of pain.

"Is that… is it bad?" she asked self-consciously and heard his hoarse laughter.

"No, my sweet," he whispered against her lips and kissed her again. "Nothing about you is bad. You are incredibly, extraordinarily wonderful." He put his forehead against hers in an endearingly tender gesture and looked into her eyes. "Does it hurt?"

Evie shook her head. It burned slightly, and she felt somewhat uncomfortable with him inside her. She wriggled a little to test the sensation, her inner muscles contracting, and heard Gabriel's pained groan.

"Does it hurt you?" she asked, wide-eyed, and Gabriel closed his eyes briefly.

"No, it doesn't hurt," he answered, his voice still hoarse. "It's just so good that I…" He paused and shook his head. "I need to move, or I might just die."

Evie blinked up at him. Gabriel stared intently into her eyes when he moved his pelvis away from her body, withdrawing his length before shoving himself full length inside her again. The contact sent tingles all along her body as his pelvis brushed against her sensitive nub. Evie moaned and put her arms around him again.

"Hold on to me," Gabriel whispered before withdrawing and thrusting in again. He moved gently out of her, then slammed himself inside again with a force that moved the bed and made Evie moan. His chest rubbed against her nipples with every movement, and the feeling of his flesh sliding against her sent ripples of sensations throughout her body until it started collecting inside her.

Evie whimpered in frustration and rocked her hips faster against his.

"Shh," Gabriel whispered. "Don't struggle for it."

He moved one hand between them and touched her swollen

nub. He circled it, still thrusting inside her along with the movement of his finger. Evie felt a fiery sensation of absolute bliss exploding inside her again. Gabriel worked above her, feeding those sparks, not letting her descend from the feeling of absolute joy. A sound, part moan, part cry escaped her, and she raised her hips before they fell limply onto the bed. She heard a low growl and felt warm liquid pour inside her as Gabriel collapsed against her.

They lay like that, breathing heavily. She flat on the bed, with her legs open wide, her arms about his shoulders, her head thrown back. Gabriel was on top of her, lying in the cradle of her hips, his delicious weight pinning her to the bed. His head lay on the pillow next to hers; his warm breath hit against her chin. Evie ran her hands tentatively against his sleek, sweaty arms and back, and Gabriel made to get up. She tightened her hold on him.

"I am crushing you," he said and kissed her lightly on her chin.

"No, I want to feel you. I like the feel of your body against mine."

Gabriel grunted before wrapping his arms around her and rolling on his back with her. "How about this?" he asked when she was comfortably settled against his chest, her head on his shoulder.

"Mm," was all she said as she closed her eyes.

She felt a light kiss on the crown of her head just before she fell asleep.

# Chapter 26

**E**vie opened her eyes and squinted against the bright light coming from the window. Why hadn't she shut the drapes all the way last night? She turned sharply and hit the hard planes of a masculine body lying beside her. She let out a tiny shriek before she remembered who that masculine body belonged to.

Gabriel was in bed with her.

He grunted something in his sleep and turned his head away from her, throwing his arm over his eyes.

Evie smiled to herself. A sheet was covering the most interesting part of his anatomy; other than that, he was completely naked. She raked him over with her gaze, studying his body unhurriedly. He was lying on his back, his abdomen and broad chest exposed to her gaze, his chest rising and falling with every soft inhale of his breath. She propped herself on one elbow and devoured the vision in front of her.

It wasn't the first time she'd seen him naked, but she didn't think she'd ever get tired of ogling him. He had a beautiful body. It was hard and lean, knotted with muscles in all the right places. The view of his tight muscles on his abdomen made her want to lick him. Evie narrowed her eyes at him. What would he taste like if she did indeed lick him? She put her hands on either side of him, lowered her head, and licked him in the middle of his flat belly. Gabriel jumped in reaction.

"What the—" He removed his hand from his face in one sharp movement but relaxed as he saw Evie crouching in front of him. His hand automatically went to cuddle her head. "What are you doing, love?" His voice was rough from sleep, and a relaxed smile split his face.

"I wanted to know what you taste like," Evie answered evenly.

"If you want to know what I taste like, that is not the place you should be licking." Gabriel settled more comfortably on the pillow and put both hands behind his head.

"Where should I be—" Evie hadn't finished her question when she felt a slight poking in her chest. She lowered her eyes and saw the bedsheet tenting over Gabriel's masculine organ. "Oh." She blushed, and Gabriel laughed.

"You don't have to, love. As much as I adore the idea, I was just jesting. Come here." He stretched one arm toward her, and Evie placed both her hands in his. He tugged her up until she was sprawled on top of him, then took her mouth in a soft kiss.

Evie ran her hands up his chest, feeling his body, studying his every muscle. Last night was like a feverish dream. She had been too confused, aroused, and excited to really feel anything other than the earth-shattering bliss he'd brought her to. Right now, in the daylight, she wanted to see and feel all of him.

## Chapter 26

She dragged her lips from his and kissed his jaw, sucking and nipping it in the process. His morning stubble was prickly and ticklish at the same time. She ran her tongue experimentally over it and heard Gabriel chuckle. Evie raised her head and looked questioningly at him.

"Nothing, love. Continue."

Having received the encouragement, Evie didn't tarry. She moved lower and kissed Gabriel on his throat, then dipped lower to the hollow at the base of his throat and swirled her tongue there. Gabriel's arms tightened on her, and he took a sharp inhale of breath. Evie smiled and ventured lower, sliding against Gabriel's body and hands. She rubbed herself against his rock-hard and hot erection and heard him growl.

"You are killing me," he hissed between his teeth.

Evie raised her eyes to his. "Do you want me to stop?"

"Not for the world." Gabriel tangled his hands in her hair and played with the strands while caressing her back.

She licked her way down to his chest and kissed him on the nipple. Then she swirled her tongue around it and sucked it into her mouth.

She raised her head and studied Gabriel's expression. His breathing was erratic, and his hands stilled on her back.

"Does it feel the same way for you as it does for me?" She took his nipple between her thumb and forefinger and pinched lightly.

"I don't think so, pet," Gabriel said with a grin. "I am afraid it's not as sensitive."

"Why not?" Evie asked with a pout. She hoped to get him as out of control as she had been the night before. She wanted him moaning and insensible. But perhaps an experienced rake like him didn't lose his control like that. Or maybe he'd just experienced it all so many times that he was immune.

"Don't overthink it, love." Gabriel chuckled. "Some body parts are just more sensitive in different people than in others."

"What parts of your body are more sensitive then?"

"Well, I know of one." He raised a coquettish brow at her.

"One is not enough. I have several."

Gabriel outright laughed at her disgruntled tone of voice. "You do indeed. And if you don't hurry it up, I shall lay you on your back and will explore all of *your* body parts."

"No." Evie jerked to sit upright. "I am not done yet. And I shall not stop until I find all of your most sensitive parts."

"Inquisitive little creature, are you? Very well, I shan't deter you."

Evie smiled smugly and lowered herself over him again. She put her mouth over his belly button and dragged her tongue over the planes of his hard body, up to the middle of his chest. He tasted like salt and musk and also him. The taste of his body was like wine to her senses and seemed to cloud her mind because the next thing she knew, she was dragging the bedsheets away from his body.

His male organ stood large and proud among the curls of intimate hair. The skin was stretched taut over it, and it was covered with veins. Evie put her hands on him slowly, tentatively at first, and heard his sharp intake of breath.

Finally, the reaction she had been waiting for. She ran her hands up and down his length, and it jumped in reaction.

"Oh, God," Gabriel groaned. He placed both hands on her head and tangled his fingers in her hair.

Evie studied his shaft curiously. It was hard and feverishly hot, but the skin was soft and velvety. She slowly lowered herself over it and licked it from the base to the tip. Gabriel's hips jerked in response. Evie smiled and took the top of him inside her mouth. Gabriel jerked again, stuffing more of him inside her mouth. She swirled her tongue around his head, and he swore. The taste of him here was the same as the skin of his abdomen, only with a bit more musk. A taste she could get used to.

Evie raised her eyes to his. Gabriel was studying her under his heavy-lidded eyes, and the moment she looked up, his hands tightened in her hair.

"Do that again," he croaked. Evie complied with a smile.

This time, she tried to fit as much of him as she could inside her mouth, lapping his length with her tongue, tasting him, moaning from the sensation. It felt incredibly erotic doing this to him, pleasuring him with her mouth.

"Squeeze me, love. Squeeze me with your hands," Gabriel instructed, and she did. She squeezed him while sucking on his length.

"Oh, for the love of all that's holy—" Gabriel muttered, and Evie couldn't help it. She freed her mouth of him and laughed.

"Oh, for God's sake, woman," Gabriel croaked as if in pain. "It's not funny."

"That's the only time I've ever heard you pray," she said between fits of laughter.

"If you don't continue," Gabriel threatened in a low voice, "I shall make *you* pray. And a lot louder."

"You promise?" Evie smiled flirtatiously and bit her lip.

The next moment, Evie was on her back, and Gabriel's body covering hers. His face was inches away from her.

"I warned you," he growled and took her mouth in a scorching kiss.

Evie immediately opened under him and spread her legs wider as he settled between them. She wrapped her arms about his shoulders, marveling at the feel of his velvety skin, the tight muscles bunching under her fingers. She wrapped her legs around his thighs and ran her foot up his calf.

Evie dragged her mouth away. "I wasn't finished playing," she pouted, breathing heavily.

"Oh, I think you are done." Gabriel crawled lower, all the while kissing her neck, her collarbone. "Now it's my time to play," he growled and took her nipple into his mouth.

Evie jumped in reaction. She heard his chuckle before he moved on to her other breast. He repeated the previous action, and Evie arched against him.

"I want to… Gabriel, I want—"

"I know what you want, love," Gabriel muttered, his voice hoarse. "Let me give it to you."

"No." Evie wriggled out from under him and sat up.

"No?" Gabriel stared at her, a puzzled expression on his face.

"It's my turn. I want to please you the same way you did me last night."

Gabriel grinned lazily. "Darling, if you please me more, I might not survive it."

Evie moved closer to him and put her hands on his shoulders, then nudged him so he fell back on the mattress. She leaned over him and whispered in his ear, "I want you insensible as you writhe beneath me."

Gabriel groaned, grabbed her by her buttocks, and squeezed. "You devious little wench," he hissed between his teeth. "You want my cock in your mouth? Then get to it and stop torturing me." He tangled his hand in her hair and pushed her down. Evie slid along his body until she was face to cock with his hot, aroused length. It jumped the moment it was at eye level with her. She took it in her hand and shoved him into her mouth. The taste of him was incredibly arousing; Evie moaned as she took more of him in.

"Use your tongue," Gabriel groaned. She did and felt his hands tighten in her hair. "Move your hands up and down and squeeze me hard. Harder. There's my girl," Gabriel kept instructing her between hisses of breath. His hips started moving in rhythm with the slide of her hands. She couldn't get enough of him, of his taste, his hot shaft in her hands and mouth. She wanted more; she wanted him begging for mercy; she wanted him to be a blubbering mess, as she had been the night before.

Tiny whimpers escaped her just thinking about it. She felt hot liquid seep between her legs, and she clenched her thighs. Her grip tightened on him as she ran her tongue over the top of his shaft.

"God, Evie," Gabriel groaned.

She raised her eyes to his face. His eyes were closed, his head thrown back, and he was writhing beneath her as if in agony. She smiled inwardly, her physical ability to smile hindered by the fact that her mouth was full of him. The thought oddly sent waves of shivers along her body and a tingle between her legs. She felt empty there; she needed him filling her. Instead, Evie dragged her mouth lower down his shaft, taking as much of him in as possible. Her mouth watered, and she sucked hard to collect the excess liquid, at the same time collecting more of his taste.

"Evie," Gabriel croaked. "I am going to come. You need to— You—" With a groan, he dragged her away from his shaft and turned into the mattress. His hands were fisted in the sheets, his body shaking as he screamed into the pillow.

Missing the heat of his body, Evie slowly lowered herself onto his back and snuggled close to him.

\* \* \*

Gabriel gazed at his wife as she ate her breakfast. She was quiet this morning, not subdued as she had been a few days ago, but content. After this morning's lovemaking, they'd shared a bath and then indulged in each other twice more. He had been certain she would be sore after last night, but she didn't seem to have any soreness at all. Well, she was athletic, so perhaps their vigorous lovemaking hadn't taken a toll on her body as much as he expected.

She looked at him and raised a brow. "Is breakfast not to your liking, husband?"

"Oh, no, it is brilliant, I am sure. Except that my wife tastes better."

Evie darted her eyes to the footmen who stood by the wall and then threw a chastising gaze toward Gabriel.

He laughed. "You didn't expect me to behave, did you?"

Evie picked up her fork with a haughty look, took a piece of fruit, and popped it in her mouth. Gabriel followed the motion with avid interest.

"I do," she said after swallowing the piece of food. "At least, in front of my servants."

"Pardon, Your Grace. I shall correct my behavior accordingly." He grinned. "So, what are your plans for the day?"

"Actually." Evie cleared her throat and placed a fork on the side of her plate. "Your father is coming here in about an hour.

308

We were going to go over some numbers from my ledgers...."

Gabriel groaned. "You'll excuse me if I'll skip the family meeting."

"I would rather you stayed."

"And I would rather he didn't come."

"Gabriel, he is your father."

"My dear wife, you came from a very affectionate and close-knit family. So naturally, you feel the inclination to flock to other family members, but I am not like that. I grew up in a cold and lonely household, and I do not wish to revisit these memories. He might be exceedingly generous with you, but he has never been so with me. Pardon me if I don't share in your enthusiasm."

"I was going to say that perhaps you should give him another chance. He was wrong; I grant it—"

"Thank you."

"But..."

Gabriel heaved a long sigh and looked at her with a bored expression on his face.

"I just wish you two spent more time together. You are more alike than you might realize," she said.

Gabriel stood. "I shall do anything for you, my dear wife, you know it. I shall kill for you, and I shall die for you, but please, do not ask that of me." He placed a chaste kiss on her forehead and stalked toward the door.

"Where are you going?" Evie's worried voice followed him to the door.

"Just out for air. I shall be back for supper. Hopefully, your guest will be gone by then."

# Chapter 27

"**A** duel, Gabriel? Are you out of your mind?" Clydesdale leapt from the chair and stared at him wide-eyed.

"The bastard dared to accost Evie. And he is not the only one. I realize I made my bed when I spent years tupping different gentlemen's wives every night, but I didn't think I'd ever be married. Now Evie is the one paying the price. If I don't put a stop to it now, she will never be safe."

"Every time I got you out of a duel was not only to save your precious arse, you know. I do not condone duels."

"So, will you be my second or not?" Gabriel raised his brow.

Clydesdale heaved a loud sigh and settled back into his chair. "Of course, I shall be your second. What do you want me to do?"

After instructing Clydesdale on his terms, Gabriel walked slowly to Evie's townhouse. He hadn't taken the carriage, as her townhouse was on the same street as Clydesdale's. Also, he wanted to make sure that by the time he got back, his father would not be there.

Evie seemed to genuinely like the old man, and since he was helpful to her, Gabriel mused he'd have to learn to tolerate him. Perhaps it was time to put the past behind him and move forward. Together with his wife.

Gabriel wondered at what had changed between the moment he took her to the hell and the moment they'd made love. His wife was a mysterious creature, but he'd never imagined that telling her he did not and would not love her would prompt such a reaction from her. Or had she heard something different in his words? Did it even matter?

As of last night, she was truly his, and he would do everything in his power to keep it that way.

Gabriel approached the house and ran up the front steps. He entered the gloomy hall and looked around. It was quiet and empty. They'd have to do something about the decor. The feel of this townhouse was all wrong. It was not the house he'd imagined his wife living in. There were no flowers, no paintings; the walls were bare. He climbed the steps and was just about to round the corner when Evie appeared in front of him.

"Oh, you're home." She smiled up at him, and he felt all warm inside. *Home*.

"Has our guest left yet?"

"Yes, a few minutes ago. And you're just in time for supper. Come." She took him by the arm and led him into the dining room.

He looked at the long dining table, then back at her. "We don't have to sit six feet apart, do we?"

"As you wish, my lord." She smiled coyly, and he grinned. He then took the plates from one side of the table and settled

311

next to her.

"Tell me, how was your day, wife?" he asked, as the footmen brought in the first course.

"Very well, husband. I've done quite a bit of work, and I honestly think you would have benefited from being present at the meeting with the earl. The investments are one thing, but as a landowner, you need to learn the boring parts as well."

"How about we strike another bargain? You deal with the boring parts, and I deal with the exciting parts."

Evie threw him a narrowed gaze. "No, there will be no bargains in our marriage from now on."

"How about wagers?"

"Gabriel," she said sternly.

"Fine, fine. I shall sit in on the meeting with you and the earl next time he comes. Are you happy now?"

Evie froze with her fork halfway to her mouth. "Truly?"

"Yes, truly."

Evie smiled widely and proceeded to eat.

"I do recognize that I need to learn about the intricacies of running our estates," he said thoughtfully. "I want to be of use to you. Besides, perhaps it might be time to let go of old grudges."

She smiled slowly. "You are always of use to me. But that's marvelous that you're willing to forgive the earl, and also, just in time. Because he is coming tomorrow for supper, so you'd see him anyhow."

Gabriel raised his brows. "You devious little wench."

She licked the food off her fork with a superior look on her face.

"Very well, I shall sit through tomorrow's supper like a good little soldier, but in return, you will let me do whatever I want to do to you in bed."

Evie swallowed hard and looked about the room, her cheeks heating rapidly. It was Gabriel's time to put a smug smile on his face.

"What else did you do today? Is there any news, gossip?" he asked, digging into his food.

"No gossip but some news. I received a letter from Sam. She invited us to spend a month or so with her in Bedford. Apparently, her estate is so beautiful now that she can't wait to show it off. And after she heard about Peacehaven..." His wife trailed off, her face turning somber.

Gabriel covered her hand with his. "We are going to rebuild it, darling."

"I know. I just can't let myself think about it for too long. Perhaps we should just let it rest for a year... or two."

The footmen cleared their plates and brought in the second course. Gabriel looked at his plate and then turned to Evie in astonishment. She blinked and raised her face to his.

"Did you not instruct the cook of your food preferences?" he asked.

Evie sputtered a laugh. "I—no. I've been so down since I came here that I've barely spoken to my servants."

"I feel like this should be the first thing you say to your cook. I don't like fish, and then good afternoon."

Evie chuckled and covered her mouth with her hand. "That is probably what I should have done. I have not briefed her on anything. I am a poor example of a mistress."

"Now that we live together, we should just bring Matilda. She cooks splendidly, and you do love her buns." He grinned.

"It is not my cook's fault. I should have instructed her on

the menu, but I was too busy—"

"Wallowing in self-pity?" Gabriel raised a brow at her.

"Yes, if you must know. Exactly that."

"Sometimes, it is healthy to wallow in a bit of self-pity."

Evie laughed. "I just felt the weight of the whole world on my shoulders. I was frightened and alone…."

Gabriel took a deep breath. "You're not alone. No matter what is going on between us, please know that from now on, you will never be alone."

Evie smiled. "I know, but I suppose I had to go through that. I needed a reprieve, sleeping in, quiet evenings."

"Oh, we can have plenty of 'quiet evenings' going forth."

Evie laughed again. "No evening is ever quiet with you."

"Very well, plenty of loud quiet evenings." Gabriel sawed into the fish and popped a piece into his mouth. "Hmm, it isn't too bad."

"Just know that if you eat it, you're not allowed to kiss me with your fish breath."

"Fish breath?"

Evie quirked her brow. Gabriel slowly wiped his hands and mouth with a napkin, then stood. Evie watched him warily. Gabriel adjusted his cravat and lunged at Evie. She shrieked and shot out of her chair. Gabriel chased her around the table, and she laughed, scrambling to get away.

Finally, Gabriel caught her in his arms and twirled her. He backed her against the table and lowered his mouth to hers. Evie averted her face at the last moment, and he kissed her cheek, then down her neck. He crushed her closer to him while licking above her bodice.

"Hm, you are far more delicious than the fish," he murmured.

"Gabriel, the servants," she whispered.

"Right." He turned toward the footmen who stood by the wall, pretending that nothing untoward was happening. "Take the food and clear out." When the servants left, he turned back to Evie. "I shall have my dessert now."

* * *

Gabriel looked at his peacefully slumbering wife. He'd tired her out before they even got to their bedchamber. Having his wife on the dining table was a different kind of delicacy, a delicacy he certainly enjoyed. Gabriel's eyelids drooped, and he just wanted to snuggle close to his warm wife and fall asleep. But duty called.

He couldn't let Bingham assume he wasn't serious about the threats he'd made. So he scrambled off the bed and sauntered toward his clothing. He got dressed quickly, hastily throwing on his shirt and not bothering with a cravat. He entered the closet and… cast up his accounts. Thankfully, the chamber pot was right there, and he didn't sully much of his clothes.

Was it nerves?

He wiped his mouth and cleaned himself up. He washed his face with the cold water left by the maid next to the washbasin and stared into his reflection. His eyes were red-rimmed, his skin clammy. He took a deep breath and left the room, swaying on his feet.

*Bullocks, what is going on?*

Gabriel slowly made his way downstairs, mounted his horse, and galloped toward their meeting place in Hyde Park. His head hurt, and there was a slight ringing in his ears. He barely held on to the saddle. He couldn't imagine the vigorous lovemaking with his wife had tired him out so much that he was hardly sitting straight.

He didn't remember how he'd made his way to the designated place without falling off his horse. The moment he reached the clearing, he fairly collapsed to the ground and cast up his accounts again.

Clydesdale reached him with quick strides and helped him up. "Good God, what is wrong with you?"

Gabriel wiped his mouth and raised his eyes to his friend. He was shaking, and his stomach was churning. "I don't know. I think I'm ill."

"You think?" Clydesdale raised his brow. "I am taking you home."

"No!"

"What do you mean, no?"

"If I leave now, everyone will peg me for a coward, and then Evie will be accosted by every vile lord in her proximity." Gabriel slowly stood on shaking legs and dusted his breeches.

"If you don't leave now, I am afraid you'll drop dead. Good Lord, Gabriel, you look half-dead as it is."

"At least then I would have died honorably," Gabriel said, his voice shaking.

"Are you an idiot? Is that what Evie would want?" Clydesdale's voice rang sharply in his head, and Gabriel flinched.

"She deserves more than being a coward's wife."

"Better than being an idiot's widow," Clydesdale said darkly.

Gabriel pushed him aside and stepped toward his adversary. He wiped the sweat off his forehead and stretched out his hand toward Clydesdale. "Hand me my gun."

\* \* \*

## Chapter 27

Evie woke up at a loud shriek. She sat up in bed and looked around the empty room. Gabriel wasn't there, and neither were his clothes on the chair next to the bed. The hurried footsteps sounded in the corridor, and then there was a knock on the door.

Evie bunched the bedsheet over her unclad body. "Come in." Her voice came out shaky. A bad feeling settled deep in her stomach. Something was very wrong.

Her maid entered, wringing her hands in front of her. "There's been a mishap in the kitchen, Your Grace."

Evie scurried from the bed and hastily drew on her robe. "What mishap?"

"One of the footmen, Your Grace. He's… He's dead."

Evie paused in the middle of tying her robe and looked at the horrified maid. The poor girl sniffed and then burst into tears. Evie ran out of the room, not caring for her state of dishabille, and hurried down to the kitchen. The servants had all collected there, silently staring at the dead footman on the floor.

"How did this happen?" Evie asked. Her hands shook, and her stomach knotted as she saw the unmoving body of her deceased servant.

"It's not my fault!" the cook yelled. "I told him not to eat it!"

Evie slowly turned to her. "Told him not to eat what?"

"The master and mistress's foods are not for servants," the cook muttered miserably.

"He ate some of our food?" Evie was confused. "And then what happened?"

"He dropped dead!"

The cook was not making any sense. "Please, call on the

doctor," Evie said to her butler and then turned back to the cook. "Mrs…" she faltered. To her shame, she realized she hadn't even learned her name. She'd lived in this house for over a fortnight, and she didn't know her servants. What a wreck she'd been. "Would you mind coming with me?"

The cook nodded, and they proceeded out of the room. They settled into one of the drawing rooms.

"I apologize," Evie said. "I haven't even learned your name. I know I have not been the perfect mistress, but I've been grieving." She tried to compose herself, but her voice was still shaking.

"Mrs. Farley," the cook answered.

"Mrs. Farley, can you tell me what happened in the kitchen?"

"We have a rule," she said, eyeing Evie warily. "We have our own food. We don't eat what we cook for our masters."

"Right, but how did the footman die?"

"He ate your fish."

Evie stilled, barely breathing. "And then he just died?"

"Yes."

Evie shot up from the chair. "Have you seen my husband?"

"No, Your Grace." The cook's eyes ran nervously about the room. Evie was certain she thought her deranged. But it didn't matter now. She needed to find her husband. Evie ran out of the room without another word. She ordered the footman not to let the cook out of his sight and hurried toward her room to change when the front door burst open, and Julie ran into the hall.

"Thank God, you are home!" she yelled. "Gabriel is headed for a duel!"

# Chapter 28

There are a few moments in one's life when time seems to stop, and the events proceed before one's eyes in slow motion. The entire scene is veiled by smoke or tears—something is obscuring the vision in any case—and all sounds recede to the background.

For Evie, one of those moments had been when she had watched her childhood home burn rapidly before her eyes. All the pleasant memories, laughter, and games of hide and seek with her family rushed through her mind.

The second time this happened was when she galloped onto the dueling field in the dead of the morning and watched her husband drop to the ground right after a shot rang out.

"No!" Evie shrieked and jumped from the horse without waiting for it to stop. She ran toward the prone body of her husband, sobbing as several episodes of her life flashed before her eyes.

First, the image of Evie's come-out ball entered her mind. She walked down the stairs, hand in hand with Mary, and her gaze collided with Gabriel's. She remembered the intense way he looked at her, his roguish smile. This was the moment she fell hopelessly in love. Next, she remembered him standing on the side of the road, his cravat covered with dirt, his eyes wide in surprise just after she threw mud at him. Their entire elopement slowly made its way into her mind again. Then, their trip to the gaming hell. And finally, his foolish declaration that he did not love her. Oh, his poor, ignorant heart.

She landed on her knees in front of him and patted his chest, looking for a bullet wound.

"I deloped! I didn't shoot him! I didn't, I swear!" The shouts came from the other side of the field. Evie turned and saw Bingham nervously clutching his pistol to his chest, muttering over and over again that he hadn't shot at anyone.

The doctor kneeled next to Evie and checked Gabriel's pulse. "He's alive."

Evie's heart slammed rapidly against her ribs. *He's alive.* "Was he truly not shot? I don't see blood anywhere."

The doctor shook his head. "Bingham shot in the air."

A deep breath left her in an audible whoosh. A gentle hand settled on her shoulder, and she raised her head to see Clydesdale standing beside her. She hadn't even noticed he was there. He stretched his arm and tugged Evie to her feet. Clydesdale blinked, obviously trying to ignore the state of Evie's attire. She'd had to wear breeches in order to ride comfortably and hastily to the dueling spot.

"He wasn't feeling well all morning, I think," Clydesdale said carefully.

"Why did you let him duel?" Evie yelled, wiping the tears off her face.

Clydesdale raised his brow. "I didn't think I had the power to stop him." He frowned, looking over Evie's shoulder.

Julie appeared at that moment and came close to her husband.

"I didn't tell you where I was headed just so you could follow me, Julie," he said. "It was in case of emergency."

Julie let out an exasperated sigh. "This seems like an emergency to me," she said sharply. "What happened? He wasn't shot, was he?"

Evie looked at the doctor. "I think he was poisoned."

He looked at her in surprise. "What makes you say that?"

"Poisoned?" Julie asked in surprise.

Evie addressed the doctor. "Our footman died this morning. Apparently, he ingested the food that was intended for us."

"Evie! Why didn't you tell me?" Julie exclaimed in horror.

"I didn't have time. I needed to find Gabriel as soon as I could." She turned back to the doctor. "But he didn't eat much of it, maybe one bite. Do you think he—Will he be well?"

"Well, if he didn't ingest much, perhaps he will. But I need to perform the bloodletting as soon as I can. We need to let the poisonous blood out. As soon as we transport him to a nice bed, I can start the process."

Evie nodded. "Good." She sniffed and wiped the remainder of the tears off her face.

They loaded Gabriel into Clydesdale's carriage and drove him to his London townhouse. Evie insisted Gabriel would be more comfortable in his own bed. She also wanted him to have his favorite cook prepare his meals when he woke up. Gabriel loved Matilda's dishes; he'd said it enough times. Besides, she wasn't about to trust Mrs. Farley with her dishes anymore.

When they laid Gabriel comfortably on the bed, and the doctor started preparing for the bloodletting ritual, Evie went downstairs and apprised Matilda of what happened. The poor woman became white as chalk, but she quickly composed herself. She prepared dandelion tea, citing that she knew it to help clear out the poisons from the body. Evie was glad to have a helping hand and was ready to try anything if it meant Gabriel would feel better.

So she watched the doctor perform the bloodletting ritual, she fed Gabriel dandelion tea when he woke up for brief periods, and she prayed for him to get better.

A few hours later, Evie sat by Gabriel's bed, changing the compress on his forehead. He was still weak, sweaty, and occasionally delirious. The doctor performed two rituals of bloodletting in one day and promised to come on the morrow as well. Evie wasn't certain it was helping. In fact, Gabriel seemed to get worse with every hour.

Gabriel stirred and mumbled something in his sleep.

"Oh, Gabriel," she breathed and moved a lock of hair away from his forehead. "Do you remember when you asked me how I can still believe in God if bad things keep happening to me? Well, I cannot say that my faith isn't shaken. But I have to believe now more than ever that you will recover." She paused and looked at him forlornly. "When Peacehaven burned down, I cried and wailed that I had nothing left... How wrong I was."

Evie reached out and caressed his cheek. Suddenly, Gabriel grabbed her by the wrist and tugged. Evie fell onto the bed with a slight yelp. Gabriel brought her hand to his lips and kissed her fingers. His lips were dry and scratchy; his breath was hot.

"Gabriel!" Evie sat up, scooting closer to him. "You're awake."

"Mm, yes," he answered, his voice hoarse.

"Here, have some tea." Evie poured some dandelion tea and fed him a few drops before he collapsed against the pillows.

"Vile drink," he said with a grimace, and Evie laughed.

"Yes, I tried it to make sure not to poison you even more, but Matilda swears it works wonders, and since you trust her, so do I."

"Poisoned?" Gabriel frowned.

"Yes, the Montbrooks poisoned the fish."

Gabriel's frown turned into a scowl. "Bastards."

"I do not disagree." She smiled slightly.

"One more reason to never have fish in the house, huh?"

Evie let out choked, nervous laughter. "Yes, well. Clydesdale had a conversation with my now former cook. Apparently, she'd been diligently blabbering information about my household situation to her former mistress. Including her concerns about the lack of nights we spent together. So Lady Montbrook sent her a packet of poison with the instruction to season the dish heavily with the powder. She said it would work like a love potion, an aphrodisiac."

Gabriel laughed dryly. He took Evie's hand in his and laced their fingers. "Doesn't she know this is the last thing I need when you are around?"

She smiled sadly. "The Montbrooks want the dukedom. And they will stop at nothing until they get it."

Gabriel struggled to sit up. "Well, we can't let that happen."

Evie placed another pillow behind Gabriel's back and helped him into a comfortable position. "I rather think the best way for us to get out of this predicament is to let them have the blasted title. Peacehaven is gone, and with it, most of the family heirlooms, everything I held dear. The Somerset townhouse doesn't feel like home anymore. The rest of the estates… I shall have to trust that the Montbrooks will take care of them."

Gabriel shook his head. "Don't even speak that way. The title and the lands are the most important things in your life; you said it yourself."

"No. I have something more important now." She caressed his cheek and pressed a kiss to his forehead. "And I'd rather not lose you too."

\* \* \*

The next day, Evie asked Clydesdale and the Earl of Winchester to accompany her to the Montbrooks' townhouse. The moment the door opened, she pushed past the elderly butler without waiting to be welcomed inside. She wasn't in the mood.

"Please ask your masters to meet us with all haste," Evie said as she entered the old and drafty house. The butler eyed her and her two tall, aristocratic companions warily and hurried away with a bow.

This was the first time she had been in the Montbrooks' residence. She looked around the bare walls and dusty interior with a grimace. A musty smell seemed to permeate through the walls.

"Well, if you wanted more evidence that your cousins are in a dire state, this should suffice," Clydesdale said, with an air of revulsion.

The butler returned just then and beckoned them to follow

him into the drawing room. The stairs creaked with every step they took, and the musty smell got worse the higher they climbed the stairs. They entered the small drawing room, empty save for the settee and a couple of armchairs.

"Would you like to sit?" Winchester indicated to the furniture in the middle of the room, and Evie shook her head.

"I cannot possibly sit still; my stomach is tied in knots." She smiled apologetically. She knew she needed to be here, needed to finally confront her cousins and put a stop to this animosity between them, one way or another. But she would rather spend this time with her husband. Her hands started perspiring inside the gloves, and she picked on the tips nervously.

About half an hour later, steps sounded outside the room. Evie turned just in time to see Lord and Lady Montbrook crossing the threshold. They stopped, looking about the room and taking in their visitors.

"My dear," Lady Montbrook said, feigning delight. "What a pleasure to see you." She stretched both hands out in greeting before turning to the gentlemen in the room. "My lords, a pleasure."

Montbrook sketched a curt bow, his gaze running from one earl to another warily. "My lords."

"Please, do make yourselves comfortable. I shall ring for tea," Lady Montbrook exclaimed as if not noticing the hostile atmosphere in the room.

"It isn't necessary," Evie said coldly. "I wouldn't drink anything in this house and wouldn't advise anyone else to."

Lady Montbrook frowned down at her. "Whatever do you mean, my dear?"

Evie slowly walked to a settee and sat down on the edge,

as regally and calmly as was possible under the current circumstances. "Let us talk candidly, my dear cousin."

Lady Montbrook raised a brow but followed Evie's lead and sat down across from her. Winchester sat next to Evie, and Clydesdale occupied the only other available seat, leaving Lord Montbrook to stand by the hearth.

"What would you like to talk candidly about, my heart?" Lady Montbrook intoned.

"Lady Montbrook," Evie said slowly. "I want to speak with you of your attempts to steal my dukedom."

Lady Montbrook's mouth fell open. "Whatever do you insinuate?"

"I do not insinuate. I speak openly. First, you tried to wed me to your son."

"A ridiculous notion. I did introduce him as your potential suitor, but all you had to do was say no."

"You told him there were two ways to become the duke. To either marry me or kill me."

"I said no such thing. How can you accuse me of this?" she exclaimed in indignation.

"After I eloped, you sent three thugs after me."

Lady Montbrook's eyes narrowed on Evie. "What you are saying is absurd."

"No, it isn't. I have a letter from a blacksmith who wed us." Evie took an envelope from her reticule. "He witnessed the entire confrontation between the thugs and my husband. He heard the bandits call you as their master by your name." She addressed the last to Lord Montbrook.

"I had nothing to do with it!" the man exclaimed.

"Even if he did," Lady Montbrook said through her teeth, "a statement from a Scot proves nothing."

"Perhaps it does not," Evie agreed. "But there is also a statement from the caretaker of my Peacehaven estate and a few villagers, who say they saw you on the estate grounds on the morning of the fire."

"These are all lies!" Lady Montbrook spat. "We were not there on that day, not even in passing. We left your wedding house party after you did."

Evie's nostrils flared. Lady Montbrook was too smug, thinking she'd gotten away with these offenses. If Evie had any doubt about who was behind the fire before, she didn't have any doubt now. They'd probably just paid some poor soul to start the fire.

"And finally, I have a statement from your former cook, Mrs. Farley, who received a packet from you with the poison you sent in an attempt to poison my husband and me."

Lady Montbrook scoffed. "A statement from a cook? She is unstable. Nobody is going to believe a word she says."

"I do," Evie said calmly.

"You have nothing," Lady Montbrook said, looking intently at the letters in Evie's hands. "None of those letters prove anything."

"You are right; they don't. But combined with my statement before the House of Lords, they will mean something. And even if they don't prove you guilty, they will make you destitute for the court bills. And I shall make certain to drag your name through the mud because I do not have anything to lose anymore."

Lady Montbrook narrowed her eyes. "What do you mean?"

"My husband is dying," Evie said, her hands fisting by her sides, her nostrils flaring. "And I am not handing my dukedom to his murderers."

A smile broke out on Lady Montbrook's face before she could contain it.

Evie felt ire rising in her throat. She wanted to throw something at the vile woman, not have a polite discussion with her. But the years she'd been groomed to be the perfect duchess won out.

She stood calmly. "This visit today was just a courtesy. I am sending those letters as soon as I get home. So you better prepare yourself for the trial."

Lady Montbrook stood slowly, her lips thinning into an angry line. "You have no proof of anything. And even if you manage to take us to court, your precious husband will be dead by then. And you will be the one entwined with the scandal! You will become a laughingstock, and so will the title you hold so dear."

"You are right," Evie agreed easily. "But if my husband dies, nothing is going to matter to me anymore. I might not survive the scandal, but neither will you."

"Evie, dear." Lord Montbrook finally found his voice. "What do you want? We shall do anything!"

Lady Montbrook shot daggers at her husband.

Evie took a step back, composing her features. "I have another letter here with me. This one is addressed to the House of Lords. And it says that I am conceding my title and my lands to my dear cousin, Lord Montbrook, on my own volition, citing my ineptitude to successfully run the dukedom."

Evie saw Lady Montbrook's eyes glint with greed, while Lord Montbrook's gaze turned hopeful.

"What do we have to do for you to send it?" he asked.

"Simple. Give me the antidote to the poison you used on

Gabriel, and I shall hand this letter to you. You can send it with the footman right now. It won't take effect for months, and there will probably be a hearing, but as long as Gabriel lives, you have nothing to worry about."

There was a beat of silence. "What if I give you the antidote and your husband still dies?" Lady Montbrook asked.

"Do you have the antidote or not?" Evie narrowed her eyes on the woman.

Lady Montbrook eyed Clydesdale and the Earl of Winchester warily.

"There is truly no choice for you, Lady Montbrook," Clydesdale spoke up. "You either hand us the antidote, or we ruin what is left of your good name."

"And seeing as how you are already impoverished. I do not think you'd want that," Winchester chimed in.

Lady Montbrook shifted in place.

"Oh, for God's sake!" Lord Montbrook exclaimed. "Give them the damn antidote! Do you want to be shunned for life? They are giving us what we wanted, anyway!"

Lady Montbrook spun on her husband. "Hold your tongue, you idiot!" She then pivoted and regarded Evie once more. "First, hand me the letters. All of them. The statements from your commoner witnesses and the one I am to send to the House of Lords."

Evie stretched her arm and handed the vile woman the letters. "You are despicable," she said.

"Yes, well... Sometimes one has to be despicable to save one's family," Lady Montbrook intoned as she ran her gaze through the letters.

*One does.* Evie swallowed. "Is it to your satisfaction?"

Lady Montbrook ripped up the statements and threw them

into the fire. Then she handed the letter meant for the House of Lords into Montbrook's hands. "Be a dear, send a footman to deliver this letter, with all haste."

She then rang the servants' bell, and they waited as a heavyset woman entered the room. "Gertrude, the powder you gave me a few days ago, the one you said to use sparingly, or it can turn into a poison. Could you bring the antidote to it?"

"Pardon, ma'am, but—"

"Just do as I ask," Lady Montbrook said, slowly enunciating every word.

The woman lowered her head in submission, curtsied, and scurried away.

Evie slowly backed away until she was flanked by her companions. "Thank you, Lady Montbrook," she said with a smile. "This is all I needed."

Lady Montbrook turned, confusion marring her face.

"The statements you just burned. They were just copies. The originals were sent to every major paper in London this morning. And yes, you are right, they are not enough to start a criminal trial, at least not against peers, but they are enough to stir the gossip. You will be shunned by the polite society you so tried to be a part of without any hard evidence. But now, I have two peers with me in the room who can testify to hearing you admit to possessing an antidote to a poison you used on my husband should this case move to trial. An attempt on the life of a peer? A hanging offense."

"You stupid cow!" Lady Montbrook cried. "There is no antidote. I used arsenic, and if St. Clare is not dead yet, it just means he didn't finish the entire dose, which is too bad. But he will die. Painfully."

"Then you will hang," Evie said coldly.

"You think after all this, you will continue to enjoy the life of a duchess? Your name will be attached to ours. Your name will be synonymous with a scandal you won't be able to shake off for years. A peer of the realm might shrug it off, but not a peeress. This is the way of the world."

Evie took a step toward Lady Montbrook. "I eloped with the most notorious rake London has ever known. I have wagered in the most scandalous gaming hell in London. Just yesterday morning, I galloped across town dressed in breeches to stop a duel. Do you truly think I am afraid of a little scandal?"

Lady Montbrook was so red she was about to burst.

"The papers with the printed statements come out on the morrow. You better leave England before they surface." With these words, Evie spun on her heel and stalked out of the room.

# Chapter 29

Evie woke up with a ticklish sensation somewhere in the region of her nose. She swatted at the air before her and heard a low chuckle. Evie sat up and looked at the smiling face of her husband. Her eyes widened, and then she fell into his arms.

"You are awake!" she breathed. "Oh, thank God, I was so worried."

Gabriel rubbed her back in soothing circles, and Evie felt a dry kiss on her hair. She disengaged from his arms and looked up at his face. "You look healthy. How do you feel?"

"I feel a lot better. Your healing techniques work wonders."

"What healing techniques?"

"Falling asleep on top of me, for one thing."

"I wasn't sleeping on top of you," she grumbled.

"Yes, you were. In fact, your mouth was perilously close to my cock, and I think that is exactly the reason why I recovered so fast."

Evie groaned.

"I know. I am incorrigible." He tugged on Evie's arms and then collected her against his chest. "But that's why you love me, isn't it?"

Evie smiled against his skin. "Umm, no. I love you in spite of that." Gabriel laughed, and Evie snuggled closer to him. "Do you truly feel better?"

"Mm." Gabriel made a sound of acquiescence that reverberated through Evie's body. Evie closed her eyes briefly, breathing him in, enjoying the heat of his body. When he had been sick last night, his skin was clammy and cold, but now he was nice, dry, and warm. He was truly feeling better.

She disengaged from his arms once more and looked at him more carefully. The color had returned to his cheeks, and he didn't look feeble anymore. "Are you strong enough? Do you think you can handle some... rougher treatment?" She bit on her lip suggestively.

"Oh, absolutely." He settled comfortably against the pillows.

Evie smiled and slapped him lightly across his face.

"Ow! What was that for?" Gabriel covered his cheek with his hand, although Evie doubted she'd hurt him at all.

"What in the world were you thinking? A duel? Truly, Gabriel?"

"I had to do it, Evie. You know I did."

"No, I do not," Evie said, exasperated.

"I couldn't let people think that you could be mistreated, and nobody would do anything about it. I can't always be there to protect you. And it pains me to even contemplate that you could be out there alone and some fop would take advantage and—" Gabriel turned away with a grimace as if he truly was in pain.

Evie placed a hand against his cheek. "Gabriel, there are

other ways you could have done that. The duel could have had more dire consequences. I can take care of myself against some fop, but what if you died? Or got exiled?"

"I will not apologize for trying to protect you."

"Very well." Evie nodded thoughtfully. "How about you apologize for lying to me—"

"I didn't lie."

"—by omission. For going behind my back and doing exactly what I asked you not to do."

"Well, in my defense, I was right; Bingham did delope. Nothing bad happened because of the duel. In fact, the only bad thing happened because I dined at your house. By the way, I told you we should have brought in Matilda."

Evie let out an exasperated sigh and turned away.

Gabriel sat up in bed and took her hand. "I am sorry," he said, and Evie looked at him in surprise. "I apologize, and I promise to never do anything that might upset you."

"I don't want you to account for your every step. But if we are to have a trusting relationship, we need to be honest with each other."

"You are right. I shall be honest with you, I promise." He took a deep breath and looked at her intently. "If we are to have a trusting relationship, does this mean we shall be living together? As husband and wife?"

"Yes?" Evie blinked in confusion. In her mind, they already were.

"Spend nights together? Perhaps work on creating a brood of heirs?" Gabriel waggled his brows.

Evie let out a tiny laugh. "What are you asking me?"

"I am asking if our bargain is done. Finished. Forgotten. If you would consider being my wife in all the meanings of the word. If you would have me as your husband."

Evie's eyes widened. "Gabriel—"

"You said... That time in Winchester manor, you said that if we had marital relations, if we spent a night together, you wouldn't be able to let me go. Now that we have... You didn't change your mind, did you?"

"No." She shook her head. "I didn't change my mind."

"Good." Gabriel nodded. "Now, remember you said that because I am not letting you go either. You are stuck with me. Forever."

Evie let out a small laugh.

"When I was standing on that dueling field, covered in sweat, my stomach tied in knots. I thought I might die. And my only regret was that I was idiot enough not to realize sooner... Not to tell you sooner." Gabriel cleared his throat.

"Tell me what?"

"That I love you."

Evie's shy smile turned into a broad grin. "I already knew that."

Gabriel raised his brow.

Evie leaned in closer to him so that their lips were hairbreadth away. "I love you too." She covered his mouth with hers and kissed him deeply.

"So, will you tell me?" he asked when he raised his head. "How did the meeting go with your cousins?"

Evie beamed up at him. "Splendidly. I threatened them with social ruin, and it felt surprisingly very... liberating. Both Clydesdale and your father did insist on leaving their footmen to watch the Montbrooks, however. And we shall have a few more guards about our estates until we are certain that they left the country. But I think it went well."

"Mm, I knew you would do it wonderfully. Never doubted you for a moment."

The door opened then, and Winchester sauntered into the room. "Son, you're awake."

"I am." Gabriel took Evie's hand and curled their fingers.

Winchester's gaze followed the action, and he smiled. "So I see you feel better."

"Yes, much."

"Good, I just confirmed with the doctor. The low dose of arsenic that you ingested should be out of your blood by now. So, he says you should be back to your regular activities as soon as tonight."

"Good news. I was just thinking about renewing my... regular activities." He threw a suggestive look toward Evie, and she pursed her lips in disapproval, her cheeks burning in embarrassment.

"Right, I shall leave then," Winchester said and turned to leave.

Evie squeezed Gabriel's hand and raised her brows.

"Father," Gabriel called.

"Yes?" The earl turned his head.

"Thank you."

Winchester gave a short nod, smiled softly at Evie, and walked away.

"That's it?" Evie raised her brow at her husband. "Thank you? There should have been a grand reconciliation! Forgiveness of all that came before."

Gabriel just shrugged. "It *was* a grand reconciliation. What did you want, tears?"

"At least a few more words than 'thank you.'" She parodied his gruff voice and Gabriel laughed.

"I am tired of talking and thinking about the past. How about we talk about the future?"

"Mm, I like the sound of that." She settled more comfortably on the bed. "What do you want to talk about?"

"Well, now that you wrestled Forton from Bingham's hands, what are you going to do with it?"

"I already have a plan. Since Peacehaven does not need the caretaker anymore, at least until it gets renovated, I thought of sending Mr. Cromwell there. I think he would be happy in a small, friendly village. He is not fond of big cities."

"Ahh, you are hoping he might find a friend there, say maybe Widow Jane?"

"Maybe." Evie shrugged innocently. "Two lonely souls could find a lot to talk about. And they both enjoy dominoes."

Gabriel chuckled. "We should visit the place again too."

Evie nodded. "But how do we explain the absence of the babe to Widow Jane?" She grimaced. "I really don't want to lie to her again."

Gabriel snaked his arm around Evie's waist and crushed her to him. He lowered his head to hers. "Then we better start working on one," he said against her lips before possessing her mouth in a fierce kiss.

# Epilogue

The season was in full swing when Evie arranged her first annual Somerset ball. People vied for invitations to the notorious couple's fete, but neither Evie nor Gabriel enjoyed dancing in stuffy ballrooms, so only three hundred people were invited.

The entire evening, Evie conversed with her guests and made certain there were enough refreshments, that the flowers didn't wilt, and the candles didn't burn out. When it was almost midnight, she finally had time to take a breath. She spotted her husband and walked toward him with measured steps, although she wanted to run to him and crash into his arms.

"Oh, I am a perfect authority on the chastity of ladies. As a matter of fact, I used to know every lady who had been chaste before her wedding because I was the one who—Here she is." He abruptly finished boasting to his friend as he noticed Evie come up beside him.

"Please, continue. You were saying that you were the devil who debauched poor, young, and unsuspecting maidens?" She blinked up at him innocently.

"None of them were either poor or unsuspecting. They all sought me out. Even you, my dear wife, or should I remind you?"

"You just did, love. Lord Vane, how are you fairing this evening?" She turned toward Gabriel's friend at last.

"It's been a long time since I've last been among the *ton*, and let me assure you, I did not miss it. However, my duty to my daughter demands that I put myself forth once more in search of a wife, and so does the duty to my title."

"Have you found any lady who caught your eye yet?"

Lord Vane's gaze lingered on one point behind Evie's shoulder before he shook his head. "I barely know anybody here. I thought you could help me. Your husband offered his assistance, but I am leery of his intentions."

Evie chuckled, and Gabriel placed a possessive arm around her waist.

"How can you doubt my skills in finding the perfect wife when I found the best one for myself?"

"Didn't you just say she was the one who sought you out?" Vane raised his brow.

Gabriel's arm tightened around Evie. She patted his hand consolingly and addressed the marquess. "So, what are you looking for in a wife?"

He shrugged lightly. "Actually, I just want a proper, reserved, capable young lady, a perfect hostess, and a caring mother."

"What you mean is you want an au pair and a housekeeper," Gabriel drawled.

Vane heaved a sigh. "Yes, my daughter needs a mother, my estates need a mistress, and I need an heir. I would not mind it if she had a tendre for me, but in my experience, that rarely, if ever, happens, so I am not going to insist upon it. I have the title, capital, and vast estates. That is usually enough for a lady to find me to be an attractive prospect. Or have the times changed?"

Evie pursed her lips in thought. "Never discount the power of love, my lord. But I shall be certain to find you the perfect bride."

"I just want someone who will set the perfect example of proper behavior and bearing for my daughter."

"Understood."

"Excuse us, Vane. I shall… er… confer with my wife about the best prospects for you and shall start introducing them to you promptly," Gabriel said and led Evie away.

"Where are we going?" she asked.

"All that talk of children and heirs has my blood pumping. I thought we should work on our own."

"Now? Here?"

"No place like here, no time like now." Gabriel grinned at her as he led her through the ballroom doors.

They rushed to the library, and the moment the doors closed, Gabriel crushed his mouth over hers. Evie held his head closer, unable to get enough of him. His hands were roaming her body, and his cock, hard and ready, rubbed against her stomach.

"Wait," Evie whispered as she tore her mouth away. "I need to get back. As the hostess, I can't just disappear; I might be needed."

Gabriel ground his pelvis against hers. "Your husband has need of you," he whispered against her lips and kissed her again.

He raised her skirts above her waist, and Evie wrapped her

340

legs about his hips. Gabriel slammed her against the door, and Evie moaned. His hands traveled inside the slit of her drawers, and he smiled wolfishly as he found moisture there.

"I see my wife has need of me, too," he growled.

Evie crushed her mouth to his, teasing him with her tongue, scraping his lips with her teeth. Gabriel undid the falls of his breeches and rubbed himself against her folds. Evie's head fell back against the cool library door.

Gabriel bit on her neck and swiftly thrust his length inside her. Evie held on to his shoulders as he worked her, thrusting in and out, banging his pelvis into her. The door rattled on its hinges with every thrust.

"Touch me, Gabriel," Evie moaned.

Gabriel placed a finger against the tiny nub above her center and circled it while continuing his wild movements with his hips.

With a short cry, Evie ascended into the realm of pure bliss. She sagged against the door, still clutching Gabriel close to her. Gabriel pinned her with his weight, holding her by her buttocks, his breath moving the hairs at the nape of her neck. They stood like that for a few moments, panting, breathing each other in, slowly coming back to earth.

All senses came rushing back to her as Evie heard strange sounds coming from the hall. It sounded like... a struggle?

"Gabriel, did you hear that?" she whispered.

"Hear what?" Gabriel's voice was slightly slurred.

"Let me down."

Gabriel withdrew his length, helped Evie adjust her clothing, and then buttoned his breeches. Evie heard the sounds again, and then a loud crack and a groan.

Evie looked at Gabriel, her eyes bewildered, before rushing

out of the room. As she opened the door, a disheveled lady ran past her. *Isabel?* Evie was about to call after her, but she collided with Lord Stanhope. Gabriel instantly grabbed him by the scruff and threw him against the wall.

"What just happened here?" he asked.

Evie decided to leave her husband to deal with the earl while she turned back to Isabel. Not knowing that she wasn't pursued anymore, Isabel ran as fast as she could. She turned left sharply just before reaching the ballroom doors.

Another shriek came and something resembling a grunt before a loud thud alerted Evie that Isabel had run into someone.

Evie picked up her skirts, but before she rounded the corridor, the door to the ballroom opened, and a couple of matrons turned into the hall Isabel had disappeared down.

"For shame!" one of the matrons exclaimed, and another one closed her eyes tight.

Evie reached the hall just at that moment and saw Isabel lying on top of a gentleman, her skirts raised above her knees, their limbs tangled. Her hair had collapsed out of her coiffure and covered the gentleman's face.

"During the ball and right in the hall!" the matron continued.

Isabel whimpered as she tried to get up. The gentleman she'd collided with unceremoniously deposited her to the side, and Evie nearly screeched in surprise. It was the Marquess of Vane.

Gabriel reached Evie at that time. He looked at the couple on the floor, then at the matrons, and whistled low.

"I suppose our work here is done, Vane. Congratulations, we've just found you a wife," he said cheerfully.

# Epilogue

## The End

If you want to read about the Marquess of Vane's Happily Ever After, Get book 4 of the Necessary Arrangements series: *An Offer from the Marquess* on Amazon.

Loved the book? Sign-up for my newsletter to get a bonus novelette:
https://sendfox.com/sadiebosque
*By signing up, you'll also get new release alerts and bonus content such as extra epilogues, deleted scenes, and more.*

Check out my new hot series The Shadows.
Steamy. Sassy. Scandalous.

Keep reading for a bonus epilogue.

# Fun Facts about this Novel

At the end of the novel, Gabriel suffers from arsenic poisoning. With the small dose he'd ingested, he wouldn't likely suffer as much as he did. However, his severe reaction was due to bloodletting and dehydration.

Evie is afraid of storms. This little quirk was taken from this author's real grandmother, who hides out in the closet until the storm passes.

Vingt-Un is one of this author's favorite card games.

About 40 percent of this novel was written before the author started writing the novella: *To Fall for a Duke by Christmas*, the love story of Evie's grandparents.

You can find more fun facts and deleted scenes from the book on my website:
    www.sadiebosque.com

# Bonus Epilogue

*A few years later.*

Gabriel looked tenderly at his wife, studying the gentle curve of her neck and the golden freckles spread upon her milky-white complexion.

She wasn't a lady to shield herself from the sun, and this was one of the million reasons he loved her.

"All done," the painter, the young artist Miss Emmeline said as she put the brush aside.

Gabriel looked up with a frown.

"Oh, finally," Evie breathed and craned her neck from side to side.

"But I am not done ogling my wife yet," Gabriel said, feigning affront. "Can't you paint us some more?"

Evie swatted at him. "You can ogle me all you want, just don't make me sit in this one position anymore. And help me up."

She raised both her hands, and Gabriel tugged her up with a great show of effort.

"My God, you are heavy!" he exclaimed and wiped at his brow theatrically.

Evie's eyes narrowed. "Be thankful you don't have to carry me around all day, unlike me, who has to lug your heir everywhere I go."

Gabriel grinned down at his grumbling wife. He bent at the waist and kissed her rounded belly. "My heir, is he now?"

"Oh, yes. I am quite certain it's a boy. Aileen never kicked like that. She was a proper lady even then. Just like her mother," his duchess said with a haughty air.

Gabriel snorted a laugh. "A proper lady... Like her mother? I'd like to meet this person you're referring to. Because the woman I am married to is a proper hellion."

Evie arranged her lips in a sensual pout. "Can we go look at the painting now, or are you going to insult me all day?"

"Insult, my dear wife? Why, it was the highest compliment!" Gabriel wrapped his arms around her waist, tugged her closer to him, and planted a demanding kiss on her mouth.

Evie sagged under his onslaught before coming to her senses. She pushed at his chest and wriggled out of his hold.

"Gabriel!" She looked so affronted he could have thought he'd killed someone in front of her. "Not in front of the artist," she said in a scandalized whisper.

Gabriel's lips twitched in a smile. "Very well, my dear, proper wife. Shall we go see the painting now?"

She gave him a nod and linked her arm with his.

They were in the duke's chambers at their Peacehaven estate. The renovation had just been completed a few months earlier, and Gabriel had bundled up his increasing wife and journeyed there for her confinement. The moment Evie stepped into the duke's—now duchess's—chambers, her eyes watered, and he knew that all that trouble he went through to renovate the mansion was worth it.

"But there's no portrait," she had said back then.

Gabriel knew she meant the old one of her grandparents. But he decided that having their own portrait made was the second-best option.

Their family portrait.

They reached the artist and peeked over her to see the painting. Miss Emmeline stepped aside with a grin.

It was beautiful.

Gabriel's eyes immediately drifted to his two girls. Aileen, their two-year-old daughter, was sitting on her mother's lap. The artist drew her first because the babe wouldn't sit still for long periods.

"We'll need to have another one made when the babe comes," Gabriel noted.

Evie looked up at him and grinned. "Perhaps when he is older." She turned to the artist. "Thank you so much. You will be invited to this house often, with every added member of the family."

"Yearly," Gabriel said proudly and received a frown from his wife.

She turned back to the artist. "And I wager all our friends are going to be commissioning their portraits from you, too."

The girl smiled and bobbed a careless curtsy.

"Yearly?" Evie pouted as she turned toward Gabriel. "You expect me to deliver you a babe every year?"

Gabriel shrugged and led his wife out of the room.

"I expect we shall be very busy making babes, so yes. It is quite possible that you'll have to deliver them yearly."

Evie pursed her lips. "That's a lot of babes."

"We can afford them," Gabriel said with a smile.

They walked slowly down the corridor, then down the stairs, with Evie running her hand along the walls. She always did that, marveling at the feel of the newly decorated halls.

Gabriel had tried to recreate the house as best he could, to preserve as many memories for of her beloved home as he could. He'd succeeded in some places and fallen short in others, but Evie kept looking at this entire place with wonder-filled eyes, making him feel as though he was a wizard, giving a piece of her childhood back to her.

They made their way through the house and finally reached the gardens. Laughter and the shrieks of their little girl filled the place, so they had no trouble locating her and her chaperones.

"Here's my little girl," Evie said, as Aileen ran toward her at full speed and hugged her mother.

Mr. Cromwell and Widow Jane—now Mrs. Cromwell—followed slowly in her footsteps.

When Evie had sent Mr. Cromwell into the little village of Forton, they had hoped the two old souls would find companionship together. However, when the first letters arrived from Mr. Cromwell, they were mostly complaints about the 'bitter old widow.'

They bickered a lot, but soon everyone realized this was how they showed affection toward one another. Mr. Cromwell and Widow Jane quickly found a kindred soul in each other. Last year, they had finally tied the knot.

Gabriel took Aileen into his arms. "How about a kiss for your papa?"

Aileen kissed him on the cheek and hugged his neck before wriggling to get out of his hold, but he held fast.

"Miss Jane! Let's climb tree!" Aileen addressed the old woman, too young to pronounce her R's properly. She bounced in Gabriel's arms, almost jumping out of them.

"How about a game of dominoes instead?" Widow Jane coaxed little Aileen.

"What's to-mi-toes?" Aileen whispered with an adorable little frown.

Gabriel tapped her nose to smooth her features, and she laughed. "It is a stimulating game that encourages the development of one's mind as well as the propensity for gambling," he said.

"Let us go, my darling. Mrs. Cromwell will teach us all," Evie said with a wink toward Widow Jane.

"Let go, Papa!" Aileen wriggled out of Gabriel's hold and dashed toward the house.

"Careful, Lady Aileen!" Mrs. Cromwell hurried after the girl.

Gabriel cocked a brow at Evie, and she sighed.

"Very well, you were right. Perhaps she's not a perfect lady. But she will be."

"She is perfect, just the way she is," Gabriel whispered, and brushed a lock of hair away from Evie's face. "And so are you."

Gabriel leaned in and captured her mouth with his. He kissed her tenderly at first, then opened his mouth over hers and possessed her in a passionate embrace. Evie's hands traveled up his body until she raked her fingers through his hair and tugged him closer.

Evie broke the kiss abruptly. She put her hand on her abdomen and took a deep breath.

"Is something amiss?" Gabriel studied her features anxiously.

"Yes. I mean, no." She grimaced. "I've been having these pains every few hours, but I think they are coming closer together."

Gabriel's eyes widened. "Are you—"

Evie smiled and nodded. "I think I am."

"You're in labor!" Gabriel exclaimed in wonder while his heartbeat accelerated and his palms started perspiring.

"Get ready to welcome your heir, my lord," his wife said with a smile, but Gabriel could barely hear her through the noise of blood rushing through his head.

Loved the book? Sign-up for my newsletter to get a bonus novelette:

https://sendfox.com/sadiebosque

*By signing up, you'll also get new release alerts and bonus content such as extra epilogues, deleted scenes, and more.*

# Also by Sadie Bosque

Necessary Arrangements Series

*Prequel Novella*
To Fall for a Duke by Christmas
Main Series
A Deal with the Earl
An Agreement with the Soldier
A Bargain with the Rake
An Offer from the Marquess
An Affair with the Viscount
A Wager with the Gentleman

The Shadows Series
Return of the Wicked Earl
Secrets of the Wicked Viscount
Curse of the Wicked Scoundrel
Ravishing His Wicked Lady
Taming His Wicked Duchess
More coming soon…

Made in the USA
Las Vegas, NV
02 November 2024

10951211R00215